Aspects of Confused Speech

A Study of Verbal Interaction Between Confused and Normal Speakers

GW00482364

LEA's Communication Series
Jennings Bryant/Dolf Zillmann, General Editors

Selected titles in Applied Communication (Teresa L. Thompson, Advisory Editor) include:

Beck/Ragan/du Pre • Partnership for Health: Building Relationships Between Women and Healthcare Givers

Cissna • Applied Communication in the 21st Century

Harris • Health and the New Media

Ray • Communication and Disenfranchisement: Social Health Issues and Implications

Shakespeare • Aspects of Confused Speech: A Study of Verbal Interaction Between Confused and Normal Speakers

Street/Gold/Manning • Health Promotion and Interactive Technology: Theoretical Applications and Future Directions

Vanderford/Smith • The Silicone Breast Implant Story: Communication and Uncertainty

---

For a complete list of other titles in LEA's Communication Series, please contact Lawrence Erlbaum Associates, Publishers.

Aspects of Confused Speech

A Study of Verbal Interaction Between Confused and Normal Speakers

Pamela Shakespeare
Open University UK

LEA
LAWRENCE ERLBAUM ASSOCIATES, PUBLISHERS
1998   Mahwah, New Jersey   London

The final camera copy for this work was prepared by the author, and therefore the publisher takes no responsibility for consistency or correctness of typographical style. However, this arrangement helps to make publication of this kind of scholarship possible.

Lawrence Erlbaum Associates, Inc., Publishers
10 Industrial Avenue
Mahwah, New Jersey 07430

Library of Congress Cataloging-in-Publication-Data

Shakespeare, Pam, 1948–
Aspects of Confused Speech : a study of verbal interaction between confused and normal speakers / Pam Shakespeare.
　　　　p.　　cm
　　　Includes bibliographical references (p.) and index
　　　ISBN 0-8058-2807-9 (cloth : alk. paper). —ISBN 0-8058-2808-7 (pbk. : alk. paper)
　　　1. Oral communication. 2. Language Disorders. 3. Dementia. I. Title
　　　P95.S495　1998　　　　　　　　98–29273
　　　302.2'242—dc21　　　　　　　　CIP

Books published by Lawrence Erlbaum Associates are printed on acid-free paper, and their bindings are chosen for strength and durability.

Printed in the United States of America
10　9　8　7　6　5　4　3　2　1

To my parents

Jessie and Charlie Shakespeare

Contents

Introduction

In this book I examine the *confused speech* of people who have been diagnosed as having dementing illnesses. The verbal and behavioral confusion that dementia generates is highly distressing for victims and caregivers alike. In terms of medical provision, and both paid and unpaid care, coping with dementia represents a huge outlay in human and financial resources. It changes lives and relationships. And clearly the imagery connected with dementia and Alzheimer's disease indicates the potency that they have in the public imagination (Gubrium, 1986). Perhaps one reason for this is that almost everyone is aware of the disorienting and often unpleasant effect that confusion has when experienced even momentarily. Confusion is not an alien concept. Its effects are glimpsed by ordinary members, even if they cannot grasp what the effects of chronic disabling confusion must be like. Indeed, when I was working on this piece of research, several colleagues and friends jokingly offered themselves up for study as being "confused speakers". I was sometimes at a loss for words when I encountered this response, having seen the distress of many confused speakers who can no longer use talk competently in their social interactions. However, such joking responses indicate an ordinary member understanding that confused talk is not set apart from the rest of talk but is a phenomenon that everyone encounters and at times produces. So, although some of the participants of this study are people who have been diagnosed as having some sort of dementing illness, the discussion has broad practical implications for anyone interested in the phenomenon of talk.

During the course of the ensuing account I hope to draw attention to some of the issues surrounding confused speech, to show that it constitutes a form of *trouble* that can highlight features of ordinary talk as well as itself being an aspect of everyday interaction. An important starting point for these discussions is the recognition that all talk between two or more people is a joint venture. It is a lived experience, it takes place in a context, and it generates further contexts. The experience of confused speech is not merely the experience of confused speakers but anyone who is engaged in interaction with them. Much previous investigation of confusion has focused on problems that people with dementing illnesses have rather than on the interactive situation in which confused and normal speakers are involved. Sometimes the questions that people are asked in order to assesss whether they are confused are far from being normal ones, for example, testing their knowledge of what it is assumed everyone should know (in the UK, asking the name of the Queen), knowledge that rarely if ever comes up for *testing* in the majority of everyday contexts. By contrast, my aim has been to consider context very seriously. Some of the contexts I discuss are institutional and on the whole my data relate to talk that might be described as *trying* (or even *testing*) for the participants. I am aware that a number of books and articles have emphasized that institutional situations may undermine the chances of communication where the contribution of confused speakers is valued. And this relates to a wider recognition of the effects of context on the *quality* of the talk produced, for example, Labov's analysis of variations in the talk of young African Americans according to who is doing the interviewing and where (Labov, 1972). In examining context, however, I want to analyze some less-than-optimum situations because I do think that they are ones to which people with dementing illnesses and indeed other categories of less-than-full members are frequently subjected. A consideration of the relation between troubled or confused talk, context, and less-than-full membership must be a potentially instructive activity.

So the shift in focus I am recommending leads to a concern with documenting how trouble of particular kinds arises in talk, how it is dealt with, how the label of confusion comes to be applied, and how all these factors are related to context. Conversations that involve confused speakers are not necessarily overwhelmed by their participation, just as conversations between normal speakers that become momentarily confused do not necessarily break down. Much of the talk is unexceptional in many respects. In part this reflects the fact that confused speakers are often competent participants in key respects, knowing their own limitations and seeking to avoid trouble. It also stems from the strategies that normal speakers often use to avoid or cope with trouble. In this way confused talk emerges from the context of normal talk as well as being defined by contrast with it.

In the book I try to keep a balance between the idea of confused talk as an aspect of ordinary talk and the idea of confused talk as talk from which confused speakers cannot easily extricate themselves. It seems to me that the key word here is trouble. Trouble is what links these two different glosses on confused talk. The sorts of trouble I outline are for the most part trouble in talk that I think will be recognized by most people. There is very little talk gone wrong that we have not all at one point or another unleashed on the world. So the fascinating question is what is it that differentiates talk gone wrong on the part of normal speakers from talk gone wrong in the hands of confused speakers? The answer to this question has practical implications for thinking about both normal and confused talk. The implications of this investigation extend well beyond the communication problems confronting professionals who work with people with dementing illnesses to those whose work or daily interactions involve talk with anyone who has been labeled in some sense as a less-than-full member.

One of the central themes of this book is that people diagnosed as confused in their speech do not all behave in the same way. In overall terms I distinguish between minimally active, moderately active, and very active speakers. I use these categories, in part, because they seem to me to be recognized by ordinary members. This differentation automatically raises questions about how much talk is normal and more generally, indeed, what is normal talk. In chapter 1, I argue that this is an issue that has not been addressed. Medical and practice-oriented investigative studies have made implicit assumptions about what is normal in order to identify the confusion of those suffering from dementia. I explain the contribution that some sociological and philosophical work can make in this respect.

In chapter 2, I discuss how I assembled my data and how I developed a point of view on them. To this end I trace the progress of the analytical categories I came to employ from the initial stages through to the final version of this text. I consider what sorts of inferential resources and contextual cues were available to participants in the interviews that I and others conducted and examine literature that explicates the different forms that interviews can take. I look at data that I use but had no part in collecting and consider the process of how I came to find them meaningful and to integrate them into the study. Finally, I spend some time examining the process of transcribing the data, which was a major stage of fieldwork in this study.

In the next chapter, I investigate the development of context during the opening phases of my interviews. I analyze the stages by which confused speakers, caregivers, and myself as interviewer strove to work out what sort of *event* this was, and to adjust their presentation of themselves for it. I also consider a couple of interviews I found difficult and which were in some respects failures, in order to begin to develop the idea of trouble as a way of elucidating the talk that was going on.

In chapter 4, I examine minimally active confused speakers. I investigate the extent to which these confused speakers conform to notions of ordinary turn taking. From this I move on to look at topic development and begin to explore the relationship between talk, troubled talk, and the identity work of people involved in the interviews.

In chapter 5, I look at moderately active confused speakers using Paul Grice's cooperative principles as an analytic framework as well as Goffman's ideas about face-work. The main focus of the chapter is on repair in talk. I examine the consequences for identity of inadequate repair work and consider in particular the problem of failing to be able to present in one's biography those facts *anyone should know.*

In Chapter 6, I consider the talk of two very active confused speakers both in interviews and occasioned activity in a domestic setting. I look specifically at the face-work done by normal speakers in such situations and at both embedded correction and correction as interactional business. I explore the extent to which these confused speakers have available to them topics of talk that are not generally available to ordinary members.

In the final chapter I draw the strings of the study together, summarizing it and considering the implications both for the treatment of people with dementia and for the nature of ordinary communcative competence.

ACKNOWLEDGMENTS

I would like to thank the clients at the psychogeriatric clinic I attended and their caregivers who were prepared to spend time talking to me and to allow me to use the meetings as part of my research. I would particularly like to thank Mr. Bruner, who recorded material for me, and Mr. and Mrs. Hoy who invited me to their home.

I am also grateful to the consultant psychogeriatrician, who kindly permitted me to sit in on his assessments and asked some of his clients and their caregivers, on my behalf, for their permission to take part in interviews with me.

Colleagues and friends at the Open University UK have been helpful and supportive: thank you to Moyra Sidell and Tom Heller for their help with the data; to Jack Clegg for technical help with the audio recordings; to Linda Johns, Mick Jones, Jan Smith, and Serena Stewardson for advice and a great deal of practical help with the presentation of this book; to Joanna Bornat and the School of Health and Social Welfare Research Committee for financial and moral support. Thank you as well to Roger Gomm, Kate and Hugh Robinson, the Discourse Analysis Group, and the Reflective Research Group at the Open University for reading and commenting on aspects of the book in its various incarnations.

I am extremely grateful to Martyn Hammersley, for his careful and creative supervision of the PhD thesis that forms the basis of this book, and for his comments on drafts of the book. I have learned a great deal from him; ranging from debates in ethnomethodology to a thorough grounding in writing and grammar. I have *tried to* absorb all these lessons (whereas originally I could only *try and* absorb them!). Also I would like to thank Paul Atkinson and Margie Wetherell, as examiners of the PhD for their reading and helpful comments.

I want to thank Jonathon Potter for pointing me in the direction of Lawrence Erlbaum in the first place. Thank you also to colleagues connected with Lawrence Erlbaum Associates: Stuart Sigman and Wendy Leeds-Hurwitz who found my original thesis interesting enough to pass it on to Kathleen O'Malley, who was then at LEA. I would also like to thank Linda Bathgate, Eileen Engel, Wendy Levin, Sharon Levy, and Sarah Scudder, all at LEA, for their help and advice.

Finally, I want to thank my family and friends for their support and interest: my parents, Angela and John Ballard, Kate Laughton, and Kate and Hugh Robinson (again!).

1

Confusion, Normality and Everyday Life

> It's the body er the body of the er body's stud is studying you know, funny little
> things, the wife like, she's telling the truth absolutely I know all that and I
> know but uhm funny little things you know I might you know keep er one of
> those like I wouldn't you know blow the gaffe if you can understand what I
> mean.

—Mr. Graham

Mr. Graham is one of the participants of this study. For the medical and caring services his confused speech raises two questions: Can he be cured and if not how can we care for him? And, of course, Mr. Graham is not an isolated example; he does not have a rare illness. The Alzheimer's Disease Society (UK) estimated the prevalence of the disease as affecting five in 100 people between the ages of 70 and 80, and 20 in 100 among people over 80; 500,000 people in the UK suffer from moderate or severe dementia (Alzheimer's Disease Society, 1990). Hamilton (1994) reported a roughly comparable situation in the USA. She cited Evans et al. (1990) who suggested that somewhere in the region of 11.3% of the population of the USA older than 65 is affected by Alzheimer's disease and that this may rise to nearer 50% in the group of people older than 85. British Government Actuary figures in 1986 suggested that, by the year 2051, 15.5% of the population would be older than 85; as opposed to a projection of 8.7% for 1991 (Jefferys, 1988, p.5). This would imply that by the middle of the next century there will be twice as many people older than 80 suffering from one of the dementing illnesses. On these projections, unless a cure for dementia is found before then, the assumption must be that provision of care will become an even more urgent problem than it is now. The issue is assuming both greater

1

resource implications and social significance and the backdrop of research endeavor increases correspondingly.

MEDICAL AND PRACTICE-ORIENTED STUDIES OF CONFUSION

Issues relating to dementing illnesses have attracted a substantial body of research and policy writing. Kitwood (1987) noted that in the 1970s and 1980s there developed a considerable corpus of literature exploring neuropathological aspects of dementia. The two main forms of research were those carried out by postmortem and tomography (photographs developed from X-rays and presented on computer as cross sections of the brain).[1] As Kitwood noted, however, the close examination of postmortem brains frames dementia solely as a medical problem. As a result of this neuropathological emphasis, there followed a period when person-centered examinations of the illness were laid aside (Kitwood, 1988). However, such technical approaches can make only a limited contribution to the treatment of the living, and a literature with more functional interests concerning dementia and confusion has therefore developed.

The concept of confusion is an umbrella term and is used to describe behavior associated with a variety of conditions including temporary illness, reaction to drugs, socioenvironmental disturbances, as well as behavior produced by specific dementias such as Alzheimer's disease or Multi Infarct Dementia (Open University, 1988).[2] A wide range of literature describes confusional states and therapeutic regimes intended to alleviate distress. Thus, some writers describe and discuss behavior of people who have been labeled as suffering from a specific dementing illness (e.g., Code & Lodge, 1987). As part of this there have been attempts to identify the features of confused talk. For example, Allison (1962) identified three different types of confused speaker:

(1) Patients who were entirely speechless, neither attempting spontaneous conversation nor making any attempt to reply to questions
. . .
(2) Patients who had little or no spontaneous talk, but who attempted to answer questions and take part in conversation initiated by others . . .

(3) Patients showing no inhibition of spontaneous talk and responding readily to questions. (pp. 135–142)

---

[1] Examples of such research include Blessed, Tomlinson, and Roth (1968); Earnest, Heaton, Wilkinson, and Manke (1979); Hawkins and Phelps (1986).

[2] In talking about people with dementing illnesses, I shall mainly use the terms *confusion* and *confused* from now on, as they are common to professional, research, and lay communities.

Consideration of confused talk has also sometimes arisen in the work of authors who consider dementias and confusion as part of a wider research concern with the lives of older people. For instance, Meacher (1972) looked at residential care and at the characteristics and problems of the confused residents. He defined a number of types of confused speech as follows:

> 1 INCOHERENT SPEECH
> This is chiefly characterized by the lack of development of recognizable ideas . . .
> (a) *Fragmentary verbalisation of private thoughts* . .
> (b) *Neologisms* . . .
> (c) *Verbal restriction* . . .
> A woman who had been removed by an attendant from the fireplace where she was fiddling with the fireguard cried out: 'Don't, don't, don't, go and go, go...go...go...' . . .
>
> 2 TANGENTIAL SPEECH
> This is defined as speech in which use of words is mainly appropriate and the ideas are broadly intelligible, but the whole statement is irrelevant to the context . . . .
> (a) *Skewing of responses to a preconceived framework of ideas* . . .
> (b) *Perseveration*
> Key words are repeated irrespective of changing reference points and from the divergence between the meaning of the words used and the inflection with which the words are spoken it is clear that the words conceal an indefinitely extensible range of ideas. . . .
> (c) *Dysfunctional word and idea association* (pp. 50-54)

I have quoted at length from this section of Meacher's book because the types of confused speech that he wrote about can often be found in my own data. Moreover, the passage underlines the fact that talk is taken as an indicator of mental confusion and, indeed, many of the features of talk highlighted in Meacher's account can also be seen in the more medically oriented work of Allison.

What is significant for my purpose, however, is that this literature identifies confused talk on the basis of largely implicit assumptions about the nature of normal talk. If talk is an indicator of mental confusion, it is also an indicator of normal status in the world. We can infer that normal talk is assumed to be relevant, locally managed, cognizant of changing references and so on. But, whereas context dependence is clearly seen as a significant issue, the problematic nature of what relevance to context actually means remains unexamined.

This parallels criticism of the use of forms of talk as symptomatic in the mental health field more generally. Thus, Blum noted:

> When jurors, psychiatrists, kinsmen, and all ordinary members decide the sanity of another, their decisions are ultimately based on a socially accredited body of knowledge that they methodically use . . . The labels

> . . . which we as observers confront are, so to speak, the end points of much socially organised activity that enters into their production. To accept such end points as points of departure for exploring the antecedent conditions or independent variables that influence the labelling process . . . is to neglect the socially organised character of the labelling process itself. (Blum, cited in Coulter, 1973, p. 113)

In much the same way, the concepts of incoherent speech, tangential speech, neologisms, and so on, are based on a *socially accredited body of knowledge* that is being methodically used: They are end points, preceded by a socially organized labeling process. But the prior methodic work required to reach these evaluations is not itself a topic for investigation within the framework of this research.

There is also a range of therapeutic literature on dementing illnesses including materials on validation therapy, reality orientation, reminiscence and so on, (see, e.g., Cook, 1984; Feil, 1983; Teasdale, 1983). Some of the names used for these therapies, *validation* and *reality* in particular, also point to the assumption of a socially accredited body of knowledge. Such materials may identify reasons for confusion, for example, "They [the confused person] forget to analyze things that are different. They forget "as if". A hand feels soft as—if it were a baby. The hand then *becomes* the baby. They lose metaphoric thinking." (Feil, 1982, p. 17)

What is implicit here is the assumption that analyzing difference and metaphoric thinking are normal. Such therapeutic regimes are based on the desirability of normal behavior and normal thinking, even though some acknowledge that "normality" may never be achieved through therapy. What is not examined, however, is the nature of that normality. It is treated as unproblematic.

Some writers have analyzed the interactions between people with dementia and those working with them. For example, Jones (1992) documented the volume of words spoken between care workers and residents. Pollitt, O'Connor, and Anderson (1989) explored the perceptions of caregivers of older people with mild dementia. And various practice-based models of working with people with Alzheimer's disease and their caregivers have been developed (see, e.g., Webb & Morris, 1994). Underlying all these approaches is a notion of the social consequences of not being a normal person; in personal behavior, relationships with others, the business of daily living, and so on. Here again, though, what is normal is left unexamined. Certain capabilities are simply taken for granted as normal, and a person's inability in these respects is treated as a sign of abnormality. Indeed, psychiatric tests may be assumed to detect abnormality even where relatives purport to find none:

('At least she's still got her faculties', a niece said of her aunt who we found, on testing, could no longer handle money and believed Queen Victoria was on the throne. 'He's a hundred percent with it', a son said of his ancient and very frail father, who according to the CAMDEX interviewer 'had no idea of the day, date or season...'). (Pollitt, O'Connor & Anderson, 1989, p. 264)

In such assessments, normal is a social construction that enables those engaged in diagnosis to find some people abnormal. Thus, the quotation suggests that a normal person knows who is on the throne, can handle money and is very clear about exactly when in the year it is. These judgments of normal rely on standardized tests and are taken to be a more valid assessment of normality than the contextualized experience of living with and being with people suffering from mild dementia. It is worth noting, however, that these instances of normality, such as handling money and knowledge of dates, do potentially involve contextualizing features that might have bearing on poor performance. For example, if one is on holiday or there is a newspaper strike, this might diminish acuity in dealing with the calendar. Nevertheless, the research interpretation emerging from standardized tests is privileged. Yet, the categories that the researchers use here *are* everyday rather than esoteric scientific categories; and, as various writers have noted, the construction of the research enterprise is itself predicated on commonsense everyday thinking (Lynch & Bogen, 1994).

In commonsense terms most people would agree that being able to do ordinary talk is an indicator of normality. It is the sort of thing that people are expected to know; it is "being ordinary" (Sacks, 1984). Most medically and practice-oriented studies of confusion use ordinary talk as a standard of comparison, and they effectively treat its features as context-free and standardized. But, as Sacks (1984) pointed out, ordinariness is an *ongoing* achievement. It is not something that is determined by the possession of particular items of knowledge. Moreover, ordinary talk involves recurrent confusions and ambiguities! There is no automatic connection between the production of confused talk and attribution of the identity of confused speaker. What happens is that normal speakers rely very heavily on context to make sense of what is being said. For example, faced with something that is unintelligible, the speaker looks to context: has the other person misheard, has the speaker been unclear in what has been said? Then they may make adjustments: speak more loudly, rephrase a question. Only if the responses continue to be unclear will the person be labeled confused; and perhaps even then only after other possibilities have been ruled out, such as that they are foreign. The medical studies do not explicate this notion of context. Instead, the abnormal stands as already problematized in a taken-for-granted way.

What is normal is a more complex business than is assumed in this literature, then. In order to understand confused talk it is necessary to have a clear sense of the context dependence of ordinary talk; and indeed, for that matter, of specialized talk such as medical or therapeutic interviews.

STUDIES OF NORMAL TALK

In order to understand the talk of those who are labeled confused, we need to understand the nature of normal talk. This points to the relevance of a quite different literature from that discussed to this point: A literature that addresses the construction of the normal as a methodic practice employed by people in the course of everyday life. Much sociology has paid as little attention to the character of mundane social interaction as the medical literature discussed earlier. However, this has been challenged, for example, by ethnomethodologists. Zimmerman and Pollner (1974) articulated this rather neatly: "In contrast to the perennial argument that sociology belabors the obvious, we propose that sociology has yet to treat the obvious as a phenomenon" (p. 80). Some philosophers have also been concerned with exploring the nature of ordinary language. For Grice, (1975), whose work I draw on later, for example, ordinary language is to be conceived afresh and to be looked at as a project in its own right; its apparent idiosyncrasies to be explored not as "undesirable excrescences" of formal language, but as legitimate structures (p. 42).

This focus on the ordinary as a project in its own right is a central feature of the various approaches on which I have drawn and I begin by looking at one of the most influential writers about everyday social interaction: Erving Goffman.

Goffman and the Interaction Order

Goffman was primarily concerned with the patterning of social activity. Psathas (1995) described him as a "theorist of co-presence" focusing on naturally occurring activities as a field in their own right. It is difficult to classify his work into any particular school of sociology: He tried to avoid being classified and, at one point, described himself as involved in conceptual eclecticism (Burns, 1992). Goffman's view of what he was trying to achieve relates to a study of what he calls the interaction order:

> Social interaction can be identified narrowly as that which uniquely transpires in social situations, that is, environments in which two or more individuals are physically in one another's response presence . . . My concern over the years has been to promote acceptance of this face-to-face domain as an analytically viable one—a domain which might be

> titled, for want of any happy name, the *interaction order*—a domain whose preferred method of study is microanalysis. My colleagues have not been overwhelmed by the merits of the case. (Goffman, 1983b, p. 2)

Under this broad banner he had a number of preoccupations. Burns noted Goffman's remark that it is in social interaction that "most of the world's work gets done" (p. 18). And in the course of his career, Goffman's work encompassed, among other things, a focus on how people behave (e.g., *Presentation of Self in Everyday Life*, 1959; *Asylums*, 1961; *Stigma*, 1963b; etc.), a concern with occasions and focused interaction (*Behavior in Public Places*, 1963a: *Frame Analysis*, 1975), and investigations into what people say (*Forms of Talk*, 1981). Throughout his life his emphasis on social interaction led him to treat all of these areas as interconnected. This emphasis, and the recurring motif of face-to-face work, make his writings a rich source of insight for my study.

Goffman is concerned with *what kind of self* emerges in everyday social interactions and explores the implications for individuals of their success or failure in self-presentation. And he is concerned about this across a broad spectrum of social activity. In a late paper in which he presented a critique of conversation analysis and explored felicity conditions, referring to an imaginary conversation between John and Marsha, he said the following:

> To be sure, when John directs an assertion or question to Marsha, and Marsha responds by remaining silent, or changing topic, or turning from John to direct her opener to Mary, Marsha's act can be perceived by all three as a behavioral comment, a reply in effect. But analytically speaking, to say that in context no answer is an answer is simplistic. Information derived from Marsha's failure to address John's utterance verbally, that is, canonically, is information given off, not given; it is (on the face of it) expression, not language. (Goffman, 1983a, pp. 48–49)

So for Goffman the context of self-presentation is wider than talk. People both give information in their talk and give information off in the way they go about their talk. Because of this breadth of concern with the interaction order, and the fact that the theme of self-presentation recurs throughout his work as a superordinate organizing category, it is possible to take and use concepts from very different periods of his work and I have done this for my study.

Within his consideration of the interaction order, Goffman constantly orients to ritual and to the moral dimensions of the actor's performance. Indeed, it has been suggested that he sees this orientation as the crux of sociology (Schegloff, 1988). The article "On Face-work: An Analysis of Ritual Elements in Social Interaction" is a good example of his analysis of face as grounded in ritual (Goffman, 1969). For Goffman, the person is a "ritually delicate object" (p. 24), a "player in a ritual game" (p. 25) who is able to "castigate himself *qua* actor without injuring himself *qua* object of ultimate worth" (p. 25). He contended that "One's face, then, is a sacred thing, and the expressive order required to sustain it is therefore a ritual one" (p. 14). Goffman is interested in the moral dimension of both ordinary and extraordinary social behavior. Indeed the idea of *faultedness* runs like a thread through his work. Williams noted that this first appeared in his 1953 thesis, and it was still evident 25 years later when Helm criticized Goffman for changing the term *repairable* (coined by Schegloff) to his own term *faultable*. Helm claimed to be irritated by this because it did not enhance Goffman's analysis (Williams, 1988). However, Williams (1988) pointed out the following:

> Although it is true that the data in this paper are recordings of naturally occurring talk, the interest that Goffman displays in this data is very firmly located in that part of the framework which is concerned with the presentation of self, most particularly with issues concerning the appearance of interactional competence. The use of the term 'fault' here is part of a vital link to this concern. It May be recalled that a rather elderly term in his vocabulary is that of 'faulty person', an individual who brings offence to interactions, causing others to feel ill at ease. (p. 78)

Goffman's preoccupation with the moral dimension is supported by an enduring interest in how remedy and repair are used to overcome problems for the moral order that a "faulty" or ambiguous identity poses. He cited numerous instances of how people attempt to pass as ordinary when their identity is impaired in some way, or how they undertake interactional work to redeem their own identity or that of others.

I want to draw attention to three concepts Goffman used that are pertinent to my interest in confused speakers: identity, stigma, and face. He argued that people bring to occasions an identity that distinguishes them from everyone else and is used by participants in a dynamic sense during interactions:

> When a stranger comes into our presence, then, first appearances are likely to enable us to anticipate his category and attributes, his 'social identity . . . We lean on these anticipations that we have, transforming them into normative expectations, into righteously presented demands. (Goffman, 1963b, p. 12)

Goffman suggested that clustered around these "righteously presented demands" is a characterization of what he called a virtual social identity. The attributes that an individual could be proved to have can be called an actual social identity. Thus, as an interaction proceeds, we can expect there to be an alignment process going on between participants' virtual and actual social identities: Initial identity markers may be reappraised.

Identity may be threatened during the course of an interaction in a number of ways. It May be threatened at the outset when an individual brings an already impaired identity to it. In this case people may be seen as stigmatized:

> The Greeks, who were apparently strong on visual aids, originated the term *stigma* to refer to bodily signs designed to expose something unusual and bad about the moral status of the signifier. The signs were cut or burnt into the body and advertised that the bearer was a slave, a criminal or a traitor—a blemished person, ritually polluted, to be avoided, especially in public places. (Goffman, 1963b, p. 11)

Stigma is a mark on the identity that brings with it moral opprobrium in social interaction. People who are stigmatized are disadvantaged in ordinary everyday interactions and because of this they may try to pass as nonstigmatized (Goffman, 1963b). Stigma can be an overarching identity feature.[3] As Goffman (1963b, p. 14) noeted, this depends on whether the difference from others is already known about (in which case identity is discredited) or whether it is concealed (in which case identity is discreditable). The latter point reveals that threats may also emerge during an interaction if the identity an individual puts up for him or herself is discredited, and this is often made manifest in interactional negotiations relating to the face of the individual concerned:

> The term *face* may be defined as the positive social value a person effectively claims for himself by the line others assume he has taken during a particular contact. Face is an image of self delineated in terms of approved social attributes . . . (Goffman, 1969, p. 3)

Face is a construct recognized by ordinary members and is a term used by them to describe many social encounters. People recognize issues related to their own face, and face-saving devices used by others; and they can act socially to save face for themselves or for someone else. Indeed, mutual protection of face is a moral obligation for participants in the interaction order.

In terms of everyday tacit understandings face is an interesting concept because its visibility depends primarily on its violation or enhancement. Goffman (1969) acknowledged the affective connotations of *face*: "he cathects his face; his 'feelings' become attached to it" (p. 3). The loss of face is a painful matter for the person concerned. Face, when disturbed, becomes a matter for accounting:

> If the encounter sustains an image of him that he has long taken for granted, he probably will have few feelings about the matter. If events establish a face for him that is better than he might have expected, he is likely 'to feel good'; if his ordinary expectations are not fulfilled, one expects that he will 'feel bad' or 'feel hurt'. (Goffman, 1969, pp. 3–4)

---

[3] Indeed, the subtitle of the book Stigma is Notes on the Management of Spoiled Identity (Goffman, 1963b).

In this quotation we see a concern with what marks out and makes apparent particular aspects of presentation of self. Goffman pointed to certain forms of activity as facilitating the emergence of underlying images of self. These images can be situationally affected. Although most ordinary events and activities are taken for granted, some become marked and affect the image one has of one's self, often in a way that is perceived negatively. An actor may become embarrassed (a situation particularly relevant to this study because one of the associated states that conventionally accompanies confusion is embarrassment) and Goffman (1972) noted a series of interactional consequences of embarrassment, where people may lose their poise and are out of face in situations that do not necessarily expose their deficiencies, but which do expose incompatible roles or lines. Other authors have examined embarrassment in institutional settings: Heath (1988), for example, noted the problems that embarrassment brings to participants in medical examinations when the medical frame is momentarily broken, for instance, when the patient sees the doctor attempting to engage in eye contact during a breast examination.

Goffman (1969) observed that face needs to be considered beyond the current situation but also suggested the following:

> There is, nevertheless, a limitation to this interdependence between the current situation and the wider social world: an encounter with people whom he will not have dealings with again leaves him free to take a high line that the future will discredit, or free to suffer humiliations that would make future dealings with them an embarrassing thing to have to face. (p. 5)

So presentation of self, identity, and face are situationally significant as actors weigh up the consequences of performing creditably or discreditably in the current situation. Whatever the outcome of such rumination, management of identity and presentation of self are not disinterested, dispassionate activities. Goffman's discussions of face and stigma indicate this, suggesting a significant amount of interactional labor devoted to the maintenance, concealment, or promotion of certain identity features during the course of encounters. Goffman's analysis of the centrality of this identity work, both to interaction and to personal presentation, has provided influential resources drawn on by other writers (e.g., Brown & Levinson, 1978; Leech, 1983).

In all of his preoccupations, Goffman maintained a highly individualistic style and approach in his scholarship. Burns (1992) suggested that his work is devoted to the following:

> . . . Uncovering what happens in trivial and commonplace, or peripheral or bizarre, corners of social conduct, depicting its mechanism and its working in almost painfully elaborate detail—and then peeling off more and more of the covering of seemingly normal behaviour and

relationships to reveal similar or analogous structures and processes at work throughout the whole order of society. (p. 16)

In peeling off the layers, Goffman's work is full of illustrations. Indeed, on an initial reading one might think he was adding layers rather than peeling them off. His books and articles are replete with footnotes citing newspaper articles, television and radio programs, fiction and nonfiction books of all kinds, as well as anecdotal asides and small tailor-made case studies. He classified social activity in a multidimensional way. His lengthy essay "Remedial Interchanges" contains 66 footnotes that range from references to Schulz's *Peanuts* cartoons and *Mad Magazine* through to primate behavior, silent film comedies, and the testimony of the Boston Strangler (Goffman, 1971). Using such a diversity of sources, Goffman drew attention to the pervasiveness of social order. For him, nothing can be taken as insignificant in the analysis of social interaction. It is, however, as though we come upon the process of his thoughts halfway through the operation. The initial observation and classification have been done. Now, as an audience, we witness the spelling out of the classifications and their illustration in such a wide spectrum of events and situations that it is difficult to understand how they cannot apply. Schegloff noted that although Goffman's work is generally supposed to indicate a deeply empirical stance, the dense empiricism is often drawn on from elsewhere and not cited in the text itself (Schegloff, 1988). Moreover, Goffman rarely talks about his own research strategies (Drew & Wootton, 1988). Additionally, as Sharrock and Anderson have noted (1986), his writing does not accommodate how people *do* everyday tasks (including work) other than by considering the presentation of self qua actor. In other words, it begins at a stage beyond description, it begins with conceptualization: The machinery of description is missing.

My own view is that, for other researchers using Goffman's work, the dearth of sustained empirical usage and research methodology is no bad thing. The work provides an illuminating perspective on the nature of human social interaction that can inform other studies, and I have made considerable use of it in this study.

Ethnomethodology and the Taken for Granted World

Also preoccupied with inquiry into the everyday world is ethnomethodology, a branch of sociology established by Harold Garfinkel in the 1950s. The genesis of ethnomethodology lies in Garfinkel's work on a study of jurors. He perceived that the jurors he was studying used a series of rules, procedures, and principles that were commonsensical: That is to say, they brought a set of resources into the jurors' room that were essential for them to be able to decide the cases (Taylor & Cameron, 1987).

Garfinkel's work was a reaction to what he saw as some fundamental problems with the structural-functionalist sociology generated by Talcott Parsons and his associates. In his graduate work with Parsons, Garfinkel found the following:

> The overall trajectory of Parsons's theory of action, established in *The Structure of Social Action* and maintained throughout his career, was towards a treatment of action in terms of concepts which were almost wholly 'external' to the point of view of the actor. Action was to be analysed as the product of causal processes which, although operating 'in the minds' of the actors, were all but inaccessible to them, and hence, uncontrollable by them. (Heritage, 1984, p. 22)

Parsons assumed predetermined roles for actors in a social situation. Actions are governed by institutional rules and moral norms reflecting an overall value consensus: When people confront certain situations they follow the rules, that is, they behave appropriately, if they have been properly socialized. So, for Parsons, behavior is a product of internalized norms and values. For Garfinkel this approach was deeply problematic. He wanted to know what kind of norm or rule it would be that would tell us how to act in a situation. What for Parsons was an automatic process was for Garfinkel one that always requires interpretation.

Moreover, Parsons dealt with norms as if they were scientific constructs: He did this because he sought to explain people's behavior as the product of norms. But for Garfinkel they are rules that members use. Members are not cultural dopes or puppets, but active agents whose work accomplishes rationally accountable action: A complex and recursive process of interpretation is involved. Garfinkel defined cultural dopes as "the-man-in-the-sociologist's-society who produces the stable features of the society by acting in compliance with preestablished and legitimate alternatives of action that the common culture provides" (Garfinkel, 1967, p. 68).

As Taylor and Cameron (1987) suggested, whereas traditionally actors are seen to internalize rules, from an ethnomethodological point of view they "design their behavior with an awareness of its accountability" (p. 102). It is not that rules do not count: People use them to construct and account for their actions, but they are not scientific concepts. Rather than explaining people's actions, rules actually constitute this behavior through the accounts that are given of it.

Garfinkel's fundamental insight is that rules can never say in so many words what ought to be done where and when in a way that is completely exhaustive. Sharrock (1977) provided the illustration of a "No Parking" sign. People understand what the rule about this is but they are also aware that there are circumstances where the rule may be legitimately broken, for example, when a fire vehicle requires access. He noted that people can "see the meanings and implications of rules that are nowhere spelt out" (p. 552).

Talk and accounting in talk is, therefore, one of the central features of social life and a central analytic tool for Garfinkel and his colleagues:

> Everything that matters is present in overt behaviour, present in talk; sense-making *is* telling that sense, and sense-making is possible only because social settings and activities are organized and managed in ways that make their orderliness evident and accountable, ways that give a sense of coherence and planfulness to the social world. (Garfinkel, cited in O'Keefe, 1979, p. 196)

And Garfinkel emphasized this antimentalist approach by saying that "meaningful events are entirely and exclusively events in a person's behavioural environment . . . Hence there is no reason to look under the skull since nothing of interest is to be found there but brains" (Garfinkel, cited in O'Keefe, 1979, p. 193).

For Garfinkel, being able to handle natural language and to provide accounts is a central element of belonging to human society. As Heritage (1984) observed:

> Garfinkel approaches the topic by stressing that understanding language is not to be regarded as a matter of 'cracking a code' which contains a set of pre-established descriptive terms combined, by rules of grammar, to yield sentence meanings which express propositions about the world. Understanding language is not, in the first instance, a matter of understanding sentences but of understanding *actions*—utterances— which are constructively interpreted in relation to their contexts. This involves viewing an utterance against a background of *who* said it, *where* and *when*, *what* was being accomplished by saying it and in the light of what possible *considerations* and in virtue of what *motives* it was said. (pp. 139–140)

Thus, every moment of interaction is rich with complex interpretations of context and action by the actors. For example, to be involved in a conversation as a piece of social action is to be involved in an ongoing accomplishment. And, of course, even if some actors do not choose to consider who said what, where and when, nevertheless others will build such considerations into their interpretations.

In his early ethnomethodological work, Garfinkel (1967) suggested that a sensible way to examine the social world was to look at trouble in order to discern underlying patterns in everyday communication and social intercourse:

> Procedurally it is my preference to start with familiar scenes and ask what can be done to make trouble. The operations that one would have to perform in order to multiply the senseless features of perceived environments; to produce and sustain bewilderment, consternation, and confusion; to produce the socially structured affects of anxiety, shame, guilt and indignation; and to produce disorganized interaction should

tell us something about how the structures of everyday activities are ordinarily and routinely produced and maintained. (pp. 37–38)

This intention was carried out in what are called the breaching experiments. As we have seen, Garfinkel suggested that in everyday talk people do not rely on precise prespecified meanings. Instead, understanding is rooted in the occasioned interpretation of vagueness, or what he called indexicality, and in retrospective and prospective contextualizing. Such understandings "furnish a background of seen but unnoticed features of common discourse whereby actual utterances are recognized as events of common, reasonable, understandable plain talk" (Garfinkel, 1967, p. 41).

The breaching experiments were designed to show up this phenomenon. One, for example, required students to carry out experiments in their everyday interactions with people in which they sought to apply the level of precision in relation to concepts that would apply in science:

The subject was telling the experimenter, a member of the subject's car pool, about having had a flat tire while going to work the previous day.

(S)   I had a flat tire.

(E)   What do you mean you had a flat tire?

She appeared momentarily stunned. Then she answered in a hostile way: "What do you mean, 'What do you mean?' A flat tire is a flat tire. That is what I meant. Nothing special. What a crazy question!" (Garfinkel, 1967, p. 42)

The breach takes place within a very ordinary and recognizable situation. Here S responds to E in an annoyed way as though E should be a rational person who is perfectly capable of understanding what a flat tire is but who is choosing for some unknown and possibly malicious reason to misunderstand. To question the ordinary usage of talk is an action that is quickly sanctionable.

However, breaching is not necessarily followed by a break in social interaction. This is evidenced by Garfinkel's experiments with the game of tic-tac-toe, in which the experimenter rubbed out the lines or added in new ones. Here, people sometimes just waited to see what he would do next, assuming that all would become clear, or they developed or extended the rules to make sense of such behavior (Sharrock & Anderson, 1986). In another breaching experiment, when students were asked to behave as lodgers in their own homes, other family members had various explanations and rationales, for example, that school performance, illness or emotional problems may have affected their behavior.

In some cases relatives adjusted, treating the whole thing as a comedy routine, whereas others sought to establish new rules, as is illustrated by one father's comments: "I don't want any more of *that* out of *you* and if you can't treat your mother decently you'd better move out!" (1967, p. 48). However, in the experiment there were no cases in which the behavior did not create an interactional problem that needed to be accounted for. Indeed one putative and insightful experimenter refused to take part because her mother had a heart condition (1967 p. 47).

As we shall see, confused talk represents a sort of natural breaching experiment. It disrupts ordinary patterns and causes problems, though it does not usually result in the breakdown of social interaction. In this way the situation of confusion and members' handling of it can be seen under the ethnomethodological rubric as a topic—a problem to be investigated rather than merely evidence of deviance.

Conversation Analysis and Types of Talk

One of the products of ethnomethodology was conversation analysis, which began with the work of Harvey Sacks and his collaborators Emanuel Schegloff and Gail Jefferson. Schegloff said of his experience of reading one of the former's early papers:

> There is a distinctive and utterly critical recognition here that the talk can be examined as an object in its own right, and not merely as a screen on which are projected other processes . . . The talk itself was the action, and previously unsuspected details were critical resources in what was getting done in and by the talk; and all this in naturally occurring events, in no way manipulated to allow the study of them. And it seemed possible to give quite well-defined, quite precise accounts of how what was getting done was getting done—methodical accounts of action. (Schegloff, 1989, p. 190)

Heritage (1984) noted that such analysis is, at its roots, concerned with the competence that underlies ordinary social activities, and Sharrock and Anderson (1986) confirmed this, noting that convesation analysts are looking to notice "what anyone would notice, to see the glaring and obvious things" (p.70).

It is perhaps difficult today to recognize the novelty that conversation analysis had when it was originally developed. Sociologists and other social scientists had not devoted much attention to the details of verbal interaction; and, perhaps surprisingly, neither had linguists. They had tended to concentrate on the study of grammar, very often using invented sentences as their data. (As Zimmerman [1988] noted, invented sentences cannot replicate context.) Sacks' emphasis on the study of naturally occurring conversations was a reaction against this earlier work. Sacks was interested, above all else, in what went on in the details of ordinary life: "He aimed to construct accounts of how the 'technicians in residence' at the conversational worksite assemble their ordinary communicational activities" (Lynch & Bogen, 1994, p. 74).

And in his work (and the work of his collaborators too) he remains, as Psathas put it (1995) "descriptively close to the phenomena" (p. 71) a position, as we have seen, that is rather different from that which Goffman took up.

A number of sophisticated formulations were developed to explain how people handle conversation as a piece of interactional work. *Turn taking* is one basic feature of conversation that has been dealt with in considerable detail by conversation analysts. In an article which has become a landmark, Sacks, Schegloff, and Jefferson (1978) began by stating 14 grossly apparent facts about ordinary conversation:[4]

1. Speaker change recurs, or, at least, occurs . . .
2. Overwhelmingly, one party talks at a time . . .
3. Occurrences of more than one speaker at a time are common, but brief . . .
4. Transitions from one turn to a next with no gap and no overlap between them are common . . .
5. Turn order is not fixed, but varies . . .
6. Turn size is not fixed, but varies . . .
7. Length of conversation is not fixed, specified in advance . . .
8. What parties say is not fixed, specified in advance . . .
9. Relative distribution of turns is not fixed, specified in advance . . .
10. Number of parties can change . . .
11. Talk can be continuous or discontinuous . . .
12. Turn-allocation techniques are obviously used . . .
13. Various "turn-constructional" units are employed . . .
14. Repair mechanisms for dealing with turn-taking errors and violations obviously are available for use. (pp. 10–11)

The body of their article is devoted to developing a model of turn taking that accommodates these facts. Participants follow various rules of turn taking in order to conduct conversation and at any stage in a conversation both current speakers and listeners are guided by this sequence of rules. The writers present a model that they think accounts for all possibilities of how turns can be allocated, notably selection of another speaker by current speaker and self-selection by current speaker.

In one of his lectures, Sacks further elucidated the complexity of turn taking (Sacks, 1995a). Whereas in a two-way conversation a speaker sequence of ABABAB is unproblematic, the same type of progression is untenable in an ordinary multiparty conversation. ABCDABCD does not, for example, accommodate B wanting to speak to A again immediately

---

[4] Lynch and Bogen (1994) suggested that a large corpus of conversation analysis work has coalesced around this original article, and thus turn taking has come to be defined as one central feature of the discipline.

after being addressed. Nor does it allow for C to ask B for clarification after she has misheard. So speaker selection techniques in multiparty conversation need to be flexible enough to permit local and immediate management of the talk. And Sacks and others have identified a number of devices that contribute to the orderly and flexible execution of turn taking. Preeminent among these are *adjacency pairs*. These are paired utterances where an utterance of one type (a first pair part) expects a second utterance of an appropriate type (a second pair part), for example, an offer and an acceptance, a question and an answer, and so on (Sacks, 1995a, p. 525). Sacks noted that such devices provide a vehicle for current speaker to select next speaker and that they play a role in what Goffman called remedial exchanges. Thus, a failure to understand can be remedied by the production of a first pair part "What did you say?" In this way, local problems of conversational order can be dealt with (Sacks, 1995a, p. 525). Sacks also noted that the use of the adjacency pair sequence can be extended into three- and four-utterance constructions that guide turns over a longer stretch of talk. Consider the following sequence:

> Are you going to Birmingham?
> What did you say?
> To Birmingham.
> Yes.

This can be described as {Q [q-a] A}, with the middle two utterances being referred to as an *insertion sequence*. Sacks (1995a) observed that the insertion sequence is one lawful occasion when turn taking can accommodate a question following a question, but that not any question can follow a question.

One of the features of adjacency pairs is that the second pair part is *conditionally relevant* on the first pair part and not merely adjacent to it (Schegloff, 1972b). The occurrence of a first pair part of a particular kind sets up the expectation that a relevant second pair part will occur. And such an expectation has moral force. However, this does not absolutely constrain the second pair part; for example, an invitation can legitimately be followed by either an acceptance or a refusal (both responses "fit" an invitation). But, as Levinson (1983) noted, not all potential, available, and appropriate second pair parts are of equal standing, and participants will prefer to make one response rather than another according to specific criteria. This construction is referred to as a *preference* (Levinson, 1983). Preferred second pair parts such as acceptances to invitations tend to be structurally less complex and to require little or no additional accounting by the respondent, whereas dispreferred second pair parts such as refusals to invitations tend to involve qualifications and hedges (Bilmes, 1988; Brown & Levinson, 1978; Levinson, 1983; Pomerantz, 1984). We can see the relevance of this to turn size in that a refusal to an invitation is likely to involve a longer turn than would be taken by an acceptance.

A substantial body of conversation analysis work builds on the idea of sequencing: On the introduction of the first topic in conversation, on signaling forthcoming stories that are going to require a long turn, on the problems of changing topic, on the openings and closings of talk, on the turns other participants are legitimately able to take during the course of a long utterance by one participant, on the telling of stories and many other aspects of mundane conversation (see e.g., Jefferson, 1978; Sacks, 1995a, 1995b; Schegloff, 1972b; Schegloff & Sacks, 1974).

Another important strand of conversation analysis work, however, is how people do the work of describing. Sacks (1963) suggested that the task of the conversation analyst is to develop a formal machinery to describe description. The question is how to produce descriptions so that people can understand them, given that they often will not have access to the referents of those descriptions. Sacks' concept of *membership category devices* is a central feature of this strand of conversation analysis. People refer to each other and to objects categorically: In this way *membership* of categories is assigned. Moreover, depending on context, people are able to group categories together. As Silverman (1993) noted, any ordinary member is able to infer that "The X cried. The Y picked it up" (p. 80) is more likely to be about a baby being picked up rather than a teacher. Sacks' classic exemplification of membership category devices is a child's story: "The baby cried. The mommy picked it up". Sacks asserted that hearers will hear this as a story about the baby's own mother picking up the baby and analyzes how this comes to be (Sacks, 1972).

In doing the work of description, ordinary members have available a variety of correct ways in which they could describe an event, and they must select from these one that is appropriate for the situation, context and audience. In a discussion of the formulation of place, for example, Schegloff (1972b) observed that "the selection of a locational formulation requires of a speaker (and will exhibit for a hearer) an analysis of his own location and the location of his co-conversationalist(s), and of the objects whose location is being formulated (if that object is not one of the co-conversationalists)." (p. 83)

Thus, the apparently simple act of referring to some place requires assumptions about where one is, who one is with, and what one is doing at this current point in the conversation. In talking about characterizing an event, Sacks (1995b) noted that "Come to dinner" is only a partial description of the event that will take place but is preferred over "Come over and have a drink of water" or "Come over and sit on the living room couch", both of which activities are also likely to take place during the course of the evening. He suggested that *dinner* is a first preference invitation. That is to say, if dinner is included in the invitation for the evening's events, then the person inviting needs to say so, otherwise it cannot be assumed that it is included.

The work of describing must always be partial. Just as no rule can ever be exhaustive, so no description can ever be exhaustive: It must disattend to some of the potential referents in an event or situation. So an appropriate formulation from a series of correct ones is partial (because there are other correct available formulations). However, although descriptions and rules are not exhaustive and do not take into account every contingency, people nevertheless manage to understand each other in a way that is adequate for all practical purposes, even given the mistakes and ambiguities with which ordinary talk is littered. Thus, the methods by which people formulate appropriately are another central concern of conversation analysts and ethnomethodologists, and considerable work has been done in this area (see, e.g., Livingston, 1987, Sacks, 1995a 1995b; Schegloff, 1972b; Sharrock, 1974).

As conversation analysis developed, many writers progressed from looking solely at naturally occurring conversation and became interested in institutional and specialized talk, where the relationship between preallocation of turns and local management of talk is important (e.g. J. M. Atkinson & Drew, 1979; Drew & Heritage, 1992; McHoul, 1978, 1990); etc.). As Zimmerman (1988), following from J. M. Atkinson, observed:

> Particular orders of interactional activity in a society may require the modification of the procedures employed in everyday talk because the conditions of interaction in institutional or organizational settings differ to some degree from those encountered in everyday conversation. (p. 424)

With this interest there was a change in orientation from a focus on identities that are intrinsic to ordinary conversation, such as current speaker and next speaker, to identities that are extrinsic to the conversation, that is to say, identities that in some way involve preallocation of turns, for example, *teacher*. However, Heritage (1984) suggested that mundane conversation remains an important baseline for all analytic endeavour in the area of talk. In talking about the application of conversation analysis to institutional data he said the following:

> Not only is mundane conversation the richest available research domain, but also . . . comparative analysis with mundane conversation is essential if the 'special features' of interaction in particular institutional contexts are to receive adequate specification and understanding. (p. 240)

Discussion of specialized talk is often based on assumptions about the nature of an ordinary conversation. For example, Suchman and Jordan

(1990), in an article about interactional troubles in face-to-face survey interviews, looked at:

> The differences between the survey interview and ordinary conversation, focusing on the survey instrument's external control over who speaks and on what topic, prohibitions against any redesign of questions by the interviewer and special requirements placed on the form of answers, problems of question relevance and meaning, and failures in the detection and repair of misunderstanding . . . In what follows we look closely at just how the survey interview is "in the manner of a conversation" and, more important, how it is not. The constraints on the interview we observe that distinguish it from ordinary conversation are all imposed in the interest of *standardization* . . . Stability of meaning, the real basis for standardization and ultimately for validity, requires the full resources of conversational interaction. (pp. 232–233)

Subsequent headings in the article reflect this basic structure, for example "Local versus external control", "Recipient designed questions", "Requirements on the answer", "Establishing relevance" and so on. Much other work on institutional talk shows similar recourse to terms originating in analysis of ordinary conversations.

However, for some analysts the movement to analysis of institutional talk poses substantial problems. Schegloff (1992) observed that institutional conversation analysis is an attempt to "effect a rapprochement" (p. 102) between conversation analysis and more traditional sociological concerns with social structure. He was concerned with the analytic problems that this presents:

> Even if we can show by analysis of the details of the interaction that some characterization of the context or the setting in which the talk is going on (such as "in the hospital") is relevant for the parties, that they are oriented to the setting so characterized, there remains another problem, and that is to show how the context or the setting (the local social structure), *in that aspect*, is procedurally consequential to the talk. How does the fact that the talk is being conducted in some setting (e.g. "the hospital") issue in any consequence for the shape, form, trajectory, content, or character of the interaction that the parties conduct? (Schegloff, 1992, p. 111)

Schegloff argued in the same article that some studies in institutional conversation analysis demonstrate this procedural consequentiality inadequately and thus fall prey to the same sort of criticism that conversation analysts originally directed at conventional sociology: That it imposes arbitrarily external categorizations on members' activities. My own view is not as empiricist as that of Schegloff, with his insistence that all that has shaped the interaction must be observable in the data. Although seeking to avoid a lapse into speculative analysis, I have interpreted the talk of the people in my data in terms of the context in which they found themselves and their likely responses to that. In other words, I make a broader reference to the interaction order.

Grice and the Cooperative Principle

Not all analysis of conversation is in the ethnomethodological tradition. Taylor and Cameron (1987) outlined a variety of approaches made to the study of conversation. Focusing largely on studies that centered on rules and units, they explored social psychological studies, speech act theories, functionalism and exchange structure analyses of conversation, and Gricean pragmatics, as well as ethnomethodological conversation analysis. The most relevant of these for my purposes here, apart from conversation analysis, is the work of Paul Grice.

Grice proposed a conception of communication that is focused on inference rather than the more traditional encoding and decoding model. Sperber and Wilson (1986) noted that "A *code* . . . is a system which pairs messages with signals, enabling two information-processing devices (organisms or machines) to communicate" (pp. 3–4). And they went on to say the following:

> There is a gap between the semantic representation of sentences and the thoughts actually communicated by utterances. This gap is filled not by more coding, but by inference. Moreover, there is an alternative to the code model of communication. Communication has been described as a process of inferential recognition of the communicator's intentions. (Sperber & Wilson, 1986, p. 9)

The focus on inference and on the constraints and opportunities in real conversations (as opposed to artificially created sentences) makes Grice's work sympathetic to many of the concerns of sociologists whose interests lie with the taken-for-granted world of everyday life.

Grice (1975) emphasized that there is an important difference between sentence meaning and speaker meaning in talk:

> While it is no doubt true that the formal devices are especially amenable to systematic treatment by the logician, it remains the case that there are very many inferences and arguments, expressed in natural language and not in terms of these devices, that are nevertheless recognizably valid. (p. 43)

He suggested that in order for people to understand each other, some principles of cooperation must be adhered to:

> We might then formulate a rough general principle which participants will be expected (ceteris paribus) to observe, namely: Make your conversational contribution such as is required, at the stage at which it occurs, by the accepted purpose or direction of the talk exchange in which you are engaged. One might label this the COOPERATIVE PRINCIPLE. (Grice, 1975, p. 45)

From this basic principle Grice derived a number of conversational maxims:

The Maxim of Quality:
try to make your contribution one that is true, specifically:
(i)   do not say what you believe to be false
(ii) do not say that for which you lack adequate evidence

The Maxim of Quantity
(i)   make your contribution as informative as is required for the current purposes of the exchange
(ii) do not make your contribution more informative than is required

The Maxim of Relevance:
make your contributions relevant

The Maxim of Manner:
be perspicacious, and specifically:
(i)   avoid obscurity
(ii)   avoid ambiguity
(iii) be brief
(iv)   be orderly (Grice, cited in Levinson, 1983, pp. 101–102)

Grice did not suggest that people adhere to such rules at a detailed level in ordinary conversation but that they use them as guides in producing talk. Perhaps even more importantly, they assume that speakers are orienting to these maxims. And speakers assume that hearers will assume that they are adhering to these maxims. It is on the basis of these assumptions that inferences about speakers' meaning are made, and that speakers communicate what they want to say. He also suggested that people infer at a nonsuperficial level so that utterances that appear to be noncooperative can, at some other level, be seen to conform to the maxims. He called this *conversational implicature* (Grice, 1975; Levinson, 1983).

Grice's work has been used and developed by a number of writers and is substantially referred to in sociological and pragmatic writing concerned with conversation and talk (see, e.g., Anderson & Sharrock, 1984; Brown & Levinson, 1978; Heritage, 1984; Leech, 1983; Sperber & Wilson, 1986; etc.). Additionally, Brown and Levinson (1978) and Leech (1983) made a bridge between the work of Goffman on face and that of Grice on conversational cooperation, in considering the moral dimensions of talk. This is a bridge of which I make considerable use in this study, looking at the implications of confused talk for the identities of those involved in conversational exchanges where it occurs.

MEMBERS WHO ARE "PROBLEMS"

The three bodies of work I have discussed so far all focus on the ordinary competences of everyday interaction, in both a cognitive and moral sense. Indeed, they show that these two aspects of competence can hardly be distinguished. Ordinary membership assumes a shared competence that is acted out in social activity and talk. As Payne (1976) noted:

> 'Members' are those with a shared stock of common-sense knowledge about the social world and a common competence in applying that knowledge. Membership involves a recognised competence in a natural language and observably adequate performance in identifiable speech communities. It involves having one's competence to make reasonable and sensible observations and to produce reasonable and sensible talk and activities taken for granted. (p. 330)

And Garfinkel (1967) observed: "I use the term "competence" to mean the claim that a collectivity member is entitled to exercise that he is capable of managing his everyday affairs without interference" (p. 57).

During the course of this study I make much use of the terms *members, less-than-full members, ordinary members* and *membership*. Largely speaking, I use the terms in the sense that Payne (above) describes, of recognizable competence. However membership is also used in what might be described as a much tighter way than this: I allude to the discussions by Sacks and others of membership categorization and membership category devices in talk (Sacks, 1972). I made some mention of these usages earlier in the chapter. Clearly there are connections between these two clusters of terms. Less-than-full membership can be seen by members to involve a recognizably less-than-ordinary competence. At the same time there are a number of categories of less-than-full members who are associated by the fact that they are the recipients of rather similar category-bound activity in talk addressed to them by normal members: children, people with learning difficulties, and people with dementing illnesses can all be talked to in the same way. Conventionally, such category-bound talk is distinguished by being loud, slow, familiar, and kind—all at the same time—and may additionally involve an amendment of the operation of equal interactional rights. Indeed, this cluster of activity in talk can alert us to the idea that someone present has less-than-full membership. And a retort can be made such as "Don't talk to me as though I were a child", which suggests an explicit refusal to orient to such category-bound talk, or to accept the membership being offered.

Ordinary membership is routinely assumed in much social interaction. However, there are categories of person that imply less-than-full membership. One such category is confused speakers. Indeed, the definitions just given provide, as it were, almost a blueprint for identifying such speakers merely by checking off what they cannot do, and observing that they are not able to carry out their everyday affairs without interventions from others. As I noted earlier, confused talk constitutes what one might call a natural breaching experiment: It illuminates the nature of everyday interactional competence and the work that goes on in recognizing and dealing with deviations from it. However, confused speakers are not the only category of people whose interactional competence is open to question, and I have also drawn on literature dealing with some other problematic categories.

One obvious category of less-than-full members is children. In some senses studies of the socialization of children have long been seen as a social scientific test ground for demonstrating a society's mores, whether in older anthropological studies like those of Margaret Mead (e.g., Mead, 1943, 1963), or some of the feminist critiques of socialization (see Belotti, 1975). A number of studies of children have been done in ethnomethodology (see, e.g., M. A. Atkinson, 1973; Mackay, 1974). One of the most important of these for my purposes is Speier's (1969) study of childhood socialization. He observes that:

> One of the basic jobs of mothers (and fathers too) is telling their children what they are "supposed to do". . . communicating to their children what "rules" they are expected to know and use, whenever it is deemed necessary or advisable to do so. (p. 1)

An underlying theme of Speier's thesis is that communication of rules goes on primarily in explicit directives and prompts:

12. Mo.	Andrea, Andrea ((calls)) Come here please. ((calls))
13. A.	Yes, mommy.
14. Mo.	Say hallo to her.
15. A.	Hi Hampton. (Speier, 1969, p. 186)

1.	Hey Mike! ((Goes over to staircase and looks up.))
2.	What? ((From top of stairs.))
3.	You can't go anywhere until you <u>say</u> something to me.
4.	Oh, Hel-lo ((Comes down stairs.)) (Speier, 1969, p. 177)

In the process, attention may be drawn to the shortfalls in children's competence. A parental directive publicly exposes them as not having said "Hallo". But allowances are made because people do not expect children to be fully competent. For the parents, public exposure has its credit side too: demonstrating to the world that the socialization is properly in hand. These processes also socialize the child to accountability. That is to say, they draw the child's attention to those things that he or she is doing that will be remarked on. The child learns that not only should 'Hallo' be said when he or she comes in but also learns, in time, that if it is said this will become unremarked behavior which is, in the main, a desirable outcome.

There are many points of comparison between the sorts of examples and situations that Speier examined and those in my data. Because children are not effectively full members, much of their lives is spent in social interactions that offer them directives concerning how to achieve full membership. Confused speakers too are offered such directives. There is a difference, however. Broadly speaking, the role of the person with confusion points in exactly the opposite direction to the role of the child, as Speier explicated it. The child's role is constructed in terms of building toward a competent persona. The confused person's role is constructed in terms of a retreat from competence. In this sense, what I focus on in my study represents a mirror image of what he was concerned with in his. Incidentally this comparison with children is one which can be identified in caregivers' concepts too. Taraborrelli (1994) quoted one caregiver as saying of her dementing mother, "They're not your baby who's going to grow up . . . you know with a baby it's only going to be like that for so long and then that's it" (p. 32).

Other work on children is also illuminating. There has been a small amount of conversation analysis work dealing with classroom talk: For example, Payne and Cuff's edited collection (1982) included papers on storytelling, dealing with latecomers, starting the day, and adolescent-adult talk as a practical interpretive problem. Other classroom research has focused on the problems of question and answer sequences, modifications to turn taking, and so on, largely from the point of view of the interactional limitations placed on children in classroom talk (Hammersley, 1986a, 1986b; McHoul, 1978, 1990). This work essentially relates to how teachers "do" being teachers and how children "do" being pupils, and to the resultant distribution of interactional rights between full and less-than-full members.

Researchers also examined other groups who are, in some way, not accorded full membership. For example, Coupland, Giles, and Wiemann's collection (1991) on miscommunication encompasses groups of people who can be seen not to be accorded full membership rights because of aspects of their status: nonnative speakers, and older people, as well as children. Particularly interesting from the point of view of this study is research relating to people with dementing illnesses, mental health problems, and learning difficulties. For instance, Gubrium has worked extensively on the lives of older people, and in the field of Alzheimer's disease, focusing on how the illness is socially constructed in biographical terms (Gubrium, 1985, 1986, 1987; see also Gubrium & Holstein, 1994). In an article partly relating to the life of Rita Hayworth, the American film star (1985), he showed family members to have constructed a retrospective of her life, which implies that there were many early signs of the illness, for example the pattern of her many marriages, and her drinking excesses. This in turn implies that "looking back on it" she was always "suspect" as a full member. In a similar way, Kitwood (1993) presented a number of sociopsychological analyses that draw attention to the construction of *us* and *them* categories in relation to people with dementing illnesses, suggesting that any behavioral aberrations of *us* as normal people are discounted and ignored while those of sufferers are seen as indicative of their condition. Again we can see that deviance can be construed as a momentary and explicable straying or disruption of the interaction order for normal people but as part of a chronic stigmatizing process for nonnormals.

Other studies have focused on the competences of people perceived to have other types of mental health problems (e.g., Coulter, 1973; Chaika & Alexander, 1986; Rochester & Martin, 1979;). Some highlight how incompetence is socially accomplished by being assigned to certain members by others or, on occasion, being jointly produced. For example, Pollner (1975) and Coulter (1975) both investigated the methods used by members to reject perceptual accounts of others that are at odds with their own commonsense knowledge. Similarly Lynch (1983) explored the methods by which ordinary members organize their dealings with people with mental health problems who remain in the community. Holstein (1988) in an examination of court proceedings at involuntary commitment hearings suggested that, depending on the plea they are making, lawyers construct talk with defendants to elicit competent or incompetent responses. These studies have in common an interest in how full members deal with less-than-full members, using normality as a benchmark for judgments, a feature, too, of this book.

Another group who often has less-than-full membership is people with learning difficulties. A number of studies in this area indicate the importance placed on "passing as ordinary" by many of those seen as less-than-full members. Hughes and May (1986) discussed the relationship between staff and trainees at an Adult Training Center, suggesting how both construct a pattern of ordinary behavior and how "doing" ordinary behavior is valorized by the trainees, in the desire to be recognized as full members of society. Yearley and Brewer (1989) explored the competence of people with learning difficulties in a residential context, as it relates to face and stigma. They noted substantial competence in ordinary conversation among residents in terms of turn taking, topic changes, and so on. However, when confronted with visitors, residents often use a monosyllabic pattern of talk: a tactic which, although guarding against loss of face by nonexposure, also threatens it. In a similar way, Edgerton (1967) discussed the *cloak of competence* that people with learning difficulties don in order to maintain face and pass as ordinary people. Such passing often includes elaborate embroidery on a biography that is essentially institutional (and therefore may be perceived as abnormal and stigmatizing), sometimes aided by the acquisition of photographs and memorabilia that are completely unconnected with the individuals' past life—but which are intended to facilitate a demonstration of normality. Most less-than-full members, then, are aware that *normal* counts and that they will be judged by others on how well they can replicate normal behavior.

CONCLUSION

The confusion resulting from dementing illnesses is commonly recognized as a problem, and one that has attracted a substantial body of research, much of which has been medically or practice-oriented in character. In such studies confusion and its medical aetiology are central. As a result, the contexts relating to ways in which confusion and normality are judged and the inferential work required to reach the point of assigning these categories are not explicated. Underlying the research is a commonsense understanding of confusion that is never made a topic of enquiry.

I want to suggest that commonsense understandings of confusion and accompanying understandings of normality are problematic and require investigation. In this chapter I have pointed to a literature that can facilitate such an investigation. Goffman's work and its preoccupation with the interaction order is important, particularly the concepts of identity, face, stigma, and faultedness. Ethnomethodology is central, too, with its interpretation of people as rule users rather than rule governed. Garfinkel's breaching experiments, which highlight the idea of troubles as revealing the otherwise unnoticed character of the normal, are relevant especially because confused speakers can be seen as the perpetrators of natural breaching experiments. But the relevance is broader than this because we all, now and then, become embroiled in conversational breaching experiments; on occasion we all cause trouble in talk.

Conversation analysis, with its two main foci on turn taking and description work, and Grice's work on conversational cooperation also provide major analytic resources on which I draw in this study, throwing light both on confused speakers and also the sort of confused talk normal speakers may become involved in. The final category of relevant literature I use in the study involves categories of people who are treated as less-than-full members: The interest of writers in this field has often been in how full members deal with less-than-full members, and how the latter attempt to pass as ordinary, issues that are central to my own research. Most of the literature I have cited and use in my analysis should be appropriate not only for examining the sort of confused speaker I identify in the study, but also for throwing light on the ordinary confusions of talk between normal speakers.

The different traditions on which I draw do not necessarily fit comfortably together. An example of the tension between traditions occurs in Schegloff's suggestion that Goffman's orientation to moral concerns and ritual (a central feature of his sociology) undermines his analysis of social action:

> 'What minimal model of an actor is needed' he [Goffman] asked . . . 'if we are to wind him up, stick him in amongst his fellows, and have an orderly traffic of behavior emerge?'. But he surely recognized that such a traffic is the product not only of the drivers, but of the properties of the vehicles, the roadways, the fuel, the traffic system, etc. (Schegloff, 1988, p. 94)

Schegloff observed that Goffman remained committed to the drivers rather than the traffic system. Yet it seems to me that both approaches are useful in order to understand the problems that surround confused speech. At an utterance-to-utterance level, confused speech can be interpreted as a momentary trouble, a traffic problem; however, it can also be seen as a chronic trouble at the level of an actor's performance in a variety of situations—in other words, as a driver problem. These are the two axes around which my investigation is organized. For some readers *the traffic problem* may be their main concern, in the sense that they are primarily interested in the issue of momentary troubles in talk. I hope this study elucidates that issue. But more generally, I think the intersection of these two axes presents a richer analysis of confused talk than either axis taken separately.

2

Assembling and Processing the Data

My original interest in the talk of confused speakers arose from my own ordinary member understanding that what people says sounds simple but usually turns out to be complex. I had always been interested in why talk goes wrong. Right at the beginning of this research I was actually investigating entirely another subject, the collective history of housing cooperatives as told by members. After conducting a number of interviews, in the lengthy process of transcribing I found I kept returning to confusions in the talk—how people did not understand my questions or how I did not understand their answers and how that was apparent in the talk. And then I got involved in how repair took place and how the talk got tangled up and then untangled. By this time I came to the conclusion that my real interests were actually how confusion is manifest in talk! So my first forays in the direction of confused talk arose out of talk between normal speakers.

Fortuitously, my interest in confusion was further stimulated by my work as a lecturer at the UK Open University. At about the time I was collecting data for the history of the housing cooperative I changed jobs, moving departments within the University to develop a course called "Working with Older People" (Open University, 1990). For this I undertook the task of writing some materials about mental health problems in old age. In the reading I did for this course there was a great deal of reference to confusion, and I became particularly interested in some materials from an earlier Open University course, "Mental Health Problems in Old Age" (1988), which outlined behavior aberrations of people with senile dementia.

There followed a period of confusion on my own part, as I began to explore the possibility of examining extreme forms of confusion by collecting life histories of people suffering from dementia or comparing the characteristics of life histories told by people suffering from dementia with those of people who were not. In the end, though, I realized that what I was interested in was how confused talk differs from normal talk; and, in particular, how people are found to be confused by normal speakers and how the latter are able to demonstrate their continuing normality in conversations with confused speakers. I should say that although this chapter focuses very much on data emerging from talk between normal and confused speakers, there are, in my view, many additional laminations involved in working up the data into their final form of extracts used in the study. The process of working up the data, as we shall see, provides a number of opportunities to commit some of the players to the category of normal and others to the category of abnormal.

COLLECTING THE DATA

Given the nature of my new research focus, I required audiotaped materials featuring confused speakers. I was able to gain access to three such sources of materials: interviews I conducted with some confused speakers and their caregivers, previously recorded interviews carried out by colleagues, and some domestic interaction between one confused speaker and her caregiver. My data consist of about 10 hours of audiotaped materials, all involving people who had been diagnosed as confused, engaging in verbal interaction with normal speakers. During the course of analyzing these data, it became increasingly obvious to me that the settings in which the talk took place were important. And so now I am going to provide as much relevant information as possible about the circumstances in which the data were collected, and about the types of talk they involve. In addition, I want to reflect on the process by which I came to have a point of view on these data.

Interviews in a Clinic

In locating people with whom to talk, my only initial criterion was that the system (i.e., medical and social services) should have labeled them as confused. I wanted to listen to people whose confusion had been recognized by others as an ongoing problem. This constitutes a large category of people, because not only are there a substantial number of sufferers from various kinds of dementing illnesses, but in older people organic illnesses such as influenza and bladder infection may generate what the medical profession calls confusion. In the latter cases, as the illness retreats, so too does the confusion. Although talking to people suffering from short-term confusion would have met my criteria, they would have been difficult to locate, interviewing them while they were feeling very ill would not have been legitimate, and I would probably have been a burden on caregivers. Instead, I decided to focus on people who had already been diagnosed as suffering from long-term confusion. This group of people often acquire the label of *confused* as a half-way house prior to some other diagnosis, for example Alzheimer's disease or Multi-Infarct Dementia (Open University, 1988). The diagnosis of confusion does not imply the total absence of lucidity, but rather that there is a high likelihood that some daily talk will be confused.

I contacted a consultant geriatrician known to Open University colleagues and he invited me to attend clinics he conducted for the assessment and treatment of people suffering from confusion. I arranged to go to one of his psychogeriatric clinics for several mornings and interview whoever was there and was willing to be interviewed. In the case of all the people concerned, both the consultant and I asked if they would be prepared to be interviewed by me, and I also asked permission to make and use audiotapes of the talk for my research. Where the confused speaker appeared not to understand my request I specifically asked the caregivers for permission as well.

I have changed most first and all last names of research participants in this study and most place names or other identifying details in the transcripts, such as the names of local companies. I have also maintained the form of names used by clients and caregivers, thus, when they used first names, I have done the same. (A full but anonymised list of all the participants in my research recordings can be found in Appendix A.)

Each time I visited, I spent the whole morning at the psychogeriatric clinic, sitting for part of the time in the waiting room or consulting room and the rest of the time in an anteroom to the consulting room where I interviewed clients and their caregivers. On the days I was present, the procedure for a visit to the clinic was standard. Clients and their caregivers would check in at reception and then go to the waiting room where a helper gave them drinks and chatted with them. They were then conducted to the consultant's room. The consultations were follow-ups, for people who had already seen the consultant. Each session lasted about 20 minutes and involved the consultant, another doctor, a social worker, and a community psychiatric nurse (plus myself if I was sitting in). Occasionally, the client was taken away from the consulting room during the session for a test of some sort.

When I was present, the consultant usually introduced me as someone interested in communication, and said that I wanted to have a chat with the confused speaker afterward. At the end of the assessment I took the client and caregiver to the anteroom. Occasionally, if I was already talking to one confused speaker and their caregiver and could not sit in on the next assessment, I was introduced to the people concerned by the consultant or the social worker after my previous talk was over. After talking to me, the client would go to the day center in the same building for lunch or to wait for an ambulance to take them home.

The Setting of the Psychogeriatric Clinic. In analyzing the tapes from the clinic, I was able to rely both on my everyday knowledge of encounters of this type, and my memory of these events. I was able to recall the physical features of the setting and when I heard nonverbal noises on the audio tapes I could recall what generated some of them. The following account relies partially on this recall and is not entirely focused on the tapes themselves. However, one of the processes of analysis in this study, as it relates to my own interview data, is to try to step outside this reliance on ordinary recall.

Much work on the study of language has emphasized the importance of context. This is true, for example, of a great deal of sociolinguistic work (see, e.g., Giglioli, 1972; Gumperz & Hymes, 1972) and also of the body of work referred to as *pragmatics* (see Levinson, 1983). Thus, in understanding the talk that took place in the clinic, and in particular my own interviews, some clarification of the nature of that context is required. It was a context in which talk was central. The confused speakers and their caregivers normally encountered a process and setting in which talk was an essential component, albeit usually talk that was initiated and orchestrated by others. Use of space and timing was controlled by the talk and the main event itself was an assessment through talk. Moreover, the illness—the confusion—was displayed through talk on this multifaceted occasion, where participants were called on to discern which types of talk were appropriate for which stage in the event.

A number of studies have explored social interaction in a clinic setting and have drawn attention to the significance of that type of setting to actors (see, e.g., Sharrock & Anderson, 1987; Silverman, 1987; Strong, 1979). In his study of a variety of clinic sites, Silverman (1987) emphasized the importance of site as a place where the career trajectory of patients and the disposal of the case are played out (p. 10). Sites present patients and medical staff with both opportunities and constraints for "doing" patient career or disposal of cases. Silverman noted (pp. 264–269), for example, that the desk, couch, and side room may each contribute toward a definition of some social situation: The family may assert their own structure in the seating arrangements and handling of the child; the couch may be seen as medical territory, with the child being taken there by a nurse; the side room may involve negotiations about "ownership" of the child. Thus the settings in a clinic may be seen as interactional resources that contribute to the joint production of an event that can be called *a visit to the clinic*.

In the case of the clinic I attended, the setting could also be seen as an interactional and contextual resource. An overall impression was of a quite institutionalized setting. The clinic was housed in an old Victorian school, decorated extensively in pale green gloss paint and lustrous tiles, equipped with plenty of institutional paraphernalia such as files lying around and pervaded by the smell of cooked lunch.

The waiting room, consulting room, and anteroom in the psychogeriatric clinic were all linked to each other by doors, as well as each room having a door to the public part of the day center. Thus clients did not have to go back into the public day center during the course of their contact with health care professionals or myself (unless they went for some kind of test). At each stage in the process they were introduced or conducted to the next room by a member of staff or myself. Each room was there to be seen as a subsetting of the clinic, and the people in each room (including myself) were to be seen as associated with the clinic. By the time the clients and their caregivers arrived to talk to me, they were in at least their third subsetting of the psychogeriatric clinic.

A visit to the psychogeriatric clinic was also a temporally organized and bounded occasion. The first stop was the waiting room. Here, usually, the helper engaged clients and caregivers in conversation, informing them that the doctor was already here, or that appointments were running late, and so on; in other words, temporal markers were established about the main event, the consultation. This was interspersed with the sort of talk people tend to have while they are waiting: the weather, the traffic, and so on. This is talk that, as Turner (1972) pointed out, embraces the maximum number of participants, as any category member may be expected to have view on them. At this point in their visit, participants were not talking in their specialized capacity as clients and caregivers. They were being offered membership of a broad category, that of people-in-waiting.

Confused speakers and their caregivers were then conducted at an appropriate moment (i.e., deemed appropriate by the consultant) to the consulting room. Here a series of temporal organizational comments by the consultant and others contextualized the event: about when the client attended the clinic last; about the previous history of the client; about what was going on currently; often concluding with "Is there anything else you would like to ask?" This was an agenda-led activity.

Following this, clients and caregivers were taken to the anteroom to see me, and I too made temporally appropriate remarks. Moreover, my comments often reflected my marginal position in the proceedings: apologizing for holding people up, thanking them for giving me their time, and concluding with remarks about not wanting to detain them any longer. As I have noted, the confused speakers and their caregivers had already experienced the setting before the visit when they met me, and my interviews were very much embedded in the spatial and temporal organization of the clinic. The final episode of the morning for clients was often lunch and social activities in the day center, marking an end to the official medical business of the day. This was organized as respite for caregivers, providing them with some time to themselves.

In various ways, then, geographical and temporal markers structured the organization of a visit to the psychogeriatric clinic, highlighting the main event and indicating to some extent the status of the various participants. For example, it would have been unlikely that I would interview clients before they saw the consultant because this might upset the timing of the morning, which was primarily organized around what was considered an appropriate pacing for the consultant's work. At the same time, my interviews were closely associated in both spatial and temporal terms with the consultation.

Previously Recorded Interview Materials

A second type of data came from two colleagues at the Open University who had carried out and recorded interviews with people suffering from confusion. Initially, I listened to these interviews merely as a way of familiarizing myself with a variety of examples of confused talk. But as I listened to the interviews I realized that, from the outset, I was able to identify something as being very wrong with the conversations. And yet the interviews were in very different contexts from my own. Consequently, I began to explore them more exhaustively, and found quite soon that they could be perceived as rich sources of data for the project; not least because the contexts involved were so different.

These data present an analytical problem, of course, because I do not know the specifics of the settings in which they were collected. Nevertheless, they too require an examination of context. With these data my sense of context has to be constructed from what I hear on the tapes, although I have also talked to both my colleagues about the interviews.

Tom's Interview. The first set of materials relate to an interview carried out by Tom Heller for the Open University course "Mental Health Problems in Old Age" (Open University, 1988). These interviews were recorded by the BBC (British Broadcasting Corporation), who produces most of the Open University's television, audio, video, and radio material. I have four versions of this interview: the unedited tapes, the edited course audiotape, the BBC transcript, and my own transcript taken from the unedited audio tape.[1] Even given this array of material, the inferences I can make are confined to what is said, nonverbal noises,

---

[1] For the purposes of the final analysis I have used my own transcripts of the unedited interviews.

my own understanding of BBC interviews, talking to Tom, and my own commonsense notions of what is going on.

The first version I heard of this interview was a finished product ready for the course. The edited interview is a highly polished affair. Its place in the course is to explore the difficulties and problems of people with dementia and their caregivers. The first activity in the course relating to the interview takes the following form:

> Listen now to the first section of the audio cassette which features Mr and Mrs Graham who were interviewed by a member of the course team in their home in a working class district of a northern city.

> You will hear them talking about some of their current difficulties and problems. This gives a limited picture of their lives, but at a first meeting with new clients or patients many professional workers will only gain a similarly limited picture.

> As you listen, note your answers to the following questions:

> 1. What do you think are the main physical and mental health problems which seem to affect either Mr or Mrs Graham?

> 2. Which other problems and difficulties do they appear to have? (Open University, 1988, p. 17)

I quoted this activity in full to emphasize that the edited tape and the whole original recorded interview were made for a very specific purpose.[2] Given this purpose, Tom sought to stimulate talk on the part of Mr. and Mrs. Graham that would, in some way, provide the data required for the activity: Or at least he would have looked for a general direction that the interview might take, in accordance with the direction of the written material. He had a specific shopping list of things to talk about. To achieve the course's requirements, he wanted substantive information from the couple, but also to demonstrate the idiosyncrasies of Mr. Graham's talk and self-presentation. He wanted Mr. Graham mainly as a respondent, that is, as someone who displayed talk that was of interest. For Tom's purposes, in being a respondent Mr. Graham needed to show he was confused, in order to illustrate for students some of the trials of that condition. Indeed, the rationale for his inclusion is that he is to be heard as a confused person. Just occasionally, Mr. Graham also acted as an informant, that is, offering information about confusion and his experience of it. But Tom wanted Mrs. Graham primarily as an informant, to offer information about Mr. Graham and his confusion.

---

[2] Later activities in the course take up the issue of biography in relation to Mr. and Mrs. Graham and invite students to consider how threatening the environment is for the couple.

From my talks with Tom and my own experience, I can make some assumptions that help me to further understand what is going on. I can assume that there were other people present apart from Tom and the Grahams (at least the BBC producer and possibly a sound recordist as well). I can speculate about nonverbal clues on the tape, for example that the off-microphone groanings are Mr. Graham rather than the sound recordist or Tom: sound recordists and interviewers, as a general rule, do not groan at interviews and, if they do, it is usually edited out! I also know from my own experience that in sound recordings for the BBC interviewers are encouraged to nod their heads rather than to say "yes" to interviewees so that the editing will be easier to do. As Pearce (1973) suggested, in relation to broadcast interviews, the aim is for the interviewee to provide a monologue. Here the absence of verbal acknowledgment on the part of the interviewer can be seen to facilitate, for the audience, concerted slabs of one-person talk. I can also speculate that the lack of background noise is because clocks, and so on, were removed from the room in advance. Furthermore, people were instructed not to point at things but to spell them out. A BBC sound interview is calculated to remove as much deixis as possible. Such an interview is a highly formalized version of people talking to each other.

All these speculations are to do with my interpretation of the context in which the recording was made. However, although I may dismiss the small number of "mmms" and "yes" answers on the tape as due to a particular situational constraint, rather than to the way normal speakers speak, either to each other or to confused speakers, it is more difficult to dismiss the groaning even within such a tightly constrained situation. The groaning, it seems to me, is an important aspect of this conversation. It is not something that can be edited out (even if this were thought to be desirable) because it goes on in parallel with the rest of the conversation. As I noted in chapter 1, Sacks et al. (1978) suggested that whereas overlap commonly occurs in conversation, talk by more than one speaker at a time tends to be brief. Turn taking is a central supportive feature of this notion. The simultaneous occurrence of talk and groaning suggests that this conversation is not quite normal.

The ecology of the conversation is highly specialized. Just as deixis is controlled in the sense of lack of artefacts (no clock, no external noise), so temporal markers are highly formalized too. The interview schedule drives the encounter on. Tom's organization of the talk is very much around questions ("I'd just like to ask you a question about . . .", "Can I ask your wife a few questions please?"). Temporality, in the sense of what will happen next, is frequently dealt with in terms of some allusion to the format or direction of future questions, or by reference to questions that have already been raised in the interview. Tom is clearly identified as being in charge:

Extract 1

Tom:	Mr. Graham, can I ask you, how old you are Mr. Graham?
Mr. Graham:	Sssssss eighty six I think it is, isn't it Lily?
Mrs. Graham:	Can I speak?
Tom:	Yes, sure
Mrs. Graham:	He was born in 1899.

Tom speaks first, choosing the next speaker. Mrs. Graham tells Tom the age of her husband rather than directing her answer to her husband (who had asked the most recent question about age). The answers are for Tom; Mrs. Graham speaks for her husband, having sought permission to speak from Tom. This is a rather structured interview, then, carried out under circumstances having features that depart in various ways from those of everyday conversation.

Moyra's Interview. Another colleague, Moyra Sidell, conducted several interviews with people suffering from confusion while researching for her PhD, (Sidell, 1986). Although her main emphasis was on services for older confused people she decided to visit some of them to remind herself of the problems such a condition brought for their everyday lives. Moyra lent me a number of taped interviews, some of which are only a few minutes long and some almost inaudible. (Permission for research use had been obtained.) However, one interview—that with Tilly—was long, clearly audible, and immediately stood out to me as an interaction between a normal and a confused speaker. Moyra had already visited Tilly several times when she conducted this interview with her at her home, so the encounter formed part of a continuing relationship.

As I developed the transcript of Moyra's interview with Tilly, it became apparent that the physical setting and the activity that accompanied the interview feature more prominently than in my own interviews or in Tom's. There are temporal markers in the encounter that are interview oriented, but there are also temporal markers that are domestic. There is a lot of getting up to fetch things, mention of things "over there", cups of tea, and cakes. Ointment is fetched and discussed, rooms in the house are visited and talked about. Moyra, on the whole (apparently), remains stationary with her tape recorder, unless invited to move. Tilly's "ownership" of the setting is evident. It does not seem surprising that Tilly has a reasonable hold on the conversation, because even given that her speech is confused, her possessions can occasionally bear the burden of her side of the conversation. If a tin of ointment is produced as a nonverbal statement, Moyra is obliged to remark on it, in effect to reply; and if it keeps on being produced, Moyra has to keep on replying. The conversation is more locally managed than other data I have discussed so far. Indeed, the encounter is *moved on* by making tea, by domestic events, by Tilly's possessions that are present in the apartment and produced by her for comment by Moyra. The ownership of the physical setting by Tilly is a main platform of the conversation, and counterbalances Moyra's ownership of the interview format. This contrasts with a more formal interview setting where the environment is either controlled by the interviewer or has been neutralized so as not to impinge on the talk, and where respondents have little they can own except their own talk. In this case, the juxtaposition of the different types of ownership is particularly interesting in that much of the talk focuses on Tilly's rejection of the apartment as her home, whereas much of the action (making tea and so on) centers on her ownership of the location and the props it contains.

In the conversation between Moyra and Tilly, there are a number of disputes. Tilly believes her sister Martha to be alive. She also believes that she is not currently in her own home (i.e., at the time when the interview is being taped). Moyra contradicts Tilly and tells her that her sister is dead and presents evidence to try to persuade her that she *is* in her own home. My hearing of the interview is rather like the situation described by Rawlings (1988), who talked about her research involving recordings of therapists and patients talking together. Rawlings sums up the directive she discovered herself to be operating to as "Hear therapists talk as reliable but uninteresting, and hear patients' talk as unreliable but interesting" (p. 174). The patients' statements are to be seen as evidence of their problems, whereas the therapists' statements can be seen as evidence of their seriousness and legitimacy. Just as Rawlings contextualizes what she knows of therapists and patients to give her the local knowledge to interpret what is being said, so in my hearing of the tape I found myself contextualizing what I know of Moyra and treating her as the person who has the reliable opinions in this conversation; even though it is not her house or her sister about whom they are talking. Moreover, this contextualiztion of the interview reinforces the view that whatever Tilly says can be interpreted as yet more evidence of *her problem* and her unreliability. In other words, in listening to this tape, I take the benchmark of Moyra's talk as representing the normal and ordinary world against which I then assess Tilly and her less normal and ordinary world.

Recordings of Domestic Interaction

The final batch of data is very different in character from the others. At one of my early interviews at the psychogeriatric clinic I met Mr. Bruner, whose wife had dementia. He remarked that he had often thought of taping his wife at home, and when I said that I would be interested in such a tape, he offered to record "the interesting bits" for me. I did, however, ask him if he would use the tapes to record some quite lengthy uninterrupted stretches of talk. I sent him some audiotapes by mail and he recorded two C90 tapes for me. This provided me with access to some talk that would otherwise have been difficult to obtain, and again increased the number of contexts I was able to examine in this study. Even though Mr. Bruner had offered to tape this material for me, I explained what I was doing and asked permission from the couple to use the tape for research purposes. Mrs. Bruner appeared to have no interest in this request and the permission was negotiated with Mr. Bruner. However, during the recordings themselves, Mrs. Bruner is not always oblivious to the tape recorder. On a number of occasions she asks why Mr. Bruner is setting it up, and each time he uses some (possibly) obfuscating answer, for example "So I'll be able to hear you", or "To play you some music." However, these responses seem to satisfy her and she then appears to have no further interest in the recorder.

My lack of contextual knowledge is even more pronounced with the Bruner tapes than it is with the recordings made by Tom and Moyra. Given that I was not present and that some of these recordings are focused on activity that is not primarily verbal, I can only infer what went on. Mr. Bruner appears to have decided to switch on the tape recorder mainly during periods of daily household routines: getting up, housework, having lunch, going to bed, and so on. As a result, there is a high level of deixis, particularly during episodes when Mrs. Bruner is being dressed or put to bed.

There are some quite long stretches of uninterrupted recorded talk in this collection of data, often when Mr. Bruner leaves the tape recorder on when he is doing something out of the room.[3] Geographic proximity (or not) of the couple seems to be extremely important to Mrs. Bruner, and the ecology of the conversation is salient for an analysis of their talk. The other episodes on the tapes appear to constitute episodes that Mr. Bruner regards as interesting. And some of the interesting episodes are very brief; noises on the recording indicate when he has stopped and started the tape and sometimes there is only a minute's talk before there is the characteristic bang of the tape recorder being switched off.[4]

---

[3] Indeed, it is interesting that Mr. Bruner's choice of material to record includes a substantial amount of talk that takes place when the two people are not copresent, a selection that in commonsense terms seems likely to focus more on purposeful *get something done* conversations rather than casual chat. People chatting tend to be physically copresent as well as interactionally engaged (except when on the telephone) .

[4] There are a number of abrupt high-pitched starts to some of the talk, not all of which appear to correspond with Mr Bruner switching it on for *an interesting bit* (i.e., during a lunchtime sequence when the couple appear to be together). This led me to wonder whether the tape recorder was voice activated.

So what I have here are some selected episodes of talk taking place in a domestic setting between people who know each other well, one of whom apparently is not cognizant of the purpose of the exercise at the time it takes place. There appears to be no attempt on Mr. Bruner's part to orchestrate the encounters for the recording in the way that he actually talks to his wife. His talk can be seen to be limited to that which is appropriate for mundane domestic occasions, with the imposed constraint of talking to someone whose practical reasoning abilities seem to be limited. Again, there is a strong thread of (the) routine as a benchmark from which to commence interpretive work.

Comparing the Situations

In all the situations in which my data have been collected, the relationships between talk, activity, and setting are an important issue, in terms of beginning to get a point of view on the conversations. For example, in the clinic where I conducted my interviews, the setting encourages a particular sort of interview format. Whereas I had anticipated fairly casual conversations, the context suggested *medical interview* as an overarching available category of organization for those involved. The situation was more complicated in the case of Tom's interview. We might expect that a conversation at home would be informal, perhaps involving the interviewee getting up, moving around and doing things. However, we find that the interview in the Graham home does not conform to this expectation. The conversation is guided and managed, and could be seen to have the explicit intent of making it understandable to people listening to an educational tape for the first time, as well as being orchestrated by the technical concerns of the BBC. By contrast, Moyra's interview with Tilly is closely related to physical activity. Although the encounter is recognizably an interview, the temporal and geographical markers demonstrate it to be a domestic and social event too, an event on which Tilly puts her own mark. Moyra's interviews are confirmatory of other strands of her work: she can allow events to unfold, she does not have to pursue a particular theme. Finally, Mr. Bruner's task is to *tell it how it is*: His intention is to produce an interesting tape for me as a researcher. "Important" and "interesting" are terms he uses to embrace both himself and myself as members of the same group of people (people who will see this talk as significant). Although the recordings are not selective in the sense that an interview format controls the talk, they are examples of types of talk that Mr. Bruner sees as relevant to my research.

In the study, therefore, I have used data from a number of rather different sources. I was directly involved in the collection of some data; other data had been collected for projects other than mine, and with no particular intention of multiple harvesting. One set of data was collected for me after a brief discussion about my research undertaking. Although, as I have explained, some of my data has involved substantial inferential problems, the diversity of the data seems to me to be a strength of the study. Effectively, I was presented with data from four different sources: Each person who gave me data did so because they thought they represented confused talk in some way. So my data were united by the feature of being heard by those who had collected them as *confused*. My problem, then, was exactly how this confusion was recognizable.

TYPES OF TALK

One of the most important points to arise from discussion of confusion and normality in chapter 1 was that the identification of talk as confused, and the features that make it confused, are context dependent. Given the variation in the character of the contexts from which my data come, this means that careful attention needs to be given to the relation between settings and types of talk.

In the case of my interviews, the people entering the anteroom to meet me could reasonably have expected to be required to engage in an interview. And interviews do have certain essential characteristics that, as I shall suggest, may be part of an ordinary member's stock of knowledge:

- Interviews have a specific start point when business gets under way ("If I can just begin with")
- The interviewer must have a reason for the interview (whether to gather information, select personnel, provide entertainment, etc.) although the interviewee may not always know what this is, or may be mistaken about it. According to purpose, therefore, interviewees can be deemed to have failed if they have not been appropriately informative, been appointed, been entertaining, etc. And, generally speaking, it is the interviewer who defines the success or otherwise of the occasion[5]
- Topics are likely to be preallocated by the interviewer, based on the purpose of the interview
- There is preallocation of the right to ask questions on the part of the interviewer, and of the obligation to answer questions on the part of the interviewee

---

[5] As Tolson (1991) noted, Dame Edna Everage, the well-known Australian television personality, has an eject button to dispose of boring guests!

- A record of some kind is usually generated, (whether by television cameras, written evidence such as a curriculum vitae, audiotapes, etc.), usually for the interviewer's benefit
- The interviewer generally initiates the interaction
- There is some concluding point after which the interview can be deemed to have finished.

However, to list essential features of interviews does little in the way of clarifying the nature of the contexts involved. Whereas members' commonsense knowledge and experience may encompass a large repertoire of possible occasions, it does not cover all the potential combinations of setting, personnel, and talk. Such an understanding is something that proceeds on a step-by-step, *wait and see* basis as the occasion unfolds. There is no determinate relation between physical setting, institutional context, and particular forms of talk. People have to work out what is appropriate behavior on any occasion, and do this on the basis of their member's knowledge of different types of occasion and the forms of talk and participant roles associated with them. Moreover, contexts can be constructed and reconstructed during an occasion.

One consequence of this is that instantiations of particular contexts are not always straightforward: they may have more of the character of mixed cases. In other words, there may be some ambiguity or uncertainty about the nature of the context on the part of those involved in it. There are, for example, many different types of interviews with which people may be familiar, such as medical interviews, survey research interviews, media interviews, employment interviews, and so on. Moreover, within each, there are different interviewing strategies. Yet, although the interviewee may only have a slight sense of these complexities, he or she must make sense of what sort of interview context they are in. And of course, in doing this to one degree or another they also determine what sort of interview context it is. In my interviews, people may have expected to face another medical interview, given the institutional location and the fact that the consultant acted as a gatekeeper. At the same time, the consultant's introduction may have suggested a research interview. And some people may have had experience of such interviews in the past, along with a range of other types of interview that they may draw on, consciously or unconsciously.

Some expectations of an occasion may not quite fit with what the interviewer is seeking. For example, ethnographers have noted that elite groups such as politicians may do *only one type of interview*, partly because of issues of secrecy but also because their concern is to express their ideas for consumption by potential voters (Dexter, 1970). Briggs noted a number of possible dissonances between interviewer and interviewee, such as the refusal of the interviewee to take a subordinate role, and the problem of invalid presuppositions on the part of the interviewer (Briggs, 1986). All of these misalignments of expectations can lead to the purpose of the interview as required by the interviewer being subverted.

It is worth exploring some of the ways in which different types of interviews vary, as this can give some sense of the resources on which participants in my interviews (and those in Tom's and Moyra's interviews) might have drawn. Interview talk can be seen as a methodic practice, but a practice that is adjustable depending on the nature of the interview (Silverman, 1973).

Interviews

Interviews are a very commonly available form of event and many people have experience in taking part in them. Moreover, the people I talked to had already been through an interview procedure with the consultant psychogeriatrician (even in the unlikely event of never having had any other medical interview). Most people, too, have seen media interviews: national television and radio news interviews; talk show interviews, the products of newspapers and magazine interviews. The interview, then, is a readily available category of activity that members can employ to understand interactional situations and guide their own behavior in them. It is a recognizable interactional format even if people are not fully cognizant of its purpose, just as being requested to tell someone the time is a recognizable interactional format even if one is not aware of why someone wants to know. However, although there may be common features in all interviews, there is some variation in format. Moreover, different participants may orient to different formats. First, I look at a type of interview that I, myself, drew on as a resource for the interaction—the loosely structured ethnographic interview.

The Ethnographic Interview. Ethnographic interviews are generally much less structured by the researcher than other kinds of research interviews. Open-ended questions tend to be used, and rather than following a prespecified set of questions, the interviewer asks questions that follow up relevant issues mentioned by the informant in previous responses. Ethnographers will usually have an agenda of topics they want to find out about but will endeavor to encourage interviewees to introduce and develop topics as well. Burgess (1988) described ethnographic interviews as "conversations with a purpose", indicating that they draw on the resources of ordinary conversation for their conduct. Although such interviews are not ordinary conversations, those taking part have resources to be able to do both conversation and interviews and to be aware that in this situation it is permissible to do both.

In such interviews researchers are concerned with generating significant analytical categories as they go along, rather than starting out with predefined categories:

> The qualitative goal . . . is often to isolate and define categories during the process of research. The qualitative investigator expects the nature and definition of analytic categories to change in the course of a project. (McCracken, 1988, p. 16)

McCracken went on to suggest that "For one field [survey research], well defined categories are the means of research, for another they are the object of research" (p. 16). This has implications for the conversational repertoire that ethnographic interviewers use:

> Ethnographers do not decide beforehand the questions they want to ask, though they may enter the interview with a list of issues to be covered. Nor do ethnographers restrict themselves to a single mode of questioning. On different occasions, or at different points in the same interview, the approach may be non-directive or directive, depending on the function that the questioning is intended to serve. (Hammersley & P. Atkinson, 1983, p. 113)

So, as researchers locate significant categories they may need different conversational tools to pursue these. However, whereas they may want to set up an occasion to elicit information relevant to their research, they also want the situation to be natural, and what they assume this means is that talk approximates in some ways to an ordinary conversation. For example, as with all interviews, questioning is a major format borrowed from ordinary conversation. However, on the whole, in ethnographic interviews a particular type of questioning is found. Many sociological textbooks of the 1970s and 1980s advise against the use of questions that can only be answered by "yes" or "no". They suggest that to ask such questions encourages confirmations or disavowals as proper responses. The occasion of loosely structured interviews, particularly in qualitative research, is one that requires the interviewee to talk: The aim is to get informants to talk in their own terms about some topic and not just respond monosyllabically. Consequently, questions that require fulsome answers are recommended.

Although this type of interview parallels ordinary conversation in not preallocating topics, it relies on the interview format, leading to question–answer sequences, with the interviewer as questioner and the questions designed to elicit extended talk on the part of the interviewee. None of the literature suggests that the interviewer says "You are supposed to talk for longer than I do and be relevant and interesting to me" but this is an implicit imperative and makes it rather a one-sided conversation. Moreover, the interviewer needs to produce the kinds of questions that will stimulate the kinds of answers that he or she wants and has a series of criteria by which to judge the success of the interview.

The interviewer's role is not that of a coconversationalist. What actually happens is that the methods chosen ape a sort of idealized view of ordinary conversation by imitating question types that generally get certain kinds of responses in such conversation. Thus, a string of "yes" or "no" answers from the interviewee may be seen to result in a failed interview, where the performance of the interviewee can be categorized as unhelpful and that of the interviewer as incompetent. Interestingly, the concept of such interviews as "failures", has been explored mainly from the interviewer's point of view and then in terms of remedial action—rarely from the point of view of what is being accomplished by the interviewee.

This interpretation of criteria of good interviewing suggests that underlying explicit instructions about methods of interviewing mundane ordinary member assumptions are taken for granted. Some are manifested literally in instructions about what sort of person to be, for example, to be an empathic listener who is both understanding and supportive of the respondent (see, e.g., Mishler's discussion which draws attention to this, 1986, pp. 29-30).

Such an approach implies aspects of self that should be withheld that is, those that are contentious. Underpinning this is an idea that people who are sympathetically understanding get more out of others than confrontational people. However, this is to map out a persona for the interviewer that is not automatically to be found in all individuals; not everyone is sympathetically understanding in their social lives, just as not everyone warms to being treated sympathetically. Moreover, some people are very successful at getting others to talk by dominating them. Approaches such as that I have just described illustrate methods as containing instructions about how to talk and who to be—both indicators of the operation of preallocation in talk, looking to an outcome not generally anticipated in ordinary conversation. Indeed, Garfinkel noted:

> One of the tasks involved in "managing rapport" consists of managing the stepwise course of the conversation in such a way as to permit the investigator to commit his questions in profitable sequence while retaining some control over the unknown and undesirable directions in which affairs, as a function of the course of the actual exchange, may actually move. (Garfinkel, 1967, p. 98)

Because interviewees are alerted to the fact that this is not a completely normal conversation, they can choose to acknowledge the implicit agenda or to be irrelevant when the agenda does not fit with what they want to say. Thus, we might suggest that "failure" in an ethnographic interview can occur where the interviewee operates stronger *local management* of the talk than the interviewer operates *preallocated management*.

The case of my own interviews is a good illustration of the complexities surrounding the concept of context and appropriate types of talk for a given occasion. Although I would say that these interviews approximate to a loosely structured ethnographic pattern, this is not an unproblematic categorization. I wanted to engage in conversation primarily for the purpose of collecting samples of confused talk. Hence, there was little or no need for any guidance on my part—in a sense "anything would do". This meant that, were it possible, a casual conversation would do as well as an interview. Indeed, I felt that this would have been the ideal. However, even at my first interview it became apparent to me that I could not be a casual participant. Partly as a result of my performance, and partly because of the context, I was very much cast in the role of interviewer. My contacts with confused speakers and caregivers were occasioned as interviews, in meetings that were officially set up. They were not occasioned as casual chance encounters between strangers where a conversation might arise. The conclusion that the occasions were interviews was reinforced for me as I listened to the tapes when I became aware that I was hearing *interviewer, interviewee* rather than *casual participants*.

In fact, what happened was that I adopted an approach in which the questions were designed, primarily, to stimulate the confused speaker to talk about matters of interest to them in their own terms. Because I behaved like an interviewer and was treated as an interviewer, this had implications for the roles of the other participants. It introduced an additional element of ambiguity. An example of this can be seen in the life history questions I asked when talk proper began (after introductions and so on). Life history questions are an opening gambit in a wide range of conversational situations, both formal and informal, when people meet for the first time (at interviews, at parties, on trains, etc.). However, I was talking in a setting with people who had just emerged from a series of encounters where the nature of the talk was preallocated and where the temporal and geographical markers were there to be interpreted institutionally. And they had also come to the anteroom specifically for an interview with me. Moreover, all of my questions took a "life history" form so that it could well have appeared to participants that the interviews never properly got started.

The key questions for the participants, presumably, was "What sort of occasion is this and what role should I play?" Although I was myself oriented toward something that might be described as an ethnographic interview, this was not an absolute constraint on the proceedings. Indeed, I would suggest that, in fact, it is fairly unlikely that an ethnographic interview would be a guiding format available to participants arriving at an interview with me. There were a number of other more widely available forms of talk that probably shaped how people saw the context, their own role, and my behavior. I begin with the most obvious one: the medical interview.

Medical Interviews. Unlike some interviews, the interviewer's participation in the medical interview is often initially at the instigation of the patient (although after the initial consultation, the doctor may control the frequency and timing of future interviews). In common with other interviews, it has specified start and end points, usually orchestrated by the doctor. It involves a specialized environment, often an institutional one (but even if taking place in a patient's home may require a specialization of the environment: privacy, washing facilities, and so on).

Such interviews constitute talk as social action, because they are part of the process of diagnosis. In talk, the doctor asks most of the questions and can judge certain answers, questions, and comments by patients to be irrelevant. In addition, a record of the medical interview is made, but only according to what the doctor deems relevant; and traditionally that record is for professional purposes, and not for patients.[6]

The literature on medical interviews (particularly within the medical profession itself) has traditionally ignored their interactive and social constructional nature. "Physicians are viewed as collectors and analyzers of technical information elicited from patients. A patient is, ideally, a passive object responding to the stimuli of a physician's queries" (Mishler 1984, p. 10).

This contrasts with the ethnographic interview where, ideally, the stimuli are distributed via both interviewer and interviewee, and a passive interviewee renders the interview a failure. In the 1970s and 1980s, a substantial amount of sociological work was conducted on the medical interview—on how a diagnosis is constructed and how accounts, are developed within that context (Cicourel, 1987; Fisher & Groce, 1990; Mishler, 1984; Sharrock & Anderson, 1987; Silverman, 1987; Strong, 1979). Within the corpus of work that was developed it was suggested that there were some variations in the structure of the medical interview. For example, Stimson and Webb (1975) emphasized the involvement and relative control of the patient, and Strong (1979) noted a variety of different medical interview formats.

Building on the work of Silverman and Torode, Mishler suggested that there are different *voices* in the medical interview: the medical voice and the patient's *lifeworld voice*:

> A "voice" represents a specific normative order. Some discourses are closed and continually reaffirm a single normative order; others are

---

[6] The 1991 Access to Health Records Act in the UK has, of course, increased patient access to records.

> open and include different voices, one of which may interrupt another, thus leading to the possibility of a new "order". . . . Disruptions of the discourse during [medical] interviews appear to mark instances where the "voice of the lifeworld" interrupts the dominant "voice of medicine." (Mishler , 1984, p. 63)

This interpretation of medical interviews leads us to look at the notion of what a valid topic of discussion is. For the patient to provide new topics is not generally valid in the medical interview, although he or she is, at certain points, expected to give accounts. However, unless these accounts are deemed valid by the doctor, it is likely that the latter will begin to ask questions that orient them in a more appropriate direction that he or she deems fit, or move to bring them to a close. Mishler noted that: "responses are not simply answers to questions but also a reflection of the interviewer's assessment of whether a respondent has said 'enough' for the purpose at hand" (Mishler, 1986, p. 55).

The important point here is that it is the doctor's *purpose at hand* that is paramount. In the same discussion, Mishler (1986, pp. 54–55) noted that doctors often encourage short responses and leave insufficient pause to allow the patient to become discursive. The accomplishment of being a patient lies in knowing how much to offer when.

At other times (often as the doctor is closing down or coming to the diagnosis), the patient is largely restricted to acknowledging what the doctor has said and can be seen to be in a situation that is controlled by the interviewer. Of course, these discursive conventions do not entirely control patient behavior. However, it is instructive that patients often ask questions or raise topics as they leave (after the interview has ended). This suggests that they may have read the situation in the interview as providing no valid openings for what concerned them. Asking such questions on the threshold of the room gives them an ambiguous status between the two worlds, offering the doctor the opportunity to hear the question as a lifeworld question or as a medical question.[7] This points to a sophisticated understanding on the part of patients about how openings and closings relate to the structure of the interview and an equally sophisticated strategy for preserving face.

Within some medical interviews, there are occasions when the lifeworld view of the patient is encouraged by the physician as the dominant voice. One of these is when the professional wants to see how the client is performing in terms of communication (i.e., stroke or concussion victims, suspected cases of depression, putative schizophrenics). Here, people are frequently asked questions about the taken-for-granted nature of the world in order to confirm that they have

---

[7] The image of the threshold has been used in social anthroplogy in discussions of rites in which a person passes from one status to another, and fits quite aptly here too.

the usual lifeworld knowledge. Of course, there is a paradox: To ask about taken-for-granted aspects of the world potentially marks the situation out as one where some accounting needs doing. As the doctor floats his or her hand in front of the patient and asks "How many fingers have I got?", those who are not too distressed might feel inclined to ask "Is this a trick question?" Usually, in medical situations, the interviewer has no obligation to say why she is asking questions about the taken-for-granted world. Thus, Fisher and Groce (1990) described a fairly common medical pattern that does not require doctors to give complete accounts. For example, they may offer an apology for hurting the patient in an examination, but no explanation as to why they are doing the examination. There is also often a certain suspension of the expectation that the patient will understand. Breaches of common understanding may be tolerated up to a certain point, on the assumption that the doctor has some esoteric knowledge that the patient cannot expect to understand. Overall, whatever the voice used, the goal for the doctor is to categorize the interviewee in terms of medical discourse, and the dominance of this discourse is routinely assumed by the doctor (and by many patients) from the outset.

Survey Research Interviews.   Given that I was introduced as a researcher, another sort of interview that may have informed participants' orientations is the survey interview. Most people have had experience with market research or other survey research interviews at some time.

Survey research often uses a highly structured question schedule in interviews that are standardized: That is to say, the questions are written in advance and trained interviewers administer them in a way that attempts to be comparable across interviews. The emphasis is on achieving an identical procedure for each interview so that no individual response is distorted by extraneous factors. If respondents cannot understand questions, or have some other query, the interviewer usually has a series of standardized prompts he or she can use to amplify the question. The methodological literature suggests that the interviewer's role should be specific and nonjudgmental, thus avoiding a whole series of interactions that people might expect in the course of ordinary conversations:

> Many situations merit the description 'interview', but we can in the present context confine ourselves to that in which the interviewer is neither trying to help the informant nor to educate him, neither to gauge his suitability for a job nor to get his expert opinion: the situation where she . . . is simply seeking information from, and probably about, him and where he is likely to be one of many from whom similar information is sought. (Moser & Kalton 1971, p. 270)

Similarly, questions are developed to anticipate and avoid all the pitfalls that characterize ordinary conversation. Ambiguous and multiple questions are to be avoided, for example, as are words with different meanings that sound the same:

> Words so opposite in meaning as these two might be confused:
>
> - Do you favor or oppose a law *outlawing* guns in the state of Maryland?
>
> - Do you favor or oppose a law *allowing* guns in the state of Maryland? (Converse & Presser, 1986, p. 14)

The implication is that the risk of mishearing can be obviated by using phonically dissimilar words. Converse and Presser suggested, then, that questionnaire writers should be clear and avoid formulations that might confuse or mislead the respondent. These are effectively instructions for modifying at least some of the talk that is likely to take place. For example, the authors also recommended the avoidance of double negatives, implicit negatives, overlong lists, dangling alternatives, and so on (Converse & Presser, 1986). An ordinary conversation provides all sorts of opportunities for such constructions and thus for participants to misunderstand each other. But, because such conversation is jointly constructed, participants can work together to understand what is being said, using self-correction, other-correction and preventative work to remedy any problems. This joint work relies on continual reading of the conversation *at this point in time*, so that both retrospective and prospective interpretive work is going on. Indeed, the remedial work in ordinary conversation is both context-shaped and context-renewing. By contrast, such work would be seen as undesirable in survey research interviews where roles need to stay the same and where local management must not take over.

The format of the survey interview and the methodological literature surrounding it effectively create a blueprint for how to go about such interviews. However underlying the method proper there are methodic practices that are taken for granted, for example:

- The interviewer's topic choice is determined in advance by the question schedule
- The interviewer's turn size is predetermined in advance by the question schedule
- The interviewer need not be the person who has constructed the questions
- Any attempts to locally manage the conversation by the respondent are responded to only by predetermined utterances, the interviewee's participation is highly constrained

- The feedback the interviewer is able to give is limited to nonjudgmental phrases like "thank you"
- There is usually an "any other" category that accommodates oddities that cannot be taken into account within the interview format
- Even misunderstanding and breakdown of the conversation can be accommodated by the coding *don't know,* which can cover both a negative answer to a question and a refusal to cooperate.

In a sense, the survey research interview can be seen to attempt to take care of the huge array of instructions Heritage spoke of in his discussion of normative views of rules. It is an attempt to exhaustively cover all the possible contingencies in the interview:

> Whilst a normative structure . . . is imaginable for a simple greetings situation, it requires little insight to see that given the enormous complexity of talk and interaction and the endless variability of the circumstances in which they occur, the normative theorist is inexorably drawn into equipping the actor with a huge array of instructions—enough, in fact, to deal with every empirically possible contingency in social life. While such a proposal may be unconvincing, still less convincing is the notion that the entire population is uniformly equipped with such instructions such that each member is capable of commonly identifying, without error, every circumstantial nuance requiring a change of conduct. (Heritage, 1984, p. 113-114)

In the survey interview, one party to the transaction (the interviewer) offers all instructions to the other party (the interviewee) and every circumstantial nuance should be accounted for through the standardized questions and prompts. As Mishler (1986) noted, the survey research interview is seen in stimulus–response terms and as behavior; problems are treated as technical, to be solved through precise methods. The context of the interview and the inferences to be drawn from interactional work involved are rarely acknowledged. Suchman and Jordan (1990), in their work on survey research methodology, suggested that compared with ordinary conversations, "the survey interview suppresses those interactional resources that routinely mediate uncertainties of relevance and interpretation" (p. 232). Among other examples, they noted that the format of questions and their pursuit by the interviewer can "escalate routine troubles" into troubles that are expressed in the form the interviewer is interested in. By this they mean that the interviewee's attempts to fit into criteria offered (these often being elaborated by the interviewer with a series of increasingly detailed qualifications to the original question) may lead him or her to cast around to elaborate answers that might have remained focused on the mundane in an ordinary conversation. In other words, it is difficult for a respondent to resist the framing offered in a survey interview whether it is relevant in their terms or not. Suchman and Jordan also commented that it is difficult for the interviewer to listen for misunderstandings in any way other than by the use of prepared prompts, whereas in ordinary conversation, "successful communication is not so much a product of avoidance of the misunderstandings as of their successful detection and repair" (p. 238).

In relation to my interviews, confused speakers and their caregivers who considered the possibility that this might be a survey interview would have looked to my responses and verbal interaction for "instructions" about how to respond and, indeed, what to respond. They would, however, have received little guidance from these.

Media Interviews. I want briefly to discuss media interviews because these are perhaps the type of interview people encounter most frequently, through watching television, listening to the radio, and reading newspapers. In media interviews, interviewees are there for some purpose related either to their enduring fame, an event of moment they have been involved in or have witnessed, or their expertise. There are special features about them, or about their lives, that are the point of the interview as far as the interviewer is concerned. Those who are being interviewed are generally aware of the reason for the interview and know that only certain accounts are valid on their part. M. A. Atkinson (1973) noted that for a celebrity to fill the interviewer in on the details of his famous life as though he were an ordinary person can only be seen as coy by those listening. Similarly, an interviewer is expected to know what is not appropriate, such as asking famous persons like Elizabeth Taylor what they do for a living. For different reasons, experts are rarely asked to establish their credentials. In most media interviews there simply is not time for this, so it has to be done by announcement. Merely to have been chosen for an interview can authenticate an expert. However, having been chosen, experts are supposed to disseminate their knowledge both wisely and simply enough for the average person to understand it, taking the context into account. And these tasks relate both to the purpose of the interview and to the projected audience for it.[8]

The boundaries of valid topics can be points of contention in media interviews, and interviewees may refuse to answer certain questions: Such disagreements often center on whether an issue should be discussed generally or a specific case cited.[9] In some types of media interviews the interviewer appears to have license to press more firmly,

---

[8] It is interesting how experts coped with explaining the derivatives market in the wake of the Barings Bank fiasco in the UK in 1995. Their wholly unsuccessful attempts reflect Lynch and Bogen's comments on the problems of addressing explanations to "anyone'" (Lynch & Bogen, 1994).

[9] In a radio interview I listened to recently about a social services scandal, the interviewer was pursuing the case of a man with learning disabilities who had been sexually abused, and the interviewee responded at least five times by saying "I can't speak for individual cases but I can say this about our policy."

for example, in political interviews, which often tend to be adversarial, whereas in others such as chat show interviews, the interviewer is not expected to press an interviewee (except on special occasions such as the interviews with the film star Hugh Grant after his arrest for lewd conduct in a public place in 1995).

In watching such interviews, people may see that there are all sorts of rules of conduct that relate to the status of the interviewer (i.e., neutrality; see Clayman, 1988), the subject of the discussion, what can be said and what should be left unsaid, the status and style of the interviewee, and so on. They may also come to see that the purpose of the interview gives the interviewer license to ask things that might not be referred to in ordinary conversation with strangers, but also gives the interviewee license to respond in kind. However, media interviews are also organized and edited for an audience, a circumstance that does not generally apply to other types of interviews (although a medical consultant may conduct an interview in front of students). Pearce (1973) noted that some issues arising in broadcast interviews relate to editing needs, such as the required length of the interview, whether the interview is going to be broadcast as a discrete entity (for example, a program devoted to an interview with one person) or whether it will be excerpted in a news program (e.g., the national news), and so on. He also noted that the modification of interviews by the editing process may present a final product that is a more coherent account than a live interview. All of these factors may facilitate an impression of a requirement for polish and sophistication as a model for an interview.

My interviewees, and similarly those of Tom and Moyra, may have been guided in their orientation to their meeting with me by these various commonsense models of the interview. However, as I have stressed, my aim was to approximate a casual conversation, and even though I was forced to present this in the form of an ethnographic interview, the concept of conversation seems likely to have played a role in the behavior of the confused speakers and their caregivers (as, indeed, it did for me). Moreover, as I pointed out earlier, part of my data comes from a domestic situation and is very much in conversational mode. So one common issue to consider in the data is how they relate to models of conversation.

Conversations

As I noted, there is some agreement among conversation analysts that ordinary conversation can be seen as a base line, with other types of talk as licensed deviations from it. Heritage (1984) suggested that all social interaction shows organized patterns of "stable, identifiable structural features"(p. 241). Such features are social in character and independent of personality or other individual characteristics:

> Knowledge of these organizations is a major part of the competence which ordinary speakers bring to their communicative activities and, whether consciously or unconsciously, this knowledge influences their conduct and their interpretation of the conduct of others. Ordinary interaction can thus be analysed so as to exhibit stable organizational patterns of action to which the participants are oriented. (Heritage, 1984, p. 241)

Nofsinger (1991), in a summation of research in the field, suggested that three characteristics are seen by many authors to be significant features of conversation. It is:

- *Interactive*: two (or more) people take part, and it exists in real time on a turn by turn basis
- *Locally managed*: during the course of interaction the people involved decide who speaks, when, and for how long
- *Mundane*: it is commonplace and practical.

To this Heritage (1984) would add two other features:

- Conversation is both context-shaped and context-renewing: What people say cannot be understood except by reference to the context, including the context of the immediately preceding remark; but what they say also creates the context for the next part of the conversation, and so on
- That nothing in the conversation can be dismissed as insignificant as a matter of course.

Levinson (1983) saw conversation as having a detailed and elaborate structure of which people are not aware, and defined it as follows:

> *Conversation* may be taken to be that familiar predominant kind of talk in which two or more participants freely alternate in speaking, which generally occurs outside specific institutional settings like religious services, law courts, classrooms and the like. (p. 284)

Conversation as the basic model for other types of talk can also be seen to involve participants in roughly equal interactional rights. Conversation is organized" more flexibly [than more specialized forms of talk], enabling more universalistic 'rights' to participate" (Lynch & Bogen, 1994, p. 79).

Specialized Ordinary Talk and Chat. Even if conversation stands as a baseline for other types of talk, within ordinary conversation itself there are more specialized versions of talk and people routinely recognize all talk as being of some *type*. Cheepen (1988), for example, attempted to pin down some characteristics of what she called *chat*. She viewed a chat as having four elements :

- An introduction—at the beginning and ritualized in form.
- Speech-in-action—seen as functional comments like *Mind that might be a bit hot*, or environmental comments like *I see you've got a new hi-fi*. In speech-in-action participants articulate what aspects of context can and should be attended to in the conversation.
- A story—a sequence of utterances that comes in the basic format state–event–state, and involves specifying who the participants are, temporal location, and evaluation: The story may be told by one person or jointly achieved.
- A closing—coming at the end, and again, formulaic.

She noted that speech-in-action is often turned into a story with the cooperation of both speakers; that stories take up the greatest time in the conversation; that speech-in-action can primarily be seen to link stories; and that stories may not necessarily be news. She also suggested that although an introduction may not always be necessary, it appears that there always has to be a closing (Cheepen, 1988).

Ordinary chat can be seen to be interruptable, low status talk; it is a mode of talk that is considered nonserious and nonthreatening (although, of course, it can always turn into something else). Tolson (1991) noted the orientation of chat to the personal and private rather than the institutional and public. When people are interrupted in a chat they may well say "We were just having a chat", an utterance that both acts as a closing and implies that it can be put on hold for some other form of talk.[10] Ordinary chat is deemed to be possible anywhere as long as the context does not indicate a requirement for some other kind of behavior (as in the case of the idle chat in the classroom) and as long as participants are agreeable to this form of talk (and there are occasions where one participant may want a chat and another does not, as in lifts, on trains, and so on).

Chat can be modified by preallocation of topics or, on occasion, by a preallocation of interactional rights or choice of suitable context. Even within casual informal talk, participants may signpost special kinds of talk that is not just chat, as when people with a close relationship in difficulties might say one to the other "We need to talk about this", thereby indicating the seriousness of the situation. Indeed, it can be seen that when a type of talk is named at the start of an interaction (or prior to it) it is being given a designation of specialized conversation even if there is no institutional context. "We'll discuss this later" indicates the

---

[10] Turner (1972) noted the use of "just" as playing down the importance of the conversation to others.

requirement for a more suitable (specialized) environment than the current one for the proposed talk.

Research work on children indicates that modifications take place both in ordinary and institutional conversation when some participants have fewer interactional rights (Speier, 1969). Indeed, Strong (1979) noted the ways in which children are routinely excluded from the main talk in clinic consultations where they are patients, and Watson (1992) commented on this more broadly in relation to adult-child interaction, by observing that ethnomethodologists see the concepts of "adult"and "child" not so much as things with an independent existence as collections of conventions which are used to establish and reinforce nonsymmetrical relations between grown-ups and children.

Role can be taken initially to be a procedural convention relating to how we might behave in certain situations. However, because every encounter presents a unique configuration of circumstances, aims, and contingencies, we need always to formulate a role we think appropriate, in light of what is going on. Accepting the role of child means formulating a performance that acknowledges the interactional rights of others: It is part of the interactional work that children do. Yet, depending on the degree of asymmetry they perceive, children may take more or fewer interactional rights (perhaps more with parents and fewer with adults whom they do not know). Limitation on interactional rights can be seen to operate, too, in other forms of specialized conversation, for example, with older people or disabled people where normal speakers may speak on their behalf. All this is to demonstrate that even within the notion of ordinary conversation, there is some variation. Indeed, within any conversation there are ways of shifting the context so that it can move into a different mode ("To be serious for a moment", "Well, enough of that").

I have noted during the course of this chapter that several interactional formats may be available to participants in what are ostensibly interviews. Even when people are orienting to a particular *role format*, which Strong (1979) referred to as the whole ceremonial order of the situation, they sometimes suspend the rules and lapse into other identities that might normally be expected to be latent, given the situation and the current role format. Potter and Wetherell (1987) noted "Because people go through life faced with an ever-changing kaleidoscope of situations, they will need to draw upon very different repertoires to suit the needs at hand." (p. 156)

We might also add that, even within a role format as apparently occasioned as an interview, participants may discern a shifting situation and therefore call on different roles and repertoires at different points in the interaction. One aspect of this is the occurrence of what I call parachat.

Parachat. Even in formal settings and interviews, ordinary conversation may be initiated at various points when a range of devices from the ordinary conversational repertoire is used, for example, inconsequential topics of conversation, remarks about the weather, biography, physical setting, and so on. Parachat can take place both in sociological interviews and in such settings as medical interviews, and indeed in less serious formal situations. Tolson (1991), in a discussion of broadcast chat in television quiz shows, suggested that it "introduces a suspension within the 'main' discourse, whilst a 'subsidiary' discourse (an aside, a metadiscursive comment) is briefly formulated" (p. 179). It is interesting in light of this that in certain quiz shows, such as the UK television show "Have I got news for you" (and the radio show "The news quiz"), the reverse is true: the formal business of question and answer serves merely as a platform for extended and witty chat. This is pointed up by the fact that the scores of the participants are largely irrelevant, a situation most unlike the radio quiz "Brain of Britain", where the scores are central to the intention of the program. This may, perhaps, be explained by the fact that the participants in "Have I got news for you" are effectively professional entertainers and that their chat is their professional talk. In most professional settings, however, the availability of chat as a type of talk is constrained and not appropriate to most of the occasion. It may be seen as a form of talk that lies both at and within the boundaries of an occasioned event: It has to be strictly delimited or the professional may not be seen as taking his or her role seriously and the occasion of the interview may be undermined. Nevertheless, the use of chat by the professional indicates that a discourse other than the professional discourse can be used, constituting a controlled handling of lifeworld discourse.

Some distinguishing features of parachat are as follows. It is talk that acts as a boundary marker: It can take place at the beginning or end of specialized talk and can be expected to terminate for more specialized talk. It tends to be initiated and terminated by the professional. It can take place in parallel with the interviewer's or professional's control of the environment, for instance while the tape recorder is being set up or while the dentist is drilling, and thus may imply unequal interactional rights and be sustained even without the participation of the respondent. (It is very difficult to respond with your mouth full of drill.)

Parachat may also occur when there are alterations to the environment that are not under the control of the professional; for example, when the window cleaner appears at the window during an interview (Cheepen, 1988). Such chat indicates that this lifeworld interruption is attendable to. It may ostensibly replace professional talk that is, replace the dominant expected discourse with another, as when the consultant apparently chats inconsequentially in order to establish whether or not you have got a concussion or in order get across a health promotion message. Indeed, there are occasions where ordinary talk is called on almost as a euphemism, where the mild term chat is substituted for sterner descriptions of talk such as *dressing down* or *telling off*, For example, when one's employer says "I think we need to have a chat about . . ." one knows that this is not, in fact, going to be a casual chat. Here, topic or purpose has been decided in advance by someone of superior status. Whether any of the features of a chat are likely to apply—that it should be nonthreatening, that there is relatively equal participation, and so on—depends on other features of the context. Participants are, on the whole, sophisticated in their understanding of the sort of instruction that "I think we should have a chat" encapsulates in particular circumstances: For example, they may well read such an opening as a warning of bad news.[11] Directives such as this capitalize on ordinary members' understanding of the functions of different types of talk and their ability to take advantage of this. This sort of chat is not the same as *ordinary chat:* It is differentiated by the status of the participants, the institutional context, and possible preallocation of topics. Thus, parachat may place the lifeworld in an ambiguous context. People may fear to make lifeworld disclosures during periods of parachat because they can see that such disclosures may be reframed by professionals within the dominant discourse.

In most situations in which parachat takes place, the interviewer or professional instigates the chat and if the respondent fails to appreciate this condition, the occasion may become problematic. To continue to chat when the interview proper has started, to fail to revert to specialized talk when the window cleaner has been acknowledged, to try to respond fully with the drill in your mouth, and so forth, all create interactional troubles.

So, parachat is something that takes place in relation to the main event: Before, after, or during. Its status is defined by the interview. We would not generally speak of an interview interrupting a chat. For those taking part, the placement of parachat is a significant contextual resource. At the beginning or end it may be interpreted as lifeworld chat. In the middle, during the course of the interview proper, participants may contextualize it in a different way and see it as being "used" in some way by the professional.

---

[11] A friend of mine was invited to the doctor's who told her he just wanted to have a chat, prior to breaking the news that one of her parents had a terminal illness.

Parachat seems to me to be a sort of hybrid category of talk, having some features of specialized talk but replicating casual talk as well: It may be a form of talk that exists in a sort of symbiotic relationship within any interview. Such symbiosis must be significant for those involved, because rules and roles vary depending on the type of talk people see themselves as being involved in. As will become clear later, one of the significant characteristics of my own interview data for this project is that although I was interviewing in a subsetting of *a visit to the psychogeriatric clinic,* a medical setting, what I was producing was parachat: It is possible that this situation could be seen by other participants as puzzling, anxiety-provoking and possibly as devious. Additionally, it may have alerted participants to problems of frame within the interview.

TRANSCRIBING THE DATA

As I collected my audiotaped data, I began to listen to the tapes and to try to monitor the process of coming to have a point of view on it. For the purposes of the study, it became necessary for me to transcribe the data so that I could use extracts in the final study, and the transcript extracts that resulted are, in some senses, an embodiment of a point of view.

Ochs' article "Transcription as Theory" (1979), which examined the transcriptions of interviews between adults and children, played an important role for me in suggesting some of the problems related to the issue of transcribing. Ochs challenged the notion that hard data, such as tape recordings, escape the criticisms leveled at intuitive data: The problems, she said, "are simply *delayed* until the moment at which the researcher sits down to transcribe the material from the audio- or videotape" (p. 44). She went on to cite a number of transcription issues that relate to assumptions about power and control within a conversational episode. These include looking to the left hand side of transcripts for the *opening up* of interaction, the assumption being that the first move sets a frame for the conversation and (in the case of her own research) the presentation of the adult as the intitiator with the child as respondent. The situations Ochs described have some similarities with my own data, where people who are competent (initiators or normal speakers) ask questions of those who are seen as incompetent (respondents or confused speakers). Thus my interview data involved sets of more powerful and less powerful people, and this had a bearing on how I went about the task of transcribing.

Transcribing is like making a map of the terrain: A detailed ordinance survey map serves a different purpose from the map one draws on the back of an envelope of how to get to the house from the railway station. However, both attempt to capture features of the terrain relevant to the purpose for which the map is required. At the outset of the map–making process one might outline major features and then consider scale, detail, and so on as refinements for a particular purpose. A variety of types of transcription are used by ethnographers, and even within a discipline such as ethnomethodology people make transcriptions for very different purposes. For example, Goodwin (1987) used highly detailed transcription for work on "forgetfulness as an interactive resource" whereas Schegloff's (1972a) more categorical work on "formulating place", at times uses a more simple set of transcription conventions.

In this section, I look at both practical and conceptual issues that arise from the process of transcribing. I was impressed with Speier's discussion of how to make a transcript and acknowledge it here as a checklist for my own discussion of some of the issues important to me (Speier, 1969). I discuss the process of transcription with my own interviews in mind and also comment on important issues relating to the process of transcribing the other data I used.

A First Transcription

I transcribed all my data myself because I wanted to plot the process of my understanding of the tapes. The quality of the tapes that formed my data varied and I could not always clearly hear what was going on. I had the most troublesome tapes amplified and transposed on to new tapes; but, even so, I had occasional problems hearing what was said. I tried to do a first transcription within the week that followed the interviews, although this was not always possible. For each 10–minute stretch of data recorded it took me roughly an hour to do a basic transcription. I typed my transcriptions directly onto my computer, finding this an easy way to adjust the text when I suddenly "heard" whole phrases as I listened to the tapes again and again.

On my first transcription of each tape I attempted to document only a basic schema of turns, allocating these to the correct people and merely paraphrasing parts of the conversation that were lengthy discussions between myself and caregivers. I used a new line for each new speaker and ran what they said on without a paragraph break until someone else started to speak. I used dots (…) to indicate pauses and slashes (//) at the end and beginning of turns where there were overlaps. I noted groans, external noises such as laughter, bangs, instances of indexicality, and indications that someone was nowhere near the microphone with bracketed comments (bangs, laughter, afar, etc.), attributing groans and noises to specific individuals when I was sure who it was. If I could not understand or hear any parts of the tape, I noted this with question marks (?????) or (mutters). Here is an example of the sort of arrangement I used for my first phase of transcription:

Extract 2

Mr. Bruner:	(??????)
Pam:	So I like I co don't live with anyone whose got dementia (noises) and I can't know what its like//
Mr. Bruner:	//No no//
Pam:	//And to talk to them//
Mr. Bruner:	//No no//
Mrs. Bruner:	//This is sore Dave (she's had a blood test on the inside of her arm)
Mr. Bruner:	Yes it will be for just a little while and then it'll soon be better.

My main problem at this first stage of transcription was not being able to understand all the talk I could hear on the audiotapes, and this was a problem with tapes from all my sources. One tactic I used to cope with parts of the tapes I did not understand was to replay and listen to unintelligible parts several times and another was to leave the tape a few weeks and then come back to it. Sometimes these tactics would do the trick and it would suddenly occur to me what was being said. Also, as I became more familiar with some of the tapes, I began to see what it was that was probably being said (putting these revelations in brackets). I was able to make more meaning of the whole transcript as I went on: I was building up a context.

The problem of inaudibility of parts of the tapes was exacerbated by the fact that a number of people to whom I talked were very soft spoken. Additionally, my own transcription labels for talk that I could not understand varied and I tended initially to think of confused speech as unintelligible mutterings. I have to confess, looking back on my first round of transcribing, that whereas usually I wrote (?????) when I could not understand what normal speakers said, I tended to write (mutters) for the people I perceived as having confused speech. Sometimes I revised this on a second transcription, sometimes I did not. Analytically, the difference between *unintelligible* and *inaudible* is a moot point. It is rather like who *owns* a silence. In using the term *inaudible* one might attribute an inability to hear what others have said to problems of sound reproduction or environmental noise; and so the concept is interpretable as the hearer's problem. However, to say someone is unintelligible is to attribute the deficit to the speaker. As I noted earlier, I had an underlying expectation that certain people would be more intelligible in interviews than others. I did not expect confused speakers to be intelligible, and thus saw the problem residing in them rather than in deficits in my own hearing. And so in this early transcription work, I used ordinary member reasoning to attribute unintelligibility to confused speakers and inaudibility to normal speakers.

Another problem was the level of detail in which to render the transcript. This was partly to do with the issue of deixis. I found I was providing more imaginative descriptions of what I thought was going on in my colleagues' interviews compared with my own. Having been present at my own interviews, my recall assured me that a jumbo jet had not driven into the side of the building while I was talking to people. I could remember incidents that generated some of the nonverbal noises on the tapes: Those that I recalled being attended to by confused speakers I transcribed (a car going by), those that appeared immaterial (my bangle making a metallic noise against the table) I did not. However, the Bruner tapes and Moyra's tapes also had quite lot of nonverbal noises and here, of course, I had no recall of what was going on. I included more of these noises in my initial transcript and made attempts to infer whether they were relevant to the talk or not. A case in point arises in Moyra's conversation with Tilly:

Extract 3

Tilly:	Aye?
Moyra:	Your Deep Heat you were going to show it to me. [12]
Tilly:	Oh yes (long pause, 17.4 seconds accompanied by some foot falls and rustling) this piece of carpet's mine you know.
Moyra:	I know oh that's it is it?

Given my initial knowledge of Tilly as an older women with confused speech, I might expect that a conversation involving her would not, perhaps, follow normal rules or necessarily follow on topically. I might expect that she would speak about some rheumatic ointment and then move without a topic link to talking about the carpet. But I also need to know that Moyra is with Tilly in her apartment and that a contentious issue—whether this is Tilly's apartment—has just been extensively discussed. On returning from fetching the Deep Heat ointment, the carpet becomes another piece of ammunition for Tilly's argument. In this light, Tilly's remark is a further demonstration on her part that although the furniture is hers, the apartment is not.

Developing the Transcripts: A Dynamic Process

My early transcription work showed me that the process whereby one comes to see something as significant in the data is a complex one. In her article on local knowledge, Rawlings (1988) made some observations about her relation to the transcriptions she produced. The remark I empathize with most is "I spent a good deal of time looking at some of the detailed transcripts of meetings I had collected without any real idea of what I was looking for" (p. 158). In other words, I began without any

---

[12] Rheumatism ointment.

well-formed questions. Anderson and Sharrock (1984) noted, in relation to some work by Schegloff, that once the data are collected the solution is there: "The analytic task is to discover what problem the corpus is a solution to" (p.108). This process of seeking a problem, or of not knowing what I was looking for, was accompanied at this first stage of transcription by using my computer to try out different ways of arranging the transcript to give me new ways of looking at the data. For example, I used two columns for the main speakers and put the interviewees' talk in the left-hand column. And at one stage, when I was analyzing Moyra's interview with Tilly, I stripped out all of Moyra's talk to check whether Tilly's talk made sense as a monologue.

In the process of developing the transcripts, I began to do some more detailed transcriptions. This was largely a result of beginning to know what I was looking for. And this came about in two ways. Firstly, it resulted from beginning an analysis that used some of the central concepts of conversation analysis and other analytic traditions: adjacency pairs, insertion sequences, face, identity, and so on. That is to say, I used some readymade concepts that could bring order to the data. This can be seen as a function of my becoming acculturated into being (at least a novice) conversation–discourse analyst and thereby finding a specific way of seeing the data. Using these concepts, I went through my hard copy of the transcript and made pencilled annotations, picking out small segments I wanted to examine in more detail. For example, in one segment involving summonses and answers, I used a stopwatch to time gaps between them and developed a layout for this piece of transcription that emphasized the issue of timing.

As I listened to the tapes, I realized that I was imposing categories on the speakers as well as on the talk. These categories corresponded roughly to that of respondent (as displaying talk that was of interest) and of informant (as offering information about some subject of interest). As potential informants, some people were reliable and others were unreliable. However, there was, in my developing understanding, an almost perfect correlation between confused speakers and unreliable informants. So, for example, when confused speakers put forward facts of some kind I listened for dissonances, corrections by normal speakers, and other evidence to support the view that these speakers were interactionally incompetent; in other words, I was using my ordinary member everyday commonsense knowledge that these speakers were hearable as confused and that the context would offer up some evidence that this was so. I might also say that for the purposes of the study, confused speakers were treated as reliable respondents, in that they fulfilled the requirement of displaying talk that was interesting because it was confused.

All this clearly has implications for my own interpretation of the status of the participants. This dawning realization of the way that I was listening to the tapes was reflected in the transcription process; thus, I tended to produce less detailed transcripts for people I was interested in as informants and more detailed conversation analytic transcripts for people I was interested in as respondents. So, the selection of transcript conventions and the mode of analysis were, as it turned out, a function of each other.

Secondly, having done my basic transcription and picked out fragments for detailed transcription, I also began to explore the data as complete conversations. It became clear to me that it may be significant that people with confused speech "sat out" whole segments of the conversation. This suggested that in the early stages of transcription, I had understood confusion to be manifested in short stretches of talk and had not looked at the whole conversation as a significant unit. So I went back and transcribed the remaining talk on the audiotapes, including stretches of talk between myself and caregivers. It also became important to do this because by then minimal answers (most noticeably "yes") were becoming a major preoccupation of the study, as a distinctive feature of some confused speech, so I wanted to know in detail how much different confused speakers talked.

Finally, when I lighted on materials that I decided to use in the final text, I went through transcripts again, attaching to them some conventions taken from Jefferson's transcription system (outlined in Schenkein, 1978). This process, in turn, often uncovered yet other new features of significance in the data. Primarily, these additions related to ways of annotating overlaps at the beginning and end of turns (see Appendix B for transcription conventions used). Although Jefferson's system is generally accepted to be the most comprehensive available for conversation analysis, many authors have tended to offer a selected version suitable for their own purposes and those of the reader (e.g., Potter & Wetherell, 1987; Silverman, 1993). At certain points, notably when focusing on sequence, I use aspects of Jefferson's conventions. Elsewhere, when I am concerned solely with the substance of what people say, I present transcript in the form of a simple dialogue.

Transcripts and Selectivity

Ochs noted that making a transcription is a selective process: It reflects the theorizing and definitions of the researcher (Ochs, 1979). Indeed, in some respects, we can see making a transcript as in itself being the "fieldwork" of the conversation or discourse analyst. Zimmerman (1988) noted "Transcription is observation: the noticing and recording of events of talk that might otherwise elude analytic attention" (p. 413). In addition, the layout and presentation of the transcription is there to be read by ordinary members according to cultural conventions. Thus, Ochs suggested that the page layout of top to bottom, left to right will be seen to present certain nontextual information: Incidents represented higher up the page take place before those lower down; when a sentence does not make sense to a reader he or she will return to the immediately preceding sentence and then to the one before that in order to ascertain relevance, and so on. In relation to research on children, Ochs observed that, in adult terms, what they say is often irrelevant and that therefore a transcript of children talking to adults requires a reader to "suspend the expectation that sequentially expressed utterances are typically contingent and relevant" (Ochs, 1979). I would suggest that this is often also the case with confused speakers. Moreover, it is a major device for spotting that something is "wrong" with an account when it is not sequentially relevant, as in statements to the police and so on. Similarly, the left to right layout of pages of text represents words to the left of other words on the same line as having been produced earlier. Speier noted the way that names of participants are used in transcripts— transcribers produce consistent titles for the participants rather than veering between, for example, *Adult 1, Man, Father* , and personal names when transcribing the talk of one person (Speier, 1972). Indeed, to change titles of participants in the middle of a transcript might be seen as making a marked point of some kind. All this is to suggest that the transcriber's task is to generate a transcript that not only selects data for a research problem but also acknowledges an awareness of the cultural conventions that accompany the act of reading. Researchers do not only develop, use, and read transcripts as researchers but also as ordinary members. Thus, ordinary members' reading of a transcript or any text needs to be oriented to in the act of transcribing.

After reading Ochs, it is easy to fall into the trap of trying to produce a transcript that transcends all cultural conventions and bias! This belief is comparable with that outlined by Briggs (1986) in relation to interviews:

> The claim is that the influence of one or more of a range of independent variables, such as the age, gender, race, political views, personality, or interactional style of the researcher and/or interviewee, can "bias" responses to questions. The assumption here is that if you could strip the interview situation of all of these factors, the "real" or "true" or "unbiased" response would emerge. (p. 21)

There is no such thing as a truly interpretation-free neutral transcript: If there were it would make no sense (Psathas & Anderson, 1990). If something is to be represented textually in English, it has to go on a page and it has to be organized in some way, and readers will read the conventions in order to give themselves a context—that this talk came before that talk, that the same set of participants is involved throughout, and so on. This is textual contextualization. As P. Atkinson (1990), noted more broadly in relation to ethnographic texts "Ultimately there will be no escape from conventional forms of some sort" (p. 175). It seems to me that what is necessary is to try to be aware of the conventions that one uses and to allude to them as and when they are germane to the direction of the analysis.

I chose to produce transcripts with a left-hand column denoting names, and a right-hand column under which talk proceeded in turns, each turn being concluded by a paragraph end. It appeared to me that this conveyed the sense of the conversation as a continuous narrative. But it also enabled me to read the left-hand column vertically to get a sense of the sequencing of turn, particularly the interventions of caregivers.[13] I hoped that by doing this I would avoid too much emphasis in the transcribed talk on *initiators*. I also decided to name most of the people involved rather than designate them as *wife* or *daughter*, as caregivers acted as informants in their own right on many occasions.

I think it is important also to note that in producing these transcripts, I was producing documentation of the incompetence of some of the people concerned. For me this was a central feature of the talk and I wanted it to be apparent to anyone on a first reading. Thus, in my selectivity I did not choose to produce transcript details of other features that would have made the text any odder to read. For example, one aspect of talk I did not attempt to capture at the first transcription (or later) was regional accent, although a number of the people I interviewed had quite strong accents. P. Atkinson (1992) noted the problems of attempting a faithful rendition of regional accents, in particular that this can be seen to patronize speakers. So in disattending to accent in my transcript, I edited out this aspect of the talk for the reader. However all transcripts disattend to some aspects of talk, even highly detailed ones.

I chose not to produce the very detailed transcripts sometimes seen in conversation analysis (where the only way I, at least, can make sense of what was said is to try reading out loud what is on the page when the sense appears to be obscure on a first reading). I wanted to transcribe the text so that it is readable as confused on a first reading by an ordinary member, just as listening to the tapes or being at the interviews would lead the ordinary member to understand it as confused speech.[14] It seems to me that this is no more a piece of artifice than any other decision made

---

[13] For ease of reference, I also frequently numbered utterances in extracts, again subscribing to a common assumption that the order of the numbers will be seen as in some way significant in the analysis.

[14] Jefferson (Schenkein, 1978) aimed to produce "a system of notation and transcription design intending to produce a reader's transcript—one that will look to the eye how it sounds to the ear" (p.xi). Not all conversation analysts appear to have used the conventions to this end.

about how to transcribe. It is a decision to produce a particular sort of map; what is important is to articulate this so that people have the key to read the map.

The selection of transcript excerpts as illustrations for the study is another stage in the process of generating a text. As in other accounts, the extracts in this study are there to be read as significant in some way. If the study is about confused speech, the reader is alerted to find confused speech in the extracts, but not to find it in the quotations, which are there to be read as expert testimony![15] Because most of the extracts are short—the implication, for the reader, is that confusion can be discerned in momentary episodes, although as Zimmerman, noted, transcript extracts "will preserve more information than might be utilized in a given analysis" (p. 415). Moreover, most of the short interview extracts begin with an utterance from a normal speaker. So, even in the choice of extract, the kinds of bias that Ochs discussed can be generated. Although I may have escaped the "left-hand column opening up" bias, I have not escaped the notion of the first remark (by a competent participant) as framing each episode of talk. However, in my interview data, the competent participants actually do speak first most of the time, producing questions that require a response from the respondent, and this is a significant issue for me to deal with in my analysis. The exception to this is the Bruner data where Mrs. Bruner begins many of the episodes of talk, and I have reflected this in my choice of extracts.

Also, of course, much transcript material has been left to one side and never transcribed beyond the first stage. Examples have been chosen for the final text that are considered paradigmatic in some way, that represent the problem and act as the resource for its solution (the solution being my analysis). At the same time they offer a member's solution: My solution is then the elicitation of what the member's problem was. This process of selection is not evident in the transcripts that appear in the study, although the analysis, I hope, will explain why the data that are presented are germane.

CONCLUSION

The progress of this research study from people talking to production of this book involved much "working up" and a constant interplay between my ordinary member assumptions and category-bound activity related to research endeavor.

---

[15] See Anderson and Sharrock, (1984), and Richardson, (1990), for remarks concerning the construction of learned articles.

In this chapter, I described the emergence of my research focus and outlined how my data were produced. In the case of the interviews I carried out, I explored the significance of the clinic setting by looking at spatial and temporal markers and at the ways in which the interviews were located in this context. As regards the data collected by two Open University colleagues, I outlined their problematic nature in that I could only infer from the audiotape and from discussions with the interviewers what went on. I compared the two pieces of data, pointing out that in Tom's interview, the physical setting had been largely neutralized (even in the unedited version), whereas in Moyra's interview it remained a significant feature. I suggested that in the former the structure of the event as an interview was dominant whereas in the latter, episodes of domestic interaction were also involved. Nevertheless even the nomenclature I have used above—*Tom's interview* and *Moyra's interview* —is clear evidence of inferences that I made on the basis of these two pieces of talk. The selection of domestic interaction between Mrs. Bruner, an older woman with dementia, and her husband–caregiver was partly based on Mr. Bruner's ideas about what would be interesting and relevant to me as a researcher. I emphasized the importance of physical and domestic settings in these recordings and observed that they often focused on events that were not primarily verbal. All the sources of data were collected as demonstrations of confused speech. The research problem was how this is recognizable in the data.

There is a variety of formats of talk available to participants in the events that comprise my data. In my own interviews, I adopted a loosely structured ethnographic approach, a model that was probably not available to the interviewees. Medical, survey, and media interviews are also possible guides for participants to use in their own performance and, indeed, some events have a mixed or ambiguous character, deriving from a number of different types of formats. Conversation may also provide a format for talk, but may itself also come in a number of varieties, for example, ordinary chat or specialized or parachat that occurs in situations where institutionalized talk takes place.

Transcribing can almost be looked on as a phase of fieldwork. One's relationship with the participants may effectively develop during this period, for example, as one is affected by ordinary member views of their relative credibility. In my case, I was initially ready to hear confused speakers as unintelligible when I could not hear what they said, whereas hearing normal speakers as inaudible in similar circumstances. Moreover, the transcription process can involve problems of inference in situations where the transcriber has not been present: For me the tapes of Tom, Moyra, and the Bruners represented substantial inferential problems.   I outlined broadly how I assimilated inferences about physical settings into my transcripts.

The process of transcription in the development of this study was a dynamic one that continued throughout the research right up until I was writing final drafts. I did not know what I was looking for at the beginning: Coming to find more in the transcripts was generated by trying different approaches to transcription and analysis. Usually, at any one time, my collection of transcribed materials contained items at very different levels and stages of completion and was being pursued to bring out different points and to draw on different analytical traditions. In fact, the way I dealt with transcripts can be seen as a metaphor for the different traditions on which I drew in this study. On the one hand, I have undertaken some analysis that, as Sharrock and Anderson (1986) suggested, is more interested in utterances than speakers, and is thus very much in the tradition of conversation analysis. In other places, though, I placed the speakers as actors at center stage, following more closely Goffman's orientation in seeing the performance of the actor and the interaction order to which it is related as a central focus of analysis (Goffman, 1959, 1963a, 1963b, 1972, 1983, etc.). The transcript extracts employed in the study reflect this, being different sorts of maps for different sorts of terrain. (In a sense this is the traffic–driver divide again.)

Overall, what I have done is to explore the various laminations built on the experience of some specific people talking to each other through the working up of the data and the analytic to-and–fro that was involved up to the point of the production of this book. We can say that in working up the data, a multiplicity of routine everyday activity and ordinary specialized activity (in the methodic practices of a particular sort of research) is involved. I would draw attention to the fact that the requirements of the various interactional situations were not overwhelmed by the presence of confused speakers. Normal speakers find ways of making sense of situations involving confused talk. In some ways the confusion is contained (just as it is in momentarily confused situations). Similarly, in the working up of the data, the transcription and analysis of the confusion is contained within a framework where *normal* is the primary organizational concept.

3

Openings

In this chapter, I examine in more detail the question of how the context in which the data for my own interviews was constructed, by focusing on one particular part of the interviews—the openings. Of course, social interaction has to begin somehow. Many social encounters have recognizable openings—conventional greetings, associated body language, and so on, but these rarely predict the exact sequencing and unfolding of subsequent interaction. And, in most situations, finding a way in, a part to play, and so forth is a function of the way participants interpret and develop context, no matter how apparently predetermined a social encounter is.

As will become clear, the nature of my meetings with confused people and their caregivers cannot be taken for granted. Although the participants entered the anteroom with some contextual information, what they encountered there was not a clearly defined and unchanging context but one that had to be reevaluated and reconstituted depending on what happened during the course of the interaction. Given this, we must ask: What work did participants do to bring about the kind of interactional events that resulted? What sorts of occasion did people anticipate? Was it seen as a medical interview, a research interview, or a conversation: Or was it a combination of all three? If it was a combination, how did people identify which mode of talk to take up to begin with? We can suppose that ordinary members have a stock of knowledge about the type of situation *this* might be and that each interactional moment opens some doors on typing the occasion while closing others. Whereas the situations I describe in this chapter might be novel in some respects for the participants, they work to integrate the novelty into a framework of already understood experience. However, in undertaking this process there is, of course, the potential for interactional troubles. As with subsequent chapters, a great deal of the text is, in fact, taken up with outlining features of social situations that are in many respects recognizable as ordinary. The presence of confused speakers is not an overwhelming and confounding factor: It does not move the situations of which I speak into some sort of incomprehensible netherworld.

In the chapter, I explore these issues by examining the initial stages of interviews with Mr. and Mrs. Hoy, Mr. and Mrs. Toll, Mrs. Inman and her daughter Mrs. Grace, Mrs. Bowles and her son, Mr. and Mrs. Pugh and their daughter Mrs. James, and Cora and her nurse.

FOCUSED INTERACTION AND MEMBERSHIP

I want to begin with a broad outline of possible features of social occasions, using some of Goffman's descriptions. All interactional events are cooperative achievements. They depend on parties' interpretations and willingness to comply. One of Goffman's central concerns is how social occasions of various kinds are established through the activities of participants. He developed a set of types of context to map the spectrum from asocial to socially cooperative behavior. At one end of this spectrum is a gathering, "any set of two or more individuals whose members include all and only those who are at the moment in one another's immediate presence" (Goffman, 1963a, p. 18).

Goffman distinguished this from social situations proper, which take place when "mutual monitoring occurs, and lapse when the second last person has left" (Goffman, 1963a, p. 18). Then there is what he referred to as focused interaction. This consists of "the kind of interaction that occurs when persons gather close together and openly cooperate to sustain a single focus of attention, typically by taking turns at talking" (Goffman, 1963b, p. 24).

Goffman (1963a) argued that focused interaction often takes place within social occasions. These are:

> bounded in regard to place and time and typically facilitated by fixed equipment; a social occasion provides the structuring social context in which many situations and their gatherings are likely to form, dissolve and re-form, while a pattern of conduct tends to be recognized as the appropriate and (often) official or intended one—a "standing behavior pattern". . . . Examples of social occasions are a social party, a workday in an office, a picnic, or a night at the opera. (p. 18)

A social occasion offers the possibility of episodes of focused interaction flowing and merging into each other, of a situation where monitoring is taking place, as well as various people being gathered together. Any putative social occasion that does not involve focused interactions will be accounted a failure, as at a party where people only monitor each other or a social outing where participants do not talk to each other. The examples of social occasion cited by Goffman are large scale and might be seen to encompass, in the case of my own data, an entire visit to the psychogeriatric clinic rather than merely a talk with me. Clients' visits to the clinic did involve gatherings that formed, dissolved, and reformed: Moreover, they were usually constituted to involve focused interaction— in the waiting room, in the consulting room, and in the anteroom. Indeed, in the assessment and anteroom, focused interaction was usually a primary requirement. And thus we can see that it is in many ways typical of an extended consultation between a variety of professionals and clients. My experience of the occasion of a visit to the clinic was that generally focused interaction was easily and promptly accomplished in the various subsettings, particularly the assessment room and the anteroom. Certainly, in my interviews focused interaction was achieved satisfactorily in all but two cases. However, to achieve focused interaction is not in any way to define what kind of interactional event is occurring. This requires other interpretive work.

In maintaining a standing behavior pattern appropriate to the occasion, participants spend time making sense of what is going on, and this includes categorizing the people they are with, because this influences their perception of the situation. Speier (1973) pointed out that a key issue:

> about terms that label persons into social positions is that the manner in which such terms are used by cultural participants is decided in each and every case of human interaction. The relevance of this term over that particular term is always enforced by participants when doing things together. It is never simply an issue of which is the one and only correct term, *but rather it is always an issue of which, among many competing terms, is the relevantly correct one for the occasion.* (p. 37)

Here Speier drew on the work of Sacks, who pioneered the analysis of membership categories. Sacks saw membership category devices as ways of signalling and discerning in talk situationally appropriate interpretations of category words. Thus, "babies can't walk" refers to them from the point of view of being at a certain stage of life. "The baby's mother fed it" indicates a baby in a particular familial relationship. Sacks (1972) defined membership category devices as:

> containing at least a category, which may be applied to some population containing at least a member, so as to provide, by the use of some rules of application, for the pairing of at least a population member and a categorization device member. A device is then a collection plus rules of application. (p. 332)

Following from Sacks, I define category-bound activity as that which is seen to be appropriate to a membership category (Sacks, 1972, p. 335).

Knowledge of membership category devices and of appropriate category-bound activity is a central part of the stock of commonsense knowledge that members share about the social world, and a common competence in applying it defines membership of society in generic terms (Payne, 1976).

The promotion of focused interaction and membershipping work are functionally related in that "sustaining a single focus of attention, typically by taking turns at talking" (Goffman, 1963a, p. 24) will involve an understanding of the circumstances in which one is likely to be called to take a turn at talking, and this in turn requires an understanding of the relevant membership categories of participants. All such work will also be functionally related to contextualizing work.

THE CLINIC CONTEXT

The clinic context, which I outlined in chapter 2, can be seen as a resource for membership categorization work on the part of all participants, providing clues as to possible and appropriate category-bound behavior. Such membership categorization work may precede the beginning of focused interaction and, indeed, even the occurrence of a gathering. Indeed, we may suggest that many institutional and professional contexts will offer up resources for membership categorization at the beginning of meetings between, say, social workers and clients, architects and clients, nurses and patients. In my own case, although I did not have precise information about the ages, symptoms, and diagnoses of all the clients to whom I talked, the clinic context furnished me with some information, for example, about the diagnosis of confusional disorder that had already been made. In addition, because I sat in on a number of assessments, listening to what had been said by clients and caregivers, and had also been briefed by the consultant, I did on occasion have some knowledge of prior circumstances of the lives of the clients. For example, at the outset of my own interviews with them I knew that Mrs. Hoy was in her late 60s and had begun to manifest signs of dementia in her early 50s, and that Edith, Mrs. Bowles, and Mrs. Inman had all suffered from confusion for some years. And I knew too, that Mrs. Pugh had only shown signs of confusion for a few months. It should also be noted that I assumed that the prior information I received from the consultant and the assessment was accurate and relevant in this situation. In other words, the context led me to accept the information and treat it as germane.

The clients and caregivers were in a similar situation at the outset of the encounter, in the sense that they had a resource of previous interaction and knowledge related to the clinic context with which to make sense of the situation. For example, they knew something about the possible format of the encounter: Prior to my interviews, clients and caregivers had been involved in periods of *focused interaction* during the visit to the clinic. Indeed, focused interaction as an activity "to sustain a single focus of attention" (Goffman, 1963a, p. 24) might be seen as one aspect of category-bound behavior linked to the categories of health care workers and clients in a health care setting. People expect encounters with health care workers in their professional capacity, and indeed with other professionals too, to involve bouts of focused interaction. It might be expected that everyone at such an occasion will do a lot of "paying attention" specifically to identify when it is their turn to talk. Thus, one category-bound expectation clients and caregivers may have had on entering the anteroom is that there was bound to be some focused interaction (unlike a waiting room where focused interaction may not necessarily take place). Conversely, if, on arriving in a professional environment people are ignored, kept hanging around, or focused interaction is otherwise delayed, then in their role as clients they may see themselves as ill-used. Indeed, one of the current markers used in quality assurance procedures (in the UK) is a negative valuation placed on the delay in the commencement of focused interaction between professional and client, or provider and customer, for example, delays in answering the telephone.

Caregivers and clients had also had been briefed by the consultant before meeting me (or, if I were sitting in on the consultation, my mission had been explained). From my experience of sitting in on assessments, I knew that my concerns were introduced by the consultant as those of someone interested in communication who would like to talk to clients after the consultation, if they were willing. This suggested that the interaction was likely to take a particular direction and that there was a purpose in hand, but also that participation was ostensibly a matter of choice rather than obligation. The latter is significant because generally speaking, once someone had arrived at the clinic, the *choice* of being involved or not in the events that constituted a visit to the clinic was generally not offered. Moreover, clients and caregivers did not, in normal circumstances, leave the medical interview to talk to a researcher. More typically, the talk they might engage in after a medical interview was sociable talk with the members and staff of the connecting day center, and would be unlikely to be preceded by a suggestion on the part of the consultant that the day center staff would like to have a talk with them. So the proposed talk with me offered more than one novelty—being a matter of choice (although, of course, the choice was offered by the consultant— a person in a role associated with managing and directing other people) and it also involved a modification to the agenda of the clinic visit. As a result of this, participants probably faced a problem on entering the anteroom, concerning what sort of focused encounter they were to participate in. However, the novelty of the situation may also have offered an inferential resource, in the sense that it implied the appropriateness of a wait-and-see attitude. Yet, although novelty provides such an inferential resource, at the same time there is the possibility of working on it to render this context orderly and understood again (see, e.g., Sacks, 1984, on the extent to which people work to make novel events fit within the category of ordinary).

It seems likely from all this that participants would anticipate the event as being oriented to *my* interests, organized by an agenda set by me. They would also know that I saw them and their lives as in some way relevant to my interest in communication—thus alerting them to a way of prioritizing their own knowledge and experience for the event. Because of the emphasis on my interests they might also think that the first move would likely to be assigned to me and that me having a talk with them might well be a particular kind of talk. Silverman (1993) noted the following:

> Many kinds of activities are commonsensically associated with certain membership categories. So, by identifying a person's activity (say 'crying'), we provide for what their social identity is likely to be (in this case a 'baby'). Moreover, we can establish negative moral assessments of people by describing their social behaviour in terms of performing or avoiding activities inappropriate to their social identity. For instance, it may be acceptable for a parent to 'punish' a child, but it will be unacceptable for a child to punish a parent. (p. 82)

What we might expect to follow from this is that because I wanted to find things out, this would be an interview, and would involve the category-bound behavior associated with interviews—that I would start things off with a first question and that a series of category-bound activities would be expected to follow—questions on my part, answers on theirs.

All of these factors had implications for the membership categories of those present and for the presentation they made of themselves during the encounter. Such factors were there to be interpreted by those present as part of the process of coming to see it as a certain sort of situation. The notion of what exactly *this situation* was, and therefore of what a normal version of such a situation can be seen to be, is crucial to my analysis and is given attention throughout this study. However, I should also note that exactly the same question was germane to the actors concerned. The question is not merely one to be imposed retrospectively by the analyst. As Zimmerman (1988) noted, "the field of data is not just capable of being ordered by analysis, but . . . is in the first instance *ordered* by the methodical activities of the social actors themselves" (p. 415). The generation and interpretation of context is a methodic practice central to social interaction.

THE INITIAL CONTACT

As I noted, as with any occasion, participants may have been able to draw on a number of inferential resources. But that still left the sort of occasion that was to take place uncertain and a matter to be negotiated. In chapter 2, I discussed a number of interview formats (medical, survey, media, ethnographic) on which participants may have been able to draw to inform their conduct in this situation. I also suggested that ordinary chat and professional chat or parachat may have been formats that could inform the event. Indeed, all of these are commonly available formats on which substantial numbers of people might draw in a research or professional encounter. But, as with any event, to suggest that a number of interactional formats are available to participants still leaves them with the crucial work of identifying which format is appropriate. Of course, in every situation people must work out what type of focused interaction is appropriate and use whatever inferential resources are available to do so. For example, J. M. Atkinson and Drew (1979) analyzed the phrase "Be upstanding in Her Majesty's Court for Her Majesty's Coroner" at the opening of a session in an English Coroner's court. They observed that those present have several methods for recognizing this as the first statement to which everyone should attend: It is recipiently designed for everyone; it is acted on by other personnel who can be recognized as familiar with the court's proceedings (by their placement or uniform) and so on. Similarly, M. A. Atkinson, Cuff, and Lee (1978) examined how people recogonize particular utterances as ways of starting a meeting. They noted that the interpretive work required in hearing a phrase like "Right: er" is linked to an understanding of the status of the person uttering it and to its juxtaposition to the next utterance "Are we ready to go again?" These are situations where a particular utterance is monitored and can be seen to indicate a starting point for focused interaction on the part of some interactants and, at least, the paying of attention by others.

Out of the diversity of prior interaction and established commonsense knowledge, the focused interaction of the whole court or of the meeting needs to emerge, a structure where certain people talk at points when it is deemed appropriate for them to do so in ways that are appropriate to both the occasion and the category of person they need to be for the occasion (e.g., those in the gallery pay attention to those taking interactional turns but do not take turns themselves). So both these analyses deal with how authority is recognized, why one person's actions are interpreted as legitimate, and why another's may not be. In both situations, the interpretation of the opening utterance is linked in some way to other inferential resources that are monitored.

As I noted in the case of my interviews, the end of the assessment marked the completion of one period of focused interaction. The move to the anteroom may be seen to continue the visit to the psychogeriatric clinic but denotes the beginning of another phase of interaction within the whole occasion. My interviews all began at the end of the assessment session when either a member of the assessment team or I took the client and caregiver into the anteroom. The movement from one room to another was to be seen by participants as indicating the beginning of a new phase of the visit and the continuing official nature of the visit was reinforced by the fact that they were conducted by personnel with formal roles (or someone associated with those personnel), not left to find their own way. Indeed, how and when people are conducted around institutional premises may be seen as a substantial inferential resource connected not only with *the next stage* of any visit but also with the status of the participants. Thus, perhaps, we may imagine that a professional working in a private capacity may orchestrate the visit so that clients are courteously seen to the external door of the premises, whereas in other less auspicious circumstances people are left to find their own way out. It is also interesting that being shown out is open to both positive and negative interpretations, depending on context: The difference between being shown out and being escorted off the premises is substantial.

In the context of the psychogeriatric clinic, I did a certain amount of inferential work about people I was meeting for the first time as the consultant or social worker ushered them into the room. Firstly, I assumed that these people were seen to be relevant to my project by the consultant (who was the person who could define people as confused or not). Secondly I did *not* assume that the presence of two people together was merely happenstance; I recognized them to be together rather like Ryave and Schenkein (1974) noted that people can be seen to be together when they are walking down the street. Putting these two points together, the presence of two people suggested that at least one of them could be subsumed under a less-than-full membership category of medical pathology, or incompetence. Only in circumstances where full membership will be questioned or denied are people generally accompanied by others to a medical interview.[1] So I was assuming that at least one person was "normal" and one person "confused" and not that these were cases of *folie à deux* or *folie à trois*, or two or three normal speakers. Indeed, the orchestration of visits by professionals that involve

---

[1] Children, people with learning disabilties, and people who may be about to receive some serious medical news that challenges their membership as full fit members may all be accompanied.

caregivers or other parties in some way interested in the client
constitutes a substantial part of professional work. (Note Silverman's
1987 comments about the orchestration of the conduct of parents and
families in visits to a pediatric clinic.) When there is one "normal" person
and one client, questions immediately arise for the professional: how the
client's problem is to be unfolded and negotiated, how each person will
be spoken to, what status their replies will be given. Similarly for the
caregiver, the question of how to "do" being a normal person
accompanying a confused person arises. Indeed, more generally,
whether "normal" and "not normal" are pertinent categories or not, the
client who is accompanied by someone else may present an interactional
challenge to any professional (as may the respondent who is
accompanied by someone else in a research context).

Generally, after coming into the anteroom, the consultant or social
worker introduced me to client and caregiver(s) and then left. The
introduction could be seen to serve as further evidence that clients and
caregivers were being passed on to someone else with whom they were
expected to interact as part of the clinic context. Following the departure
of the clinic personnel, there was a period of settling down. Two of the
clients, Mrs. Hoy and Edith, used wheelchairs, so that spaces had to be
made and people to be disposed around a fairly large table. During this
phase, I did not have the tape recorder on and so I can only rely on my
recall and brief notes. However, the pattern here was that I thanked
people for taking the time to stop and see me. So although the encounter
began with a *managed handover* (and thus suggested the continuation of
the authority of a medical encounter), it immediately proceeded as an
event where I presented myself as someone with no particular right to
demand an encounter. I want to note that focused interaction was
generally achieved nonproblematically immediately upon the entry of
the client and caregivers into the anteroom. Talk commenced and turns
were taken. There were, for example, no lengthy silences in response to
my introduction of myself.

At this stage too, I began to form impressions of the people who had
come into the room (and had already done this at the assessment, if I had
sat in on it). I formed an impression of the various participants as
nervous, depressed, pleasant, and so on (both clients and caregivers); in
other words, I assigned identities to them (Goffman, 1963b). Indeed, my
ordinary members' judgments of aspects of self-presentation created
some difficulties for me in that my own construction of the experience of
confusion prior to this was such that I found it unlikely that being
pleasant and laughing a lot would be associated with being confused. On
the other hand, being nervous and depressed seemed to me to be
eminently suitable emotional states in which to be if one were confused,

or even if one was caring for a confused speaker. In fact, Edith and Mrs. Hoy, who were both pleasant and apparently amused by the proceedings, were probably the least normal speakers; whereas several more competent speakers appeared to be markedly depressed. The important point is that from the outset I was doing interpretive work on the self-presentation of the participants; interpretive work rooted in prior commonsense reasoning of the virtual identity of people suffering from confusion; work requiring modification as the occasion proceeded (Goffman, 1963b).[2]

THE INTRODUCTION OF THE TAPE RECORDER

After we were seated, I asked permission to use the tape recorder. I did not explain that I wanted to carry out a research interview before the tape recording began. I think that this order of development in the interaction may once again have suggested someone with the license to begin proceedings without a contextualizing explanation (e.g., in the same way that a nurse taking a blood sample during a consultation might not offer an explanation).

The presence of a tape recorder operating in a conversation is not congruent with it being an ordinary conversation: Its use may be seen as a category-bound activity. People do not normally record talk. Talk is usually transitory and can only be recreated imperfectly through the recall of the members who have been present. Ordinary people generally only tape record from the radio and records: People who tape record live social interaction are members of distinctive social groups, those who for some reason want to put what is said on record. This relates to one of Garfinkel's breaching experiments, where an interviewer revealed that they had a tape recorder on their person and were taping the interview: For participants a tape recorder presents *a breach of expectancy*—although the conversation is between *us* a record implies new and as yet unknown possibilities for the conversation and new and as yet unknown listeners (Garfinkel, 1967).

When people do record interactions, generally their identity needs to be validated in some way. If someone came up to you on the street, switched on a tape recorder, and started to interview you, you would want to know who they were. Their activity would need to be validated by membership in some appropriate group (local radio, school child doing project, newspaper reporter). Those who professionally occupy a

---

[2]Recall the point made by Kitwood (1993) and cited in chapter 1: The behavior aberrations of normal people are not seen as significant, but those of people with of dementing illnesses are seen as connected to their illness.

medical setting can both legitimize the lengthy interrogation of one person by another and validate a record of this event. Researchers do not have quite so much license. At the beginning of a research interview, the tape recorder has to be introduced. This introduction is part of the ethics of the role of the researcher, and at the same time implies the explicit introduction and definition of this particular role.

My tape recorder became something of a force in the interviews, despite the fact that recordings were never played back for any of the participants. It acquired some moral energy of its own. It remained in sight throughout the interview and was referred to occasionally. It had some significance for those involved in the occasion, at least at the beginning, as is shown here by one caregiver's comments to his wife:

Extract 1

	((Beginning of recording))
Pam:	(Just put that on) ((Loud cough)) Find that I haven't got it switched on or something like that yes it is this is its little ears for recording ((Laughs))
	[
Mr. Pugh:	Ignore it=
Pam:	=Yes (.) just ignore it erm [...]

The utterance contains an anthropomorphic reference on my part to the tape recorder as having ears, and this can be seen as giving *the recorder* responsibility for hearing and thus allowing me to distance myself at that time from being the person who is making the record. Occasionally, reference to the tape recorder recurred later in the interview, again by two caregivers:

Extract 2

Mr. Bowles:	No no that was a saga from last year that's another story and I'd rather you didn't tape record it=
	[
Pam:	No no
Mr. Bowles:	=It's I mean you don't really want to hear about it I've just recited it in there you see=
	[
Pam:	Yes
Mr. Bowles	=You know I mean I don't want the name of the company=
	[
Pam:	No no
Mr. Bowles:	=That I went down to=
	[
	No no
Mr. Bowles:	=What it amounts to is ((tape off for about 3 minutes)) It was a very unfortunate experience=
Pam:	[
	Yes
Mr. Bowles:	=Now you can understand why she gets confused.

Extract 3

Barry:	It just proves a point here while we've got this tape on=
	[

| Pam: | | Yes |
| Barry: | = That if your system and your body is out of sequence it does affect you. | |

In Extracts 2 and 3, the tape recorder was again identified as a *listener* for whom I was responsible, this time by caregivers. This may also have implied to them, at least, that my membership category was something that had some continuing existence after this meeting, in the form of listening to the tape. In one sense, at least, the record of this event was viewed as dangerous or potent knowledge and I and my membership category, as a researcher and as a worker at the Open University, were associated with that (Hughes, 1977). My emphatic "no" answers expressing agreement with Mr. Bowles in Extract 2 seem to reinforce the idea of the potency of tape recording.

The recordings generally began as I talked about setting up the tape recorder. At the outset of the recording, I sometimes described the technicalities of the tape recorder to the confused speaker (compare this with the mode of distancing myself from the recorder in Extract 1). Below is one of three similar exchanges:

Extract 4

Pam:	((Low)) I'll put it over here. <u>Do you</u> mind if I put it over here because I've got a very loud voice((laughs))
	[
Mrs. Hoy:	Yes=
Pam:	=And you've got quite a quiet voice=
Mrs. Hoy:	=((Low)) Yes.
	(4.0)
Pam:	So (2.0) Do you want to hold it?
	(2.0)
Mrs. Hoy:	((Animated)) Ye:s=
Pam:	=Would you like to hold it?=
Mrs. Hoy:	=((Animated)) Ye:s
	(2.0)
Pam:	I'll put it in your hands (1.0) <u>Oh</u> you've got a biscuit there (Look there's a little pot)=
Mrs. Hoy:	=Yes=
Pam:	=I think that's quite a clean saucer I'll put the biscuit on it=
Mrs. Hoy:	=Yes=
Pam:	=OK=
Mrs. Hoy:	=Yes thank you=
Pam:	=Can you see the wheel going round?=
Mrs. Hoy:	=Ye:s=
Pam:	=Can you?=

I commented about the loudness of my voice and the quietness of other people's voices and placed the tape recorder according to my assessment of this. In an ordinary unrecorded conversation, not being able to hear is usually dealt with locally at the time that one of the participant's voices sinks to inaudibility. Here, as the interviewer, I attempted to orchestrate the conversation for subsequent hearings, that is, so that I would be able to hear the conversation on tape adequately when I listened to it again. Accommodation was made so that the tape recorder could do its job (the job the interviewer wants it to do—to record adequately the answers of the confused speakers). The equipment was oriented to the person with confused speech. At the beginning of none of the interviews did I, as the interviewer, mention that the caregivers had quiet voices. I defined the people to be involved in the conversation (or at least the conversation in which I was interested) as myself and the confused speaker, and positioned the tape recorder accordingly.

There was an aspect of global management from the outset, therefore. The focused interaction was not intended to develop into a conversation where caregivers could join in, just as those seated in the gallery are not seen as having the right to join in at a court of law. This could be seen to relate to Rawlings' maxim about hearing therapists as reliable but uninteresting (see chapter 2; Rawlings, 1988). My anticipation of hearing caregivers as uninteresting was so powerful that I did not organize the environment to hear them at all! And this piece of organizational work on my part in tape recording contrasts with the organization of ordinary conversation, where generally speaking we do not anticipate in advance that some of those present will not be ratified to speak. However, when caregivers did speak, I did not attempt to alter the environment by, for example, switching the tape recorder off. Thus, I acknowledged their self-ratification.

Given that I was hoping for an informal conversation where participants had relatively equal status, this raises the question of the extent to which this piece of early interaction relating to the tape recorder could be seen to indicate that this was a joint venture between myself and the confused speakers. The most obvious marker of a joint venture might be seen to be the use of pronouns, for example, by using "we". However, using the term "we" may not necessarily imply a joint venture (Payne, 1976). In the case of a teacher, use of "we" can be seen as a rhetorical device designed to legitimize a situation where there is a power differential. "We" are not actually joined together as members of the same category.[3] Very often, however, I used use the pronoun "I" during this activity and thereby my authority to set up the form of the encounter was taken for granted. For example. Extract 1 denotes "I" as the person who is responsible for adjusting the tape recorder. My requirements in relation to the tape recorder had priority, but I did offer involvement to some of the confused speakers: I offered the tape recorder to both Mrs. Hoy and Edith to hold. They were to play a role in looking after the tape recorder, but very much a subordinate one. In fact,

---

[3] Indeed 'we' may be used in a classroom in an ironic sense as in "I wonder if we are all paying attention Jenkins?"

later in the interview, Edith turned off the tape recorder and there was a mad scramble on the part of both Barry, her son, and myself to turn it back on again: an indication that turning off the tape recorder was not a valid activity for Edith to engage in and thus casting doubt on the notion of collaboration. For an interviewee to turn off a tape recorder or to ask for it to be turned off, there has to be a reason that is contextually valid. Mr. Bowles' reason (Extract 2) related to some delicacies regarding the acquisition of a piece of electrical equipment. In seeing himself as required to contextualize something his mother had just said, he considered it necessary to say something compromising. But when Edith turned off the tape recorder it was not deemed to be contextually valid, because no reason was given for the action and no valid reason could be inferred by the other participants. And yet as soon as their involvement became more than token, a problem was generated for me. Edith ceased to treat the tape recorder as a toy and usurped my function as the controller of the recording. In hindsight, I think that this all implied an interesting commentary on my ordinary member assumptions about those present. I gave the tape recorder to these participants almost in the sense that I would give a toy to a child (as a less-than-full member) to keep it occupied. Their involvement with the machine was, at most, token. In previous interview work I have done with people who might be considered as full members, for example, with bereaved people, the thought of giving them the tape recorder never entered my head. However, I do think the notion of interviewees as comechanics battling together with the researcher into taming the technology offers possibilities for further research into membership categorization!

In various ways, then, the opening sequences of these interactions are set apart from casual, mundane conversations:

- They are recorded and thus are not ephemeral in the manner of ordinary conversations.
- The recording of the event may imply to clients and caregivers that this is some kind of official event, possibly an interview.
- The talk of the people with confused speech is seen to be important to me even before I have heard what they are going to say.
- I demonstrate that I am not so interested in a record of what people other than confused speakers say (though when caregivers begin to take turns—usually very early on—I do not turn off the tape recorder, which suggests that I see any interaction that takes place within this setting as worthy of a record).
- I take responsibility for monitoring the immediate environment in ways I define as related to the generation of the conversation.

In these respects, I said and did things related to my membership category as a researcher at this event (reinforced by how I had earlier been introduced) that implied I had a right to control the situation for my purposes. We might suggest that, even though mutual monitoring was going on, as the interviewer I took a lead role in establishing the nature of the focused interaction and its recording. And this fact could be taken to indicate my "legitimacy" as a member of a category of people who have the right to do this. Moreover, the act of my dealing with the tape recorder suggested that certain category-bound activities must happen before the meeting proper could begin. People can normally be assumed to be aware that this category-bound activity both prefixes and signposts the *real reason* for the meeting: the reason for which the record is going to be made. The setting up of a formal occasion is one of its distinctive characteristics and this may provide cues as to the membership categories of those present.[4] Much of what I have so far described can equally be applied to any occasion being recorded. Indeed, the status of the participants may well be reinforced by their involvement (or not) in the setting up of the equipment. The paradox here, recognized by Mr. Pugh and myself in Extract 1, is that even though it significantly changed the nature of the event and assigned to me and others specific membership categories, the tape recorder was to be ignored, suggesting perhaps, that participants were expected to behave as if this were a nonrecordable ordinary conversation; and this implies, at the outset, a certain amount of ambiguity about the nature of the occasion.

THE REASON FOR THE CONVERSATION

It is apparent from this discussion that the clinic context, the initial contact between myself and clients and caregivers, and the setting up of the tape recorder all provided resources from which participants may have been able to infer reasons for the conversation they were about to have. Indeed, many interactional formats rely on such inference to provide an informal justification. For example, in ordinary conversations people do not often give explicit reasons for what they are saying or doing (or the direction in which they are taking the conversation). Much of the time they do not need to. It is assumed that other participants will be able to infer such reasons; if not at that moment, then later. Similarly, in some formal situations, medical ones among them, participants may infer reasons for the conversation rather than being given them. This process may be facilitated if they are offered a particularly powerful context. Strong (1979) developed the concept of *role format* to refer to the

---

[4]Informal conversations rarely have prestarts. Where they do, people talk about getting their cups of tea, getting comfortable, and so on: Such prestarts usually anticipate that some news is going to be told and indicate that people are getting ready for it.

whole ceremonial order of an institutional setting. Such a role format, as defined, offers participants cues as to what sort of frame to operate within. Some role formats are so powerful and operate within such a broad spectrum of commonsense understanding that reasons are not required, and we might suggest that the ceremonial order surrounding going to the psychogeriatric clinic may belong to that category. This may have been the reason why at the outset of my interview with the Bruners, Mr. Bruner took the initiative in interpreting the reason for the conversation, making inferences from the tape recorder's presence, and suggesting that it would not record the reality of Mrs. Bruner's illness, thus linking the interview to the reason for being at the clinic. Again, there is an underlying assumption that a necessary and defining methodic practice in a medical context is in some way the recording of the illness. Similarly, on more than one occasion, I too used the sequence of events of a visit to the clinic to begin the conversation, offering my absence from what went on in the consulting room as a way of legitimating my talk without exactly giving a reason:

Extract 5

Pam:	Right=
Mr. Bowles:	=( ) You're asking questions what have you you=
Pam:	=No I just wanted to, having missed the whole of the preceding er twenty minutes, I mean I was just going to ask you about erm I mean things like wh wh you know er do you come from Jessop?=
Mrs. Bowles:	=No from the north.

An opening such as this could be seen as belonging either to medical talk or to ordinary talk. However by suggesting that I had *missed* the whole of the previous 20 minutes (the business of the assessment), other participants may have been able to infer that it was in some way my business too (because only people who claim some right to be at an event or interest in it can claim to have missed it) and thereby that this conversation should continue in a medical frame. So, being aware of the ceremonial order of the clinic enables participants to produce appropriately recipient-designed talk for their coconversationalists without necessarily giving reasons for the conversation.

My most protracted attempt to explain the reason for the conversation was with Mr. and Mrs. Pugh:

Extract 6[5]

1. Pam:	Like Doctor Brown said in the other room I'm I'm looking at erm how people's speech might change if something you (.) know if they've had an illness like p'haps you might have had and so I was interested in the sorts of ways that people talk. Is that worrying you? ((The tape recorder))=
2. Mrs. Pugh:	= ((Quickly)) No no
	[

---

[5] This extract follows on immediately from Extract 1.

3. Pam: Shall I put it to one side?
                                                             [
4. Mrs Pugh: No=

In Extract 6, the beginning of Utterance 1 is a justification for what I am
going to do. It is a reason in my own terms but it also carries part of its
weight from the explanation that the consultant gave in the assessment.
My reason for the conversation shelters under the wing of the doctor's
relationship with this client. This further reinforces my social identity as
official in some way, and is intended to legitimize subsequent questions.
In seeing the doctor, the client has become a special case of someone
who, at least temporarily, can release her claim on full membership, but
has become a subject for investigation.

However, although I was being assimilated into a medical role and
made use of it, I did not have any specific medical authority. Moreover, it
was not a medical interview that I wanted to carry out and this was
signaled by the fact that I engaged in the procedures (asking permission
to set up the tape recorder, and in some cases giving a reason for the
interview) that would not normally occur in medical interviews. In this
respect, I too suffered from some role confusion, and my exhibitions of
confusion may have been, in themselves, confusing to other participants;
not least because they would be unlikely to expect confusion or
embarrassment on the part of an interviewer in this sort of context.

THE FIRST QUESTION

The next thing that happened in the interviews was an opening question
posed by me to the confused speaker. A first question is, of course, a
likely marker in any interview situation. This first question was often
quite abrupt in relation to the prior conversation. This might be seen as
appropriate by participants, given that in interviews the move from the
warm up stage to the interview proper can often be quite sudden:
Indeed, many professional situations involve abrupt shifts from
preliminaries to the purpose at hand, and there was no reason for the
participants to suppose that there was anything odd in that procedure
here. But this interpretation, of course, is part of the work of seeing the
occasion as an interview. Such sudden transitions made by particular
participants in certain contexts may be seen as an indication of their
interactional rights. Such rights do not suggest that the person in charge
will say more than others: Indeed, many interviewers say less than
interviewees. What is implied, however, is that they have a right to
control the agenda, to intervene to ask questions that demand topic
changes or modifications, to ask for clarification, to draw the interview to
a close, and so on. In research interviews, even if there is no schedule of

questions, there is some notion of global management and some preallocation of interactional rights. Subsequently, topical connectors are not absolutely necessary in an interview because the interviewer retains the floor after each response to a question.

The placement of questions in talk may be seen to be of significance for participants. Normally we may suppose that if a reason for the conversation has been given, it contextualizes at least the immediately following exchanges. Moreover, we might suggest that all early talk in a conversation may be used as a resource for contextualizing purposes, and that if a reason is not given, people may infer reasons from early questions, just as they infer reasons from the physical setting, participants' presence, and so on. However, in this case, the nature of the questions added to the potential ambiguity. Here are some examples of the first couple of *inventory type* questions I ask.

Extract 7

Pam   So you were saying in the other room that you were born in Linton, do
             you come from around Jessop? [. . .]
             Your wife was saying when you were in there that you'd been to
             Majorca? [. . .]
             Were you brought up in this area are you from the Midlands? {. . .]
             Where were you born? [. . .]
             Do you come from round Jessop? [. . .]

The nature of the questions I ask may be seen as heightening the abruptness of the start of the interview, and potentially adding to the ambiguity of the situation. Participants have to figure out from prior context an interpretation of why I ask "Where do you come from?" or "Have you always lived around here?" and so on. They have to interpret an occasion where questions such as "Where do you come from?" can legitimately be asked and what sort of a member will ask them. What is potentially puzzling is that these questions, although purportedly the beginning of the interview proper, are in content the type of questions that would be at home in a *conversation* among strangers. Only in the unlikely event of my interviewees being familiar with life history or oral history interviews would these initial questions seem like interview questions. Moreover, because this was the type of question I continued to ask throughout the interview, the hypothesis that this was initial parachat would have been abandoned at some point. Their persistence, and the resulting implications that they are the type of questions of which the whole interview will be composed, may well have conflicted with expectations about the likely nature of the interview. At the same time, they approximate in some respects the type of questions that sometimes occur in medical interviews where someone's cognitive functioning is being assessed. In these ways, the ambiguity of the event in which participants were involved persisted.

Faced with such ambiguity, the decision about how to answer any question relates to occasion and membership. We might suggest that an opening question of an interview or conversation would be recipiently designed so as to facilitate the possibility of a successful answer. Questions such as those cited in Extract 7 are built on the assumption of a shared stock of knowledge that events concerning life history are a legitimate opening topic for a conversation or an interview with someone whom you do not know. Indeed, in much the same way as Turner(1972) noted that a choice of certain topics (e.g., the weather) embraces the largest possible number of participants, so too we could expect that common life history questions would have a good chance of a successful answer from a large sector of the population, that is, they are questions that *anyone*, *everyperson* or ordinary members should be able to answer. Even given that, in commonsense terms, memory is accepted as a variable attribute, we would still expect a fairly high success rate by beginning a conversation or interview by asking people questions about major events in their lives. So I constructed my first question of the interview on the commonsense assumption that the people to whom I was talking had ordinary member's access to their own biography. Holstein (1988) talked of the way that some lawyers construct their talk to emphasize the competence of those they represent in involuntary commitment proceedings. I was doing something similar in offering questions that could easily be answered by anyone. As I made clear in the previous chapter, this was all I thought was required, given that my aim was simply to obtain samples of confused talk.

However, even though the questions I asked were there to be heard as easy, and perhaps in a less ambiguous context might have been seen as *warm up* questions, the context of the talk on this occasion may also have offered another interpretation. One legitimate scenario for life history questions is in a medical encounter: Thus, on an utterance-by-utterance basis, participants in these interviews may well have seen these questions as having some medical authority. By presenting myself under the auspices of a medical approach, my opening and subsequent questions were there to be interpreted as medical. In relation to the various possible interactional formats, we can suggest that if this were to be a medical interview, such opening questions could not only be construed as life history questions, but also possibly as memory test questions. If I begin by probing life history, well so too do consultants: If I ask memory test questions a similar interpretation is possible. And such an interpretation may make such questions seem not easy, but anxiety provoking. And indeed, three out of six people did not or could not answer an opening question about their own history.

So far I have suggested two possible inferences that might have been drawn from my opening questions: That they were easy *everyperson* questions and that they were medical testing questions. In both cases, they may have provided inferential resources to participants as to the nature of the conversation. I also want to cite one sequence, at the beginning of the interview with Mrs. Pugh, where I think I offered an ambiguous stimulus in another respect in the opening question that I asked:

Extract 8

Pam: =Erm so what it sounds a bit silly really so er ((laughs)) I just wanted to
                have a brief talk with you erm about say for example erm were you
                brought up in this area?=

This utterance attests to the difficulty of introducing a first topic without making the explicit link that I was interested in the competence of Mrs. Pugh's talk. The use of "It sounds a bit silly really" seems to relate quite closely to Schegloff's (1980) discussion of what he called *pre-delicates* —the signposting of talk or questions to come that may be uncomfortable such as "Can I ask you a personal question?" Additionally, we could suggest that "It sounds a bit silly really" can be seen as some sort of moral positioning, in the sense that I should be heard as a silly person and thus, that any responses to my silly questions will not be judged harshly because I am placing the interviewee in a delicate position. This is somewhat similar to the moral positioning discussed by Silverman in relation to HIV counseling (Silverman, 1994).

As I noted in chapter 2 "I just wanted to have brief talk with you" suggests some preallocation by the speaker, thus claiming authority. On the other hand, "just" possibly acts as an indication of *merely* (not to be seen as important), perhaps aligning the conversation with casual inconsequential talk and thus assigning equal interactional rights. The use of "for example" suggests a model of some sort is going to be offered and this contrasts with the idea of a naturally occurring, locally managed conversation (although examples might be required in an ordinary conversation, the requirement is usually for clarification of something that is being discussed). Overall, I seem to have wreathed my prespecification of the talk in embarrassment and ambiguity.

A PROBLEM FOR CAREGIVERS: A ONE-TO-ONE INTERVIEW OR MULTIPARTY TALK?

I suggested that participants may infer that there are a number of possible interactional formats for this event. The clinic setting, the initial contact, the business of the tape recorder, the reason given for the conversation, and the first question can all be seen as resources with which any participant can do inferential work in regard to the nature of what is happening, but without any very clear determinants. There is, however, a further complication. As noted, much of my activity in the early part of the interview was oriented to the client, who I expected to be the person with whom I would be interacting. Yet caregivers were present during the whole of this period and, for them, the question may not only have been "The beginning of what?" with regard to the encounter but "How am I to be involved, if at all?" So one decision that they had to make was whether they were, in fact, ratified to participate. How caregivers took their cues over this varied. One caregiver, for example, did not join in until addressed by the confused speaker at turns 37 and 38.

Extract 9

| 37. Mrs. Bowles: | =And the village Cartwright Street was quite long wasn't it?= |
| 38. Mr. Bowles: | =Yes= |

Mr. Bowles only enters the conversation on the invitation of his mother. This could suggest that, as far as he is concerned, the talk hitherto has been satisfactory, (not in any way challenging his identity, or that of his mother), and indeed, his response would indicate that it still is. It may be that he does not initially perceive the occasion to be one where multiparty talk is appropriate, though an invitation by the respondent for him to talk is cannot easily be ignored.

In contrast, other caregivers began to contribute to the talk very early on in the proceedings. It seems to me that this provides some clues as to their understanding of an appropriate interactional format for the occasion at that point in time. For caregivers to intervene at all indicates that they saw contributing their own talk (and thus transforming the conversation into multiparty talk) as within the legitimate range of possibilities for *this sort of occasion,* whether they saw it as a medical interview, a research interview, or an ordinary conversation. There were a number of specific types of interventions by caregivers:

Extract 10[6]

17. Pam:	Do you you listen to music at home?
	(1.0)
18. Mrs. Hoy:	Well I like it yes=
19. Pam:	=What sorts do you like?
	(1.0)((Bangs from tape recorder))
20. Mrs. Hoy:	O:h (3.0) ((laughs)) It's a long while ago.
	(2.0)
21. Pam:	What do you listen to?
	(4.0)
22. Mr. Hoy:	You like Foster and Allen don't you?
	(1.0)

---

[6] Continues on immediately from Extract 4, which involved setting up the tape recorder.

23. Mrs Hoy: Mm yeh=

This suggests that very early on in the proceedings, Mr. Hoy formed a working knowledge of what is required on the part of the participants, and may (from past experience) have realized that his wife is not going to be able to provide it. He may have oriented to the *five* lengthy silences that precede his intervention and have interpreted these as noticeable absences of answers (i.e., silences that would be heard as significant by participants as implying that the respondent will not or cannot answer, and so on; Schegloff, 1972b). He may also have concluded that Mrs. Hoy would have problems with answering open-ended questions, because his intervention produces a closed question. Mr. Hoy's early intervention is not an isolated case:

Extract 11

Pam:	[...] I was interested in in what people what people can remember and things about their childhood So (.) Can you can you do you come from round Jessop. Do you come from the Jessop area? (3.0) Were you brought up in Jessop? (4.0) No.
	(4.0)
Edith:	( ) I <u>don't</u> know=
Pam:	=Where were you brought up?=
Edith:	=((Mutters))
	(3.0)
Barry:	Where were you born?

Here Barry intervenes to pose a question to his mother. It can be seen that although I have posed four questions, all phrased slightly differently, they are interspersed by a total of 14 seconds silence and a negative answer on Edith's part. Barry's question reduces the scope of the field somewhat (after all, if someone had moved home, say, 10 times in the first dozen years of their life, then answering such a question could be tricky). Again, as in Extract 10, the silences could have been a key factor for the caregiver in making an intervention. In each case, questions might be seen to facilitate some identity work on the part of the respondent. However, other early caregiver interventions were not precipitated by silences on the part of the confused speaker:

Extract 12

	((Beginning of recording))
Pam:	[...] Do you come from round about Jessop?=
Mrs. Inman:	=I've always lived at (Betchworth) Biddington=
Mrs. Grace:	=No you lived in Biddington when you were young:er Mum you've always lived in Jessop since you've been married=
Mrs. Inman:	=Oh <u>yes</u>=

Extract 13[7]

| Pam: | [...] Are you from Staffordshire? |
| | (.) |

---

[7] Continues on from Extract 5.

Mrs. Pugh:	From Staffordshire yes =
Pam:	=Where do you come from?
	(.)
Mrs Pugh:	Er Norton no er Stanall ((Laughs nervously)).
Mr. Pugh:	You live at Stanall now=
	[ ]
Mrs. Pugh:	Oh erm
Mr. Pugh:	Clayton where you was born?=
Mrs. Pugh:	=Clayton.

Mrs. Grace enters the conversation to correct her mother while Mr. Pugh enters to help his wife provide fuller biographical details. In both Extracts 12 and 13 there are prior attempts to self-correct on the part of the confused speaker, and incorrect self-correction may be seen as legitimizing entrance into the conversation by others. More broadly, the need for correct presentation of biography can be seen as a possible justification for a caregiver entering the conversation.

So far we have two types of initial interventions from caregivers: reformulations of my questions in situations following noticeable silences, and corrections of answers by confused speakers. Each of these interventions implies that the occasion requires an orientation to my agenda. Caregivers did not choose to do *something else* with the conversation. Rather, they made interpretations about what was appropriate to the context and sought to effect a realization of it. This is underlined by the next extract, which shows the caregiver considering the talk both from the point of view of the interviewer and of the interviewee:

Extract 14

Pam:	Your wife was saying when you were in there that you were in that you'd been to Majorca (.) for your holidays.
	[
Mrs. Toll:	No he's been to Wales=
Pam	=You went to Wales=
	[
Mrs. Toll:	To Wales
Pam:	=Where where did you go in Wales?=
	(1.8)
Mr. Toll:	((Low)) Where was it?=
Mrs. Toll:	=To Llandudno=
Mr. Toll:	=Llandudno.

Mrs. Toll seems to be concerned with establishing that my initial question is based on an erroneous assumption. She intervenes to correct me, suggesting possibly that one thing that interviewers should do is be technically correct when they reiterate statements others have made. She may have assumed that Mr. Toll will not be able to take on the task of correction, or alternatively that my incorrect information (attributed by me to her) reflects on her truthfulness (in terms of Grice's maxim of quality). The second half of Extract 14 implies that Mr. Toll appreciates that correct answers are appropriate to the occasion, even if he cannot give them. I discuss this issue in greater detail in subsequent chapters when I come to the main part of my interviews.

For the caregivers the nature of the event was beginning to emerge on an utterance-by-utterance basis, with each utterance providing more contextualization. I accepted the entry of the caregivers into the conversation and this acceptance was there to be interpreted as another clue to the nature of the conversation. If, at the first intervention by caregivers, I had said "I wonder if you would mind if Mrs. X tried to answer the question for herself", I may well have closed down the possibility of a multiparty conversation; but I did not, and this had consequences for how the interviews evolved. And, of course, the caregiver continued to monitor the conversation in case they should be selected to talk or should wish to select themsleves.

INTERACTIONAL PROBLEMS

In most of the interviews I conducted, focused interaction was deftly accomplished by most participants. Regardless of whether confused speakers were monosyllabic, or could not remember their own life histories, or whether I was embarrassed or caregivers intervened, a single focus of attention (usually oriented to my questions) was achieved almost immediately. However, occasionally focused interaction was not achieved. Take, for example, the case of the Bruners:

Extract 15

	((Beginning of recording))
Mrs. Bruner:	[...] Hey mi duck hey=
Pam:	=Right=
Mrs. Bruner:	((Looks at the tape recorder)) That's it then
	[
Mr. Bruner:	Sometimes thought about
	putting my tape recorder=
	[ ]
Mrs. Bruner:	Dave.
Mr. Bruner:	=on when we're at home.
Pam:	Yes.
	=[[
Mrs. Bruner:	Oh:h: h: h.
Mr. Bruner:	(She isn't always quiet)=
	[
Pam:	Yes.
Mr. Bruner:	=She isn't always she doesn't=
	[
Mrs. Bruner:	Hey ay: y
Mr. Bruner:	=You know like she is at the moment.

Two-party interaction was quickly achieved in this encounter between Mr. Bruner and myself. However, as can be seen, Mrs. Bruner's talk was, at least to begin with, not oriented toward the turns of the other two participants, but away from them. Here, if verbal interaction was to take place immediately, the onus was on normal speakers and, indeed, this imperative may have acted as a motivation for Mr. Bruner to participate from the outset.

There was also one case where I was unable to satisfactorily set up the tape recorder, present a reason for the interview, or to get many questions answered at all (these being a whole series of conversational projects requiring focused interaction). Cora, who was in her mid-70s; came into the room with a young nurse in her early thirties. I had not been present at the assessment and have no idea whether or how focused interaction had been achieved there. During the course of her stay in the anteroom with me, Cora hardly sat down at all, and spent most of her time roaming around the room and heading for the door. At times her voice is quite difficult to hear on the recording because she was moving around so much. At the outset there was some question as to whether she was deaf, and on the audiotape the pitch and modulation of my own voice can be heard to alter as I try to determine whether Cora can hear me.

There was a small section at the beginning of the encounter where I tried to set the tape recorder up :

Extract 16

Pam:	CAN I PUT THIS HERE?=
Cora:	=Eh=
Pam:	<u>Can I put this here</u> ?(3.2) <u>Can you hear me</u> ? (.)
Cora:	((Low)) Eh=
Pam:	=((Low)) Can you hear me?=
Nurse:	=(Drink)=
Pam:	=Can you hear me? (1.7) ((Low)) Can you?
	(1.0)
Cora:	((Low in tone)) (Mmmm mon)

The setting up of the tape recorder is ignored by Cora and its significance in relation to my membership category is therefore apparently ignored. By roaming around the room Cora also preempts my attempts to control the environment. Acknowledgment that a recording is to be made in no way features in her actions, unless we can see her attempts to escape from the room as related to it. In fact, we can suggest that this almost fails to be a situation at all, as mutual monitoring does not always take place.

This is not an anarchic piece of discourse, but my questions are rarely answered because Cora resists. My definition of the situation is never successfully imposed. As I already noted, rights to the definition of the situation may be a characteristic of certain participants, for example, an interviewer. My persistence in trying to put the conversation on the rails is equalled only by Cora's resistance. She is not amenable to the particular interactional format I offer. She is not even amenable to being party to a gathering. She does not want to be copresent in the room with me.

The recorded conversation is 79 turns long, during which I get only a couple of my questions answered.

Extract 17

Pam:	Where are you going back to? (4.7) Where do you live?=
Cora:	=Pardon=
Pam:	=((Desperately)) WHERE DO YOU LIVE?=
Cora:	=Just down here.

Notice here that although the response is likely to be correct, the formulation is not that of someone answering an interview question about where they live ("In Stanall" or "sheltered accommodation in the village"); in other words answering according to the project of the questions or as Sacks (1995a) put it "what you can see that the question wants to find out, is something that controls how you answer it" (p. 56). I should add that the refusal on Cora's part to answer at all or not to answer according to the project of the question increases the desperation in my voice as the interview goes on and sets it apart from all the other interviews.

I do not succeed in establishing a topic at all with Cora. However, although a single focus of attention is not established, turn taking is regular and evenly patterned as the following extract shows:

Extract 18

Pam:	Do you come from Carbridge?
	(2.5)
Cora:	What?=
Pam:	=Do you come from Carbridge?
Cora:	=(GA:RBAGE?)=
Pam:	=CARBRIDGE. Do you come from CARBRIDGE?=
Cora:	=Ah I ain't stopping at them=
Pam:	=No where do you come from?

During the conversation, Cora usually speaks after an utterance has been addressed to her. Sometimes her answers come back after a pause or she misses one turn and I have to repeat a question. Although regular in occurrence, many of her answers have no obvious propositional content. The number of adjacency pairs where a question by me is followed by an (unproblematic in my terms) answer by her is only four in the entire recorded conversation. And of these four, only one is an adjacency pair that has *not* been preceded by another adjacency pair, of which the second pair part was "what", "eh", and so on. For example:

Extract 19

Pam:	Are you hot?=
Cora:	=What?=
Pam:	=Are you hot? (1.0) Do you want to take your coat off?=

Cora: =Yes=

There were a number of cumulative chains of double adjacency pairs:

Extract 20

Pam: Where do you live? (2.0) Where do you live? (.)
Cora: Uh?=
Pam: =Where do you live?
                          (1.0)
Cora: (What did they te:ll you?)

Almost half the conversation (38 turns) is devoted to four- and six-turn clusters of repeated questions and obscure (from the interviewer's point of view) or propositionally empty answers. So although we have some of the constituents of focused interaction, we do not have all of them. Although there is turn taking there is little cooperation.

Cora's main line of resistance is her talk and activity centered on trying to leave the room. Note that in his study of people with dementia in a Dutch residential home, Coenen (1991) said, "The sense of time is not absent in the residents' experience" (p. 325). And he went on to talk about preoccupations residents have with *I have to go.* Similarly, we can see that Cora has a real sense of purpose in her desire to leave this interview. As part of a number of her turns she says "Come on" (i.e. a command or request to leave) mainly to the nurse (or occasionally to me) 12 times, and other sentiments relating to going another 3 times (i.e. "Are you going to stay here?"). Nearly all these directives are addressed to the nurse (who she chucks under the chin several times) and most of the time her tone is quite urgent. The nurse rarely responds. One of the categorical imperatives of my membership as an "official" is that people pay attention to me. Cora pays scant attention to me. I am not a person she identifies as being able to facilitate what she wants to do. I am therefore of no further interest.

With the exception of mentioning to me that Cora has a thing about moving or cleaning the furniture, the nurse hardly speaks. She does not attempt to get Cora to answer my questions. She does not interpret my questions for Cora. On the other hand, she does not respond to Cora's requests to "Come on" either. Indeed, it is I who breaks first:

Extract 21

Cora: Come on you (If you're going there) come on.
                          (1.0)
Pam: I think you might as well actually=
                                   [
Cora: COME ON
Pam: Thank you very much.
Nurse: ((Laughs))
                     =[[
Cora: (Where you going then   )
Pam: ((Low)) don't want to hold your morning up any longer ((Laughs))
                THANK YOU VERY MUCH FOR YOUR TIME.
                          (4.0)

Cora: Come on look here (what I've been all opening).

The nurse's main acknowledgement of me as an interviewer in action is to keep Cora in the same room (not necessarily near the microphone). However, there are also moments in the interview with Cora when the nurse deliberately seems to efface herself, realizing perhaps that as long as Cora's focus of interaction is on her, it cannot be on me. For example, she looks away slightly when Cora is berating her and only answers Cora monosyllabically as though not to encourage her. At the same time, she does not in any way help Cora to identify herself as a person being interviewed. There are only three people at the gathering, and a multiparty conversation or a two-person conversation are the only possible combinations to produce focused interaction. The episode is composed of three different interactions: Cora and I talking, Cora and the nurse talking, and the nurse and I talking. Of these three interactions, those involving Cora and myself involve no single focus of attention.

One other interesting thing shown by this brief encounter is how important it is to the definition of the role of interviewer to be able to establish focused interaction. Interviewers who do not establish focused interaction have not succeeded. My suspicion is that in informal social circumstances, as one of the participants, I would have withdrawn from this conversation substantially sooner than I did. Consider the number of substantive questions I put in a conversation consisting only of 79 turns:[8]

Extract 22

Has it been good weather here?
Where are you going back to?
Where do you live?
Where do you live?
In a house?
What sort of house?
Have you always lived round here?
Have you always lived round here?
Do you come from round here?
Do you come from Carbridge?
Do you come from Carbridge?
Carbridge do you come from Carbridge?
Where do you come from?
Where were you brought up?
Where were you br. Where were you brought up?
Where did you live when you were little?
Where did you live when you were a little girl?
Where are you going to go now?
Where are you going to go now?
Where are you going to now?
Where do you live?
Where do you live?

---

[8] This extract was not transcribed to show turn construction, only the number of substantive questions I posed during the interview.

Where do you live?
What's this lady's name?
What's this lady's name?
What's this lady's' name?
When you come here do you always come by ambulance ?
When you come here do you always come by ambulance?
Is it in walking distance?
Could you walk to where you live from here?
Do you stay here for your lunch ever when you come here to see the doctor. Do you stay for your lunch?
How long will the ambulance be?
How long will the ambulance be until it arrives? Does it? Is it later in the morning?

Seventeen turns are devoted to my questions (containing a total of 33 questions). Cora's answers are usually "eh" or statements that indicate her resistance to the interactional format on offer. But I still persist. In normal social circumstances (i.e., casual conversation), a person receiving so little encouragement might be seen at best as intrusive and at worst as incompetent. Again, this suggests that, my intentions as to casual conversation notwithstanding, the interactional format I am offering participants is very much an interview. In persisting with Cora, I am taking up my interactional rights as interviewer. It is my membership of the category of interviewer that enables me to carry on. Indeed it may have obliged me to carry on claiming membership of that particular category in order not to be seen as an incompetent ordinary conversationalist.

I want to close this section by noting that at one point fairly late in the conversation with Cora, it all became too much for me and I began, involuntarily, to laugh at my own complete failure to be able to "do" an ordinary interview. It is interesting that Cora immediately asked "What are you laughing for?" This implies that she *was* monitoring the behavior of other participants, but because she apparently did not see it as an interview at all, the perception of me as failed interviewer was not available to her as an object of humor.

CONCLUSION

In this chapter, I explored many interactional issues surrounding the openings of formal or semiformal encounters, whether between normal speakers or normal speakers and confused speakers. My concern has been to examine the way in which the interviews I carried out were jointly constructed from the outset, and in a couple of cases failed to get established. Ultimately, I was concerned with how encounters get going and how context is generated and developed by participants.

Most of the preoccupations of the chapter can, I think, be applied to *openings* quite broadly. Prior information, potential formats of talk for specific contexts and assumed interactional rights, the setting up of technical equipment, reasons for the conversation, opening questions— these all provide inferential resources for the participants in a broad spectrum of social situations. Although confused speakers were copresent in these early stages and participated in various ways, for the most part their performance did not dictate the nature of the occasion. However, I have also begun to hint that the presence of confused speakers may contribute to interactional troubles and offer an opportunity to consider underlying assumptions which shape interpretations of events. The cases of trouble to which I have alluded— Edith turning off the tape recorder and Cora refusing to be interviewed—were both highly instructive in helping me think about my prior expectations of *normal versions* of these events. When I first began to analyze my data, I dismissed the interview with Cora out of hand. In my mind it was a failed interview. Even though I was, in fact, looking for confused talk, my underlying ordinary member assumptions about requiring focused interaction were so strong that I could not admit something that did not appear to be focused interaction as data. I had not anticipated anyone purposefully avoiding focused interaction. Rather, I suppose, I assumed that any lack of focused interaction would manifest itself in catatonic behavior. I could admit myself as an ambiguous stimulus causing some interactional troubles but not as a rejected stimulus! It was not until I was able to put trouble on the table as an analytic device that I was able to overcome this reluctance. As I noted elsewhere, trouble is not a concept reserved only for occasions when confused speakers are present. As I emphasize throughout this book, I see trouble as a device that can highlight normal versions of events.

My hope is that from reading this chapter, readers can see practical implications in terms of talk they have themselves encountered. The opening stages of interviews and more casual talk involve substantial contextual work. Much of it is unmarked never becoming interactional business. Indeed, in none of my interviews did anyone say "Why do you ask?" when I began my life history questions, and yet that is a very simple question, the answer to which might do a lot of contextual work very quickly. People are often prepared to wait and see, even if they are presented with an incomprehensible or problematic situation.

The appropriateness of talk must always be judged in relation to the context in which it occurs; contexts have to be established and are not always unambiguous or uncontested. From this point of view, in theoretical terms, the identification of confused talk becomes more complex and difficult than it is presented as being in the literature. Yet, as members, we have no difficulty in identifying it. Subsequent chapters are concerned with resolving this apparent paradox.

4

Minimally Active Confused Speakers

The amount of active engagement and participation in a conversation is related to its nature and how people perceive their role in it. Different types of talk may imply differing interactional responsibilities and rights among participants. In a mundane conversation, the degree of local management suggests that such rights and responsibilities are not allocated in advance, but unfold as the context unfolds. Nevertheless, depending on the development of the conversation, the interactional rights of some participants may become more potent at particular points. For example, if someone proposes to tell a story, this may involve extended rights to talk, involving a greater likelihood of being selected as speaker for several subsequent turns as people dissect the import of the story and seek further testimony from the teller. In more formal situations speaking rights may be preallocated. But whatever the formality or otherwise of the situation, there is a balance to be struck between the prescribed system of turn taking and the inevitable contingencies and unpredictabililty of talk in progress—as topics develop and are managed and repairs are effected. Even where people operate in highly prescribed settings, the nature of their talk is not and cannot be wholly controlled in advance. Philips (1992), for example, observed in relation to legal talk that although various judges' talk may be routinized, individual judges alter and vary sequences and the sense of what they say to different people. Additionally, as I already suggested, any formal interactive event may permit circumstances where the dominant discourse is temporarily replaced by, for example, parachat, and we may assume that such a development might alter interactional rights and responsibilities.

Thus, in examining particular encounters, any student of social interaction will need to consider the overall context, how formal the event is, the extent to which interactional rights and responsibilities are likely to be preallocated, moments at which the dominant discourse is forsaken for another one, and so on. Of course, they will also need to pay detailed attention to the fact that the participants are "technicians in residence at the conversational worksite" (Lynch & Bogen 1994). In the case of my own data, we might inquire whether all the technicians are fully proficient, or at least whether the talk orients to the full competence of all the technicians present. And that question is not by any means limited to the sort of data I am presenting here—in any situation where some participants may be accorded less-than-full membership, the question of how the technicians treat each other needs to be examined.

In this chapter, I use data from my interviews at the psychogeriatric clinic—a situation in which we can assume that achieving the purpose of the meeting presupposes focused interaction and that there are certain expectations about the allocation of responsibilities for the control and maintenance of the interaction; though as we have seen, these are by no means unambiguous. I would suggest that many elements of the situation I am going to discuss are those of a fairly ordinary version of a meeting between a researcher or professional and client. The fact that there is a question mark hanging over some of the speakers does not alter the fact that it is a conversational worksite with a variety of features recognizable as being associated with such a site. Moreover, the trouble caused by some of the speakers may, in fact, throw into relief ordinary expectations of such events.

The degree of participation and type of active engagement in these interviews varies across the people with confused speech who were interviewed. Broadly, three different types of speakers feature in my data; these types reflect those I mentioned in chapter 1 as being identified by Allison (1962):

- Minimally active speakers.
- Moderately active speakers.
- Very active speakers.

In this chapter, I introduce the notion of levels of participation in conversation and then examine some aspects of the talk of minimally active confused speakers. The interview situations I outline I have already suggested were in some ways ambiguous. Given the medical setting, participants may have seen themselves as being tested, and this may generate particular, perhaps defensive, forms of talk. Such interviews are a type of interactional situation that confused speakers encounter from time to time. On the other hand, my own involvement may have cast doubt on the medical nature of the situation. My question, then, is how can we understand the type of talk that goes on?

I focus on four minimally active confused speakers whom I interviewed. Mrs. Hoy had suffered from a dementing illness for many years and was accompanied by her husband. Edith, whose confusion was also of long duration, was accompanied by her son Barry. Mrs. Pugh had only recently been diagnosed as confused and came with her husband and her daughter, Mrs. James. Mr. Toll came with his wife.

PARTICIPATION AND INVOLVEMENT: A PRELIMINARY OVERVIEW

The categories of speaker activity I offered earlier are not merely analytical categories. Members recognize different levels of verbal participation in talk. There are ordinary member assumptions about the extent to which various participants will participate. I noted previously the relatively equal participation that is acceptable in ordinary conversation, but I also pointed to certain modifications to this format when some members, such as children, have limited interactional rights. Participation is a matter for comment and adjustment within specific conversations, and more globally. This is illustrated by common sayings such as "Couldn't get a word in edgewise", "Cat got your tongue?", and "Vaccinated with a gramophone needle" (see Dingwall, 1980). However, participation alone is not the only factor to be considered: Involvement, too, is pertinent. Conversation is occasioned activity, which Goffman (1963a) defined as follows: "To be engaged in an occasioned activity means to sustain some kind of cognitive and affective engrossment in it, some mobilization of one's psychological resources: in short it means to be involved in it" (p. 26).

Involvement can be described as the degree to which people are committed to their chosen or assigned role in the interaction. What degree of involvement is required, and is desirable, varies according to role, and may also be a matter for local negotiation.

Participants may try out varying degrees of participation and involvement in an event. Perhaps we can say that a concern for participation and involvement appropriate to one's identity need not necessarily be maintained throughout an occasion. Conversations, parts of social occasions, have their peaks and troughs; and there may be times when individuals feel that they have less of a vested interest in what is being said than at others times. Within any conversation, participants have varying opportunities for dipping out at different points, not bidding for a turn when they are able to, or making minimal contributions to the topic at hand. It depends on the type of conversation. In a classroom, such a relaxation of involvement is easy for pupils, if risky. There is always the chance that they will be asked a question. It is much safer to dip out of a lecture. In a multiparty conversation too, there are possibilities for one party to be quiet and enjoy a microsleep. But there are risks attached, particularly because one of the characteristics of such conversations is that any individual speaking may choose to address any other individual. A two-party conversation of whatever sort probably offers the least opportunity for relaxing one's involvement, because each participant is, as it were, always on call to be the next speaker.

Participants may also seek modifications to the participation and involvement of others. As people establish context in a conversation, and assign identity to participants, they may engage in strategies to encourage those they see as participating inappropriately for a person of that status in that type of conversation to modify their behavior. Thus, children may be encouraged to "pipe down", that is to participate less, or to "pay attention", that is, to become more involved: Such directives may be seen as comments on how appropriate membership is constructed. Members may use devices to sanction an oscillating interest in maintaining identity, as when others say "You're quiet today", or invite a comment from a particular participant to indicate that they see that person's identity as currently being involved. This means that participants need to be ready for any turn that is offered or requested.

All this is to suggest that because the events I discuss in this chapter are ambiguous, we might expect people to try out varying degrees of participation as they work toward defining the event. We can propose that this presentational work should be observable in social interaction and specifically in talk. So the degree of participation and involvement may in some way be reflected in the machinery of how people take turns and manage topics in the conversation. I move now to a discussion of the mechanics of turns and turn taking in my interviews with minimally active confused speakers. This provides a framework for looking at degrees of participation and involvement.

Much of the data of this chapter are recognizable as talk in which normal speakers, too, may engage at times. Labov (1972) discussed research interviews with young African American boys, noting that in particular interview circumstances, the boys were practically monosyllabic. It is interesting that monosyllabic responses were seen by some researchers as an indication of particular membership characteristics. Labov and his coresearchers altered various aspects of the interview environment and effected a situation where fuller responses were forthcoming and consequently membership redefined. For the purposes of this chapter, I want to remain with the monosyllabic responses and continue to tease out what goes on there, and the membership implications.

TURNS

In chapter 1, I noted that Sacks, Schegloff and Jefferson (1978) developed a list of *grossly apparent facts* about turn taking. They argued that these can be seen to be the result of ordinary members' ability to identify points in the conversation when a new turn is appropriate, their understanding and use of turn sizes, and their adherence to a set of rules for the allocation of turns.

In order to be able to participate in talk successfully, individuals need to be able to identify points in the conversation when a particular turn might be complete, thus giving them a chance to hold on to the floor if they are already talking, or to enter (or reenter) the conversation if they are not. Sacks et al. (1978) called these points *Transition Relevant Places* (shortened to TRPs from now on). In relation to this concept, we could define a turn in more than one way. It could be defined as a turn unit, that is, a word that has the projectability to be seen as a complete utterance and have a TRP. Within such a definition, one person might have a number of turns within one utterance (passing through a number of TRPs when they managed to keep the floor). Or a turn might be defined as the utterance that one person makes before another person takes over the floor, either at a first, or subsequent, TRP. For the purposes of the following discussion, I define turn in the latter way.

In an ordinary two-party interview, we might expect interviewer and interviewee to each have half the turns, so first, I want to note that minimally active confused speakers tended to have fewer turns than might be expected in a one to-one-interview. Figure 4.1 shows the percentage of turns taken by various speakers in my interviews.

Client	Caregiver	Interviewer
Mrs. Hoy 25%	Mr. Hoy 33%	Pam 42%
Edith 18%	Barry 48%	Pam 34%
Mr. Toll 36%	Mrs. Toll 23%	Pam 41%
Mrs. Pugh 42%	Mr. Pugh/Mrs. James 21%	Pam 37%

Figure 4.1. Percentage of turns taken by all participants.

As I noted in chapter 1, conversation analysis tends to pursue two main interests—the machinery of turns and the machinery of description. Thus, for any student interested in talk, the distribution of turns in a multiparty conversation is likely to be of analytic interest. In the case of my own data, the distribution of turns is significantly related to the nature of the encounters, and there is some breach of expectancy. Each of the minimally active confused speakers had fewer than half the total number of conversational turns, even though in an interview involving two people an equal distribution of turns might reasonably be expected because the floor is shared between them.

However, as we saw in chapter 2, caregivers often entered the conversation, turning it into a multiparty conversation. In that chapter too, I explained that I hoped to establish something along the lines of a loosely structured ethnographic interview that offered interviewees an invitation to talk; it will be noted that although in most cases I took more turns than the interviewee, in no case did I take more turns than the interviewee and client together. As we shall see, this distribution of talk is a significant feature of these interviews and has implications for definitions of membership in interviews.

It is worth noting that even though taking a smaller percentage of turns than might be expected, most minimally active confused speakers recognized TRPs even when it was difficult to understand how they were using their turn, as is shown in this extract:

Extract 1

1. Barry:	Your mother, what's your mother's name?
	(3.5)
2. Edith:	((Mutters expressively))=
	[
3. Barry:	Normally she'd just have it straight off=
4. Edith:	=((Mutters expressively))=
5. Barry:	=And what's Grandad's name?
	(.)
6. Edith:	Grandad?=
7. Barry:	=Grandad what's Grandad's name?=
8. Edith:	=Name name ((Mutters expressively)).
	(.)
9. Barry:	Who's Tottie then?=
10. Edith:	=Ma mi mother=
11. Barry:	=Oh that's your mother is it? Tottie=
12. Edith:	=Yes.

In many respects, this sequence conforms to the grossly apparent facts as outlined by Sacks et al. (1978). Speaker change recurs, on the whole only one of the pair is talking at a time, there are slight gaps and slight overlaps, turn size varies, and so on. By and large Edith orients to TRPs. Even in Utterances 2 and 4, she mutters expressively and this may be interpreted as an attempt to take her turn. There are no discernible words in these mutterings; they mostly sound like the kind of expressive babble small children make who want to join in the conversation but do not have the words. However, perhaps we can take it that Edith still operates in such a way as to respond if she is addressed. So even though one of the participants here may be seen as a less-than-full member, the machinery of turn taking is still evident. I hope to show in the course of this chapter that *modifications* in turn taking are also evident and to suggest that such modifications may be associated with handling less–than-full membership in talk.

Sacks et al. (1978) saw TRPs as a motivating feature in conversation. One of the main reasons that people listen is so that they can identify when they can, or need to, speak again. When they do not listen, they do not know when TRPs are going to occur. In order to be able to recognize TRPs, particularly in terms of whether turns are complete, people need to be familiar with the possible units of talk that can occur. Nofsinger (1991) noted that Sacks et al. (1978) suggested that turns are constructed out of four different sizes of unit:

- A single word; for example, "yes".
- Phrases several words long that do not constitute a sentence; for example, "at the hop".
- Clauses that have all the necessary components to be a sentence (subject and predicate) but do not constitute a stand-alone sentence; for example, "the woman at the computer".
- Full sentences.

Additionally, special conditions exist where the speaker intimates that he or she is going to have a longer turn than might normally be expected, often involving the telling of a story. For example, Sacks observed that "Something terrible has just happened" does at least three jobs: It gets the space to build a multisentence length utterance, it tells the listener how to listen for the end of the story (i.e., presumably when something terrible has been described), and it helps the listener by indicating an appropriate response to the story (Sacks, cited in Benson and Hughes 1983).

When we come to the sort of turn construction units confused speakers use, not surprisingly perhaps, we find that the majority of the minimally active confused speakers use very short turns, often the smallest unit that can be followed by a TRP, namely, a word. Figure 4.2 shows the percentage of various turn construction units in the total talk of four minimally active confused speakers. In that figure I calculated as a percentage of their total turns the relative frequency of different turn sizes for each confused speaker. The line entitled *other* represents utterances where it was not possible to understand what the

	Mrs Pugh	Mr Toll	Mrs Hoy	Edith
No. of turns	53	43	152	87
Word	53%	58%	78%	38%
Phrase	17%	12%	8%	12%
Clause	4%	0%	3%	1%
Sentence	19%	23%	8%	15%
>Sentence	8%	5%	1%	5%
Other	0%	2%	0%	29%

Figure 4.2. Percentage of turns taken by turn size. (Values do not sum to 100% because they are rounded off.)

turn construction units might be. From Fig. 4.2 we can see that in each case the majority of turns are one word in length. To take the case of Mrs. Pugh, of her 53 utterances, almost 3/4 are turn units shorter than one sentence. In an interview where the interviewer is encouraging the respondent to talk, this would normally suggest that the interviewer has not been successful, or the interviewee not cooperative, or both.

Figure 4.3 shows again the percentage of different turn sizes turns for confused speakers and also percentages of turn sizes for caregivers and interviewer (based on aggregates over all four interviews).

It will be noted that caregivers and interviewer have relatively similar profiles, the bulk of their turns being one sentence or longer. The use of a series of minimal answers by confused speakers can be compared with my own use of them as interviewer, where such answers function typically as continuers in a monologue by caregivers. Here, such responses can be seen to acknowledge the rights of another taking an extended turn. Indeed, we might expect that in an interview situation, it would be the interviewer, who is encouraging talk from others, who would have the largest proportion of minimal utterances. Here, however, this is not the case. So a judgment about the appropriate and frequent use of the minimal answer "yes" is highly dependent on context. We all

	Confused speakers	Caregivers	Interviewer
Word	57%	19%	24%
Phrase	12%	11%	4%
Clause	2%	4%	3%
Sentence	16%	38%	43%
>Sentence	5%	24%	21%

Figure 4.3. Percentage of turn size by different categories of participant.

recognize it as a common conversational strategy that is appropriate in some situations (e.g., as I suggested, interviewers or hearers offering continuers), but as ordinary members we also understand that certain conversational circumstances require fuller answers. In such circumstances, to answer only "yes" comes to be seen as clumsy or uncooperative.

Having mentioned percentage of turns taken, use of TRPs, and size of turn taken by participants, I want now to move on to the process by which turns are allocated. In a two-person conversation the factors that affect conversational exchange are turn size and TRPs, who speaks being allocated on an ABABAB basis, if it is to be a conversation rather than a monologue. However, although two different two-person conversations may share an ABABAB pattern, they may be very dissimilar in how turn size is distributed and how TRPs are used. For example, a lengthy exchange in a court of law between lawyer and defendant might involve one person having long turns and the other person having very short turns.

When a third party enters the conversation, turn-taking rules become more complex. In all the conversations discussed in this chapter, caregivers were involved, so it is also necessary to examine the principles of turn taking in multiparty talk. Sacks et al. (1978) proposed a linked set of rules that they say account for all the possibilities in focused multiparty talk. They noted that there are two forms of speaker allocation: Current speaker can select next speaker and next turn can be claimed by self-selection. From this they generated a series of rules that were formulated as follows by Levinson (1983):

> Rule 1 – applies initially at the first TRP of any turn
>
> (a) If C selects N in current turn, then C must stop speaking, and N must speak next, transition occurring at the first TRP after N-selection
>
> (b) If C does not select N, then any (other) party may self-select, first speaker gaining rights to the next turn
>
> (c) If C has not selected N, and no other party self-selects under option (b), then C may (but need not) continue (i.e. claim rights to a further turn-constructional unit)
>
> Rule 2 – applies at all subsequent TRPs
>
> When Rule 1(c) has been applied by C, then at the next TRP Rules 1 (a)- (c) apply, and recursively at the next TRP, until speaker change is effected (p. 298)

Psathas (1995) cited Coulter in emphasizing this as an ordered optionality system: that is to say, it is not specified what any party must do but rather what options may be selected.

Given that the interactional events being discussed were interviews, we would expect that turn allocation would occur primarily by means of the interviewer selecting the next speaker and then self-selecting at a subsequent TRP, and this is, indeed, what occurred most of the time. Extract 2 is taken from an interview with Mr. and Mrs. Toll and represents a stretch of multiparty conversation. I want to show, to begin with, that the turn-taking patterns within this extract are appropriate to a loosely structured ethnographic interview:

Extract 2

1. Pam:	Wh wh er where did you go in Wales?
	(1.8)
2. Mr. Toll:	((Low)) Where was it?=
3. Mrs. Toll:	=Llandudno=
4. Mr. Toll:	=Llandudno=
5. Pam:	Ha had you been there before?
6. Mrs. Toll:	((Low)) Years and years ago.
	[
7. Pam:	Did you enjoy it?
8. Mr Toll:	((Low))Yeh.
9. Pam:	Did you have the good weather?
10. Mrs. Toll:	Take take your hand down from there.
11. Mr. Toll:	((Takes hand down)).
12. Pam:	Did you have the good weather?=
13. Mr. Toll:	=Yeh.
	(.)
14. Pam:	You're looking very sun tanned=
15. Mr. Toll:	=Yeh=
16. Pam:	What's Llandudno like? I've never been there=
17. Mr. Toll:	Oh its nice.
18. Pam:	Is it (.) What what does it look like? Is it is it erm is it hilly country?=
19. Mr. Toll:	=Yeh=
20. Pam:	=Is it and a seaside?=
21. Mr. Toll:	=Yeh.
	(1.2)
22. Pam:	Is is there a promenade?=
23. Mr. Toll:	=Yeh.
	(1.7)
24. Pam:	So you walked up and down the prom=
25. Mr. Toll:	=Yeh
	(.)
26. Pam:	Who did who did you go with?
	(3.6)
27. Mr. Toll:	Went with you didn't I?=
28. Mrs. Toll:	=Yeh me and who else?
	(3.2)
29. Mr. Toll:	I don't know=
30. Mrs Toll:	=Brian.
	(1.0)
31. Mr. Toll:	Aye Brian=
32. Mrs. Toll:	And Sue=
33. Mr. Toll:	=Oh with Sue yeh=
34. Mrs. Toll:	Take your hand off your mouth Fred, we can't hear what you're saying.
35. Mr. Toll:	((Takes hand down))
36. Pam:	Who's Brian?
37. Mr. Toll:	Mi son.
38. Pam:	Your son. What does what does Brian do?=

39. Mr. Toll:	=What?=
40. Pam:	What's Brian's work?
	(2.7)
41. Mr. Toll:	He works as a mechanic

In turn allocation people may be selected or select themselves for the next turn. As each turn has two ends, this means that it is possible to produce four possible types of turn sequence. These are illustrated Figure 4.4, along with the distribution of these turns types among the participants featured in Extract 2. In many respects, in terms of turn allocation, Mr. Toll behaves appropriately for a loosely structured ethnographic interview, being almost always selected, rarely selecting others, and overall being the most selected speaker. As interviewer, I am only selected once by another speaker (when Mr. Toll apparently does not hear one of my questions). My prime pattern is to self-select and select others. Interestingly, Mrs. Toll is the person with most variability in turn-allocation profiles, appearing in all four cells of Fig. 4.4. This points to her mediating role, at different times picking up the role of both interviewer and respondent with their different characteristic turn allocation profiles.

When we come to the size of the turns that Mr. Toll takes we find that his behavior is, perhaps, less appropriate for an ethnographic interview format where the interviewee is expected to do the bulk of the talking. Out of his 19 turns in this extract, on the three occasions when Mr. Toll self-selects, he only reiterates what the previous speaker has said. Seven turns consist of "yes" answers and another two of nonverbal responses to an instruction. Thus, he does not self-select at TRPs to answer my questions. Nor is this an isolated example of taciturnity in

1. Speaker self-selects and subsequently selects next speaker		2. Speaker self-selects but does not then select next speaker	
Pam:	14	Mr. Toll:	3
Mrs.Toll:	2	Mrs. Toll:	3
Mr. Toll:	0	Pam:	0
3. Speaker is selected and then selects next speaker		4. Speaker is selected but does not select next speaker	
Pam:	1	Mr. Toll	13[1]
Mr. Toll:	3	Mrs. Toll:	1
Mrs. Toll:	1	Pam:	0

Figure 4.4. Selection of speakers in Extract 2.

---

[1] I included the two nonverbal responses (11 and 35) here where Mr. Toll took his hand down from his mouth when instructed. Although they do not really constitute a turn in terms of Sacks et al.'s criteria, they are nevertheless a significant part of this interaction. This broadens my interporetation to

minimally active confused speakers. Again, I suspect that an investigation of turn profiling of this type can act as an effective preliminary analysis for considering membership issues in relation to a broad spectrum of talk.

Implications of Minimal Turn Size for Turn Allocation

The predominant pattern of talk on the part of the research participants who were minimally active in their talk was as follows:

Interviewer:	Talk followed by TRP (Rule 1(a) – selects respondent)
Respondent:	Takes up turn allocation, often after a pause, responds very briefly (does not allocate another speaker, or self-select to continue) TRP.

This sequence is discrete but can be repeated to build up into a chain, as shown in Extract 3 where I self-select as next speaker after each of Mrs. Hoy's responses (Rule 1b):

Extract 3

1. Pam:	What so what sorts of songs do they sing here?
	(2.0)
2. Mrs. Hoy:	Crystal Chandeliers=
3. Pam:	=Do they?
4. Mrs. Hoy:	Ye:s
	(0.8)
5. Pam:	And do you lead them when they sing that?
	(.)
6. Mrs. Hoy:	Ye:s
	(.)
7. Pam:	Do yo you come here several days a week?=
8. Mrs. Hoy:	=Yes.

Here Mrs. Hoy recognizes TRPs at the end of questions four times, although her response to one is after a pause (Utterance 2). In the whole conversation of 612 turns, there are 84 pairs of turns like this between Mrs. Hoy and myself. Utterance 2 is one of the few times in the conversation where Mrs. Hoy offers an answer other than "yes"; and perhaps here it is significant that Mr. Hoy has mentioned that she liked this song six utterances previously and we have been talking about it for all the subsequent turns. Thus, we can see that this minimally active confused speaker recognizes TRPs, and can fill in a turn slot, but that this is usually only with a brief response.

Most of Mrs. Hoy's turns are a single word, usually "yes"; and this response has consequences for the selection of the next speaker. That is to say, a speaker who chooses a single-word turn does not self-select a next speaker, or (usually) select someone else as speaker. A single-word turn like this honors the obligation of responding to a turn allocation

---

Goffman's concept of *information given off* (see ch.1) – that not all meaning in social interaction is to be found in talk alone.

from another, but it does not involve bidding for or allocating another turn. It always permits, indeed requires, another speaker to self-select as next speaker. An unqualified "yes" answer can only do the job of confirming. A continuing string of "yes" answers can be seen in a number of ways, as (a) implying others have the right to allocate turns, (b) imposing an obligation on others to allocate turns, or (c) permitting the conversation to peter out.

Other single word responses perform a similarly limited job. "No" can only refuse (however, "no" is more rarely a single-word answer, because it is often followed by hedges and qualifications as a dispreferred answer). A repetition of what someone has just said provides no additional information on the part of the speaker (as shown by Extract 2). A term of address can only direct or redirect. For example, if Lyn asks Paul "Are you and Sally going to the theater tonight?", Paul may turn to Sally and say "Sally?" in a questioning tone. The turn is used to redirect a question by selecting another speaker, not to respond to it, a pattern that is observable with some minimally active confused speakers. So single-word responses can only minimally answer a question or can be used to redirect it.

Each of these options suggests a strategy involving little personal obligation and minimal participation or involvement in the conversation. Goffman's (1963a) description of what he calls an involvement contour is useful here namely, "between beginning and end there is often an 'involvement contour', a line tracing the rise and fall of general engrossment in the occasion's main activity" (p. 18).

Goffman focused on general engrossment, but for individuals, their own involvement contour may depend on the topics of conversation; in establishing topics that hold their own interest, modifying topics introduced by others, and contributing in order to establish a relation between the topic in hand and an identity that is available to them. In these terms, the involvement contour of minimally active confused speakers remains at a low level, not meeting what would normally be expected in ordinary conversation on the basis of Grice's maxims, or in a loosely structured ethnographic interview. Interestingly, it is perhaps not so far from what is required of interviewees in some highly structured interviews.

The Minimal Answer and Preceding Utterance

We need to establish next whether the nature of the preceding questions was such as to require only minimum answers; in other words, whether confused speakers, in fact, had the leeway to produce fuller answers. In this interview conversation, it will be seen that such a consideration is likely to be of interest to any analyst examining the degree to which participants expect or are expected to talk in specific situations. This investigation is related to the nature and functions of various types of questions.

Questions as first parts of adjacency pairs strongly expect an appropriate type of response—an answer. Thus, whoever the next speaker is, in normal circumstances, he or she would expect to give an answer. This means that whoever becomes next speaker has to identify a TRP at the end of a question and to appreciate that they have been selected or self-select as an appropriate person to speak next: This requires monitoring the preceding turns for the upcoming TRP and listening in this turn to see what action might be required in the next turn and also, of course, for what sort of response would be appropriate.

Part of understanding what sort of response is appropriate involves an ability to discern the type and length of answer that is suitable for specific types of questions. A variety of question and answer formats have been identified, for example, yes–no questions; questions offering alternatives questions ("Are you doing this or that?"); and WH questions (why, where, what, who, when, etc.).

All of these appear in the data I collected and are, of course, all commonly recognizable in all types of conversations. In the way they are posed yes–no questions are restricted in the scope of the answer they require (Hausser, cited in Bauerle, 1979). As Goody (1978) noted "These are complete propositions: in English they differ from statements only in the inversion of word order" (p. 23). Thus "You like country music." becomes "Do you like country music?" One proposition is put forward in the question and the answer required is either an affirmation or denial of its truth. If the question is turned back into a proposition, then it is a complete statement standing on its own. Alternative questions are really a variant on yes–no questions, offering the respondent an opportunity to choose one of the two propositions that have been offered. In the answer, no departure is required from what has been in the question. This can be compared with questions that Goody points to as being incomplete propositions, for which the answer provides the missing clause. Thus the question "How many people were at the party?" may be represented formally as "? (X number of people were at the party)" (Goody, 1978)). WH questions fit into this sort of format. Thus "What do you do at the day center?" is a question for which the answer is to provide the missing clause—"? (What you do at the day center)".

Whatever type of question is posed, we can suggest that in an interview situation, respondents may be alerted to the possibilities of appropriate turn lengths. However, for the most part, in a loosely structured ethnographic interview they will find that whatever the format of the question, its project is such that a long answer is permissible. Indeed, even those questions that are yes–no questions can be construed in this situation as questions whose project encourages more than one-word answers. One might also expect participants to monitor the extent to which lengthy responses are acceptable, for example, according to whether the interviewer seeks to reenter at the first TRP.

Given that my orientation was to produce an ethnographic interview, most of my questions were invitations to talk. Many are incomplete proposition questions. They offer the opportunity for participants to choose to take lengthy turns and presuppose a turn that will be *at least one clause long* (because incomplete proposition questions ask for a missing clause). And yet, typically, my questions get short responses from minimally active confused speakers, either the minimum single-word answers that are required of yes–no questions or minimal disclaimers or silences after incomplete proposition questions. Even if people do not have the resources to answer questions, there are options open to them to facilitate a response to an invitation to talk. For example, Mr. Toll might have chosen more frequently to select Mrs. Toll as next speaker; thus acknowledging that discursive answers were being invited and choosing a next speaker whom he knew could fulfill this requirement. But, largely speaking, neither he nor any of the other minimally active confused speakers did this; they continued to respond in a minimal fashion throughout.

Overall, participants need to be able to choose appropriate turn sizes for specific occasions. In terms of a loosely structured ethnographic interview, we can propose an involvement contour on which the most proactive (involved) approach that can be taken is to self-select to talk in a turn longer than a sentence and indicate the telling of a story, and at the end of that story to select another speaker. At the other end of the scale of involvement we have the least active approach (short of not participating at all), which is to be selected by another speaker, to reply only in one word, and then not to select another speaker. In the situation of a loosely structured ethnographic interview, the interviewer might be expected to be proactive in terms of self-selection and other-selection in terms of turn taking, whereas the interviewee might be expected to be proactive in choosing to take long turns. However, if an interviewee does not understand what they have been asked, they may require the interviewer to increase their active involvement in the talk and explain. So, either way, depending on context, people might alter their involvement contour. However, in the case of my data, minimally active confused speakers chose to produce minimal answers even in circumstances where they had been invited to talk. They were neither proactive, nor did they in any way amend their involvement depending on context.

Of course, even though single-word responses may be seen as inappropriate for the circumstances, they still perform certain functions for those producing them. By giving single-word responses minimally active confused speakers behaved in such a way as to reduce to the minimum their obligations to the conversation, while nevertheless remaining as participants. In a sense, the frequent use of the minimal answer "yes" might be seen in certain circumstances to offer up its own little breaching experiment. Whereas in a survey research interview it might not breach expectancies, in an ethnographic interview it does. My feeling is that this understanding is discernible by any ordinary member who might reflect on an interview encounter and describe it as being like "trying to get blood out of a stone." And it is to an exploraton of reasons why this judgment might apply that I now turn by considering the consequences of this strategy for topic management in these interview-conversations.

TOPIC MANAGEMENT

So far, I have noted that minimally active confused speakers rarely self-select and that their answers are very brief. The implication of this is that they have little involvement in the development of conversational topics. After all, one can only do a limited amount of work with a single-word answer, primarily to react to the topics of other people's choosing. This means that the other participants must play a substantial part in maintaining the conversation through the introduction and development of topics.

A number of authors have noted the difficulty of defining topic (see, e.g. Sperber & Wilson, 1986) and the bulk of conversation analytic work on topic seems to launch right in, ignoring any attempt at definition. I am tempted to do the same. However, I want to note what Schegloff and Sacks (1974) said:

> If we may refer to what gets talked about in a conversation as mentionables, then we can note that there are considerations relevant to conversationalists in ordering and distributing their talk about mentionables in a single conversation. (p. 242)

In their work they emphasized the importance of placement in the analysis of utterances noting that: "a pervasively relevant issue (for participants) about utterances in conversation is why that now?, a question whose analysis may . . . also be relevant to find what that is" (Schegloff & Sacks, 1974, p. 241).

Thus, understanding of topic is related to its placement in a conversation. Ordinary members can be seen to be aware of the problem of introducing mentionables at the right moment. As I noted, Sperber and Wilson (1986), in their discussion of relevance, outlined the methodic search made by participants for the links between this sentence and the last one, to the one before that, and finally to more encyclopedic contextualizing knowledge. This enables them not only to make sense of the conversation, but to structure their current talk so as to reflect the order and presentation of previous topics. Thus, to successfully develop topics or introduce new ones participants must be able to integrate them into the flow of talk. As Levinson (1983) remarked on the subject of topic shift: "if A has been talking about X, B should find a way to talk about Z (if Z is the subject he wants to introduce) such that X and Z can be found to be natural fellow members of some category Y" (p. 313).

If participants cannot do such overarching work smoothly, there are devices for mentioning something when the moment has passed or the topic is otherwise out of time. We can suggest that ordinary members have the resources to recognize topics that are not adequately contextualized in the foregoing talk, and that such topics will be seen as problematic. The next two extracts demonstrate two problematic topic introductions by a minimally active confused speaker. Mrs. Hoy rarely self-selected in the conversation, but almost all the occasions when she did were topically problematic in some way:

Extract 4

[Mr Hoy has just been talking about Blackpool.]
Pam: Did you go to the illuminations?
Mr. Hoy: Oh yes she went to the illuminations didn't you?
Mrs. Hoy: =Yeh=
Mr. Hoy: We went to er=
Mrs. Hoy: =Brightling Abbey
Mr. Hoy: I took early retirement[2]
                                            [
Pam: Where sorry?=
Mrs. Hoy: =Brightling Abbey=
Pam: =Brightling Abbey what's that like?=Mrs. Hoy: =Well it's er just
                          (.) it's not er big.
                                            [
Mr. Hoy: It's a (   ) park isn't it?=
Mrs. Hoy: =Yeh.

Extract 5

[After talk about Mrs Hoy's sister.]
Pam: ((Addressing Mr Hoy)) And does she live round here?
Mr. Hoy: No she's er=

---

[2] Out of context, this statement by Mr. Hoy seems as problematic as those by Mrs. Hoy. After listening to the extract, I took it to be related to why they might have been to the northern holiday resort of Blackpool other than during the summer season.

Mrs. Hoy:	=You're about sitting on the spot where to be yeh.
Mr. Hoy:	She's been gone fifteen years.

In both of these cases, Mrs. Hoy self-selects as next speaker at a point when Mr. Hoy has hesitated (which can be seen as a TRP so that participants can self-select to fill in the rest of the answer, thus continuing the topic or seizing the opportunity to develop it). So self-selection at such a point can be seen as quite appropriate. Also, categorically, the introduction of Brightling Abbey is not a completely disconnected topic: It can be seen as *another place that we have been*. So Mrs. Hoy has actually got quite a lot right with this self-selection of turn. Unfortunately, she does not quite bring the topic development off successfully. The progression from Blackpool (X) to Brightling Abbey (Z) via some connecting topic (Y) is absent in Mrs Hoy's talk. Even though there is some topical connection, the mechanics of developing topic have been omitted. And this is reflected in my own utterance "Where sorry?", as I have not been alerted to the topic shift in the preceding talk. Even after lengthy consideration, Extract 5 yielded no topical connections: Mrs. Hoy's rules of relevance did not reveal themselves to me as a normal speaker. We might suggest that if this is to be regarded as a conversation such abrupt topic changes mark it as odd in some way. Indeed, in the same paragraph as that cited above Levinson (1983) noted Sacks' remark "that the relative frequency of marked topic shifts . . . is a measure of a lousy conversation" (Levinson, 1983, p. 313).

As I noted, these conversations in the psychogeriatric clinic were also interviews. It is important to note here that, like much else in the data, the management of conversational topics is influenced by the interview format of the encounter. Taking Sacks' lead, one possible criterion of an interview could be that it is a *lousy* conversation. Thus, topics might be fixed antecedently by the interviewer's agenda, and relevance from one utterance to the next may be partly predefined in these terms. So, in the case of an interview-conversation, perhaps, this lousy structure is generally more obvious. However, where minimally active confused speakers are participants, the bare bones of the interview may be even more exposed: Topic progression depends either on the interviewer (or on other normal speakers) or it depends on the confused speaker and is faulty. Any notion of *articulation* of topic progression from X to Z by way of a superordinate category Y has to be accomplished by the normal speakers. For this reason, too, topic control and development tend to be carried out by the interviewer or caregiver. In the conversation with Mr. and Mrs. Toll, a third of adjacency pair second pair parts produced by Mr. Toll are monosyllabic. If one were to strip a transcript down and reprint only the confused speaker's contribution it would be very difficult to establish what issues the conversation deals with. For example, here is a sequence of Mr. Toll's contributions taken from the middle of Extract 2:

Extract 6

13.	Yes.
15.	Yes.
17.	Oh it's nice.
19.	Yes.
21.	Yes.
23.	Yes.
25.	Yes.
27.	Went with you didn't I?

Goffman (1981) noted the following:

> Observe that although a question anticipates an answer, it is designed to receive it, seems dependent on doing so, an answer seems even more dependent, making less sense alone than does the utterance that called it forth. (p. 5)

In Extract 6, the impetus of "yes" derives solely from the sense of the question. It adds no more to the conversation than confirmation. It gives no clue whatsoever about topic. Unless a stretch of talk were very formal (e.g., certain types of cross examination in a court of law), or perhaps a survey research, or counseling interview (see Garfinkel's counseling experiment, 1967), if the talk of individual speakers were printed out, some kind of notion about what is being said might emerge from that of any one person. This is because participants would answer according to the project of the question, or they would fill in the clauses of incomplete proposition questions and these would be ways of developing and initiating topics.

However Mr. Toll, although taking on the role of uttering the second pair part, provides no material for me to build on as first pair part speaker. In order to continue this line of questioning all my first pair parts have to emerge from my own train of thought and my own experience of holidays. If we now look at the turns omitted from Extract 6 we find this collection of questions from me:

Extract 7

12.	Did you have good weather?
14.	You're looking very sun tanned.
16.	What's Llandudno like? I've never been there
18.	What does it look like? Is it hilly country?
20.	It is and what a seaside?
22.	Is there a promenade?
24.	So you walked up and down the prom.
26	Who did you go with?

This extract shows me building up some kind of picture of the holiday in Llandudno. It involves talking about the topography of the place, some reference to how the time was spent on the holiday, and who went on it, an evaluation of how much good the holiday had done (a sun tan). In other words, I am developing a story about the holiday but with little assistance from Mr. Toll.

In a sense, Mr. Toll is safe in this conversation, in that all that he has to do is a second pair part in response to a first pair part. If he does not provide any extra information he will not be quizzed on it. If he does not initiate a first pair part he does not have to decide to whom to address it, form it into an appropriate first pair part, risk someone not understanding it, and so on. In short, the less topic development he engages in, the less he is exposed. The less he wrestles with the machinery of description, the less his operation of it will be called into question.

So, topic management can be more or less successful depending on the resistance or cooperation of the confused speaker with the normal speakers. And here I speak of cooperation in a less precise way than that used by Grice (1975) and those who have developed aspects of his work on principles of cooperation and implicature. On the whole, the cooperation of the minimally active confused speaker in the story I outlined involves complying with a structure presented to him by a normal speaker: By not deviating from it or proposing any alteration to it, he minimizes his own exposure. Of course, this then raises the question of whether always sheltering within the conversational competence of others challenges one's own competence and thus defeats the object of the exercise: That is, allowing others to *operate the machinery* instead of being responsible conversational technicians themselves (Lynch & Bogen, 1994). I return to this question later.

Nevertheless, minimally active confused speakers also may offer what might be called passive resistance to topic development, making it difficult for the interviewer to present any semblance of normal conversational appearances. For example, Extract 8 shows my turns in the opening phase of the conversation with Mrs. Pugh:

Extract 8

1.	Were you brought up in this area? Are you from Staffordshire?
3.	Where do you come from?
7.	And I don't know Staffordshire at all. What's Tibstone like?
9.	What was it like when you were a child?
11.	Can you remember your childhood?
13.	And how long have you been there?
20.	Do you have brothers and sisters?
22.	Not even . . . you were an only child in Tibstone and where did you go to school?
24.	Drinkworth.
26.	What sort of school was it that you went to?
29.	Were there a lot of children there? Was it a big school?
33.	Small.
35.	How many classes were there?

37.   When you were in the other room your husband said that you used to
                        do a lot of gardening that was before you came. Has the flat got a
                        garden?

Here I develop the topic structure with a series of separate little
pyramids (Staffordshire, childhood, school, these all falling under the
banner of history; I then shift to a completely new topic together with an
acknowledgment of the shift: the garden). I take 15 of the 40 turns, Mrs.
Pugh takes 17, and Mr. Pugh and Mrs. James, the daughter, take 8 turns
between them. Mrs. Pugh uses 5 of her 15 turns to say she does not know
or cannot not remember, in response to my questions:

Extract 9

8.   I don't know I never go down there I never (????)
10.   Oh I can't remember that.
12.   Not much really I mean (???)
14.   Oh (sighs) I don't know.
37.   Oh I don't know. I couldn't tell you.

These comments account for a number of her longer turns. They do not
answer the questions; they are accounts or excuses for not answering the
questions. Three more of her turns are used to confirm answers given in
her stead by relatives. Thus, in this small segment of 40 turns she has less
than half the turns and, of these, half are either attempts to deter the
interviewer from carrying on with that topic or merely confirm what
others have said on a topic. Her responses to my other questions are
usually in the form of a single word. In all she gives no help with topical
development except by closing down my various lines of questioning.
The possibility of developing a story is denied to me because of the
refusal by Mrs. Pugh to accept the topics I choose. Thus, whereas
minimal "yes" answers permit the interviewer to continue to build a
story of some kind, for the confused speakers excuses or disclaimers can
act to move toward closure; a series of them *wrong foot* the interviewer,
suggesting that he or she has in some way chosen the wrong frame for
their questions. I would like to suggest that much of the foregoing
analysis, although relating specifically to minimally active confused
speakers, can be applied more broadly. Certainly, I think it may be
applied to what researchers may describe as an unsuccessful interview.
But additionally, there is an argument that this sort of pattern is also
frequently evident in situations of defensive talk where one party does
not wish or intend to proffer many aspects of their identity as topics for
talk, or to respond to the overtures of others regarding their identity as a
topic for talk. This leads me into discussion of the identity work that
takes place in these interviews through the presentation of biographies.

IDENTITY WORK

Having demonstrated some of the distinctive characteristics of the talk of this group of minimally active confused speakers in the given circumstances, I want now to consider how identity work relating to them is done. I focus this discussion partly on the relation between the interview situation and identity, and partly on the way that normal speakers, primarily caregivers, represent confused speakers in and through talk.

The Interview as a Location for Identity Work

In this series of interviews, I decided to use life history as a topic for talk. For each person, I sought a unique history, being oriented toward a notion of personal identity as defined by Goffman:

> While most particular facts about an individual will be true of others too, the full set of facts known about an intimate is not found to hold, as a combination, for any other person in the world, this adding a means by which he can be positively distinguished from everyone else. (Goffman, 1963b, p. 74)

This unique history or personal biography contributes to personal identity and in normal circumstances to social identity (i.e., wife, father, etc.). Yet identity depends not only on the uniqueness of the facts about someone, but also on presentation. For most competent members, presentation of historical self is something that the current self might be expected to do. When adults prompt small children to answer questions about themselves, the suggestion is that even children are able to identify salient features about their history that are pertinent to presentation of self in the here and now.

In the discussion that follows, I rely heavily on M. A. Atkinson's work on "lifetimes" (Atkinson, 1973). Presentation of self in the present and self in the past (biographical matter) is a matter of competence. Presenting one's identity is a methodic practice rooted in interpretive work involving ordinary member assumptions about how lives are socially represented. Our life stories and conventional lifetime formulations are commonly used resources in ordinary talk and extensively used by most of us in the way we position ourselves in talk and determine the positions of others. One of the topics with which Atkinson deals is how people select particular lifetime formulations to suit the circumstances. For any occasion, there are doubtless a number of correct formulations that can refer to time, space, place, and biography. However, not all possible formulations will be appropriate to the occasion. The occasion to which I refer, an interview in a psychogeriatric clinic, requires an understanding not only of how ordinary members generally relate biographical issues, but also of what sort of biography might be required in these particular circumstances. Indeed, any particular occasion may require an equally distinctive biography.

One common practice when one meets someone new and wants to find out something about them is to ask *everyperson* questions: That is to say, questions that might suit a very large possible population. Such questions indicate something about the relationship between the two people, that neither knows much about the other. However, in fact, of course, clues are frequently offered at the outset that enable people to choose appropriate everyperson questions: For example, one is unlikely to ask a man what his experience of childbearing is. In my own case, at the outset of these interviews I had sometimes gleaned some knowledge from sitting in on the consultant's assessment and I was aware that I was talking to older people who are recognizable as having a lengthy life history on which to draw. And I was also introduced to caregivers as husbands, wives, daughters, and so on. So I knew that I could ask everyperson family questions. The respondents and caregivers knew something about me—that I was interested in communication; and they had been told my name and the place where I work. They would also have been able to recognize features about me such as my age and gender (e.g., that I was a middle-aged woman and not a child). All these features could be expected to influence the types of questions that I asked.

External indicators of recognizable personal attributes notwithstanding, we can expect that people can generally be assumed, for example, to have been born and brought up somewhere, to have gone to school, to have had a job or looked for one, possibly to have married and have had children, and so on; so that general questions on these topics would suit the circumstances of a good many people. As M. A. Atkinson (1973) noted:

> Using a particular lifetime formulation is in effect claiming its recognisability for particular hearers . . . certain lifetime formulations have a common currency aspect in that they have high recognisability potential such that they are usable anonymously. Examples of such formulations may be the following common biographical markers: When I was a child, On my twenty-sixth birthday, When I was at school. (p. 97)

The asking of such questions, then, invites responses that use common everyperson biographical markers combined with particular details. Indeed, lifetime formulations as a form of "currency" in social interaction of a formal nature are quite pervasive: From the practice of filling in an assessment form as a way of guiding the first phase of social interaction with a client, through to life history case study approaches that structure much social work (and the weight given to what a client chooses to reveal); from the requirement of using some lifetime formulations to position witnesses and defendants in a court of law through to the questions that both probe and structure *family life* in market research. I should also note the practice in work-related appointment interviews, which are conducted on an equal opportunities basis, that certain questions about personal biography cannot be asked; in other words the *acceptable* biography for the occasion is controlled through questions.

In the case of my interviews, everyperson questions can be seen as an invitation to the respondent to develop a particularistic biography, within a highly recognizable biographical framework. I began my interviews with a commonly used developmental notion of the biography of the people concerned, starting with their childhood, and so on, thus offering a format for the unfolding of the biography. I tried also to make personal connections with the area under scrutiny. For example, in the interview with Mrs. Pugh, when the name of a local village came up, I said that I had once taught there. And with other respondents, when we talked about playing cards, I mentioned to two people that I, too, play cards. This can be seen as the modeling of a particularistic biography, as an encouragement to the respondents that we have found a community of interest, thereby indicating appropriate future formulations in this area.

We need to note that my own use of biography to establish and further communities of interest may have contributed to the ambiguity of the situation for other participants. First, negotiating communities of interest around biography can be seen as a feature of ordinary chat. Second, even if the occasion is seen as an interview, this is not something that all interviews would involve: In a television political interview, for example, only the biography of the interviewee is seen as appropriate for exposure.[3] Third, when professionals establish communities of interest with clients, it comes under the heading of professional or parachat, not the main business of the interview (and it would be seen as inappropriate for the client to continue to follow this line once the interview proper had begun). These multiple possible interpretations might be seen as a significant consideration by participants in these interviews.

However, even though ambiguous, this interview format does offer a number of cues as to what sort of identity to present: a developmental biography as a framework, filled in with particular detail and presented to someone who is known not to know these details. But as I have noted earlier in this chapter, the characteristic responses of minimally active confused speakers were short and often propositionally empty. When

---

[3] Occasionally, the interviewee may well come back with remarks about "You media people" as a biographical riposte.

someone answers only "yes", the interviewer carries the burden of formulating the biography. From an ordinary member point of view, constant "yes" answers can be seen as failure to recognize that which is appropriate to tell, or as constituting an inability to provide the relevant information. Either way, the participant fails to enter into the telling of a particularistic biography. If no particulars are filled in, the discussion continues to be highly generalized. The absence of a unique history, or the unwillingness or inability to use it, contributes to the social identity of people suffering from confusion.[4] They are no longer able to construct a personal identity for themselves. The social identity of confusion becomes an overall explanatory identity supported by gaps or absences in personal biography and personal identity. It can be seen to account for everything.

Caregivers and Identity Work

The burden of developing a biography for the confused speakers did not fall entirely on me. Caregivers made considerable contributions. It is important to see what type of person the confused speaker was being presented as by the caregivers. We can suggest that caregivers are likely to have become accomplished in *bringing off* the identity of the confused speaker. After all, it is probably a daily occurrence for them to take part in multiparty conversations that involve the confused speaker, other people, and themselves.

In the interviews under discussion, caregivers were able to develop a much more specific story line than I could as interviewer. For example, they could work backward from something that they knew should be known and relevant to the confused speaker, and then pose questions to which they could then get an appropriate answer. Indeed, this points to an almost formal knowledge of the kinds of issues entailed in adjacency pairs, namely, that normal people can give answers to questions, can accept invitations, and so on. Here the environment is being manipulated so that the confused speaker can also do this; choosing the way that questions are put, invitations given, and so on, and by offering subject areas where there is a good chance that specific questions will be answered. Particularistic biographies now begin to be filled in, whether by the asking of particularistic questions or by the supply of particularistic answers. However, caregivers can only give answers to the extent that they know them. They cannot have had the life experience of the confused speaker, although spouses and children may have shared a great deal of their lives with the person, and children have been told stories about the confused speaker's life. Thus, the presentation of the

---

[4] Such an absence might also, of course, lead to the conclusion that someone has something to hide.

biographies of minimally active confused speakers is shaped by the necessarily limited knowledge of those speaking for them. It is interesting that in my failed interview with Cora (discussed in the previous chapter), biography had a minimal place and was not used by her nurse, the caregiver, to hold things together. Presumably the nurse could not make good the biography, offering only very minimal information about Cora being obsessed with polishing things.

I now identify a number of ways in which caregivers interacted in the interview situation to contribute toward the presentation of the identity of confused speakers.

Answering for the Respondent. Caregivers try to ensure correct answers by using a number of routes. In some instances they effectively put forward the answer themselves. For example:

Extract 10
1. Pam:	What have you got in the garden? (1.0) What sorts of flowers?
	(3.5)
2. Mrs. Pugh:	It's er=
3. Mrs. James:	=Some roses=
4. Mrs. Pugh:	=Roses=
5. Mrs. James:	=Fuschias.

Mrs. James' response demonstrates that she has the resource of some particular knowledge of her mother's life, and it can be seen not only as an answer but also as a model for future responses. Indeed, in Utterance 4, Mrs. Pugh repeats what her daughter has just said, a repetition that can also be seen as an acknowledgment that the respondent is under some obligation to answer the interviewer herself, even if an answer by another intervenes. Another type of response is one that reformulates the answer as a sort of narrative at one remove from the confused speaker:

Extract 11
1. Pam:	[...] What sorts of roses have you got?
2. Mrs. Pugh:	Ah all sorts.
3. Mrs. James:	You've got miniature ones=
4. Mrs. Pugh:	=Got some miniature ones=
5. Mrs. James:	You've not got as many as you used to have. You used to have a lot of roses.

In Utterance 2 "all sorts" can be seen as a comprehensive but brief answer that effectively closes down the topic (particularly when Mrs Pugh does not opt to continue her turn at the TRP that follows the word "sorts"). In effect, it is an everyperson response to an everyperson question.[5] Again, a kind of modeling effect takes place and in Utterance 4, Mrs. Pugh once again repeats her daughter's response. Mrs. James,

---

[5] It is interesting that everyperson answers to everyperson questions may be seen as evasive — maintaining anonymity in a situation where particularity has been invited.

however, although not answering in the place of Mrs. Pugh, also engages in some topic development on her mother's behalf, reformulating the answer into the second person. Looking back at Extract 10, it can be seen that even the two one-word responses that Mrs. James offers are collectively more than a minimal response: They are the seeds of future topic development, suggesting that she sees the respondent's job of identity work as being about producing more than minimal responses.

In this interview, Mrs. Pugh's husband and daughter chose mainly to adopt the role of speaking for the confused speaker, and although they developed her answers or elaborated on her minimal responses, they did not greatly facilitate her performance or help her extend it. Significantly, I think, the interview was fairly brief.[6] It may also be revealing that Mrs. Pugh appeared to be very unhappy about her identity as a confused speaker: it was, I understand, a fairly new identity for her, (and possibly a temporary one), and her relatives appeared to have not taken on the role of restructuring that identity by means of substantial assistance. The current identity of the confused speaker notwithstanding, the exchanges in this interview suggest that the details of *normal* history and *normal* identity are the salient ones.

Pressing the Respondent. A more strenuous example of a caregiver facilitating identity work can be seen in the case of Mr. and Mrs. Toll. To illustrate this, I want to look again at some lines taken from Extract 2, lines that I have not yet commented on. They are presented here in Extracts 12 and 13 where I have also noted the preceding lines for each:

Extract 12

9. Pam:	Did you have the good weather?
10. Mrs. Toll:	Take take your hand down from there.
11. Mr. Toll:	((Takes hand down)).
12. Pam:	Did you have the good weather?=
13. Mr. Toll:	=Yeh.

Extract 13

33. Mr. Toll:	=Oh with Sue yeh=
34. Mrs. Toll:	Take your hand off your mouth Fred, we can't hear what you're saying=
35. Mr. Toll:	((Takes hand down))
36. Pam:	=Who's Brian?

We can perhaps interpret these two exchanges as adjacency pairs. Utterances 10 and 34 are first pair part commands that are responded to by Mr. Toll taking his hand down from his mouth: There are, as it were, two nonverbal second pair parts (Utterances 11 and 35). The exchanges demonstrate the normative strength of adjacency pairs, as Mrs. Toll tries

---

[6] Partly because, unlike other caregivers, Mr. Pugh and his daughter did not engage in metatalk about Mrs. Pugh's condition.

to ensure that Mr. Toll is *fit* to answer the question. In the case of both commands, Mrs. Toll self-selects to begin the first pair part; both commands ensure that Mr. Toll can answer subsequent questions and keep the channels for communication open. Presumably, Mrs. Toll also sees her husband's behavior as potentially offensive, if only at the level that not to produce a second pair part after a first pair part is a noticeable absence. The monitoring and control of someone else's physical management of self is something that we would expect of those in charge of others, indicating that the management of self should be directed to the matter in hand. Because Mr. Toll takes his hand down, it can be seen that he perceives Mrs. Toll as an appropriate person to make such an utterance, and that it is appropriate for him to act on that command. It would not, I think, have been appropriate for me to put forward such a command or even to reinforce it (i.e., "Yes take your hand down" would have been rude). However, Mr. Toll does not take his hand away until his wife has instructed him to do so. Perhaps he does not see his behavior as potentially offensive. Or, possibly, he wishes to put a smokescreen over any second pair part he produces (maybe a lack of clarity of speech is a more acceptable form of absence because at least it implies a reply even if it is not audible). Perhaps also, if in doubt, hearers assume that there has been a normal response and that the problem is at their end. The point is that Mrs. Toll takes on a controlling role, having established that it is necessary for Mr. Toll to be heard in this situation. Rather like a teacher, she adopts interactional rights that assume that an unclear answer such as mumbling into one's hand betokens a fault in the production of the answer on the part of the speaker. In all, it is a more explicit direction about how to play the role of interviewee than the modeling work that goes on with caregivers elsewhere.

Another example of Mrs. Toll's monitoring can be seen in the following extract, again taken from Extract 2:

Extract 14

26. Pam:	Who did who did you go with?
	(3.6)
27. Mr. Toll:	Went with you didn't I?=
28. Mrs. Toll:	=Yeh me and who else?
	(3.2)
29. Mr. Toll:	I don't know=
30. Mrs. Toll:	=Brian.
	(1.0)
31. Mr. Toll:	Aye Brian=
32. Mrs. Toll:	=And Sue=
33. Mr. Toll:	=Oh with Sue yeh=

In this case, Mr. Toll does not make a mistake but had he not, in Utterance 27, selected Mrs. Toll to speak, there might have been a noticeable absence: After such an event, it is possible that whatever happened next would have placed him under greater pressure. Given that he appears to be aware that he cannot ask the interviewer to intervene (because an interviewer could not know the personal details of his life), his choice is to invite his wife to become a respondent too. Mrs. Toll then immediately turns herself into a first pair part speaker allocating her husband a very circumscribed set of second pair parts indeed, which confirm information to which I, as an interviewer, have no access. The consequence for Mr. Toll is that he is given a hard time: The answer is not just presented to him, he has to work for it. By aligning herself with the role of interviewer, Mrs. Toll presses him in his role as respondent. It will be noted that in order to do this, Mrs. Toll needs to know the details of the holiday. When she asks "Who else?" (Utterance 28), it is a format that, as interviewer, I could perhaps use because it can be seen as an everyperson question (most people go on holiday with others). However, her next two utterances are the names of the other people who went. She knows when to draw the exchange to a close, something that I could not have known.

Mrs. Toll's contribution acknowledges that Mr. Toll's repertoire is likely to be limited, even though she pushes him to fulfill more properly the role of an interviewee. We can see that in some respects, Mrs. Toll's handling of the situation is a rejection of the identity of *confused* for her husband. She attempts to get him to perform normally: to be a fit respondent who spells out enough details of his biography to do this. In many respects she is asking him to conform to a number of Grice's maxims in terms of quality, quantity, and manner (Grice, 1975). Indeed, her formulations in Extract 14 almost suggest that she is making Mr. Toll cooperate.

Reformulation. An option used by another caregiver was to extensively reformulate my questions by presenting biographical details of his wife's life within his own questions. This pattern links with topic management: A prior statement was translated into a different type of format that could be followed by a speaker who was unable or unwilling to engage with the current format. Such reformulation alters the talk to maintain coherence and topic. It would have been perfectly feasible for the caregiver in question, Mr. Hoy, just to answer my questions for Mrs. Hoy. However, he usually established a situation that was a continuation of an interview with its question-and-answer format framing questions in such a way as to enable Mrs. Hoy to take part. Mr. Hoy played a very vigorous role in the development of a conversation, and it was one that took place as if between normal speakers. The work that he did in his participation in the conversation was almost preventive, being so well organized as to avoid remedial work ever having to take place. Indeed, when remedial work did take place, it tended to be Mr. Hoy's corrections or amplifications of what I said (presumably perceived by him as far too complicated), so that his wife's responses could be maintained as per normal.

The device of conditional relevance was exploited by Mr. Hoy to develop a form of talk with his wife that *passed* her as normal in the conversation. A substantial portion of this interview consisted of questions of a kind that had a very high expectation of a specific type of answer. In fact, there was often a cumulative structure, as the following sequence shows; and this cumulative structure was largely due to *stage management* on the part of Mr. Hoy. The extract includes an initial question by me:

Extract 15

1. Pam:	What were what were the names of your brothers? (5.2) Can't remember?
2. Mr. Hoy:	There were (Simon) weren't there?=
3. Mr. Hoy:	=Yeh=
4. Mr. Hoy:	=Jack=
5. Mrs. Hoy:	=Yeh=
6. Mr. Hoy:	=And Nigel
	(.)
7. Mrs. Hoy:	Yeh
	[
8. Mr. Hoy:	Weren't there?
	(1.0)
9. Mrs. Hoy:	Yeh.

In this sequence, after my initial question to Mrs. Hoy (Utterance 1), Mr. Hoy self-selects to take next turn. But note that he does this following a turn involving a lengthy pause, after which I put a second question, offering a let out. But a noticeable absence has been generated. A noticeable absence has some influence on turn-taking rules and gives other speakers the right to enter the conversation (because they can give the answer, maintain the topic, or cover over any state of embarrassment). With his next two utterances (4 and 6), Mr. Hoy says the names of two of the three brothers; these are statements in Goffman's terms (Goffman, 1981). Finally, he repeats part of his original first pair part (Utterance 8 repeats part of Utterance 2). In their placement, both "weren't there?" questions can be seen as tag questions: questions commonly connected with the end of a turn and which act to select the next speaker (Levinson, 1983). Like yes–no questions, tag questions require answers that are limited to confirming the previous assertion. In the case of this sequence, the answer to the original question can only have a limited number of components, the brothers' names. One can expect people to have a small enough number of brothers to be able to name them (it is not like being asked "What were the names of the people who attended the cup final?"). Thus the first pair part in Utterance 1 indicates the expectation of a limited answer.

Such sequences read more like a cross-examination than part of a casual conversation or ethnographic interview because they are highly repetitive. If the minimally active confused speaker is forever replying "yes", then roughly half the turns will be repetitive and the variety that locally managed conversation involves will be lost. The strategy also breaks down into the smallest available turn sizes what otherwise might have been one second pair part ("Who were your three brothers?", "Simon, Jack, and Nigel"). Again, the normal speaker develops the topic by translating the talk into an interview format. The extract has similarities with the elicitation of answers from a class of children (Mehan, 1986). The questions are posed in such a way as to almost eradicate the possibility of Mrs. Hoy getting anything wrong. Mr. Hoy can be seen to present first pair parts that are elicitations and that require only acknowledgments. He produces a series of single-word statements, each of which could be seen as an answer to the original question. The overall effect is to generate a multiple-turn answer. And, because Mrs. Hoy acknowledges each statement, she is an accomplice. After intervening, Mr. Hoy settles the talk down into a two-way conversation. During the interview, attempts that I made to establish two-way communication with Mrs. Hoy were often cleverly preempted by means of this intervention strategy by Mr. Hoy, for example:

Extract 16

Pam:	What else do you do here when you come here (.) at this day center?=
Mr. Hoy:	=Shouts bingo numbers out don't you?
	(.)
Mrs. Hoy:	Yes=
Mr. Hoy:	=And she makes things.
	(.)
Mrs. Hoy:	Yeh.
Pam:	What sorts of things do you make?
	(2.5)
Mr. Hoy:	Makes some lovely things don't you? Pictures don't you?

The assumption or rule here is that the first pair part must be of a very specific type to permit Mrs. Hoy to participate competently by contributing a second pair part. The initial intervention here is more prompt than in Extract 15; its promptness suggests it is a device to avoid a noticeable absence. If Mrs. Hoy is offered very few or no alternatives she can participate. In the previous examples, the first pair part, with its tag question indicates a very tightly defined answer as in "didn't you?", "weren't there?", "don't you?" This strategy combines controlled turn allocation with very consistent first pair parts. Little varies in the formula over long stretches of the conversation. Yet by these means, a story is told for Mrs. Hoy with her complicity. She *passes* as an ordinary member.

Another way in which Mr Hoy accomplishes the passing of his wife in the conversation is to intervene with very specifically designed questions:

Extract 17

Pam:	What do you listen to?
	(2.7)
Mr. Hoy:	You like Foster and Allen don't you?
	(.)
Mrs. Hoy:	Yeh=

The intervention that Mr Hoy makes has the particular characteristic that it is a question specifically designed for Mrs. Hoy. Conversation analysts suggest that all talk involves what Sacks et al. (1978) called *recipient design*:

> The talk by a party in a conversation is constructed or designed in ways which display an orientation and sensitivity to the particular other(s) who are co-participants. In our work we have found recipient design to operate with regard to word selection, topic selection, the admissibility and ordering of sequences, the options and obligations for starting and terminating conversations and so on. (p. 43)

Thus, the notion of recipient design defines a situation where speakers frame their utterance so as to be appropriate for certain aspects of the context, especially for who the other participants are and what they have just said (Schegloff & Sacks, 1974). Recipient design is important in talk involving confused speakers, and particularly so with minimally active speakers: The extent of its use can mean the difference between them passing as members in the conversation or being seen as incompetent. Such recipient design is not merely to suit the listener but to ensure that some interaction does take place. Mr. Hoy designs his questions explicitly for his wife. They contain the answer so that an appropriate second pair part for Mrs. Hoy is just "yes". In Extract 17, my question is recipient designed too, but it does not turn out to be appropriately designed for Mrs. Hoy. Successful recipient design for Mrs. Hoy, apparently involves not only the direct address to her ("you") but also a specification of the complete answer to the question within the question itself. In Goody's (1978) terms this is the presentation of a proposition in its original form. The framing of the interrogative is done as a tag question, and it occurs at the end of the turn, thus minimizing the chance that Mrs. Hoy will have forgotten that a question is being asked. Indeed, we can even suggest that as long as Mrs. Hoy can participate to the extent of saying "yes" to the tag question "wasn't it?", she needs no other resources to be able to participate.

Recipient design as practiced by Mr. Hoy almost preempts the need for repair work. The reiteration of the second pair part as "yes" also provides a model for me as to how to structure future first pair parts, namely, put everything that has to be said into them in an order that ensures the greatest chance of "yes" being the utterance chosen by the confused speaker (an expedient that Mrs Toll also adopts).[7] This strategy takes various guises. Sometimes it is a takeover of the interviewer's initial question, a sort of rerun of the first pair part involving very precise recipient design. And the recipient design *looks both ways*. It reformulates my first pair part, reducing it to a size and scope that can be answered by "yes" (i.e., it assumes that there is only one category or type connected answer at which Mrs. Hoy is efficient) and at the same time it acts as a second pair part to my original question. So a sort of chain is developed:

Pam:	Question (first pair part)
Mr. Hoy:	Answer (second pair part) *as* question (first pair part)
Mrs. Hoy:	Answer (second pair part)

The fact that this recipient design strategy looks both ways is sometimes made explicit, as in the following example:

Extract 18

Pam:	Did you go to the illuminations?
Mr. Hoy:	*Oh yes she went to the illuminations didn't you?=*
Mrs. Hoy:	=Yeh=

Here Mr. Hoy starts off by answering a question I have posed to Mrs. Hoy, speaking for the confused speaker and referring to her as she: But during the course of the utterance he changes the utterance from a second pair part (i.e. , the response to my first pair part question) to a first pair part directly addressing Mrs. Hoy with the tag question "didn't you?" This recipient design strategy often involves some topic development on the part of Mr. Hoy. For example, consider the following extract:

Extract 19

1. Pam:	And what sorts of flowers were there in it?
2. Mrs. Hoy:	Oh the there the flowers were big.
	(.)
3. Pam:	Big big.
4. Mrs. Hoy:	Oh yes.
5. Mr. Hoy:	*She used to have some lovely flowers didn't you=*
6. Pam:	=Did you?=
7. Mr. Hoy:	*=She used to have a flower garden at the bottom=*
8. Pam:	=Really=
9. Mr. Hoy:	*=And she used to do it all herself.*
	[
10. Mrs. Hoy:	Yeh.

In this sequence, Mrs. Hoy's response in Utterance 2, although a correct possible response to a query about *sorts* of flowers, could perhaps be seen as an unconventional one. Mr. Hoy does not correct his wife but he moves the topic on to further mentionables, doing so in a way that

---

[7] It is interesting that in the latter part of the interview, I adopted this strategy quite frequently!

maintains her participation. So Mr. Hoy takes on a variety of voices in order to facilitate his wife's participation in the conversation. At times he appears to combine the voice of both interviewer and respondent, modifying turn-taking rules in order to do this.

Taking a broader view of the interviews as a whole, we can point to the adoption by caregivers of utterances that are questions but which at the same time contain enough information to build up into some sort of biographical story in answer to my questions (or what they believe my interests to be). Recipient design here means being able to convey enough information in questions to carry the biography of the confused speaker. This throws into doubt the ability of the interviewer to be successful in talking to the confused speaker. Everyperson questions will not work because of the specificity of recipient design required. The successful questioner is required to know both the biography and the capabilities of the respondent in order for a narrative to be developed.

Mr. Hoy's substantial interventions, which seemed designed to pass Mrs. Hoy off as normal in the conversation, can be seen as a structured way of helping her (and him) avoid loss of face. He is assisted in his task by Mrs. Hoy's compliance: She can still be relied on to present a second pair part for each first pair part. Equally important, by restricting herself to minimal second pair parts she avoids potential danger. Were she to engage in some topic development herself, the carefully built edifice might come tumbling down. The rare but problematic topic developments, evidenced in Extracts 4 and 5, illustrate this. However, this adds up to a presentation of Mrs Hoy's self that is managed more by her husband than by her. The fact that the biography has to be constructed by someone else in her presence, undermines it as a successful personal biography (although another reading of this situation is that Mr. Hoy construes himself and his wife as *we* in this situation and not as himself representing her).[8]

As I demonstrated, Mr. Hoy manages his wife's conversational interactions very tightly. He presents elicitations and she acknowledges them. As far as the substance of these conversational interactions is concerned, although she almost always only acknowledges what he says, her world is presented to her (and to me) as one in which she has a positive degree of participation, a world, in fact, on which she acts, as this extended version of Extract 16 shows:

Extract 20

Pam:	What else do you do here when you come here (.) at this day center?=
Mr. Hoy:	=Shouts bingo numbers out don't you?
	(.)

---

[8] This is a reading that incidentally can be seen to fit some of the creative turn taking I discussed earlier in this chapter.

Mrs. Hoy:	Yes=
Mr. Hoy:	=And she makes things.
	(.)
Mrs. Hoy:	Yeh.
Pam:	What sorts of things do you make?
	(2.5)
Mr. Hoy:	Makes some lovely things don't you? Pictures don't you?
Mrs. Hoy:	((Whisper)) Yeh.
Pam:	Oh and things like cards=
Mr. Hoy:	=Yeh.
	[[
Mrs. Hoy:	=Yeh.
Pam:	Birthday cards and=
Mrs. Hoy:	=Yeh=
	(.)
Mr. Hoy:	She made a Valentine card for me didn't you?
Mrs. Hoy:	Yes.

So now we have two strata of *as ifs*. First, Mr. Hoy has constructed the conversation as if his wife were participating as a normal participant and, second, he has constructed an agenda of events and activities that demonstrate that she does indeed take part normally in everyday life. And the following extract suggests a further aspect of the presentation of her self:

Extract 21

Mr. Hoy:	You just imagine people like Maisie if I just sat her in a chair at home after I got her ready in the morning.
Pam:	Yes.
Mr. Hoy:	It must be a long day for some people.
Pam:	Yes yes.
Mr. Hoy:	I always make it you know I put her in the chair.
Pam:	Yeh.
Mr. Hoy:	As I say when I ( ) do jobs I put her a record on I always put a record or the radio.
Pam:	Mmm.
Mr. Hoy:	She'll sit and listen while I do the work.
Pam:	Yeh.
Mr. Hoy:	As soon as I've done my work I put the dinner on and I take her a walk out to the shops don't I?
Mrs. Hoy:	Yes.
Mr. Hoy:	We go a nice walk round.
Pam:	Mm.
Mrs. Hoy:	Yeh.
Mr. Hoy:	Then er have a quiet afternoon and then if the weather's nice I take her another walk out at night she loves to go a walk round.

Mr. Hoy reports how he has constructed for his wife a daily routine that assumes her participation as a normal person, including her need for stimulus like anyone else. He has projected a continuation of the old Maisie into the current Maisie. Some of the literature on Alzheimer's disease remarks on the fact that it is very common for caregivers to suggest that the dementing person no longer has their real identity:

> She's not the person I married: she looks much the same, but she's a different person now. In one sense she's dead already—but still here in another. (Alzheimer's Disease Society, 1989, p. 12)

Caregivers may well mourn for the person who has gone away before they actually die, even while he or she continues to live in physical terms (Alzheimer's Disease Society, 1989). What seems to be involved here is that the presentation of self of the person with Alzheimer's has so little consistency with their presentation of self down through the years that the effort to maintain the sense of the continuity of self ceases to be worthwhile. Identity is lost or it becomes inconvenient for other people and challenges their own identities. This does not seem to be the case with Mr. Hoy, however, who skillfully stage-manages the situation to present his wife as a person who is still *as normal.* Mrs. Hoy obligingly presents no information to the contrary. This double act is accomplished in an environment that is not in itself quite normal. My interviews are a bit odd, but even so, Mr. and Mrs. Hoy present a joint performance in which she is constructed as a participating member. Furthermore (and my biographical approach may have emphasized this), Mrs. Hoy is given a normal past too, which is connected to a normal present by continuing preferences (one of the staples of identity): *she has always enjoyed going for walks* and so on.

Problematizing Identity. My final case of identity work relating to minimally active confused speakers involves Barry and Edith. It seems to me that here some rather different identity work is being done from the cases I have discussed so far, where normal identity was being oriented to.

In the interview, Barry takes over the role of being the person who speaks to Edith very early on. In fact, he intervenes to take a turn directly after my first (recorded) question to Edith. He then sets up a series of biographical questions that he expects Edith to be able to answer ("normally she'd be able to answer this"):

Extract 22

Barry:	Where were you born [...] Was it in Wolverhampton?
Edith:	Yes
[...]	
Barry:	Who's Tottie then?
Edith:	Ma mi mother.
Barry:	Oh that's your mother is it?
Edith:	Yes.
[...]	
Barry:	What's your father's name?
Edith:	My father's Baines.

This sequence (of which there are many similar ones in this interview) is comparable to what Dunn (reported in Goody, 1978) referred to as training questions:

In some middle class families almost everything parents say to children from about twelve months to two or three years is turned into a question. She [Dunn] calls these training questions, as they are not about the child's wishes and feelings but rather set problems. (Goody, 1978, p. 25)

In this case, the *set problem* has a wider reference, which is Barry's attempt to demonstrate to me the degree of recall that Edith has. Of course, this says something about how he perceives the nature of my interests. In Extract 22, most of Barry's questions are of the everyperson variety, suggesting that in his structuring of questions he has almost taken on the role of an interviewer unfamiliar with the interviewee. He disengages himself from his personal knowledge of Edith's history. Compare this with how Mr. Hoy might have formulated a couple of the questions in Extract 22:

You were born in Coventry, weren't you?
Your father's name was Baines, wasn't it?

The tag questions that Mr. Hoy uses not only give firm directions to his wife, they express a familiarity with the facts of her biography. Within a family, one would not normally expect people to use everyperson questions: It has a touch of the breaching experiment about it (Garfinkel, 1967). Indeed, part of the work of family members is to position themselves as exactly this, namely as people who are familiar with individual other members of the family. Everyperson questions are a correct and appropriate formulation for an interviewer, but could be seen as inappropriate for a relative.

A more pronounced example of Barry distancing himself from his role as a person familiar with Edith is shown in the following extract:

Extract 23

Barry:	Yes how old are you then now?=
Edith:	=Me?=
Barry:	=Mmm=
Edith:	=(How do you know?)
Barry:	Well how old are you?
Edith:	Ye do ye d I don't know that.
Barry:	You don't know who am I then?
Edith:	(Em) (2.7) ((Mutters))
	(2.0)
Barry:	Who am I then?
Edith:	Aye?
Barry:	((Low)) Who am I?
	(2.0)
Edith:	You like it.
Barry:	I like it but who am I?
	(11.9)
Pam:	I think perhaps [...]

As an interaction among intimates, this is very difficult to normalize. It perhaps could be one where a parent had dressed up and was trying to get a child to say who they thought the character was or something like that. But otherwise it places Barry in the situation of apparently not knowing something that people are generally expected to know: Who they are. And all this is for the purpose of demonstrating that Edith does not know people who she should know. Unlike Mr. Hoy, Barry does not always steer clear of questions that he knows that Edith cannot answer. At some points in the interview, he asks her questions that she answers incorrectly. For example, he asks if she is married and she says "No"; if she has any children, to which she replies "Yes"; and then eight utterances later he asks her again and this time she says 'No'. In his commentary to me, Barry says "Some days I'm her son Barry, some days I'm Uncle George, some days I'm her father, some days she doesn't know me at all." Presumably some of Barry's lines of questioning are deliberately intended to demonstrate what he already knows: That there are defects in Edith's ability to present her biography. However, it is interesting to note the Catch 22 situation in which confused speakers often appear to find themselves: that questions are asked of them that sometimes fly in the face of context. For a mother to be quizzed by her son about her family is a rather peculiar situation. Family members may possibly use a device like this to invite stories: "So Granddad lived in the East End did he?" but Edith does not respond to such questions as invitations to tell a story. Additionally, because she is a confused speaker, no one feels that they have to account for this oddity in the questions. It appears that aberrant talk on the part of a normal speaker can be excused here because of its metapurpose.

Although Barry is prepared to expose deficits in Edith's knowledge that are material to her identity, this is not an all-or-nothing strategy. He also constructs questions that ensure a good chance of Edith successfully answering them, and he comments on her successful presentation of biography and identity, as this next extract shows:

Extract 24

1. Barry:	What's Granddad's name? (2.3) What's your father's name?
2. Edith:	My father's, my father's Baines.
3. Barry:	Baines is it? (2.4) *You know that do you?*=
4. Edith:	=Yes=
5. Barry:	=What's his name what's his Christian name?=
6. Edith:	=He'd give you a fight=
7. Barry:	He'd give you a fight would he? *You can remember that can you?*=
8. Edith:	=Yes=
9. Barry:	=What's your father's name?
10. Edith:	((Mutters)) Mi dad=
11. Barry:	=What's your dad's name?=
12. Edith:	=((Mutters))
13. Barry:	What's your dad's name?
14. Edith:	My dad's?
15. Barry:	Yeh.
16. Edith:	Baines.

17. Barry:	*Do you remember that?*=
18. Edith:	=Yeh.
19. Barry:	What did your dad do?
20. Edith:	((Mutters))
21. Barry:	Was he in the army was he an army man?=
22. Edith:	=Yes he is=
23. Barry:	He's in the army is he? What did he used to do in the army?=
24. Edith:	=In the army he was a soldier=
25. Barry:	=He was a soldier was he?
	(1.2)
26. Edith:	Yeh (2.7) Didn't you know that?

In asking whether Edith's father was in the army, we can suppose that this question implies that he *was* in the army (it is unlikely that the questioner would have asked a series of random questions about possible occupations). The question being engineered in this way thus gives Edith the chance to answer minimally and correctly. In his questioning, Barry also draws attention to Edith's competence in presenting her biography. In the previous extract , I italicized comments in Utterances 3, 7, and 17 that focus on her knowledge and memory. Such remarks appear to commend Edith for these abilities; as if to say "I wouldn't have expected you to know/remember that." Yet, biographical resources are available to all ordinary members. In talking with others we can assume that we and they have in common access to details of biography; but this common access is not generally a mentionable item. I suspect that in normal circumstances people make comments like Barry's only when a memory feat is prodigious or unexpected. In commending Edith for being able to remember ordinary things, Barry marks out generally unmentioned aspects of what is considered to be ordinary competence, making them remarkable and drawing attention to the fact that when Edith does something ordinary and competent it is worthy of attention.

In their talk, members also need to identify the particularizing features of biographies that are not part of a common stock of knowledge available to all members and to accommodate for members for whom they are unlikely to be common knowledge. So it is worth mentioning that Barry is not always responsible for talk sequences that show Edith's biography to be problematic. It is something that she can also demonstrate for herself. In Extract 24, Utterance 26, where Edith expresses some incredulity that Barry may not know a fact that has just been mentioned, one interpretation is that she might be seen to be contesting the distanced persona that her son has developed. It is not clear whether she asks this question because she thinks Barry, as her son, should know the answer, or whether she thinks everyone should know. (This is, again, almost like Garfinkel's [1967] breaching experiments where students were asked to behave like lodgers and where family members became suspicious or cross or both.) On another occasion she asks me a similar question:

Extract 25

Pam:	Where is the (.) you don't know where the farm is now?=
Edith:	=No=
Pam:	=No=
Edith :	=You don't know?=
Pam:	=I don't know where it is either no [...]

People need to understand that their particularized biography will come as news to some people, and the two previous examples may suggest that Edith is not aware of which categories of people will find aspects of her biography news. Indeed, we might say that if she is not always aware that her son *is* her son, then the issue of what comes as news to whom must be, for her, a very complicated one. On the other hand, if she does not know whether she knows people, perhaps the issue of news has ceased to be an issue for her at all .

In his interviewing, then, Barry does not present his mother entirely as if everything were normal. He pays attention to problematizing the identity. His representation of the situation is that it is like being with a baby:

Extract 26

Pam:	What sort of conversational strategies do you try to actually keep it going?
Barry:	Light conversation obviously (6.0) It's difficult to say really baby talk I would say actually. You relate back to baby talk [...] I think what you do is go back to being in a baby situation, having a baby situation that's what you go back to because that's what they understand.

He has therefore found an identity for his mother to which he can relate. There is, however, an interesting paradox: Babies are not quizzed on their biographies, an activity that we have seen Barry undertake with his mother. Nevertheless, within this wider context of the *baby situation* he does distinguish between his mother in the situation of being interviewed and *normally*. Her presentation of self is not constant, but varies during the course of the day. To demonstrate this he asks his mother a lot of training type questions and often finishes a sequence with "Normally she'd just have it straight off, Normally she'd know all this straight off because this is the era." He insists that she is at her worst now, in the morning (when the interview is taking place). So even though he problematizes her identity, largely through setting up her defective presentation of biography, he still makes claims for her being more normal some of the time.

CONCLUSION

Confused speakers vary in the degree to which they participate in social interaction, and in this chapter I focused on a group of confused speakers I refer to as minimally active. I suggested that the presentation of the self of these speakers was to a great extent shaped by the interplay between the requirements of the interview situation, my use of the everyperson question format, and the development of particularistic biographies (often supplied by caregivers).

In the given circumstances, minimally active confused speakers do acknowledge TRPs, and respond and speak when selected, thus demonstrating some of the characteristics of normal talk. However, their contributions are usually very brief: They tend to take fewer turns than might be expected and to use shorter turn construction units than the context demands. Frequent minimal answers in an open-ended interview situation can be seen to demonstrate a minimal obligation to the conversation and a lack of context awareness of a refusal to acknowledge context.

Minimalism of this kind has implications for topic management. Minimally active confused speakers do only a very limited amount of work in keeping conversations going. Normal speakers therefore find ways of maintaining the social occasion. This almost inevitably involves them in speaking *for* minimally active confused speakers, correcting, prompting, or modeling what they take to be appropriate answers. Alternatively, and equally consequential for face, they may press respondents for a more proper rendition of this role. They may speak to the confused speakers, reformulating my questions as interviewer or generating new questions that can be answered minimally by the confused speaker. Finally, they may use the interview situation to problematize the identity of the confused speaker. Thus the deficits in the knowledge of minimally active confused speakers are manipulated in various ways by caregivers to present carefully constructed identities of the confused speaker and of themselves.

The primary requirement for the interviewees at these interviews was to be able to give some account of their own history. However, recounting one's past is a matter of competence that, of course can also be seen as a reflection of current competence in responding to occasion. A biography needs to be topically unfolded in a way that is appropriate to the occasion and for the person one is presenting oneself as. Particulars need to be filled in and to have some consistency within an everyperson framework. That is to say, biographical markers need to conform to what people recognize as possibilities for a viable biography. As Atkinson points out, you need the template of birth, school, marriage and so on against which to begin to measure individuals: the term *a late marriage* can only be understood if we understand at what ages marriages generally take place (M. A. Atkinson, 1973).

In most of the cases I discussed in this chapter, the evidence of incompetence in terms of biography is demonstrated not by what is said but by who says it. The template of an ordinary biography has been maintained, but usually only by caregiver intervention. This raises the question of the extent to which the biography and identity of a confused speaker can be viewed as competent if they are constantly being developed and adjusted by caregivers and normal speakers. One must be seen to be in charge of one's biography and identity: It comes with the territory of being an ordinary member. Commonsense practical reasoning is based on people having agency and position in the social world, and biography and identity are accounts of such agency and position. Although not being in charge of one's identity and biography may not be one's own fault, it leaves one without much currency to be able to do social intercourse.

The thrust of the chapter was to emphasize the ambiguities of the identity of minimally active confused speakers, and the extent to which these are orchestrated by normal speakers. They may be presented as competent through the work of others. One example of this is that when normal speakers make questions closed rather than open, minimally active confused speakers have a better chance of participating in the conversation. But, of course, the fact that normal speakers have to use such tactics betrays the incompetence of the confused speakers. Such work by normal speakers could be seen to imply that although the confused speakers are found wanting, the failing should not count against them. But the failings are of such a kind as to leave the confused speaker with little remainder as a person.

I think that there are wider implications to this analysis, which are about the elicitation of biographical detail from one member by another. In the cases I discussed, caregivers have to a great extent "taken charge" of the confused speaker's biography. There are issues both of context and membership involved in ascertaining the degree to which acting to elicit another's biography is appropriate. In the case of children, there often seems to be an ordinary member assumption that most of the devices I have discussed (perhaps with the exception of problematizing the identity) are appropriate with most children in most circumstances. Such devices disguise minimal response in a situation where an invitation to talk has been given, and they also model how to respond to such an invitation. Similarly, other groups accorded less-than-full membership may be prompted and directed into biographical disclosure by ordinary members who discern an occasion to require such talk. However, even when people are accorded ordinary membership, their biography is not their own exclusive conversational property. Others who are known to them may attempt to elicit specific details of which they are aware, depending on conversational context. And this again may be connected with identity work, where a hearer perceives a *biographical opening* for another participant who has not taken it up as a conversational project of their own. In such circumstances we can perhaps suggest that if a speaker who has been invited to talk about their biography now remains taciturn, he or she she is going to be seen as unforthcoming. Their participation in the conversation (or lack of it) will become marked by a noticeable absence of a response to the invitation to talk: I would suggest that this is consequential for understanding identity. The cases I discussed in this chapter were of people whose scant biographical disclosure is disguised by other participants. Because of understandings about the identity of confused speakers this biographical work on behalf of another is not deemed as pushy or presumptuous. However, where ordinary members offer up too little talk in response to an invitation to talk, other participants cannot easily take over the biography because to do this challenges the identity of another and possibly implicitly their own. To take over the telling of someone else's biography in their presence is, depending on context, one way in which to construct them as a less-than-full member. However, such a strategy may rebound uncomfortably, rendering the person who has taken over as someone unable to discern the proper conduct of ordinary membership him- or herself.

5

Moderately Active Confused Speakers

> Whatever you may think about what it is to be an ordinary person in the world, an initial shift is not think of "an ordinary person" as some person, but as somebody having as one's job, as one's constant preoccupation, doing "being ordinary" . . . a job that persons and the people around them may be coordinatively engaged in, to achieve that each of them, together, are ordinary persons. (Sacks, 1984, pp. 414–415)

As Sacks makes clear here, in an important respect, *being ordinary* is a job that people engage in on a daily basis. Furthermore, most of them have no difficulty with this task much of the time. By contrast, as I have shown, minimally active confused speakers seem to have renounced any attempt at being ordinary. Other confused speakers seem more aware of and committed to the achievement of normal interactional appearances. Included among these are those I refer to in this study as moderately active confused speakers. What I mean by this is that they often respond with turns longer than one word, frequently of one or more sentences; they seek clarification and self-select to take a turn on occasion; and finally, there are indications that some of them, at least, are well aware of the shortcomings of their conversational participation. Yet, paradoxically, because they take more part in conversations and therefore expose themselves to a greater extent, there are respects in which these conversationalists appear to be less successful than minimally active confused speakers. There are certainly a number of interactive troubles that we can observe in talk involving these speakers. Some of the problems in the talk and its repair are what might generally be called very ordinary troubles. However, the talk of this group of speakers also involves troubles that can be seen as less ordinary; these troubles focus not so much on the repair work itself but on what has to be repaired. Again, these troubles point up *what anyone should know* and thus should be of interest in the consideration of ordinary members' methodic practices.

I should say also, at this point, that many of the problems concerning what anyone should know are frequently heard used in various ways by ordinary members as sarcasm, irony, and jokes of various kinds: What anyone should know is a resource that can be utilized for implicative purposes. But almost invariably in such cases in the context of their ordinary membership the person(s) concerned are able to rely on such witticisms being seen implicatively. When someone has been assigned less-than-full membership bringing off implicative intent becomes a good deal more difficult. It is difficult to *do irony* when your membership is suspect. I hope that the illustrations used in this chapter will enable readers to reflect on the extent to which successful repair work in talk relies on full membership.

In the chapter I examine interviews with four speakers who are moderately active in their talk. I interviewed three of these speakers: Mrs. Inman had been diagnosed as suffering from confusion some time ago and was accompanied by her daughter, Mrs. Grace. Mrs. Walker, also accompanied by her daughter, Mrs. Becker, was 92 and had been referred because of suspected confusion and deafness. Mrs. Bowles, also, diagnosed as confused some time ago, was accompanied by her son. I also look at some aspects of Tom's interview with Mr. Graham. Mr. Graham was interviewed in the presence of his wife, who occasionally intervened and was also invited to speak at some points in the interview.

ORDINARY TALK

If we look at the patterns of participation of these moderately active confused speakers, we see that they are very different from those of minimally active confused speakers. Figure 5.1, provides information about relative lengths of turns. These speakers often took more turns in the conversation overall than the minimally active speakers. For example, Mrs. Walker took 190 turns in a conversation of 435 turns (44%)and Mrs Inman took 105 out of a total of 235 turns (45%). Mrs. Bowles only took 170 out of 630 turns (27%) but a substantial amount of the conversation involved her son talking about himself and she made little input to this talk. Likewise, in Tom's interview Mrs. Graham was invited to speak at length.

Figure 5.1 shows that moderately active confused speakers use a variety of turn lengths that are consistently longer than those of minimally active confused speakers, routinely producing utterances of longer than a sentence.

	Inman	Walker	Bowles	Graham
Number of turns	**105**	**190**	**170**	**34**
Word	33%	35%	23%	9%
Phrase	10%	12%	10%	9%
Clause	8%	3%	7%	6%
Sentence	32%	30%	24%	24%
> Sentence	15%	16%	36%	53%
Other		4%		

Figure 5.1. Percentage of turns taken.[1]

Such speakers thus demonstrate that they can hold on to the talk through TRPs. To take the example of Mrs. Inman, nearly half her turns were one sentence or longer, and about 2/3 of her turns were more than a minimal oneword answer. For example:

Extract 1

1. Mrs. Walker:	Yes I love whist.
2. Mrs. Becker::	How much do you win?
3. Mrs. Walker:	<u>Oh about a pound.</u>
4. Pam:	<u>Really</u>? Is that playing for pennies?
5. Mrs. Walker:	You pay thirty p for your game.
6. Pam:	Ah ah right so you win.
	[
7. Mrs. Walker:	You can get first half ladies or second half ladies=
8. Pam:	=Right=
9. Mrs. Walker	= And you get a pound if you get=
10. Pam:	[the lot.
11. Mrs. Walker:	= The highest number.
12. Pam:	Yes oh that's very good 'cos I play I play bridge but for pennies=
13. Mrs. Walker:	=That's a thing I'd love to do.

Here we see Mrs. Walker (in an ordinary member's judgment, probably the least confused speaker of all those interviewed) answering questions, that is, dealing adequately with second pair parts, taking turn at TRPs, answering according to the project of the question (Sacks, 1995a); and, in the case of Utterances 12 and 13, developing a relevant adjacent reply to a statement (Goffman, 1981). She answers my questions to provide some account of herself that is greater than the "yes" that would be literally acceptable on the basis of the questions. In short, there is nothing remarkable about this extract of talk; it is a perfectly ordinary interchange and is one of many in this conversation. Mrs. Bowles also produces talk that is normal in these respects. In Extract 2, Mrs. Bowles holds her turn through two interventions by me, producing a recipient-

---

[1] I have not included the groanings that Mr. Graham uttered at points when Tom was talking to Mrs. Graham, categorizing them as utterances away from turn.

designed response to my second intervention, accommodating the fact that I have inserted a correct and appropriate ending to her account of the pit cages.

Extract 2

Mrs Bowles:	Yes, mi dad he was an onsetter he worked at the pit but he didn't cut the coal he was on the=
	[
Pam:	Right.
Mrs Bowles:	=Chair on the cage to see the men got on and=
	[
Pam:	Up and down.
Mrs Bowles:	Exactly, that's right yes.

However, despite its structural normality, much of the talk of moderately active confused speakers nevertheless comes over, in various ways, as confused rather than normal. In this chapter, I want to explicate what it is about the talk that leads to this impression. Any conversation may have moments in it when there are confusions: What is characteristic of ordinary conversation is not that everyone always gets it right, but that when it goes wrong it is adequately repaired. In some of the data discussed in this chapter, however, the confusions tend to happen on a grand scale and in situations that would not, in normal circumstances, give rise to confusion. Moreover, a substantial amount of repair work done by the confused speakers is inadequate. I would suggest that there are requirements for normal interactional appearances other than the structural normality of talk. We can understand what some of these other requirements for normal interaction are by looking again at Grice's cooperative principle.

COOPERATION IN CONVERSATION

In chapter 1, I outlined the basic points of Grice's cooperative principle and its four conversational maxims: *quantity, quality, relation,* and *manner.* Grice (1975) went on to present, by means of analogies, some of the requirements for cooperation. For example, in relation to quantity, he noted that in mending a car the mechanic expects the helper to contribute four screws at the appropriate stage, not six or two. In relation to quality, contributions should be genuine, a spoon given to someone making a cake should be real and not rubber. In regard to relation, the contribution should be appropriate to the immediate needs of that particular stage of the transaction: If one is mixing the ingredients of a cake, one does not expect to be handed a good book. Finally, in regard to manner, the partner should make clear "what contribution he is making, and . . . execute his performance with reasonable dispatch" (1975, p. 47).

Applying Grice's maxims to the interview situation, we can suggest that in relation to quantity, the interviewer might expect, on asking an open probing question, to receive a fairly full answer, not a half-hour monologue, on the one hand, or a single-word reply, on the other. Correspondingly, in relation to quality, an interviewer might expect a straight answer to a question and not a riddle. The interviewer expects the answer that is given either to be relevant to the question that has just been asked, or to otherwise show some demonstrated relevance to an earlier part of the conversation. Finally, in relation to manner (which can be considered the *how* of conversation), the interviewer might expect the respondent to reply promptly, not to hesitate unduly, to remain seated rather than standing, not to groan, and so forth.

Any departure from the normal conditions of the cooperative principle may be seen as some kind of breach of that principle. Of course, we expect breaches in any conversation. However, what we also expect, on the whole, is that these breaches will be self-corrected or repaired in some way. But in order for this to happen, a participant must be aware of the normal proprieties as laid out in the conversational maxims.

I look at accidental breaches and situations both when people are unaware and when they are aware of what they have done. I then go on to explore deliberate breaches. All of these positions are ones that ordinary members generate and encounter. I hope, however, to demonstrate some unusual circumstances in which moderately active confused speakers take up these positions.

Lack of Awareness of Accidental Breaches

Consider the following example: In an unrecorded conversation when I sat in with the consultant at the psychogeriatric clinic a woman aged 86 contributed cooperatively, answering questions about her health in an appropriate manner, and concluded by saying something along the lines of "So while I'm now feeling much better my mother's still pretty poorly." This remark produced a certain *frisson* among those present, who all studiously avoided each other's eyes. Although it was possible that her mother was still alive (although this did not, in fact, turn out to be the case), it did present a problem to listeners. We know that people of 86 do not, as a general rule, have live mothers. We look to context and to a possible discrepancy. There is a question about the status of this remark: Is it true? The context presents the possibility that the maxim of quality has been breached. The woman presumably did not intend to violate the maxim and no one present challenged her, but the breach may be seen as having "confirmed" her confusion.

In my recorded interview material, the following extract demonstrates another accidental breach:

Extract 3

1. Pam:	So what do you do what do you do at these day centers then that you go to?=
2. Mrs. Bowles:	Er (.) I don't know really what *what* we're doing we we're just sitting around=
3. Pam:	=Yes.
4. Mrs. Bowles:	( ) I've only been once twice and er I don't er I've not got used to the people who=
	[
5. Pam:	Right.
6. Mrs. Bowles:	= Who visit and who've been going for some p'haps a few weeks=
7. Pam:	=Yes=
8. Mrs. Bowles:	=And they're used to it and they're
	[
9. Pam:	So you've got no real sense of what=
	[
10. Mrs. Bowles:	That's right.
11. Pam:	=What goes on=
12. Mrs. Bowles:	=No=
13. Pam:	=Have you been to other ones before?
14. Mr. Bowles:	Only the one no not there's one in not far from where we're living in Bessingham I live in Bessingham now.
15. Pam:	Yes.
16. Mrs. Bowles:	But when I was at home in a village that was a little welfare there=
17. Pam:	=Oh was there?=
18. Mrs. Bowles:	=But didn't I never went into the welfare but they had dances and things like that=
19. Pam:	=Oh I see.
	[
20. Mrs. Bowles:	But being an only child [...]

Because I have been referring to other day centers in my question in Utterance 1, I am assuming that any answer will be within this frame of reference. It is only in Utterance 20 that it starts to become clear that Mrs. Bowles is, in fact, talking about "the welfare" in her village when she was a child ("an only child" being a descriptor generally tied to the events of one's childhood). Mrs. Bowles is moving to a different stage in her biography without due referencing. "At home" in Utterance 16 seems a key phrase that requires me to understand that this was the home of her childhood rather than "When I was at home" in the sense of last weekend.

This raises the question of relevance. Perhaps we could say, in terms of conversation analysis, that we would expect the production of some kind of utterance that indicates a gear shift to a different range of knowledge (i.e., to mark that she has gone beyond the context offered by my questions, but that there is a link). In Sperber and Wilson's (1986) terms, possibly, she has not articulated the process of moving to what they call encyclopedic knowledge to answer a question. Moving to encyclopedic knowledge must necessarily be referenced in order to remain relevant. Indeed, there may be sanctions against this move as, for example, when people complain that someone is bringing up stories from their lives inappropriately.

The structure of a highly recognizable biography offered by the interviewer provides a broad context for appropriate relevant responses. This is perhaps more structured and offers more clues to the hearer than might, at first, seem to be the case. For example, in none of my interviews, including this one, did I pursue a biography from the person's current life and work backward. (Extract 3, which posed questions about Mrs. Bowles's current life, took place very near the end of the interview.) The order was chronological, as commonly understood, a developmental approach: born, brought up, school, work, marriage, children, moving, and so on. Within this framework, people may reasonably suppose that after questions about where they were born, they will be asked questions about their young life. Conversely, if they are asked questions about their recent biography, for example in the case of the discussion with Mrs. Bowles about which day centers she attends, we can expect that they must justify introducing other more distant aspects of their biography.

Extract 3 is not the only occasion when I had problems with Mrs. Bowles' handling of biography:

Extract 4

1. Pam:	So your family was a a mining family=
2. Mrs. Bowles:	=Yes=
3. Pam:	=Ah ah and did
	[
4. Mrs. Bowles:	But I was a lone girl they hadn't any children at all=
5. Pam:	=Who didn't?
6. Mrs. Bowles:	=I always called them dad and mum I always called them mum and dad=
7. Pam:	=Yes=
8. Mrs. Bowles:	=And previous to that I wa they adopted me you see.

In this extract, Mrs. Bowles presents her story in such a way as to create a problem for the listener. One possible inference from Utterance 4 is that the "they" she refers to were her parents and if so, the utterance does not seem to make any sense. Mrs. Bowles appears to have violated the maxim of manner, specifically the submaxim *Be orderly*. She opens up the possibility of a biographical fact that is unusual, that of being orphaned, but in such a manner as not to prepare but to confuse the hearer. Her construction of a biography at this point, far from answering the interviewer's questions without problems, is likely to require other questions to get this all sorted out.

Unfolding a chronology in an order that might present problems for listeners is something that anyone might do. However, what we would expect to happen in such circumstances is that they would, in the interests of cooperation, correct the confusion. But Mrs. Bowles does not appear to have any awareness of the problem she has created for at least one listener (the interviewer).[2] If, in such circumstances, the teller does not show awareness of the breach, then we would expect one of the listeners to correct or to ask for clarification. Here I seek clarification (and the tone of my voice is quite mystified in Utterance 5). But her response does not seem to acknowledge the significance of the question and she continues to unfold the biography in her own chosen order, where adoption is a punch line rather than a prior contextual requirement.

The following extract is taken from Tom's conversation with Mr. Graham and demonstrates accidental breaches in a situation where the questions are much more tightly structured:

Extract 5

1. Tom:	Can I ask you do you know what (.) what time of the year it is now? (3.6)
2. Mr. Graham:	What do you mean er months?=
3. Tom:	Su summer or winter or autumn?
4. Mr. Graham:	Well I I say it's (.) anticipating the spring.
5. Tom:	Right that's it, yes do you know what month it is?
6. Mr. Graham:	Yes er er er second month Jan <u>February</u>.
7. Tom:	That's right and do you know can you remember the date that it is today?
8. Mr. Graham:	((Coughs)) The date it is ((Coughs)) today somewhere about (.) 20th init Lily or something?
9. Tom:	Yes, it's a bit later that that, it's the 26th I think=
10. Mr. Graham:	=Oh the 26th yes=
11. Tom:	What about the day of the week do you know what day it is?=
12. Mr. Graham:	=This yeh it's Friday isn't?=
13. Tom:	Well that's near enough it's Thursday today=
14. Mr. Graham:	=Oh <u>Thurs</u>day=
15. Tom:	=But that's pretty good really.

In this extract, Tom asks a number of questions that can be seen to be intended to examine Mr. Graham's awareness of the here and now: about time, season, month, date, and day. Such formulations are common in assessments for people with mental health problems, where getting answers right is treated as a display of normality. These correct answers are knowledge that is publicly available to all ordinary members. To get them wrong is immediately to expose oneself as not normal in some sense; even though normal members might sometimes have difficulties with them.

In some respects, Mr. Graham can be seen to respond cooperatively. He asks a relevant question (Utterance 2) in order to check, presumably, that he can give a true answer to Tom's question (maxim of quality). In terms of the maxim of quality more generally, Mr. Graham qualifies two

---

[2] It seems likely that her son would know she had been adopted and so for him the chronology as unfolded would not presumably pose such problems. This would seem to be an indication of the context sensitivity of the maxim of manner—that orderliness is required to orient to the hearers.

of his answers with tag questions (Utterances 8 and 12) in such a way as to disclaim certain knowledge. That is to say, he suggests that he thinks these answers are true but alerts the other speaker to the fact that he may be wrong and that he is open to correction. Both these qualifiers might also be seen as acknowledging his own role in answering test questions. In each instance, Mr. Graham's response is as informative as required, providing an answer and on two occasions setting that information against the maxim of quality (Utterances 8 and 12). However, his reply in Utterance 2 "anticipating the spring" could be said to cause problems in relation to the maxim of manner, in that it introduces an unwarranted element of obscurity into the conversation. Although correct, the use of poetic rather than precise terms, given the testing nature of the questions, might be viewed as inappropriate. Overall, Mr. Graham appears to be trying to behave cooperatively in the conversation but simply cannot reliably supply the information that people are assumed to have about ordinary but key matters in everyday life. In this light, it is interesting that in Utterances 10 and 14 the tone of Mr. Graham's voice is rather similar to the tone people adopt when they have given the wrong answer in a quiz—a sort of "Oh I should have known that, I could kick myself" tone. Such a tone might be appropriate and face saving when one fails to answer a question in a quiz about the protagonists in the Hundred Years War: Indeed, the tone implies "I knew that really." However, that stance is not one that is generally expected when talking about today's date.

In the examples discussed so far, I implied that interactional problems may arise for the participants from accidental breaches of the cooperative principle. Above all, issues of face may arise. A number of authors have made links between Grice's initial work on the cooperative principle and the concept of face. Leech developed what he termed the politeness principle. If someone says "Cold in here isn't it?", this is a request to shut the window that is not as informative as it could be but, by that very fact, maintains politeness and is face saving in a way that a blunt directive such as "Switch on the heater" could not be (Leech, 1983). Brown and Levinson (1978) developed a more elaborate schema linking the cooperative principle with strategies that may be used to deal with what they called face-threatening acts. Elaborating on Goffman's notion, they defined face as follows:

> 'Face', the public self-image that every member wants to claim for himself, consisting in two related aspects:
>
> (a) negative face: the basic claim to territories, personal preserves, rights to non-distraction—i.e. to freedom of action and freedom from imposition

(b) positive face: the positive consistent self-image or 'personality' (crucially including the desire that this self-image be appreciated and approved of) claimed by interactants. (p. 66)

We might rephrase this as the want to be left alone and the want to be positively recognized. In relation to Grice's conversational maxims Brown and Levinson suggested that: "face redress is one of the basic motives for departing from the maximally efficient talk that the Maxims define" (p. 276).

However, if a participant in a conversation fails to recognize that face has been threatened, as is the case with the accidental breaches to the cooperative principle, then people's behavior, we assume, will continue on the same trajectory. This poses a problem for others present. They can either make the issue of face explicit or they can leave the breach unattended. I would suggest that people who rarely adjust after accidental breaches of the cooperative principle may be viewed as insensitive or overbearing. Ordinary member judgments are often quite sharp on this, as common sayings such as "a bull in a china shop" attest. And yet if there appears to be doubt about membership in some cases, such judgment may be reserved.

In the case of the 86-year-old woman I discussed, no attempt was made by anyone present to suggest that her mother was not alive. In one respect this can be seen to be collusion among normal speakers to allow her face to be maintained. It might even be viewed as a form of consideration for negative face, that is, not to impose on the world she has constructed for herself, which includes a live mother. But at the same time, everyone knew that she had made a serious breach of conversational cooperation, so that another way of looking at it is that the collusion was an acknowledgment that she was stigmatized, not a full member, and that there was therefore no point in requiring a repair. Repair is not a pathological aspect of conversation: It is a normal part of it. Therefore, if a repair is not required of a participant who has made a noticeable error, then he or she is not being treated as a full participant. As I noted in chapter 1, one of the questions addressed in this study is whether confused speakers are directed by normal speakers through repair and correction back into full membership or whether they are left as less-than-full members. In the case of the woman I just discussed, the nonactivity of the normal speakers can be seen as an acknowledgment of less-than-full membership.

In the case of Extract 3, I did not request correction although it took me a further utterance (about being an only child) to be able to contextualize what Mrs. Bowles meant by "at home" and thus to understand which "welfare" she was referring to. In all repair and correction work, the further away from the delict a correction request is placed, the more difficult matters become, perhaps indicating a threat to face of the potential challenger for not paying sufficient attention to be able to make the request immediately. In Extract 4, I did request correction, only to have my request ignored. Not only did Mrs. Bowles fail to appreciate that she had accidentally breached a conversational maxim, she failed to appreciate that face was being challenged, which suggests a lack of context sensitivity both in regard to her own presentation of a narrative and to the occasion more generally.

In the case of Extract 5, Tom corrected Mr. Graham on each occasion he breached the maxim of quality. If Tom was testing Mr. Graham on the basis of what normal members know, then not to correct would have been to confirm Mr. Graham's less-than-full membership. In fact, what Tom did was to occupy a sort of half way house where he both corrected and offered a saving of face to Mr. Graham by saying things. like "It's near enough." However, when one excuses people for being "near enough" where in ordinary member terms everyone should get the answers right, that too engenders face difficulties.

Awareness of Accidental Breaches

I spoke earlier of the extent to which moderately active confused speakers expose themselves in conversation. In some cases they appear to be aware that they are breaching some principle but are unable to repair or correct in such a way as to achieve adequate face redress:

Extract 6

Tom:	[...] How long have you lived here?
Mr. Graham:	((Groans for 3.8 seconds)) (3.1) Something about ten years isn't it? Nayy (2.8) twenty ohm.

In some respects this is a perfectly ordinary repair following an accidental breach and orienting to the maxim of quality: question—response—adjustment of reponse. We all do it probably a dozen times a day (What's the time?"—" Half past six, no 25 to seven"). However, we may suggest that Mr. Graham's response is seriously problematic in terms of the maxim of quality. There are aspects of biography that no adult normal speaker might feel a loss of face about not being able to recall (e.g., "Name six people in your class in your first year at school." would be a real show stopper asked of a middle-aged adult, but an answer might be expected of a seven year old). But there are other aspects that anyone would be expected to answer. Mr. Graham copes with his difficulty in this respect by indicating a margin of possible error and providing two answers. The first of these strategies would be appropriate in some circumstances, but it is perhaps questionable in this context. The production of two answers is even more problematic, not least because it is not clear whether the second was intended to nullify the first, and yet there is considerable discrepancy between them. Ten years or 20 years may be all right if we are talking about events a thousand years ago (well within appropriate margins), but it is too great a discrepancy when talking about how long one has lived in one's current house. However, even though the self-correction is apparently valid (not being challenged by Mrs. Graham), to have to correct by such a wide margin how long one has lived somewhere can be seen to threaten face. I have to also say that it is possible that someone prompted Mr Graham after he had said "ten years" because "years" ends with a slight questioning uplift and there is a subsequent pause before he says "twenty". Nevertheless, even if another person corrected him, the error from the first guess is still great enough to suggest that his information about ordinary chronological markers in his life is suspect.

A more spectacular example of problematic correction work comes from an Open University (1990) video we made for the course "Working with Older People", where an older woman talking in a reminiscence group makes several attempts at saying how many siblings she has.

Extract 7

Facilitator:	How many brothers and sisters did you have when you were small?
	[
Woman:	Er er er eight.
Facilitator:	<u>Eigh</u>t.
Man:	Oh quite big yes.
	[
Woman:	Yes.
Facilitator:	And how many left now?=
Woman:	=No oh oh yes there is there's one cos he's coming down cos=
Facilitator:	=Yes=
Woman:	Coming down to see us see er er his wife died and of course he's alone that's the only one oh no two three I think ((Laughs nervously)) No there's erm there's Alice and she's not well er and there's there's er what's the ( ) (2.0) I've forgot now I er er er I can't think you know oh my er he's coming to er give us some dinner and make a dinner for us and er he's the the boy.
Facilitator:	He's the youngest is he?
Woman:	Yeh yeh.

Again there are many circumstances in which one might use this sort of numerical adjustment: "How many people were there at the party?"— "20, no 25, just possibly 30." We can see such adjustment occurring as one reviews the scene in one's mind's eye—there must have been 10 people in the kitchen, a dozen or so in the drawing room—oh yes and there were probably about 5 or 6 in the hall. The person responding is orienting to the maxim of quality. But to have to make such an adjustment in an area of ordinary life that is seen as given, something you really should know, becomes problematic.

Such self-repair work is face threatening and in this case the woman, judging from the expression on her face, the plucking of her collar, and the hiding of her face with her hands, becomes more and more anxious as she realizes she is not getting it right.[3] The repair work is unsolicited and as she speaks she makes several amendments. However, a repair having been instituted needs to be right, because the more failed repair attempts someone makes, the more his or her credibility and face are damaged. So it may be that the clever thing to do is in some way to acknowledge the mistake but to back off from doing the repair. This woman starts to do this, claiming she has forgotten, but then continues to plough on with the disastrous self-repair work. This makes the facilitator's job difficult. In the face of continuing self-corrections, which is she to take as correct? When will the repair stop? In fact, what she does is to ignore completely all the attempts at self-correction and allude only to the woman's final statement—a common face-saving strategy. This preserves face, to some extent, and avoids the difficult issue of what full members are expected to know.

Mrs. Inman shows a different pattern of self-awareness:

Extract 8

1. Pam:	Right and can you re remember anything about that? (.) How little you were when you left there?
	(1.7)
2. Mrs. Inman:	Well I can't quite put anything really what we were like because there were were seven of us.
	(.)
3. Pam:	And where were you, sorry were where were you in a family of seven?=
4. Mrs. :Inman:	=Yes=
5. Pam:	=But which number were you?=
6. Mrs. Inman:	We were all children.
7. Pam:	( ) Were you the little girl at the end?=
8. Mrs. Inman:	=We went to school=
8. Pam:	=Yes=
9. Mrs. Inman:	( ) But it were only one building=
10. Pam:	=Right=
11. Mrs. Inman:	=That's if I'm doing it right.
	(.)
12. Pam:	Sounds alright to me and you were at school in Alderidge=
13. Mrs. Inman:	=((Low))Yes=
14. Pam:	And and so when did you move to Bessingham?
	(3.10)
15. Mrs. Inman:	It were when the I think it were when we started going to work or them things you know=
16. Mrs. Grace:	=No Mum you came to Bessingham when you got married to Dad.
	(.)
17. Mrs. Inman:	Aye?=
18. Mrs. Grace:	=You came to Bessingham when you got married to Dad=
19. Mrs. Inman:	=There's a fair bit I don't remember.

In this exchange, the maxims that appear to be violated are those of quantity, quality, and relevance. Mrs. Inman is not as informative as is

---

[3] Seeing this on video provides a strong visual reminder of how much issues of face can be manifested on *someone's face*.

required, she gives inaccurate information, and she can be seen to give irrelevant answers. However, she does recognize some of this and provides an excuse.

As I noted in the previous chapter, M.A. Atkinson (1973) suggested that in order to establish a particularized version of someone's biography, there needs to be a generalizable biography that is highly recognizable and anonymous. Here the questions posed by me are a combination of the use of a generalized biography (when someone went to school, how many children there were in the family) and particularized refinements (asking where she was placed in a family of seven), on an everyperson assumption that anyone will know their own placement in a family of seven. Although the question "When did you come to Bessingham?" permits more than one correct answer (e.g., "1940", or an answer relating to work, family or marriage and so on), Mrs. Inman chooses to say that it was related to work and is corrected by her daughter, who links it instead to getting married. So Mrs. Inman links the wrong set of biographical information to an event. She also fails to understand two of my questions completely (Utterances 3 and 5) as they begin to move on to anticipate more specific answers: Though of course, this may be a result of the way that I phrased the questions.

However, although Mrs Inman may be anxious in this situation, she continues to contribute to the conversation by offering comments on quality: She acknowledges the need to try to be correct and cooperative. Given the apparent shortfalls in her knowledge, Mrs. Inman has to try to remain cooperative while at the same time being less informative than required. She can do this, perhaps, by orienting to maxims other than that of quantity. And this may be a strategy that can be used by confused speakers in order to maintain face: to prioritize a conversational maxim they can cope with over others that they cannot. Mrs. Inman offered several such disclaimers during the interview:

Extract 9

Pam:	What programs do you like? (2.8) What program do you like? What programs do you turn on for?=
Mrs. Inman:	=I don't can't pronounce them properly when you ask like that (.) because you know I don't know [...]

Extract 10

Pam:	So what so when you go back today what will you do for the rest of the day?
	(.)
Mrs. Inman:	I can't tell you I don't know=
Pam:	=You don't know what do you do most days?
	(.)
Mrs. Inman:	Well I can't tell you much about it really.
	[
Mrs. Grace:	You [...]

We could suggest that in saying "I don't know", Mrs. Inman prioritizes the maxim of quality: She does not say that for which she has inadequate evidence and she does not say something she believes to be false. The problem with all of this is that people are expected, as a general rule, to be able to answer questions about their own history and their current lives. In substantive terms, in a conversation about one's own biography we might expect the maxim of quality to be unproblematic to the teller of the biography. Yet in Extracts 8, 9, and 10, we see problems with biographical information in a variety of contexts, not only in relation to long- and short-term biography, but relating to routine daily activity as well. The inadequacy of Mrs. Inman's knowledge is, in ordinary member terms, comprehensive: It is not just a momentary lapse. Avoidance of providing information about one's own biography raises yet more questions relating to face. Here, prioritizing one maxim over another (but having to do it frequently and in a number of contexts) can be seen to involve the unhappy tactic of trying for the least loss of face rather than avoiding losing face altogether.

So when Mrs. Inman is aware that she is in danger of not getting it right, she usually draws back from answering or makes an excuse. On other occasions she seeks corroboration step-by-step ("That's if I'm doing it right"). Although the cooperative principle is threatened very frequently in everyday conversation, normal speakers have strategies for its repair. Mura Swan (1983) discussed licensing for violations and cited such licences as "I'm trying to think", "Oh I'm sorry I really have been rambling on", "Before we were so rudely interrupted", and so on. Brown and Levinson (1978) discussed hedges used in cooperative conversation and suggested that conversational participants adjust the emphases in conversation drawing attention to the maxim to which they are orienting and guarding themselves against misrepresentation: "To the best of my recollection" (quality), "I don't know whether you're interested" (relevance) and so on (p.174). So "If I'm doing it right" can be seen as a perfectly ordinary conversational device that might be used by anyone, in certain circumstances. However, the problem here lies in the area for which Mrs. Inman is seeking the license, that is (what should be) familiar aspects of her own biography. In response to Mrs. Inman's orientation to the maxim of quality I answer encouragingly. But I am unable to provide corroboration about the knowledge itself. And I am an inappropriate person for her to ask whether she is "doing it right" in terms of quality, in this instance. Interviewers can be expected to develop a framework that is recognizable as one on which people can build their own biography, but they cannot usually comment on the veracity of any particulars that are stated.

So Mrs. Inman presents a sort of cusp case between being unaware of the maxims and therefore accidentally violating them, and deliberately breaching them for some implicative purpose. That is to say, she is aware that she has breached them, or may have done so, and that she might not be able to repair them adequately.

Other confused speakers, aware that they did not have the knowledge required, engaged in a dialogue with caregivers and asked for help to provide an answer that accommodated the conversational maxims. This indicates that an extra step is required that the confused speaker cannot provide:

Extract 11

Pam:	And so when did you move away from that village?=
Mrs. Bowles:	=When was it?=
Mr. Bowles:	=((Low)) During the war=
Pam:	=((Low)) During the war=
Mr. Bowles:	=((Low)) During the war=
Mrs. Bowles:	= ((Low)) Yes (.) it must have been.

Again, this raises the issue of how much of one's own biography one is expected to have access to in order to maintain face as an ordinary member. On the one hand, we can suggest a similar interpretation to that in Extract 6—that people should know when they moved where. On the other hand, we could say that, in this instance, Mrs. Bowles' invitation to her son to join in the conversation implies that she sees this as one of the more murky areas of biography where it is legitimate to seek additional information from knowledgeable others. We could suggest by this that Mrs. Bowles is employing face-work that brushes aside the threat to face and maintains the conversation as per normal. Indeed, the quiet low tone of all parties who take part in this exchange suggests that it is conducted as a consultation aside from the conversation—a discussion that is legitimate, not face threatening. Goffman, of course, outlined the refusal to take challenges to face as one form of face-work (Goffman, 1969). In some sense this reflects the point I noted about Mrs. Bowles' accidental breaches of which she was unaware, cases where she treated a challenge to face as an ordinary question.

Deliberate Breaches

Until now I have treated Grice's maxims as if they controlled ordinary talk or ought to do so, and have shown how confused speakers who are able to operate the basic machinery of conversational interaction often fall afoul of these maxims. However, only a little reflection will reveal that much ordinary conversation fails to meet the requirements of these maxims not just as a result of accident, but by design. Indeed, Grice himself was well aware of this. He saw the maxims as oriented-to features in conversations, not as rules that are always obeyed. For example, he posited four common violations of the cooperative principle that I have summarized in the following list (from Grice, 1975, p. 49). He suggested that people may:

- Violate a maxim "quietly and unostentatiously"which may be "liable to mislead";
- Opt out from the maxim and more generally from co-operation (I'm afraid I couldn't possibly comment) ;
- Be faced by a clash of maxims so that choosing one maxim violates another;
- Flout a maxim, blatantly fail to fulfil it i.e., exploit it.

In his examples of conversational implicature, Grice cited a number of readily recognizable conversational gambits (some of which I list here): damning with faint praise, irony, metaphor, meiosis, hyperbole, and obscurity in terms (e.g., spelling out words in front of children or dogs so that they will not understand, but the other participating conversationalists will). Implicature is a way of saying more with words than the words themselves convey. In order for it to be successful it needs to be context sensitive, as Grice's example of spelling out words in front of children illustrates: There would usually be little point in spelling out words in front of those who could already spell them and thus understand immediately what was being said.[4]

One of the things conversational implicature can do, then, is to perform some activity that does not become explicit interactional business in conversation (in the case just cited, hiding of facts or proposals from children precludes the possibility of them becoming their interactional business). In her discussion of embedded correction, Jefferson (1987) noted in relation to explicit correction that what has been going on before the correction stops, that accounting takes place during the correction (i.e., instructing, admitting, apologizing), and that after the correction, the corrected person reiterates the correction: All this suggests a distinct episode where correction becomes the business of the conversation. Jefferson went on to note that "the talk which constitutes embedded correction does not permit of accountings" (p. 95). Following from this idea of embeddedness it can be seen that conversational implicature can be used to produce social action that is not explicit interactional business. For example, damning with faint praise can be seen to perform the act of criticizing.

So, for implicature to come off, that is, for no accounting to be required, participants need to be context aware, both of the local

---

[4]Though it might be possible to imagine cases where this would be done, for example, as a challenge to the face of an ostensibly competent, literate adult. More generally though, spelling things out is reserved for certain categories of people—those who are in some way not up to speed.

environment and of the other participants. Otherwise they risk their obscurity, hyperbole, ellipsis, and so forth being misunderstood, challenged, and made accountable. Nevertheless, when accounting *is* demanded, the speaker can point back to the words themselves and suggest the action was not, in fact, performed.

Given, then, that violation of the maxims, both accidental and intended, is common and is, in fact, part of ordinary talk, why do the breaches of the maxims I examined in this chapter come across as signs of confusion rather than as ordinary talk? As I already noted, one kind of orientation to the maxims is correction. Errors may be made in relation to these maxims, of the kinds I have noted confused speakers making, but one would expect self-correction when the error becomes apparent. Moreover, when the violation of a maxim becomes part of the interactional business of conversation, then the correction must be correct. However, I suggested that moderately active confused speakers do not always engage in corrections when maxims have been breached, and when they do so they may fail to bring off the corrections effectively, one problem being the inadequacy of their correction.

The following extract illustrates some of the issues of the relation between the conversational maxims and implicature that arise in the case of one moderately active confused speaker:

Extract 12

1. Tom:	I'd just like to ask you a question about your house=
2. Mr. Graham:	=Beg your pardon?=
3. Tom:	=You've lived here a long time in this house.
	(.)
4. Mr. Graham:	Yes well what do you call a long time?=
5. Tom:	=Well you tell me how long have you lived here?
6. Mr. Graham:	((Groans for 3.8 seconds)) (3.1) Something about ten years isn't it? Nayy (2.8) twenty ohm.
7. Tom:	About twenty years.
	((Mr Graham groans for 1.9 seconds))
8. Tom:	I've noticed that the toilet's outside is that a problem for you?
9. Mr. Graham:	Erer well in a way yeyes but it's er the trou the er I don't know whether you've been out there and had a look at it have you?=
10. Tom:	=I haven't seen in seen inside it no=
11. Mr. Graham:	=No well that's for that's for you to (1.6) look inside.

In this exchange, Mr. Graham puts Utterances 1 and 3 back to Tom by asking a question (Utterance 4) that suggests that Tom has not been informative enough for him (Mr. Graham) to engage in a truthful exchange. If he does not know what a long time is then how can he answer the question as posed? Here we see Mr. Graham performing his own breaching experiment, bacause although Tom's question permits a number of both correct and appropriate answers (e.g, "Since the war", "Since we got married", "Since 1945" all of which might define "a long time"), Mr. Graham is taking a very precise view of it. It seems to me that this exchange links with Extract 5 (three utterances occurred between the two exchanges recorded in Extract 5 and 12). In Extract 5, Tom asks questions about times and dates. There, precise, correct answers are called for and each time Tom feeds back comments about correct answers. Now it seems that Mr. Graham is testing out the issue of precision again. Is it a precise answer that is required? In other words, is the maxim of quality being viewed as paramount in this situation? Utterances 8 to 11 show Mr. Graham almost modeling himself on Tom as a test questioner. Again after a topic shift by Tom he puts the problem back to Tom as test questioner (Utterance 9), just as Tom had done to him (Utterance 5—"Well you tell me"). He then goes on to offer a sort of challenge to Tom: Utterance 11, Mr. Graham's *coup de grâce*, obscurely answers Tom's question—if Tom looks inside the outhouse he will understand whether it is a problem. So he has addressed the question by thrusting responsibility on Tom. In a sense this can be seen as opting out of the maxim of quality. It is not exactly "My lips are sealed", it is more elliptical than that, suggesting that if Tom wants to discover the truth of the situation he must seek it himself. This could almost be seen as a defense of negative face, a suggestion that the social action Tom has performed with this question was an imposition: In his own defense Mr. Graham challenges Tom's face.

In continuing my discussion of implicature, I want to examine a complex example of its use that creates an impression of a confused speaker. In an interview with Mrs. Inman, a packet of photographs is produced of the wedding of her grandson, which had taken place on the previous Saturday. Her daughter, Mrs. Grace, begins to ask her various questions about the photographs:

Extract 13

1. Mrs. Grace:	Now who are they?
	(2.6)
2. Mrs. Inman:	Well that's your daughter=
3. Mrs. Grace:	=Yeh who is she to you?
	[
4. Mrs. Inman:	And that's her husband she's er aunt to me=
5. Mrs. Grace:	=She isn't=
6. Mrs. Inman:	=I mean I'm aunt to her=
7. Mrs. Grace:	=No she's your granddaughter.

We may suggest that the initial stage of this exchange is a comparable situation to that of formulating place: The formulation not only needs to be correct, it needs to be appropriate. In his discussion on formulating place, Schegloff (1972a) noted:

> The "problem" of locational formulation is this: for any location to which reference is made, there is a set of terms each of which, by a correspondence test, is a correct way to refer to it. On any actual occasion of use, however, not any member of the set is "right." (p. 81)

In Utterance 2, Mrs. Inman presents a correct formulation: It could, at a first reading, be seen as an instance of what Grice (1975) called generalized implicature:

> Sometimes one can say that the use of a certain form of words in an utterance would normally (in the ABSENCE of special circumstances) carry such-and-such an implicature or type of implicature . . . Anyone who uses a sentence of the form X *is meeting a woman* this evening would normally implicate that to be person he met was someone other than X's wife, mother, sister or perhaps even a close platonic friend. (p. 56)

For a woman to use "your daughter" to describe her own granddaughter may imply a degree of censure (as when a woman might say to her partner "Your son broke the dining room window today" in order to make a certain point, distancing herself from the behavior and aligning it with her partner). It could be seen by coconversationalists as a marked choice from a number of correct terms. However, in Utterance 3, Mrs. Grace asks her to choose an appropriate formulation, thus indicating that a marked use of the term "your daughter" is inappropriate. Her question also indicates the form of an appropriate response in these circumstances, which is to establish the relationship Mrs. Inman has with the person in the photograph. So here we have a situation where the notion of implicature is almost inverted. That is, Mrs. Grace discerns that Mrs. Inman's words are saying more than they should have. However, as the exchange goes on, Mrs. Inman fails to give even a correct but inappropriate formulation (in Utterance 5, Mrs. Grace challenges the correctness of the formulation). As the episode unfolds it appears that Mrs. Inman cannot articulate what her own relationship is with the young woman in the photograph. Such incompetence can be seen to be charming in small children when they think their own father is their grandmother's father, but adults are expected to know these things.

Talking about photographs can be seen as yet another manifestation of biography: People are expected to be able to articulate aspects of their biography from the story that photographs tell. They are expected to give a correct formulation and they are expected to be able to deal with appropriate naming of close relatives for the context. Moreover, they are expected to be able to name those in the photographs in such as way as to accommodate what they know of the person to whom they are showing the photographs. That is to say, among close family members they might say "Tommy is a devil", whereas to others they would need to say that Tommy was their grandson and that he had just buried his father in the sand when this photograph was taken. So, given a medium that might be seen to be unproblematic for most people as a platform for handling their biography, Mrs. Inman fails to perform competently.

INTERVIEWS, COOPERATION, AND FACE

So far, I have examined cooperation and face by means of a number of extracts from my data, but have only made passing comments about the context of the interview.

An interview places particular constraints on face. It is a sort of trade-off between positive and negative face on both sides. For example, in an ethnographic interview an interviewer would expect to facilitate positive face as much as possible on the part of the respondent. To do anything that may damage the face of the respondent might be seen as undermining the usefulness of the interview. On the other hand, investigative television reporters are adept at impinging on negative face, and shape many of their interactions with respondents using this tactic: They may impose on territory that is personal and private and by focusing on negative face, they provide no opportunity for the other to promote positive face. However, any interview may be seen as a potential challenge to the face, of the respondent. Questions asked by the interviewer are not necessarily predictable to the respondent, and each requires the respondent to answer in a way that maintains his or her line (Goffman, 1969). When respondents evade answering questions, it is risky because this may suggest that they are having difficulty in maintaining their line. And if they choose to answer questions, they must do so in a way that does maintain their line. Additionally, to be successful the line must be consistent with the line that should be taken at an interview. For a respondent to clam up completely certainly is a line, but not one that is appropriate.[5]

As I have suggested throughout this study, the interview is a joint construction and the cooperation and face-work of the confused speaker is complemented by that of normal speakers. As Goffman (1969) noted, "in many relationships, the members come to share a face, so that in the presence of third parties an improper act on the part of one member becomes a source of acute embarrassment to the other members" (p. 34).

In the last chapter, I considered a group of confused speakers who were very unforthcoming. The involvement of the caregivers in the conversation was, on the whole, extensive: assisting in answering questions appropriately, or asking appropriate questions for the confused speaker to answer. In the case of moderately active confused speakers we might expect, perhaps, a greater predominance of self-correction, thus obviating the need for caregivers to intervene. However, as I have shown, self-correction on the part of the confused speakers does not always solve problems of either cooperation or face. Caregivers do

---

[5] I have already alluded to the problems that arise when minimally active speakers do not speak in interviews, although not specifically in relation to face.

generally intervene from quite early on, claiming the status of interactants rather than witnesses to the event. The primary issue relating to face for normal speakers would appear to be the problem of the confused speaker's inadequate biography for the occasion, which puts the cooperative principle under pressure and raises many issues of how and when face should be maintained and by whom.

In the case of moderately active confused speakers caregivers appear to make four main types of contributions:

1. Answering for the confused speaker, largely correcting things that the confused speaker has said.
2. Prompting, suggesting new topic developments (that they know the confused speaker will be able to deal with or at least acknowledge).
3. Being corespondents, that is to say on certain occasions caregivers answer and elaborate on some of the discussion from their own point of view (not as metatalk but as a contribution to development of topics I have raised).
4. Acting as informants and engaging in metatalk with the interviewer, thus reducing the conversation to a two-person conversation, effectively excluding or marginalizing the confused speaker.

Each of these modes of participation can be viewed as significant in terms of cooperation in conversation, although they seem to have different implications for the face of moderately active confused speakers.

As *correctors*, caregivers seek to ensure adherence to the cooperative principle. This is illustrated in Extract 13 where Mrs. Grace orients to the maxim of quality by eliciting correct and appropriate formulations of a particular relationship. At the same time, though, her corrections can be seen as a challenge to face for Mrs. Inman.

As *prompts*, caregivers offer up topics that will enable the confused speaker to talk cooperatively, or topics they can develop on behalf of the confused speaker. For example:

Extract 14

Mrs. Walker:	Ye:s I'm in a bungalow one of the council bungalows=
Pam:	=I see=
Mrs. Walker:	And there's heating and cords to pull for help you know=
	[
Mrs. Becker:	Warden assisted.
Mrs. Walker:	=Very nice=
Pam:	=Sheltered accommodation I think it's called is it? sheltered (.) sheltered.
Mrs. Becker:	Yes you have a warden.
Mrs. Walker:	We have a warden=
Pam:	=Yes=
Mrs. Walker:	=And we have cords=
Pam:	=Yes=
Mrs. Walker:	=In the living room the bedroom.

Here, Mrs. Becker prompts her mother to say more about the warden. At other points in the interview she does the same in regard to a number of Mrs Walker's hobbies. In such cases, the possibility for cooperation is set up. Mrs. Becker plays an enabling role for her mother and sets up the opportunity for her to present positive face. It is interesting to note that Kemper, Lyons, and Anagnopoulos (1995) suggested that spouses and caregivers of people with probable Alzheimer's disease successfully offer contextual cues that enable confused speakers to retrieve more complete stories about aspects of their life histories. Indeed, as I noted earlier, everyperson questions an interviewer might ask cannot offer enough contextual clues for the moderately active confused speaker to develop a topic, but when they are offered fairly specific clues they can develop topics. This is to be compared with the case of minimally active confused speakers where caregivers carry the onus of topic development for their relatives.

As *corespondents* caregivers appear to be reading the conversation as accessible to them as equal coparticipants: That is, cooperation is something they can offer alongside the confused speaker. This category of caregiver interaction did not appear in relation to minimally active confused speakers, perhaps because the burden of topic development for the confused speaker was already being carried by caregivers, so possibly they were not listening to see how topic development related to them. This sort of intervention turns the conversation firmly into a three-way negotiation of cooperation, as the following extract demonstrates:

Extract 15

(Follows on immediately from Extract 11)

Mr. Bowles:	Before the war before the war=
Mrs. Bowles:	=Yes=
Mr. Bowles:	=Cos that's when my father came we came ((Door bangs obscuring talk)) cos this is my mother=
Pam:	=Right yes.
	(.)
Mr. Bowles	My father well he had emphysema we came down here (.) got to be 37 38 ( )
	[
Mrs. Bowles:	I was born in 1914.

Here, Mr. Bowles is setting the record straight biographically and giving a context for his own contribution. "This is my mother" is a marked remark. I think I did or said something in the early part of this conversation that led him to believe that I thought Mrs. Bowles was his wife rather than his mother. Or, possibly, because Mrs. Bowles asked him questions that implied a shared biography (see Extract 11), he may have thought that I would interpret their relationship as that of husband and wife. Here, Mr. Bowles can be seen to be demonstrating how his own remarks should be oriented to. He sees himself as a ratified participant in the proceedings, someone for whom face is currently active. In fact, Mr. Bowles speaks extensively about himself and his own life. Much of his talk is linked to Mrs. Bowles, their lifestyle, and so on, but some of his discussion borders on metatalk (see Extract 16) about the problems of living with someone who is confused.

Finally, as *informants*, caregivers extrapolate from cooperation in conversation to a more general notion of cooperation and competence in everyday life and engage in metatalk.[6] In some cases, they may *blow the whistle* on the confused speaker. I noted earlier that one reading of the situations in which caregivers intervene is that they see themselves as a team with the confused speaker and answer as *us*. The notion of blowing the whistle offers a counterbalance to this: Caregivers occasionally draw away from being *us*; distancing themselves from the confused speaker as the following extract shows:

Extract 16

Mr. Bowles:	She lost them (her glasses) yesterday=
Pam:	=Yes=
Mr. Bowles:	But she hadn't lost them at all she'd just put em down on the bed=
Pam:	=Yes=
Mr. Bowles:	When she'd gone to change (.) her dress and come over to go to (Belshaw).
Pam:	Mmm.
Mr. Bowles:	She'd taken them off (.) left em on the bed come downstairs and gone=
	[
Pa.m:	((Low)) forgotten them
Mr Bowles:	=To Age Action. They didn't know ( )=
Pam:	=Yes=
Mr. Bowles:	=Whether she'd lost em there=
Pam:	=Yes=
Mr. Bowles:	=Or where they were.
Pam:	So it turns into a bit of a saga.
Mr. Bowles:	It's a major production every time.
	[
Pam:	Yes yes yes.
Mr. Bowles:	I mean it was a major production this morning because I didn't realize she hadn't got them on til twenty five minutes to twelve=
Pam:	=Yes=
Mr. Bowles:	=And we'd got to be up here by twelve o'clock=
Pam:	=Yes=
Mr. Bowles:	And I didn't even realize she hadn't got them on I mean I didn't even come home until eight o'clock this morning ((Pam laughs)) I've had about an hour and a half's sleep so far=
Pam:	=And then you had to follow up the glasses and then you had to (.) yeh.
[...]	[Mr Bowles talks about his shift work for a few minutes]
Pam:	Do you find things like household tasks how do you find doing those nowadays? Are you=
Mrs. Bowles	((Low)) (I just get on with it)=

---

[6] This type of device is one I already began to develop in the previous chapter in relation to Barry and Mr. Hoy.

Pam: =Just get on with it yes is it
                                           [
Mr. Bowles: (   ).
Mrs. Bowles: Well
                      [
Mr. Bowles: You do your you do I must admit yes you get on with the pots
                      alright don't you? Do the pots and things like that.

Mrs. Bowles begins to be seen as person who is, at the least, variable in her ability to get by as an ordinary person. Her son offers two different assessments of her in a short space of time; one suggests that she is incompetent (the glasses), the other that she is competent (the pots). It is interesting that in the former case he talks *about* her and thus distances himself from her performance, this distance possibly being heightened by myself weighing in as a *member of his team* reformulating his criticisms of his mother. On the other hand, when he talks about her competence, he talks *to* her, relating himself to her performance. Note too that Mrs. Bowles allows the first account to go unchallenged, instead of saying "Get away with you" or remarking that anyone could lose his or her glasses. Although her face is challenged, Mrs. Bowles takes no action to rectify matters. We may almost suggest that in her silence she is endorsing herself as a ritually dangerous actor (Goffman, 1969). This fits with her general pattern of ignoring or failing to appreciate challenges to face.

CONVERSATION AND IDENTITY

In endeavouring to cooperate in conversations, moderately active confused speakers engage in identity work that often leads to a loss of face. Unfortunately, some of their attempts to save face, by their very nature, damage it: For example, some of the self-deprecation that goes on in answers can be seen in terms of work that both excuses and at the same time stigmatizes the speaker. Effectively, such speakers devalue their identities so that other delicts can be viewed according to the lesser standards set by the impaired identity. The face-work they undertake itself draws attention to their incapacity.

If people show themselves to be short on commonsense and biographical knowledge, and cannot account for the shortfall to the satisfaction of other members, they are likely to lose face. Indeed, Payne and Cuff (1982) suggested that commonsense knowledge "entails notions of propriety, of what persons ought to know, ought to be and ought to do" (p. 5). The cooperative principle is a medium for being able to show a sense of propriety, and conversational implicature is one way that normal competent members can demonstrate, words notwithstanding, that they are cooperating and do have a sense of propriety. But confused speakers do not always have the resources to do cooperative conversation and issues around knowledge and identity show this up. Goffman's (1969) footnote to part of his discussion on face throws more light on this:

> When the person knows the others well, he will know what issues ought not to be raised, and what situations the others ought not to be placed in, and he will be free to introduce matters at will in all other areas. When the others are strangers to him, he will often reverse the formula, restricting himself to specific areas that he knows are safe. On these occasions, as Simmel suggests, . . . discretion consists by no means only in the respect for the secret of the other, for his specific will to conceal this or that from us, but in staying away from the knowledge of all that the other does not expressly reveal to us. (p. 12 [Footnote])

The ordinary proprieties of face are jointly constructed by caregivers, interviewer, and confused speakers. The first part of Goffman's footnote can be seen to accommodate caregivers of confused speakers who know what issues can be touched on in what way in order to assist the maintenance of face. Some caregivers can be seen to be engaging in a delicate balancing act of maintaining the face of the interviewer in the encounter and preserving the face of the confused speaker by broaching *safe* topics safely; others appear to be less concerned. However, in fact, there is rarely any such thing as a safe topic, as is shown with the example of Mrs. Inman's photographs.

The second part of the footnote could be applied to the situation in which I found myself as interviewer, and this also relates to safety in conversation. One has to assume, as an interviewer, that one can ask some questions and make some comments: Otherwise interaction becomes impossible and the identities of interviewer and respondent become nonviable. My questions can be seen as an attempt to stick to safe areas. But, because the confused speaker's biographical knowledge is suspect, it becomes very difficult to know what knowledge is a safe area for discussion. Yet in everyday terms we can say that people expect there to be safe areas of conversation: It cannot, in general, be conducted as if every potential topic were a minefield. Although there are always issues of face, as a general rule, members are expected to be able to negotiate the rough and tumble of ordinary conversation. And of course, some types of face-work can be seen as a sort of emollient that soothes the bruises from the rough and tumble.

The confused speakers have two choices: Either they can say nothing or they can say something. If they say nothing, then the entrance of caregivers into the conversation raises the question of the extent to which being answered for by someone else is a threat to face; but if confused speakers say something, few topics are safe—responding is therefore also dangerous.[7] They are caught in a double bind: They are damned if they do and damned if they do not.

Sometimes the confused speakers themselves comment on the problems that their impairment brings them. This is to move from a focus on the conversation as a form of social action to it becoming a commentary. Two of the people to whom I talked did talk briefly about the experience of being confused. What they had to say appears in the following:

Extract 17

Pam:	Yes yes do you find that you lose words?
Mrs. Inman:	Yes sometimes and sometimes.
Pam:	And you can't find what you want to say. Do you know what you want to say in your head?
Mrs. Inman:	Well I do but when I get there I can't do it.
Pam:	You can't do it. What does that feel like?
Mrs. Inman:	I just put it down and just look after myself and then do it slowly.
Pam:	So that's one of the things you try to do it slowly. What other little tricks have you got for helping? You doing it slowly sounds like a really good idea and are there other things you do as well to find the words?
Mrs. Inman:	No I don't think that there's any that I can pronounce properly.
Pam:	You find you don't think that you can pronounce well. Do you lose them so that you don't know the name for?
Mrs. Inman:	No I just when it's in place like this and just wait for an answer and
Pam:	Does the answer spring into your head eventually?
Mrs. Inman:	Yes, I think it does myself I don't want to keep repeating it.

Extract 18

Tom:	Are there other things that are quite difficult at the moment?
Mrs. Graham:	No I don't think so, can't think of anything.
Mr. Graham:	It's the body er the body of the er the bodyd stud is studying you know, funny little things wife like, she's telling the truth, absolutely I know all that and I know but um funny little things you know I might you know keep and er one of those like, I wouldn't you know blow the gaffe, if you can understand what I mean.

Both Mrs. Inman and Mr. Graham demonstrate that they are aware that there is an appropriate way to conduct a conversation. Mrs. Inman talks about not being able to pronounce things properly (I think I may have misunderstood this phrase during the conversation). But not being able to pronounce the words seems to have a connection with the idea of spoken competence—almost as one would speak of not being able to pronounce a word in a foreign language. Mrs. Inman also emphasizes in several ways the benefits of keeping quiet and of waiting: She does not want to keep repeating things, she is aware that this is not appropriate conversational behavior. Mr. Graham speaks directly about not wanting to blow the gaffe: He is afraid of making a blunder, of acting tactlessly,

---

[7] Politically, those who speak out only at the behest of others are called puppets, and this suggests that having no line of one's own is problematic in terms of face.

and of exposing himself to a loss of face. For both speakers, it seems that there is a strong sense of the loss of competence. For both there is an awareness that interacting with the world now brings considerable threats.

However, the major problem with all this is that talking about blowing the gaffe is itself blowing the gaffe. Few people choose to draw attention to their potential as gaffe blowers: To do so focuses on their potential incapacity and threatens face. When people make a gaffe, a commonly used technique employed by others is to avoid reference to it, or to take someone aside from the public domain and tell them quietly. If face is to be saved, it should not be interactional business and certainly should not be put on the agenda by the gaffe blower.

CONCLUSION

In this chapter, I suggested that structural competence in talk is an insufficient condition to make an effective conversationalist. This has to be combined with an ability to fit one's personal history and identity into a conversation in such as way as to accommodate to context.

Accidental breaches are common in ordinary conversation, but subject to routine correction, thereby avoiding any threat to face. However, moderately active confused speakers often fail to correct accidental breaches or to do face-work to rectify the line they are holding; and they appear not to construe interventions by normal speakers as invitations to amend face. In some cases, moderately active speakers seemed aware of accidental breaches in cooperation but were unable to correct or repair the breach enough to constitute adequate face-work. In such situations, they often had to make quite explicit statements about their conversational capabilities, and these drew attention to their limited competence, thus exacerbating the threat to face. Deliberate breaches in conversational cooperation (if brought off) can count as embedded conversational work that possibly circumnavigates issues of face. However, moderately active confused speakers had problems with deliberate breaching: The breaches often became an explicit interactional issue and their consequent face-work generally failed.

Throughout the chapter, I drew attention to my assumption that although moderately active confused speakers are in some respects able to conduct structurally normal talk, they are unable to present their biographies in a form expected of a normal member in an interview situation. I suggested that the format of corrections and repairs is available to all members and competently performed by these speakers. However, to have to use them in the matter of one's own biography creates a situation where the speaker's statements are hearable by normal participants as *confused* rather than as isolated incidents of talk gone wrong.

I set my discussions of cooperation and face in the context of the circumstances of the interview, suggesting that conversational cooperation in an interview has special requirements. Thus, how much one says, the issue of truth, relation, and manner all have to be oriented to in distinctive ways in the interview situation. I noted in particular that conversational implicature is significant because if our words mean more than we say, then this must be context sensitive, as it is necessary to understand how much and what we can implicate when speaking to an unknown speaker (that is to an interviewer).

What implications does all this have for ordinary talk? In his discussion of frames of talk, Goffman (1975) refered to the looseness of talk and its loose relationship to the world. It permits a multitude of interpretations, misunderstandings, and usages by hearers and speakers. So confusion is an ordinary aspect of most talk including some formal talk and can both be easily repaired or used implicatively as a resource. Every example used in this chapter could have been described in a different context as being used by a normal speaker perhaps ironically, humorously, or in some other implicative way. However, I would suggest that generally in order to be able to accommodate looseness of talk as an ordinary phenomenon and to understand apparently bizarre talk as implicative, sensible, and cooperative, participants have to understand those others present as ordinary members. Moreover, they need to assume that the people present will work on understanding and developing context in such a way as to render implicative talk effective, and thus to in some way signpost its status.

Personally, I found the group of speakers in this chapter the most discomforting in my study. The semblance of normality was more pervasive than with other confused speakers (after all, here were speakers who were not *underdoing* it or *overdoing* it: None of the normal member reactions of how to deal with a lot of talk or no talk were required). Yet the very structural normality and ordinariness of the types of repair work being undertaken was pointed up by what was having to be repaired. It all seemed a bit like suggesting using a Band-Aid when someone has had their leg chopped off.

This juxtaposition of ordinary repair work on extraordinary subject matter is something that is used extensively in drama, or in ordinary talk for implicative purposes when it can very often be heard as irony. This is all right if you are a normal member: normal members have irony as a potential resource. But if your membership is in question, it may not be heard as irony, or whatever, and then you are in serious trouble. If what you say is always heard as an accidental breach rather than anything else, and moreover in an area where accidental breaches are uncommon, then you are not afforded the privilege of using the language loosely as others can and do.

6

Very Active Confused Speakers

In this chapter, I look at the final category of confused speakers I identified, those who speak a great deal. I want to draw attention to the fact that *very active speakers* is a category that is available to describe individual ordinary members. As I noted in chapter 4, there are common terms that describe very active speakers ("Can talk the hind leg off a donkey"). I think that this category of person may use turn-taking machinery, in particular, in a distinctive way. Thus, in a multiparty conversation, the very active speaker may be adept at self-selecting as next speaker at a TRP where another has not already been selected or self-selected; may be highly competent at organizing their talk to indicate that they intend to take a long turn through several TRPs; may be able to interpret various points in someone else's turn as a TRP when others would not do so and thereby interrupt; and may pursue such a vigorous policy of self-selection that there will come a point when other parties will not bid for a turn because they do not anticipate carrying the bid through successfully. Similarly, in their use of the machinery of description, very active speakers may be able to use resources that less active speakers do not use so frequently (repetition, dispreferred answers and so on). Many of the characteristics I have outlined apply to the two speakers I examine in this chapter. But there are also other features of their talk that do not occur with very active normal speakers.

The data are taken from Moyra's interview with Tilly and from parts of the tapes that Mr. Bruner recorded for me. In the recording of the interview with Tilly, the conversation begins and concludes abruptly and contains nothing that can be identified as an opening or closing sequence to the encounter. The talk involves a long dispute about who lives in the flat and whether Tilly's sister Martha is alive; an episode of making and drinking tea, although there are still echoes of the talk about Tilly's rightful home; and a long discussion about Tilly's health—hinging almost entirely on a story about some Mentholatum Deep Heat Ointment that she has found very helpful for her rheumatism. The remainder of the conversation centers on Tilly's experience in service. The conversations involving Mr. and Mrs. Bruner consist of a number of summons and answer sequences, and of talk taking place at lunchtime and at bedtime.

EMBEDDED FACE-WORK AND REPETITION

In this section, I examine Tilly's participation in the interview and the part that Moyra plays as an interviewer. I have already noted that in ethnographic interviews we expect the interviewer to talk less than the respondent. The general format of such interviews might be as follows:

A   *Interviewer*
             Opening remarks/parachat
             Respondent
             Parachat

B   *Interviewer*
             (Short) open-ended questions introducing topics
             Respondent
             Lengthy responses according to the project of the question and
             occasional inquiries as to whether this is what the interviewer wants
             Interviewer
             Continuers and occasional requests for clarification

C   *Interviewer*
             Closings/parachat
             Respondent
             Closings/parachat.

Sequence B involves repetitions of combinations of question and response throughout the interview and may also be combined with parachat when occasioned activity, such as taking tea, occurs alongside the interview. Indeed, this may supplant interview talk for a while: In which case we might expect some mini-openings or -closings to take place within Sequence B. A simple Sequence B pattern is illustrated in Extract 1 when Tilly talks about being in service:

Extract 1

Moyra:	You were telling me once that you went down to the seaside with them=
Tilly:	=Oh yes they had a house there=
	[
Moyra:	Did they?
Tilly:	=Isle of Wight=
Moyra:	=<u>Isle of Wight</u>.
	[
Tilly:	And er we used to go out bathing and all that sort of thing in the afternoon.
	[
Moyra:	Did you?
Tilly:	=They didn't make any ( ) difficulties about that=

Moyra: =No=
Tilly: =Long as you did your work and did it right nobody interfered with
                you only the housekeeper was our boss=
Moyra: =Yes.
                [
Tilly: You see.

There is nothing remarkable about this fragment of conversation as an interview. Tilly understands Moyra's first statement to be an invitation to talk about a particular topic. She answers according to the project of this statement, which functions effectively as an elicitation. She also sets her remarks about what she did at the seaside into a wider context of the responsibilities of working in service. Moyra responds with continuers, and with the exception of the first turn of the sequence her utterances are generally shorter than Tilly's.

Extract 2 also illustrates the identities of interviewer and respondent as nonproblematic: Both women are talking in a way that is taken for granted in an interview:

Extract 2

Moyra: What did you cook, what kinds of things?=
Tilly: =Well I was in the kitchen I was the vegetable maid=
Moyra: =Yes=
Tilly: =I cooked all the vegetables=
Moyra: =I see=
Tilly: Oh yes and er they er had any amount.
                              (.)
Moyra: Yes=
Tilly: =Grew their own stuff because they had big gardens you see.

Here Moyra, as interviewer, asks a question and Tilly develops and expands an answer to it. Moyra leaves Tilly to get on with this, offering only continuers. Her short turns of continuers at TRPs support Tilly in carrying on and can do only a limited amount of work, serving no part in helping to change the topic. If one is to participate only in this way, one must accept the topic management exercised by the other person, and in this extract Moyra appears to do this.

However, although the conversation maintains a recognizable interview format on a turn-by-turn basis, there are respects in which it is problematic. First, there are issues around the negotiation of topic choice and development. These can be identified by the extensive repetition used by both interviewer and respondent. Second, there are problems centering on Tilly's biography, and these relate to issues of identity and face for both Tilly and Moyra.

Repetition

Repetition per se is not an indicator of confusion. Tannen (1989) cited a considerable number of instances where repetition is an acceptable, useful, and taken-for-granted aspect of conversation. For example:

- It can amplify the amount of talk in situations where silence is deemed to be uncomfortable or unacceptable.
- It can set up a paradigm into which to slot new information: People may repeat a sentence structure several times using different words.
- It can give people a chance to think about what to say next as they repeat in some way what they have already said.
- It can create redundancy so that there is a chance people can pick up the gist of what is being said, even if they fail to understand one part of the talk.
- It can serve a referential, evaluative, and tying function connecting different parts of the discourse.
- It can serve interactional purposes: It enables listeners to show that they are listening, to show humor, and also allows a new entrant into the conversation to be informed about what is going on.

A number of these functions of repetition can be seen as potentially relating to face. For example, in the case of filling uncomfortable silences, someone's face may be being saved. Redundancy can enable people to more easily pick up what is going on and thus not lose face. The space that repetition provides can give people a chance to do the necessary face-work so as to avoid embarrassment.

We may suggest, therefore, that in some circumstances repetition can be seen as an indicator of local conversational management, which involves embedded action oriented to face that never becomes explicit remedial work. As I noted earlier, Jefferson (1987) talked about embedded corrections in this way when she suggested that some corrections do not constitute interactional business and do not require accountings. There is some evidence to suggest that in terms of topic choice and development, Moyra uses repetition to do such embedded face-work. For example, one problem for Moyra is that Tilly often ignores her suggestions for topic development, and even if she defers to Moyra's choice of topic, she very quickly returns to her own chosen topic. For example:

Extract 3

Tilly:	Cooking=
Moyra:	=You were a cook=
Tilly:	=Yes.
	(.)
Moyra:	Did you start (.) you couldn't have started off as a cook did you?=
Tilly:	Er I always had done did do cooking nothing else.
	[
Moyra:	But when you started?=
Tilly:	=Young girl young girl yes=
Moyra:	=When you started did you start as
	[
Tilly:	When I started I did that=
Moyra:	=Yes.
Tilly:	That was when (.) they're a big place you see.
Moyra:	Yes.

Tilly:	And there's a full staff well ye you have to do all sorts of things in that line.
	[
Moyra:	Yes.
Tilly:	=Vegetables all sorts of things and er er (3.5) the dishes the dishes to wash up it's *all* interesting you know.
	[
Moyra:	Yes it is.
Tilly:	And clean=
Moyra:	=But did you start off as a kitchen maid first?=
Tilly:	Yes kitchen maid.

Here Moyra can be seen to try to encourage Tilly to fill in her particularistic biography by using common knowledge that people do not take on expert roles such as cook at the beginning of their career. She uses a developmental biography to do this, using "first" and repeating the word "start". However, Tilly does not respond to this everyperson developmental approach. Tilly's refusal to grasp this framework leads to further talk on Moyra's part where she asks further questions to get her line across. She repeats herself, using the phrase "did you?" five times. A question expects an answer and if an answer is not forthcoming, the question is often repeated in one way or another. In such circumstances a normal speaker is confronted with the prospect of becoming slightly overbearing if she is to establish a topic satisfactorily. A very active confused speaker may refuse to see the relevance of an immediately prior turn and refer only to her own last remark. One can speculate that the more you pay attention only to what *you* have said in a conversation, the easier it becomes to ignore its local management. You can say what you like. But repetition on the part of the normal speaker may be seen to be a form of embedded face-work that appeals to the normal proprieties of conversation: That speakers pay attention to each other. Repetition is a demand to be paid attention to, it is two-way face-work requiring Tilly to be in proper face and requiring her to attend to Moyra's face.

On another occasion Moyra's repeated questions appear to anticipate problems regarding face, rather than to be a corrective procedure:

Extract 4

1. Tilly:	Mentholatum Deep Heat I'll show you (2.8) that's lovely ((Noises)) (14.0) I've had it here I must get home because my sister's there and I want to know if she's going to be there or what. I haven't seen her so I MUST GET HOME TONIGHT=
2. Moyra:	=Alright=
3. Tilly:	=And
	[
4. Moyra:	Where's your Deep Heat?
5. Tilly:	Aye?
6. Moyra:	Where's your bottle of Deep Heat? You were going to show it to me=
7. Tilly:	=You what?=
8. Moyra:	=Your bottle of Deep Heat=
9. Tilly:	=Aye?=
10. Moyra:	=Your bottle of Deep Heat=

Here, Tilly begins by talking about the Deep Heat ointment and then abruptly changes topic to talk about her sister Martha, who she thinks is alive and "at home" (Utterance 1). Moyra uses her turn (Utterance 2) to soothe Tilly rather than to challenge her: That is to say, at this point she appears to be deferring to Tilly's choice of topic although not offering anything specific (like a question) that would encourage Tilly to follow it up. When Tilly uses her turn to say "And", which presumably heralds more *risky talk*, Moyra uses her next turn to revert to the first topic of the Deep Heat ointment. This is not so obvious as a complete change of topic. It defers to one of Tilly's previous choices of topic but prefers one topic over the other. Moyra is then insistent, taking four turns to repeat her point.[1] She uses her turns to encourage Tilly to fetch the ointment, prioritizing the here and now over Tilly's more global topic of complaint. So if a threatening topic can be deferred (or changed), then face will have been saved without any direct challenge to the person concerned; changing topic before someone has a chance to lose face performs an embedded function, in that the conversation does not have to focus explicitly on face (Jefferson, 1987). Also, insisting on maintaining a topic that has already been in play when threatened by a risky topic is a ploy that saves people from embarrassment. We might perhaps suggest that this sort of repetitive use of turn taking may be anticipatory face-work because it takes place when people are afraid of what they may hear. It can be a sort of protection of face on both sides, stopping Moyra from having to challenge Tilly again (which has implications for her own identity) and thus saving face for Tilly.

So Extracts 3 and 4 demonstrate the use of repetition on the part of a normal speaker to establish a proper and safe topic for the respondent. As an interviewer, Moyra can be seen to have the task of introducing or following up on topics of interest to Tilly that will nevertheless allow both women to maintain face. By using repetition, she insists on some of the proprieties of ordinary conversation: not least that the speakers should pay attention to what each says.

Stories and Repetition

In this section I examine a repetitive story that Tilly tells and consider whether repetition on her part can be seen as a problem. Cheepen (1988, p. 53) noted some potential features of a story in ordinary casual conversation:

- It describes a state (of affairs), an event, and another state (of affairs).
- It specifies the participants.

---

[1] Even though Tilly is slightly deaf and there are face problems relating to how many times you can repeat a question to a deaf person, Moyra still prefers these repeats over allowing the topic to revert to a more risky area.

- It indicates a temporal location.
- It provides an evaluation.

It can be seen that the ordinary biographical talk discussed in this and previous chapters can be fitted into such a pattern. Rayfield (1972) suggested that a story should not be too simple, too complex, or confused and that it should have a beginning and ending. In his discussion of what a story is, he also noted that some stories can appear curiously unsatisfying to listeners, and cited examples of protagonists changing, changing structures, and inadequate chronologies as reasons for this.

However, in addition to providing a satisfactory structure an oral storyteller must pay some attention to his or her audience. Sacks (1995a) noted, for example, that people must get the floor to be able to tell a story and signpost that they may need several turns to do this (p. 682). Jefferson (1978), following Sacks, noted the structure that can be seen to exist in stories:

> Story telling can involve a story preface with which a teller projects a forthcoming story, a next turn in which a coparticipant aligns himself as a story recipient, a next in which the teller produces the story, and a next in which story recipient talks by reference to the story. (p. 219)

Gaining the floor for a story is less of a problem in an interview than it is in a conversation. Here, Tilly has license to talk, the short question and short statement turns of the interviewer are invitations to take and hold the floor. On the whole, the interviewer will opt to a take turn during a story only for reasons of clarification, evaluation, and so on, rather than wresting the floor from the teller to tell a second story. But we can also say that if interview talk is based on ordinary conversation, then some of the same criteria will apply as for ordinary conversation, for example, a storyteller has to monitor what she says for whether it is news to the recipient and to make sure that as it unfolds it is recipient-designed (which should include monitoring for repetition, to ensure that any repetition adds some nuance to the story, dramatically or whatever).

The Deep Heat story begins after Moyra has asked about Tilly's health (the complete story is shown in Appendix C)[2]:

Extract 5

Moyra:	[...] How have you been keeping? (.) How are you feeling?=
Tilly:	=Not too good I have rheumatism a lot=
Moyra:	I know (1.6) mmm=
Tilly:	=As long as I can keep on that's the chief thing. I've got some very good stuff.

---

[2] In Appendix C I produced a transcript that leaves out a substantial number of continuers on Moyra's part. To emphasize the structure of the story for the reader. Later in this chapter, in Extracts 7–11, a fuller transcription of parts of the story is given. However, the numbering is that used in Appendix C.

Asking about Tilly's health is not only an introduction to a topic but also an invitation to her to choose a topic within a particular spectrum. Moyra's invitation might be seen as an opening sequence and could be responded to on a single-word basis. However, placed as it is well away from the beginning of the conversation it is easier to see it as a genuine request for a named topic to be taken up and possibly as an invitation to tell a story. Tilly takes it as a request to choose a topic within the range of health topics and introduces the subject of Mentholatum Deep Heat Ointment. In the case of this speaker "I've got some good stuff" can be seen as the preannouncement of a story.[3] It offers some information but promises more in that what the *stuff* is, is not specified.

Basically the story is as follows: Tilly goes to the doctor's for some ointment for her rheumatism. She is given a tiny can of greasy ointment, which spoils her clothes. She goes to a drugstore and buys some Deep Heat ointment, having ascertained that it is a preparation many people buy. It is not greasy, she finds it very good, and resolves not to go to the doctor's again for such a preparation. The epilogue to the story, as it were, is to show the product to Moyra to demonstrate its qualities, encouraging her to use it and to recommend it to other people. The episode contains many of the characteristics of a story: a hero, a villain, trials and tribulations, and a resolution that vindicates the hero and is not therefore in its basic form unsatisfying (Propp, 1968; Rayfield, 1972). The structure of the story is binary: It is a before and after story. Tilly frequently uses the device of comparing the first product (from the doctor's) with the second product (the Deep Heat), drawing favorable comparisons for the latter, so items in the story are grouped together to perform a specific evaluative function.

However, as noted earlier, a storyteller needs to pay attention not only to the structure of the story per se but to its unfolding in terms of the hearer. Some stories are in some respects news.[4] But as the story is told, even if it is news, the hearer becomes knowledgeable about the event. In an article on forgetfulnesss as an interactive resource, Goodwin (1987) discussed how speakers talk when they are in the company of people who were also present at the events being talked about. He suggested that what might be initially seen as amendments or corrections to a conversation such as "What was that guy's name?" serve the purpose of acknowledging that another speaker present was at the events being reported: He referred to this other speaker as a *knowing*

---

[3] For some other confused speakers it could be seen as a closing down: For example, Mrs Pugh, whom I discussed in chapter 4, would have been unlikely to follow up such a statement with a story.

[4] Stories told to children may not be news, particularly stories they want to hear every night sor that they can join in. Also, some stories may become part of someone's repertoire and acceptable to significant others as likely to be told quite often. In these circumstances there are indicators that such a story is not news: groans from the hearers *Oh no not again* and so on.

	Recipient was there	Recipient was not there
Speaker knows	1	2
Speaker does not know	3	4

Figure.6.1. Knowing and not knowing: the start of a story.

recipient (Goodwin, 1987). I want to elaborate this idea of the knowingrecipient and to try to develop it in relation to the telling of a story. When a story is to be told about an event, different types of people may be present: those who were at the event and those who were not. The storyteller may or may not know which others present were at the event. Thus, the starting point of recounting of an event or situation may be represented as illustrated in Figure 6.1.

There are a number of positions that the storyteller can take. Each cell represents a starting point for the teller regarding how to unfold the story. For example, if Cell 1 represents the starting point, the storyteller can draw in the knowing recipient, asking for his or her reminiscences of the event. In relation to Cell 2, the storyteller can begin the story as news. If the storyteller does not know whether someone has been there or not, (Cells 3 and 4), again he or she is likely to begin the story as news or to try to establish whether the recipient is *knowing*. In the former case, the knowing listener has the choice to remain silent and risk problems of face if the storyteller starts romancing, or deviates from the listener's recall of the event or discovers that he or she is a knowing recipient: Or to reveal that he or she knows, that is, to make a statement that throws some light on their own identity as a knowing recipient.

In the situation of the story in question, Cell 2 should be the beginning point for the teller. At the start of the story, the speaker knows that the hearer knows nothing of it. During the unfolding of the story, however, the hearer gradually becomes a knowing recipient. This process may be facilitated by the hearer asking questions to indicate what she has not heard that she considers pertinent, and by offering evaluations that confirm her as a knowing recipient. So, as the recipient contributes to the story, she offers information about what Goodwin (1987) called her *discourse identity* (p. 118). Thus, in this story we find Moyra asking a number of questions:

Extract 6

Where did you get that from?
How much does it cost you? Is it expensive?
How much does it cost?
When did you get that?
When did you get that?
When?

Such questions might be referred to as product specifications in the sense that Moyra is trying to pin down some practicalities: They are questions about what she has not heard that may be seen to fill out the story for her. They contextualize many details of the story and attempt to elicit a more structured story, perhaps one in line with the discourse identity she sees as proper to Tilly as the teller of the story. However, the story goes on for nearly 200 turns and is really a series of presentations of the same story (in which the doctor's ointment comes out unfavorably) told repeatedly with a few variations. In terms of Rayfield's analysis, if seen as one long story it is problematic because it does not have an end; if seen as a number of stories then we can suggest that being told the same thing again and again in close proximity is unsatisfying for Moyra as a knowing recipient. For the listener, the later stories are no longer relevant or informative because nothing new and pertinent is being added. I cite a few extracts here:

Extract 7[5]

19. Tilly:	That's lovely if you've got rheumatism or anything like that=
Moyra:	=Is it?=
Tilly	=*Yes* and the heat that give out and it's clean now I went to the doctor's (.) before I get that=
Moyra:	=Yes=
Tilly:	=And he gave me some old greasy stuff <u>Oooh</u> my dear I messed up my vest and my night dress up=

Extract 8

49. Tilly:	I thought miself <u>whatever</u> muck have I got here but I soon washed it all off and threw the whole tin in the bin (.) I thought miself let me have some decent stuff and went and got that=
Moyra:	=Mmmm.
	(.)
Tilly:	And that put on I was that take all the pain away you know if you've got a headache or anything=

Extract 9

75. Tilly:	No I don't know it but that is the best stuff I've ever had (.) and you know it take all the pain away=
Moyra:	=Does it?=
Tilly:	=And you just go to sleep it's the finest thing out=
Moyra:	=Lovely=
Tilly:	=And my limbs are loose and everything=
Moyra:	=Yes=
Tilly:	=And I can move, twice now you get I got the stuff from the doctor (.) and that warn't no good at all and that messed up my night dress and all grease <u>ooh I thought a miself</u>.

---

[5] The turn numbers in the left hand column of Extracts 7–11 indicate the point at which these utterances occur in the whole story.

Extract 10

103. Tilly: No that's why I don't mind buying stuff like that but when you get that (.) I had some stuff from the doctor <u>oh</u> and that was l l grea <u>oh</u> <u>mucky</u> old stuff=

Moyra: =Was it?=

Tilly: =Messed up my vest and night dress I had to soak em afterwards.

Extract 11

151. Tilly: I keep them ((Aspirins)) by me and the stuff to ri rub on Deep Heat that stuff=

Moyra: =Mmm=

Tilly: =And that take all the pain out of my limbs if they're swollen or that doctor's stuff was full of grease and oh I thought to miself my vest and night-dress was messed up I thought this is rubbish stuff so I never go I won't go it's a waste of time to go.

As the repetitions continue, we can see that Moyra is in an increasingly perilous situation. Her own face becomes threatened. Tilly, however, appears to be oblivious to the fact that as time goes on, Moyra has heard most elements of the story before. She does not orient to Moyra's discourse identity as a knowing recipient.

As Levinson (1983) noted, conversational participants are expected to monitor throughout a conversation and to tie up all the ends: If a topic is reintroduced, it needs to be given a new slant. It is not acceptable to introduce the same topic without variation or elaboration as news. It can, of course, be done as in the apocryphal stories where each new segment begins with a motif such as "We were so poor that . . ." or where the speaker justifies the repetition, "I know you think I'm going on about the pain in my hip but yesterday . . ." Repetition is acceptable in separate conversations: One can repeat something one said in an earlier conversation in a later conversation, but repetition has to be handled very carefully within the same conversation. Tilly's monitoring of the conversation as a whole and of her own talk in particular appears to be minimal. She can do local management of the conversation on a turn-by-turn basis, but does not accommodate to the fact that she has already told a particular story earlier in the conversation. Each repetition is, for her, a fresh rendition of the story. And, of course, repeating elements of a story, mindless of the hearer, adds to the volume of talk of the confused speaker.

One device that Moyra uses to try to facilitate Tilly orienting to her discourse identity as a knowing recipient is to introduce new topics. This is evident, to some extent, in the questions I cited in Extract 6, which are asking for information about things that she has not heard before about the story. But Moyra also attempts to change topic as well:

Extract 12

31   And what about your headaches?

141   Who is your doctor Tilly?

157   For your headaches do you take those? When do you get a headache?
161   You used to cook didn't you?

Again these tactics are similar to those of the embedded corrections I
discussed earlier (Jefferson, 1987). Attempts to forestall the story do not
become explicit interactional business as they would have if Moyra had
told Tilly that she was repeating herself: To do this, however, would
have been explicitly to challenge face. But none of these attempts work
and Moyra's voice appears to have less and less energy as the story is
repeated again and again. The story is finally brought to an abrupt halt
when Tilly says:

Extract 13

Tilly: That's splendid I can recommend that to anybody (.) In fact my sister
                Martha (1.0)what's at home now er=
Moyra: =MARTHA?=
Tilly: =Yes=
Moyra: =No where's Martha?=
Tilly: =Martha=
Moyra: =Martha=
Tilly: =Mm she's at home now=
Moyra: =No she's not=
Tilly: Oh no of course she's not=
Moyra: =Yes=
Tilly: I can't forget her you know.

At this point Moyra intervenes quite sharply. Her voice is energetic. She
explicitly mobilizes her discourse identity as a knowing recipient of an
aspect of Tilly's identity, namely that her sister is dead.[6] Now, the
embedded nature of Moyra's face-work in the main body of the story is
replaced by explicit interactional work: A challenge to face. No longer is
she willing to work within the structure offered by the telling of this
story, even though Tilly has actually introduced a new element in the
story by mentioning Martha and thus moved away from the repetition.
So the story structure in which the storyteller concludes the story is
usurped. Rayfield (1972) discussed the accommodation that is made for
whole stories to be told and cited examples of stories being told in
episodes if they are too long to be told in one sitting. A *complete story*,
then, appears to be an important feature of structure. Had Moyra not
usurped the ending of the story it may never have ended if Tilly had
been left to her own conversational devices.

EXPLICIT FACE-WORK AND KNOWLEDGE

I now go on to look in more detail at explicit interactional face-work that
takes place within this conversation. As I already noted in chapter 2, I

---

[6] Please note that Extract 14, which follows in the next section of this chapter, relates to an earlier part of
the conversation than Extract 13.

listened to this tape and prepared the transcript hearing Moyra as the reliable participant and Tilly as the unreliable participant so that my interpretative framework here is of a *problem that Tilly generates.*[7] Extract 14 illustrates some of the problems that arise in the conversation deriving from Tilly's construction of her own biography.

Extract 14

1. Tilly:	Minnie or somebody oh it's
	[
2. Moyra:	Edie isn't I
3. Tilly:	[Edi no I don't think Edie is no no=
4. Moyra:	=mm=
5. Tilly:	One or the other then I wanna get home I'd rather be in my own home I WANNA BE my o I'm 80 now=
	[
6. Moyra:	I know]
7. Tilly:	=And I think I ought to be in mi own home as I won't be here in anyway in a place like this=
8. Moyra:	=But this is your flat dear Mrs Perkins lives underneath=
9. Tilly:	=I KNOW but I de I why should I be here? I'm er I was made to work here that's when ( ) the idea I got a home o mi own they now sent them chairs (.) there and brought that so now I haven't been home my sis I wanna know what is happening at the home WHERE I COME FROM.
10. Moyra:	Well we'll have to find out are you going to put this on love?
	(.)
11. Tilly:	I haven't got a kettle that leaks=
	[
12. Moyra	No no
13. Tilly:	=So I th I gotta get another one.
14. Moyra:	That's enough whoa.
	[
15. Tilly:	Aye?
16. Moyra:	That's for two of us is that enough water for two of us?
17. Tilly:	Yes I'll (put a drop more) I mean I don't know where I am where I stand or anything else about I haven't heard from Mrs Per not Mrs you know it ain't Mrs Per but I don't know I don't know what I'm go I wanna be ( ) WHY SHOULD I BE HERE? ((Clanking of crockery)) I don't want to be here. Isn't I'm 80 and don't you think I ought to be?=
18. Moyra:	=((Very quiet)) Mmm.
19. Tilly:	YES I DO.
	[
20. Moyra:	I know mmm.
21. Tilly:	I'm going to clean this kitchen the walls all down on Monday or so I thought (.) and so then everything would be alright=
22. Moyra:	=Yes=
23. Tilly:	=And then then that's done then.
	[
24. Moyra:	But this is all your stuff in here love.
	[
25. Tilly:	Aye?=
26. Moyra:	=All your (.) this is all your food and everything in the cupboards=

---

[7] It is interesting that if we were to hear Tilly as the reliable person instead it would be very easy to hear Moyra as confused. The concept of *reliable person* here seems to be extrinsic to the conversation compared with the intrinsic discourse identity.

27. Tilly:	=I know well I shan't I shall take it with me so I shan't leave nothing behind not in the food line so (you needn't worry)

                                                                               [

28. Moyra: No.

29. Tilly: (   ) I am er

                                                                  [

30. Moyra: But that's your bedroom through there.

31. Tilly: Yeh.

                       [

32. Moyra: So and er because Martha used to live here before she died=

33. Tilly: =Aye?=

34. Moyra: =You and Martha used to live here before Martha died=

35. Tilly: Yes but my dear ((Exasperated)) <u>that's nothing to do with my sister dying</u> Martha never had anything=

36. Moyra: =But she used to live here=

37. Tilly: =Martha did not=

38. Moyra: =Yes she did Mrs Perkins told me=

39. Tilly: =Martha did not used to live <u>never never knowed this place at all</u>=

40. Moyra: ((Whisper)) Yes she did.

41. Tilly: =<u>No she didn't</u> ((Exasperated)) Martha won't come here my dear she don't when she went I got when she got a home of her own Martha and I share.

                                   [

42. Moyra: I think you moved to this you see

                                          [

43. Tilly: What?=

44. Moyra: You moved to this flat you see=

45. Tilly: =She did not=

46. Moyra: =Both of you did=

47. Tilly: =Aye?

48. Moyra: =Both of you did a while ago you both moved to the flat quite a long time ago=

49. Tilly: =No no my dear my my sister Martha had never been in this place ((Banging emphatically)) no and cause she's died now we know=

50. Moyra: =Mmm yeh=

51. Tilly: =Never <u>she's never been to this flat</u> ((Banging emphatically)) (2.0) not at all ((Banging for 5.0)) she might have come if she's have been to the (club) and come here but nothing else.

                                   [   ]

52. Moyra: Yes.

In this extract, the three main points of discussion are whether the flat in which the conversation is taking place is where Tilly lives; whether her sister Martha is dead or alive; and whether Martha used to live in this flat. Within these discussions there is a dissonance: Whether Martha used to live in this flat does not seem to be connected with whether Tilly now lives in it. The whole discussion poses problems for both women because they are at odds over the status of the fact as presented by each other.

Both women seem to be engaging in explicit interactional work relating to face. To Moyra, Tilly's statements are a demonstration that she is not presenting an acceptable line, her view of herself is not acceptable. Ordinary members know where they live and can recognize where they live when they are there. They know which close relatives are alive and which are dead (unless they have lost touch with them), and when not in the presence of their live relatives they assume, for working purposes, that they continue to be alive. Such biographical and life experience knowledge should not have to be talked about and should not emerge as a matter for dispute. Once they do, they immediately become issues requiring face-work on the part of the ordinary member. But Tilly's view of her own biography and situation is as tenacious as Moyra's. As far as Tilly is concerned, she is presenting an acceptable line and she engages in face-work too, defending her line against challenges by someone who, in conventional terms, has less claim to know about these matters than she does. All of this is a basis for plenty of talk.

Tilly proposes a number of things that she intends to do. However, these intended actions are, in Moyra's opinion, based on false assumptions (i.e., Tilly's taken-for-granted is not the taken-for-granted of other members). For example, Tilly is going to clean the apartment so she can leave it with a clear conscience (Utterances 21–31). But Moyra points out that all this stuff in the apartment is Tilly's (a statement beneath which lies a taken-for-granted assumption that we keep our stuff in our own homes: That if we say that this is our furniture, people will assume we own or rent the apartment). But Tilly does not make quite the same taken-for-granted assumption. Instead, she assumes that this is, indeed, all her stuff and that she knows your own stuff should be in your own apartment and that she will take it with her when she goes to her own apartment. Here, Moyra's frame is accommodated within Tilly's frame of what is going on, rather than being seen as a challenge to it. So Moyra's claims, which, it might be suggested, can be seen as relevant support for a challenge to face for normal speakers, do not constrain Tilly—almost the reverse, they support her version of her face—and the dispute continues.

The face-work that goes on in this episode, it seems to me, is not really resolved when Tilly says that Martha is dead now (Utterance 49), because the statement does not seem to emerge from any prior work in the conversation. It is as though Tilly had just *come to*. This poses another problem for identity: Ordinary members know all the time that a relative is dead. It is not something one forgets, except perhaps in the first few days of mourning, when people may wake up in the morning and not remember. This would be generally be assumed to be a fixed aspect of one's identity.

This is to put a different gloss on the idea of the knowing recipient. Based on what she already knows, Moyra knows what she needs to hear and she needs to find a way for Tilly to present an identity that comes into line with this. As I have said, the issues at stake are, in the common understanding, not matters of opinion where a knowing recipient can be corrected: They are nonnegotiable and consequential facts. If Moyra were to accept that Tilly does not live here and that Martha is alive, it would have consequences for her relationship with the world, including Mrs.

Perkins who lives in the flat below! Moyra *cannot* accept Tilly's interpretation of the world.

So a number of identities are being contested here: not least Moyra as knowing recipient and Tilly as a displaced person with a live sister. How is the explicit interactional face-work accomplished? The discussion is again characterized by repetition and also by the extensive use of dispreferred replies on the part of both women. I already alluded to dispreferred answers in chapter 1, citing work by Sacks, Schegloff, Bilmes, and Pomerantz. Where there is a choice of conditionally relevant responses to a first pair part, these choices are not treated as equivalent by the responder: Some are preferred over others. Typically, a preferred response is a short, unqualified acceptance to an invitation, whereas a dispreferred response involves a hedge, and some kind of account (Levinson, 1983). I want to note that one of the features of dispreferred answers is that they require some qualification over and above a basic rejection, refusal, or denial. Thus, by engaging in dispreferred answers, speakers usually generate more talk than if they had used preferred answers.

In Extract 14, we find a fairly frequent construction of the pairing of statement–reply (adjacency pairs as identified by Goffman, 1981) and these too can be considered within the framework of preference structure, although whereas a request may be followed by an acceptance or a refusal (both being conditionally relevant), a reply to a statement allows perhaps a greater degree of latitude. Nevertheless, one use of a statement is that it can be offered as an assertion, and in that case we can see that a preferred reply is an agreement with it and a dispreferred reply is a counterassertion. Thus, I think that a number of Moyra's replies can be seen as dispreferred, even though they emerge from statements on Tilly's part rather than from questions, for example, Utterances 8, 24, 30, 36, 38, 46, and 48. Most of these are preceded by "but", which indicates to the other speaker that an alternative assertion is being introduced.

Tilly's counterassertions rarely contained hedges. On only one occasion does she use "but" (Utterance 35) and here it is "Yes" *but* followed by "my dear", which acts as a sort of hedge that can be heard as a diminution of Moyra, thereby discounting her answer. This response is one that challenges the relevance of Moyra's preceding statement, and thus challenges her face.

The use of dispreferred answers is accompanied by repeats of the argument on the part of both women, so that each entrenches her own position. The talk is lengthy because it centers on dispreferred answers (adding to the length on utterances) and also because it is repetitive (adding to the number of utterances). There seems to be a tension here in that one thing that dispreferred answers may be seen to do is to add to the density of the discourse, whereas one thing repetition does is to make space—to make the discourse less dense. I suspect that this tension may well be at the root of the notion of what it is to be *talkative*.

This explicit interactional work relating to face is brought about by the fact that the problem apparently cannot be dealt with by an embedded strategy. It is not possible in an embedded way to circumnavigate such serious issues. Correction cannot be slipped into the conversation by stealth. Again, I would suggest that this contributes to the notion of this being a very talkative section of the interview. Embedded correction work can be seen as a singularly elegant and economical way of handling correction, and embedded face-work is the same, deserving such descriptions as *tactful, subtle* and so on. However, when it becomes explicit interactional business, face-work is less economical, less elegant, and becomes marked behavior.

In my discussion of the talk between Tilly and Moyra, I noted a number of things that I think indicate that Tilly is a very active speaker. Some of these features are recognizable, too, in ordinary very active talk. For example, extensive use of dispreferred answers, preoccupation with one's own narrative, and so on. There is also the repetition, although I have shown that there are features of this that are structurally difficult to interpret as normal repetition. But at the same time I would suggest that as the topics of conversation unfold, it becomes evident that one of the speakers is confused. The argument about where Tilly lives and whether Martha is alive suggests areas of talk that are not generally available to normal speakers. People simply do not generally contend that someone close to them is dead when they are alive.

OCCASIONED ACTIVITY

I want now to continue the theme of too much talk by looking at a number of stretches of domestic talk involving the Bruners. For Mrs. Bruner, many ordinary taken-for-granted aspects of daily life are mysteries that she cannot solve alone. I illustrate a number of examples of this inability on her part to *get on with daily life* and of how this is manifested in a rather large volume of talk.

Summonses and Answers

Much of the talk on the tapes Mr. Bruner recorded is not, strictly speaking, conversation. It does not, for example, contain openings and closings, which Schegloff and Sacks (1974) suggested are two of the essential criteria of conversation. Instead, what takes place is a state of what these authors call incipient talk:

> There can be silence after a speaker's utterance which is neither an attributable silence nor a termination, which is seen as neither the suspension nor the violation of the basic features [of the talk]. These are

adjournments, and seem to be done in a manner different from closings.
Persons in such a continuing state of incipient talk need not begin new
segments with closing sections and terminal exchanges. (p. 262)

Nevertheless, although the Bruners' talk may be without openings in the
sense of greetings, it is necessary for the couple to focus the interaction as
talk resumes. The extracts I chose are examples of one form of adjacency
pair: the summons and answer. Examples of this are often generated by
Mr. and Mrs. Bruner when they are in separate rooms, and so the first
pair parts stand as devices to reactivate interaction again after Mr.
Bruner has been physically and interactionally absent (taking it from
Mrs. Bruner's perspective as the summoner).

Schegloff (1972b) notes several significant features about the
summons and answer as an adjacency pair: I have adapted these into the
following list :

- "Upon a summons an answer is expectable" (p. 364), moreover,
  an answer is conditionally relevant and if it is absent then this is
  a meaningful absence.
- In the completion of a summons and answer, the answer must
  directly follow the summons (compare this to the fact that an
  answer may lie several sentences after a question, or a very long
  silence, and still be construed as an answer) (p. 365).
- The summoner is obligated to speak a second time after the
  conclusion of the summons/answer that forms a first adjacency
  pair (p. 364): In this sense there are three elements—summons,
  answer and follow-up by the summoner.
- There is a limit to the number of times that a summoner may
  summon without receiving a reply (although Schegloff does not
  formulate a rule for just how many times this first pair part can
  be repeated) (p. 365).

We may also suggest other significant features of a summons. A
summons is likely to take place in a situation where the speaker of the
first pair part knows it is realistic that the potential speaker of the second
pair part can hear and respond. It must be appropriate to the occasion. It
must make the right claim on the person summoned, given the context.

Thus, a successful summons conforms to a specific conversational
format and observes the proprieties of face for those concerned.
However, we can see that there are many common social situations when
summons and answer sequences do not quite conform to this happy
state. For example, people may not reply to a summons as Schegloff
(1972b) noted:

A member of the society may not "naively choose" not to answer a
summons. The culture provides that a variety of "strong inferences" can
be drawn from the fact of the official absence of an answer, and any

member who does not answer does so at the peril of one of those inferences being made. (p. 367)

A summoner who gets no response when apparently the summoned person can hear and has the capacity to answer may infer a meaningful absence: that he or she does not have any authority with the other person, that their own identity has turned out not to accommodate the authority that they had previously thought (or hoped) they had, etc. An aspect of identity has been found wanting. The person who refuses to answer is making a comment on the identity of the summoner. Parents whose young children do not do as they say, and teachers whose pupils will not do their bidding both put at risk authoritative aspects of their identities. Because successful summoning is an integral part of these identities, it can be seen that they face a real dilemma in needing to continue with exactly that interaction that shows up their inadequacies.

In the absence of a response, the summoner is faced with the problem of deciding how long to keep summoning. Schegloff (1972b) outlined the possibility of *no answer, no person,* and noted that although he has not formulated a rule for this, this conclusion is generally drawn after three to five summonses. However, there is an interim stage before this conclusion may be reached, illustrated in Figure 6.2.

There is a point after one or two summonses and no answer that the summoner must try to construct what is going on. For example, when telephoning, one makes assumptions about how long it takes to get to the telephone. In some circumstances, summoners will know this, in others they will be unfamiliar with the place they are telephoning. There must, however, come a cut-off point after which one must draw other conclusions about the absence of an answer. If the person does not seem to be there, the summoner may stop. People do not continue to summon indefinitely until the person returns physically. A telephone summons illustrates this. You put the telephone down after 11 rings because either the person at the other end is not there (and you cannot continue because what if they have gone away on their holidays for 3 weeks?) or they are there and have decided not to reply. In the latter case, continuing to allow the telephone to ring for an hour may be seen as an unwarranted insistence that a reply should be forthcoming. In some circumstances, even though you may infer that someone is there at the other end of the telephone, you nevertheless stop summoning. For example, when you telephone the local hospital, you may conclude after 11 rings that although it is clear that the hospital cannot possibly be out, it is nevertheless interactionally unavailable in the form of a jammed switchboard.

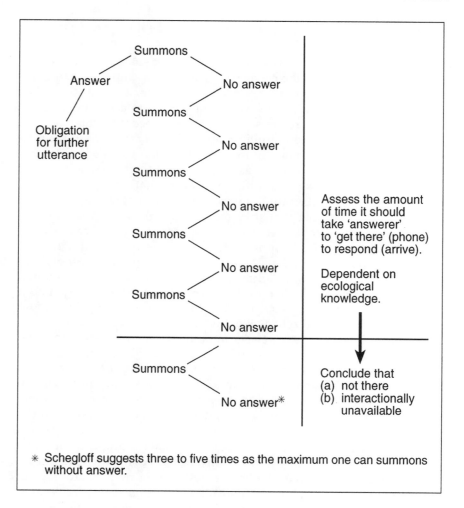

Figure. 6.2. Length of summoning sequences.

There are, however, circumstances when an extended series of summonses may be made without the receipt of an answer or the loss of face. When people are in desperate straits they may call to "anyone" to respond: When they are "lost on the moors" they may call for hours, maintaining, perhaps, an expectation that others are interactionally available: That the search party has set out or that someone is passing by, and so on. Because the interactional availability of others cannot be specified, the summoner can continue to summon for long periods because they are not summoning a specific person but rather anyone within earshot. For searchers, extensive repetition of summonses is legitimate because each could be seen to be a new occasion for the summons (as in "We've tried over there, now let's try over here").

The complexities of interactional and physical availability raise issues about different types of summonses. We may summon (a) expecting the summoned person to make a verbal response (summons to interactional availability); or (b) expecting someone to get themselves into our presence (summons to physical presence).

This distinction has important implications for what would constitute the successful completion of a summoning sequence. In one case, a verbal response is sufficient, whereas in the other it is not. Closely associated with this are implications for face. All first pair parts in adjacency pairs carry implications about the identity both of the speaker and of the person being addressed. Not everyone is allowed to ask questions in some contexts, and for any individual there may be others to whom they cannot direct questions. It seems that summonses are a very demanding kind of action, in terms of the relationship they set up between the summoner and the summoned. Moreover, the second type of summons just identified is particularly demanding, potentially leading to complaints about being *at someone's beck and call*. Within a relationship where the parties are treated as interactionally equal, both types of summons may be regarded as legitimate, although there is likely to be some conception of overuse. Any inequality in the statuses of the participants would lead to a sharp decline in the appropriateness of the summons in one direction, especially those of the second kind. A lower status participant summoning a higher status participant can threaten the status hierarchy. Moreover, summonses can threaten to turn an equal relationship into a hierarchical one. In the case of the Bruners we can reasonably assume that this is an equal relationship, or that Mr. Bruner would normally be accorded higher status, given continuing patriarchal influences within families, especially those of the generation to which the Bruners belong.

However, there are other considerations that go into judgments about the legitimacy of summonses, beside the relationship between the participants. One is some measure of the urgency and significance of the matter that the summons is dealing with. Some matters are so urgent and important that even those at the bottom of status hierarchies would be allowed to summon those at the top. Another relevant factor is the frequency of summonses. Any particular summons is likely to be judged in the context of other behavior and the implications that carries for the identities of the participants. Frequent use of summonses, especially when the justification for them is weak, is likely to become an interactional problem for one or both sides. One strategy that a summoned participant might use to deal with this is, of course, to stop responding to the summonses. That possibility is one that the summoner will usually be aware of. However, it is not, of course, the only explanation for there being no response.

So out of the initial notion of summons and answer as an adjacency pair there is a chain of possible outcomes. The strong expectation is of an answer. The persistence with which an answer is sought is, among other things, an indicator of the strength of expectation of a second pair part. The range of possible outcomes indicates that quite complex interpretive work has to be done on the part of the summoner in order to carry out a summons. Consider, therefore, the following extract:

Extract 15

1. Mrs. Bruner:	Ooh dear (1.5) ((Sound like door))
	Da:ve (1.7) Dave.
2. Mr. Bruner:	((From out of the room)) Yes love.
	(2.0)
3. Mrs. Bruner:	Oooh dear (1.4) (they do) (2.3) Dave (2.5) Dave (2.6) Dave (2.3) Dave
	((Low)) (1.2) (they do).
	(1.4)
4. Mr. Bruner:	((From out of the room)) What do you want love?
5. Mrs. Bruner:	Dave ( )
6. Mr. Bruner:	((Nearer and irritated)) What do you want?
7. Mrs. Bruner:	Dave ( )
8. Mr. Bruner:	((Here)) What do you want?
9. Mrs. Bruner:	(Cover mi feet) ain't it.

Here, Utterances 1 and 2, 3 and 4, 5 and 6, and 7 and 8 form four summons/answer adjacency pairs; Utterance 9 is what Mrs. Bruner says to Mr. Bruner when he comes into physical presence. From the noises on the recording, it is evident that Mr. Bruner is not in the same room as his wife at the beginning of the episode. It is reasonably common for a summons to take place when the protagonists are not copresent. Indeed, Mrs. Bruner's intonation, with an upward lift toward the end of her husband's name in Utterance 1, and the register of her voice, would be inappropriate for summoning someone in the same room. The register of Mrs. Bruner's voice diminishes in the second adjacency pair (Utterances 3 and 4) and it might be assumed that this is only a pseudosummons that echoes the first (not loud enough to catch someone from afar), perhaps not really a summons at all but self-talk, that talk we address to ourselves without the expectation that it will have any interactional consequences (Goffman, 1981). In Extract 15, Mrs. Bruner calls her husband eight times. Although Mr. Bruner is out of the room from Utterances 1 to 6, he does answer, indicating his interactional availability. In the case of a summons requesting such availability, this response should have been followed by the obligatory third part of the summons. However, Mrs. Bruner continues summoning. This implies that her summons was concerned with bringing about Mr. Bruner's physical presence. However, even given this, simply to continue summoning without providing any hint that there is a justification for this can be seen as being very demanding behavior. This demandingness relates not just to personal convenience but also has face implications. It threatens to reduce the relationship to that of a mistress and servant, where the summoned person is under obligation to abandon any other demands on their time.[8]

As I noted earlier, a summons can be justified by the urgency and significance of what prompts it. However, it is not easy to understand from the tape or the transcript what prompted the summons by Mrs. Bruner on this occasion. If it was that she was cold and needed her feet covered, this could conceivably be regarded as urgent and important for her, and perhaps, given their relationship, also for Mr. Bruner. However, perhaps only royalty in days gone by would summon servants to carry out personal service tasks that they could in principle do for themselves. If Mrs. Bruner sees this degree of subservience on Mr. Bruner's part as appropriate, then her challenge to his face is quite emphatic, imperious even. However, it may be given that for some reason she sees herself as not being able to cover her own feet, in which case the summons to physical presence can be seen as justified, although the refusal to acknowledge Mr. Bruner's interactional availability early in the episode remains problematic.

So the summons and answer is one major way that focused interaction begins in this household. Mrs. Bruner initiates many first pair parts of this sort. Moreover, the frequency and repetition of her summonses imply that she seeks Mr. Bruner's interactional availability for longer than any normal speaker would. Sometimes her summonses are not answered, presumably because Mr. Bruner is out of earshot or is choosing not to be interactionally available. Indeed, he observes in one of my interviews that he finds her summonses disruptive because it means that he cannot get the housework done. In the following extract, I put summonses on separate lines in order to emphasize the patterns:

Extract 16

1. Mrs. Bruner:	Dave (3.2)
2.	Dave (3.4)
3.	Where am I?
4.	Where am I?
5.	Dave (3.2)
6.	Dave (3.3)
7.	Da:ve (3.5)
8.	Where am I? (3.8)

---

[8] This is the crux of Joseph Losey's film "The Servant" where the changing relationship of master and servant is played out through the changing patterns of summoning. At the outset, the servant answers summonses in an exemplary fashion, emphasizing that his own requirements are not worthy of consideration. By the end of the film, however, he has undermined the right of the master to do any summoning whatsoever.

9.	Da:ve (3.4)
10.	Da:ve (3.4)
11.	DAVE (3.7)
12.	Da::ve (3.3)
13.	DAVE (4.4)
14.	DAVE (3.8)
15.	DAVE mmm (2.9)
16.	DAVE (3.8)
17.	Dave (4.1)
18.	Dave (4.2)
19.	((Telephone rings) (1.9)
20.	((Ringing)) Dave (4.6)
21.	((Ringing))DAVE (8.5)
22.	((Ringing)) DAVE (3.1) oh dear (6.9)
23.	((Ringing)) Eheheh (4.3)
24.	DAVE (6.0) ((Telephone stops ringing))
25.	Dave (3.2)
26.	Oh please (2.7)
27.	DA:VE (4.1)
28.	DA:VE (4.4]
29.	Dave (3.6)
30.	Dave (4.2)
31.	Da:ve (4.3)
32.	Dave (4.2)
33.	Aohh ((Possible tape break?))
34.	(Can I stay in bed) a bit longer?
35. Mr. Bruner:	Yes OK.

In this long series of summonses there are some regularities; for example, the timings are fairly regular until the telephone rings. After this Mrs. Bruner's calls to her husband lose their rhythm. To an ordinary member it might seem that the telephone ringing would present an intervening summons that possibly has precedence. Perhaps the call is seen in this way by Mrs. Bruner too: The disruption of the timing of her calls may suggest this. Although a number of episodes of summoning in the recordings Mr. Bruner made are superficially similar, the gaps between the summonses vary from episode to episode. For example, in Extract 15 when the sounds on the tape suggest that Mr. Bruner might well have merely gone into the next room, the gaps between her summonses are far shorter: But in Extract 16, when the noises suggest that Mr. Bruner may be downstairs, the gaps are longer. This indicates that in some instances Mrs. Bruner may be orienting to some of the differing requirements for summonses: Requirements that are a function of the proximity of interactants (i.e., that her husband is only in the next room as opposed to downstairs and thus interactionally more available).

When Mr. Bruner does arrive after his wife has called his name 27 times, she asks him if she can stay in bed a bit longer.[9] It will be noted

---

[9] It is possible there is a break in the tape recording here: the fact that the tape recorder may be voice-acticated, makes it difficult to tell the difference between a sudden call and a tape break.

that this time, there is no apparent justification for requiring Mr. Bruner's physical presence at all. This is the most *demanding* kind of summons of all in terms of face.

In Extracts 15 and 16, Mrs. Bruner does not begin her request until her husband arrives. So while the rules of summons and answer may have been bent a little, she still retains a sense of agency, that is, that the business proper of the summons does not begin until her husband is interactionally available even though her definition of interactional availability seems to be related to physical copresence. I have implied so far that a summons to physical presence may be seen as perhaps one that has more status and identity implications than a summons to interactional availability, and particularly a summons to physical presence that ignores the interactional availability of the summoned person. This is because it gives the summoned person no leeway to deal with the summons while they are doing what they are already doing. They have to stop and orient totally to the summoner. Mrs. Bruner's conflation of a requirement for both interactional availability and physical copresence can be seen to heighten this challenge to Mr. Bruner's identity and face.

In both extracts, there is a real disjunction between the degree of distress apparent in Mrs. Bruner's summonses and the question she asks when her husband arrives. The question eventually put is very ordinary and undistressed, the moment of stress appearing to have passed. This would suggest that Mrs. Bruner appears to have difficulty in maintaining a line from the beginning to the conclusion of a summoning sequence. I have suggested already that the sort of summons sequences she engages in threaten the face of others. But, of course, they threaten her face too. There are ways of handling summonses that can lead to pejorative assessments by others. The degree to which Mrs Bruner uses summonses might be summed up by the phrase "crying wolf". Although there are points in the local management of any conversation when some types of adjacency pairs are more suitable devices than others, there also come points in conversations (and over a period of time) between speakers who are familiar with each other when some types of adjacency pairs are seen to be inappropriate by at least one party in the talk. One example of this is when children ask questions interminably and parents get exasperated. Another is when the summons is devalued by being used too often in the wrong circumstances, as seems to be the case with some of Mrs. Bruner's summonses. For a normal speaker such as Mr. Bruner, presumably, over time the experience has been that the subsequent justification his wife presents for the summons is not sufficient to take it seriously. Perhaps, for face purposes, he has decided to not always be at her beck and call. To this end he chooses simply to be interactionally unavailable. This is an effective strategy for him because he knows that responses *from afar* are pointless and that interactional obligations only begin with physical copresence.

There is another way of looking at it though: "Crying wolf" could be seen as a way of confirming one's existence rather than merely gaining attention. In some senses, this compares with my earlier discussion about someone lost on the moors. Such calls for help are not merely calls for assistance, but are summonses for someone to acknowledge the lost person's existence. Continued existence is dependent on acknowledgment of the self by others. Summoning help on the moors would be unlikely to be interpreted by others as "Crying wolf" As the person on the moors needs someone else to facilitate their continuing existence, so perhaps does Mrs. Bruner. If no one is there with her she may not know where she is (or even perhaps who she is). This is almost an inversion of Schegloff's maxim, *no answer, no person* into *no person, no answer* (Schegloff, 1972b). If every summons is a need to reaffirm one's existence, then using constant summonses to do this would seem to be a workable strategy, if somewhat wearing for the other party. The arrival of the other party may then be sufficient to confirm one's existence, the existential question may not have to be asked when summoner and summoned are face-to-face. But this does place the summoner in a difficult situation; normal members would be required to have a *good enough* reason for having made the summons. Of course, Mrs. Bruner does always have a reason (the obligatory third statement), the conclusion to her summoning activity is structurally normal in this sense, but is her reason actually good enough to save face?

So overall, in this household there is more talk than might be expected for an occasioned activity like summoning and answering, and much of the responsibility for this extra volume of talk lies with Mrs. Bruner.

Routine Activities

There are many events and routine activities that involve questions on Mrs. Bruner's part that I think would be unlikely to be asked by ordinary members. In this section, I want primarily to discuss the occasion of lunchtime in the Bruner household, but I begin with two excerpts that show, again, how alien ordinary everyday life seems to be to Mrs. Bruner:

Extract 17

Mrs. Bruner:	What do I put on now?
Mr. Bruner:	Your bedsocks.
Mrs. Bruner:	Bedsocks are these?
Mr. Bruner:	Yeh lift your foot up.
Mrs. Bruner:	Oh I don't know mi duck.
Mr. Bruner:	Lift your foot up ( )
Mrs. Bruner:	Dave Dave.
Mr. Bruner:	There you go.

Mrs. Bruner:	Here?
Mr. Bruner:	That's right yeh that's it.
Mrs. Bruner:	This me?
Mr. Bruner:	That's right.
Mrs. Bruner:	Dave.
Mr. Bruner:	Yeh.
Mrs. Bruner:	Which side?
Mr. Bruner:	This is your side look.
Mrs. Bruner:	Here? Are you sure?
Mr. Bruner:	Yeh.
Mrs. Bruner:	How many pillows do I have? I don't have all these.
Mr. Bruner:	You do as a rule.
Mrs. Bruner:	Aye? Oh I never want all these Dave do I? Look here.
Mr. Bruner:	Well you well I'll take one away and then you'll see.
Mrs. Bruner:	Take away aye.
Mr. Bruner:	Here you are now see how you like it you had the four last night.
Mrs. Bruner:	Eyeyeey aye I don't know mi duck I can't get mi legs in.
Mr. Bruner:	Here you are.
Mrs. Bruner:	Oh oh oh.
Mr. Bruner:	Yes there you go.
Mrs. Bruner:	Am I in?
Mr. Bruner:	Yes.
Mrs. Bruner:	Dave am I in, love?
Mr. Bruner:	Yes.
Mrs. Bruner:	Oh that's better.
Mr. Bruner:	Yes.
Mrs. Bruner:	AI hey hey mmm ( ) it's awful mi duck eeny meeny miny mo Dave.
Mr. Bruner:	There you go.

The occasions of going to bed and getting up, judging from the tapes Mr. Bruner recorded, are ones that Mrs. Bruner cannot achieve without physical and organizational assistance. Here, Mrs. Bruner does not appear to recognize the sequences of events that are commonplace in going to bed or in dealing with common equipment associated with bedtime. Moreover, she does not appear to be able to monitor her own body to the extent of knowing whether she is in bed or not (on another occasion she asks if her feet are in bed). However, she does appear to understand the occasion to the extent that she knows that the end result of the operation should be that she is properly in bed. All of this is a cause for talk, because she asks questions and makes comments on issues and routines that would not normally generate talk, as the following extract again shows:

Extract 18

Mrs. Bruner:	When do I get up?
Mr. Bruner:	((From afar)) What?
Mrs. Bruner:	Dave Dave Dave Dave where are you?
Mr. Bruner:	((From afar)) I'm here I'm coming.
Mrs. Bruner:	Dave where are you?
Mr. Bruner:	(From afar)) I'm in the kitchen love.
Mrs. Bruner:	((Mr Bruner arrives)) ( ) Have I got to get up?
Mr. Bruner:	((Exasperated)) It's bedtime now.
Mrs. Bruner:	Aye?
Mr. Bruner:	It's bedtime.

Mrs. Bruner:	Is it night?
Mr. Bruner:	Yes.
Mrs. Bruner:	Are you sure?
Mr. Bruner:	Yes.

Here, Mrs. Bruner does not appear to be able to recognize for herself what time of day it is and therefore needs to ask if she has to get up. Recognizing the time of day provides a substantial resource for ordinary members to use in order to commence various sorts of occasioned activity, although the sequence shows that Mrs. Bruner is not entirely lost to a sense of occasion in that she knows that night is when you go to bed. Here again, problems with ordinary occasions call for talk that focuses on aspects of the world that are taken for granted by most normal members. It is interesting that when she asks Mr. Bruner whether he is sure it is night, this challenges even whether such knowledge should be ordinary taken-for-granted knowledge.

Lunchtime too poses problems. The Bruner's lunchtime is an event, we might suppose, that involves *doing being ordinary* (Sacks, 1984). Doing being ordinary includes doing being *the right sort of ordinary* for a particular occasion. However, in this episode there are a number of ways in which Mrs. Bruner can be seen to be failing to live up to the requirements of the situation. The complete transcription of this occasion is in Appendix D. Of course, any talk that takes place at a social lunchtime may well sound quite chaotic to an outsider.[10] But generally much apparently chaotic talk can be contextualized by the accompanying actions. Even allowing for the fact that lunchtime is likely to be quite activity based, and that in relation to these data I do not have access to the physical action that was going on in a more than speculative way, Mrs. Bruner's deviance and Mr. Bruner's attempts to prevent and deal with it are nevertheless very obvious.

Speier's (1969) analysis of mealtimes involving children is a useful starting point for this analysis, because he outlines a number of factors which delineate a meal. For one thing it is "the direct result of the planful preparation of its participants" (p. 159). They gather together in a routine way and at some point following the arrival of at least some of them the meal officially begins. Whereas the meal is the main activity of the event, as Speier suggested, other activities may occur simultaneously. However:

> It is the occasioned feature of the activity that provides its members with public understandings about the event as a sequential and temporal set of arrangements revolving around a main activity. The

---

[10] Listening to a recording of an occasion like lunch strips it of its context and taken-for-grantedness. To see something in a taken-for-granted sort of way requires us to disattend to certain elements of the occasion, for example, knives and forks being scraped along plates. Listening to a recording, we are not able, at least initially, to disattend to the things normally disattended to. Moreover, other relevant aspects of the context have been cut out.

> character of interactional and conversational development is influenced by the participants' orientation to that main purpose. Their talk is organized around that purpose in various ways, as a kind of dominant theme in the interactional structure of the occasion. (Speier 1969, pp. 160–161)

There is, or should be, a public understanding of the events, their sequence, and the chronology that surrounds dinner. Conversational topics that do not relate to the main event nevertheless have to be developed within its parameters. The meal is a demarcated occasion. In terms of focused interaction, one would expect participants to pay attention to the occasioned aspects of the meal.

So in the case of the Bruner's lunchtime, we can expect a certain amount of occasioned activity relating to the meal. We can also expect that there are ways of handling talk not occasioned by the meal itself. At one extreme, is the strict monastic order where only occasioned activity takes place at mealtimes, and at the other, the buffet party where the guests may not even address the issue of the meal if they choose not to do so. For many people lunch may be a quiet occasion. Indeed, participants may effectively be in a state of incipient talk from which actual talk will be occasioned by the next requirement of the meal or by the spasmodic introduction of topics unrelated to the meal. Marked behavior is the production of talk that is neither occasioned nor a locally managed conversation running in parallel with the meal.

Speier's work on this subject is doubly useful because he looked in particular at how children come to be socialized during routine occasions such as a family dinner—socialization involving explicitly drawing attention to those moments when they are not doing being ordinary properly. As I noted in chapter 1, the aim of the socialization of children is that they should arrive at a situation where they can participate in an occasion in a taken-for-granted sort of a way. Not to participate in a taken-for-granted sort of way is accountable, and may deny someone full membership status. Following Cicourel, Speier (1969) suggested that in some respects children are like cultural strangers who need to develop an effective sense of social structure (p.16). They have to decipher social meanings in a world of as yet unfamiliar actions and activities, a suggestion that reflects Schutz's work on *The Stranger*:

> The approaching stranger . . . is about to transform himself from an unconcerned onlooker into a would-be member of the approached group. The cultural pattern of the approached group, then, is no longer a subject matter of his thought but a segment of the world which has to be dominated by actions. Consequently, its position within the stranger's system of relevance changes decisively, and this means . . . that another type of knowledge is required for its interpretation. Jumping from the stalls to the stage, so to speak, the former onlooker

becomes a member of the cast, enters as a partner into social relations with his co-actors, and participates henceforth in action in progress. (p. 17)

At meal times the newcomer must acquire social skills—learning when to eat, when to speak, when to remain silent, when to interrupt, how to handle food, when to leave the table, and so on. But whereas an adult stranger may watch to see how to handle cutlery, how to talk, and so on, children may have little sense of occasion. That something *is* an occasion is something we learn culturally. In relation to these data, my feeling is that some confused speakers appear at times to be similar to children in having little sense of occasion and at other times to be like adult cultural strangers in that they understand there is an occasion but the nature of it is a mystery to them.

Mr. Bruner's Approach. To set the context: Prior to the meal, Mr. Bruner says "three minutes and your dinner will be ready", indicating a taken-for-granted assumption that occasions such as dinner properly *begin*. In his talk, Mr. Bruner *scripts* the features of the occasioned activity lunch. The recording of this occasion involves 103 turns. Of these, Mr. Bruner uses 28 in occasioned activity in addition to having signposted the event several times prior to this particular stretch of conversation:

Extract 19[11]

12	There you are here's your dinner.
16	I've put plenty of gravy on and there is more if you want it.
18	There's some more if you want.
20	Yes you start.
24	Do you want a drink?
26	Mmm do you want a drink?
36	No I don't think it is ((She has said it is boiling)).
40	Start a bit there.
42	You've hardly started.
44	I didn't put you a lot on because I thought you wouldn't eat it.
46	Take your time.
48	Take your time.
50	Let me cut it up for you a bit.
52	You haven't eaten much at all come on.
54	Look it's nice look at all that.
56	Come on.
64	Try and eat a bit more meat.
66	Will you have some sweet?
68	We've got you can have prunes and custard.
70	Or apple tart would you like apple tart?
72	Come on.
76	No you haven't started try and eat a little bit.
78	Well I don't know why you shouldn't be hungry you didn't have much breakfast.
84	When you've had your dinner ((She has asked if she can lie down)).
86	You can go and have a lie down.
90	[...] Eat a bit more of your meat that will do you good.

---

[11] The numbers in the lefthand column denote the place of the turns in the episode as a whole.

| 94 | It's all nice chicken. |
| 98 | OK leave it there or something I'll sort it out in a minute. |

Much of what Mr. Bruner says indicates an expectation of certain appropriate behavior for such an occasion. It is something that has a *beginning*: Once handed your dinner, you are supposed to get on with it (42, 56, 72, 76) and continue to get on with it; at the same time you are supposed to eat it at an acceptable speed (46, 48); and if you appear not able to do so, others can intervene and offer you assistance in doing so (50), although this is probably the occasioned activity of lunch only with someone who may not be able to accomplish a normal member's performance of the occasion—for example, we help children at the lunch table. You are supposed to eat an adequate meal (52) and in this household, the primary object of the first course is meat (64, 90). One of the available excuses for not eating a meal in this occasioned activity is that "it is not nice" but that excuse is not available here because "it is nice" (54, 94). There are certain other activities that are not available to you until you have finished this one (84). These utterances contain a whole series of instructions about how to tackle the meal as an occasioned activity. But all this occasioned talk on Mr. Bruner's part seems very odd in relation to another adult. It would serve very nicely as a script for lunch with a small and recalcitrant child. But normal members would be unlikely to employ quite so much talk for this sort of everyday occasioning. Of course, there is an uncertainty in the conduct of ordinary occasions as to what is allowable and therefore what is open to reasonable correction. It depends on the situation. What we have in this situation is someone who is not behaving appropriately, who has already been labeled as deviant, and who is therefore open to an abnormal degree of guidance or correction.

Mrs. Bruner's Approach. Mrs. Bruner's approach to the meal is a mixture of resistance to the occasion and behavior inappropriate to it. There appear to be a number of different ways in which she fails to understand the event. She does not appear to understand its normal structure, thus lunchtime is no longer a taken-for-granted event, but one that, for her, needs accounting:

Extract 20

3. Mrs. Bruner	[...] Is there only two of us today?
4. Mr. Bruner	Yes there's only us two today.
5. Mrs. Bruner	Why is that then?
6. Mr. Bruner	Well there's always only two of us.
7. Mrs. Bruner	Aye?
8. Mr. Bruner	There's only us two always.
9. Mrs. Bruner	Oh I don't know ma duck[...]

Here, Mrs. Bruner engages in talk that is almost identical to the kinds of talk involved in Garfinkel's breaching experiments, where experimenters breach everyday tacit understandings (Garfinkel, 1967). In Utterance 3, the question might have been one that a lodger or someone used to eating in an insititution or a group might have asked. At a private household's lunch, only the householders are likely to be present at lunch. Certainly it is not a matter for accounting when there are only a requisite number of householders, only when there are fewer or more. This also fits into discussions about preference structures as outlined by Bilmes (1988)." [In a discussion] If A is speaking to B on some subject, and A knows something unusual or unexpected about the subject which might be of significance to B, then A should mention it" (p. 163). Bilmes gave the example of going to a party: Unless told that it is a fancy dress party, people would not go in fancy dress, and if they arrive in ordinary dress and find it is a fancy dress party this may be a matter of reproach between host and guests. Thus, when nothing unusual is going to happen, speaker A has nothing unusual to mention and therefore is likely to be surprised if speaker B asks him a question about the occasion as though there were going to be something unusual about it. This is the situation that Mr. Bruner finds himself in. Mrs. Bruner has remarked on something that in normal commonsensical reasoning would not be remarked on.

There are a few instances where Mrs. Bruner does seem aware that there is some issue around her participation in the occasion. An example is when she asks "Have I got to start?" This question suggests a suspicion that something has to happen first before she can begin. Her use of the words "What's all this about?" which appear to be generated when she looks at her lunch (Appendix D, Utterance 73), may indicate that she is mystified by the occasion. At this point, Mrs. Bruner is asking for an account of that which, to an ordinary member, can be seen to be the taken-for-granted aspect of lunch as an occasion, namely, that if you do not eat your lunch it remains on your plate until something is done about it. But such words may also be used in a mildly reproving way to be read by members as some kind of a request to justify what is going on, as to why an occasion is not as it should be. It is a device often used by school teachers when they walk into a noisy classroom or when they find children obviously breaking the rules, and may be a request for an account and not for information.

Mrs. Bruner also does not appear to know where she is:

Extract 21

21. Mrs. Bruner: Oh dear don't aye? I don't know where we are ma duck aye? I don't know aye? I don't know de da dee ded de dade.

Insofar as place can be seen as one contextualizing feature of taken-for-grantedness (i.e., we always have lunch in the dining room, therefore if we are not in the dining room and are nevertheless having lunch, then it is likely to be a mentionable matter), then not to know where you are indicates that you are not able to take this event (whatever it is) for granted. Another interpretation of this utterance is that Mrs. Bruner is saying that she does not know where they are in the sense of not knowing where they are in the meal, or the conversation. But generally such utterances take place after a distraction or interruption. People do not tend to lose their place in straightforward familiar occasioned activity, and if they do, they account for it.

Mrs. Bruner is also unable to cope with choices offered in the meal:

Extract 22

66. Mr. Bruner:	Will you have some sweet?
67. Mrs. Bruner:	I don't know he her.
68. Mr. Bruner:	We've got you can have prunes and custard.
69. Mrs. Bruner:	I don't know.
70. Mr. Bruner:	Or apple tart would you like apple tart?
71. Mrs. Bruner:	((Indistinctly))I don't know.

If she does not know whether she wants a sweet or not then she does not know *which* sweet she wants and so the process of the meal is held up. In order for a meal to work, people need to eat in the right order, and to facilitate the next stage of the meal when offered a choice by choosing. It is interesting that choice at mealtimes is part of the process of socialization of children. Beyond a certain degree, refusing to choose, or choosing things that cannot be offered or that take an inordinate amount of time to prepare, can be seen as immature behavior according to certain common child-rearing principles. Choosing promptly within the available parameters is ordinary member behavior. Not to do so may be an accountable matter. Even if people cannot decide promptly, they need to make it clear that they understand that a decision is required fairly urgently.

However, Mrs. Bruner does, in fact, produce some occasioned talk. For example:

Extract 23

32. Mrs. Bruner:	It's boiling.

[...]

57. Mrs. Bruner:	Oh leave it Dave <u>don't</u> ((Crossly)) I can't eat it if you keep messing it up oh no mmm I don't feel a bit hungry.

Here, Mrs. Bruner's remarks relate to the presentation of the meal. Meals should not be boiling and they should not be messed up. In relation to messing up the meal, as I noted previously, intervention in the meal of another person is saved largely for people who have acquired the labels of being less-than-full members. Their lack of full membership and the need to get the meal eaten overrides any consideration for maintaining the face of the other as a full member (at least as far as the full member who is intervening is concerned). But here Mrs. Bruner is giving herself full membership and criticizing her husband for undermining it and thus threatening her face.

Extract 24

13. Mrs. Bruner:	Oh Lord Dave oh you've given me all that.	
14. Mr. Bruner:	Mmm yes.	
15. Mrs. Bruner:	Oh Dave I don't know where I'm going to put it (pause) I don't know ma duck I don't know mmm.	

[...]

25. Mrs. Bruner: I'm not going to eat all this lot.
[...]

45. Mrs. Bruner: [...] I can't eat no more Dave he he (pause) oh dear not yet he he mm.
[...]

51. Mrs. Bruner: Oh I'm full up mi duck he he.
52. Mr. Bruner: You haven't eaten all that much come on.
[...]

75. Mrs. Bruner: All this I ain't ate any of this.
76. Mr. Bruner: No you haven't started. Try and eat a little bit.
77. Mrs. Bruner: Well what's the good when I ain't hungry?

This raises the question of the identity work that the couple are doing. In these snippets, Mrs. Bruner uses a specific competent identity that relates to the occasion. As Speier (1969) noted, people need to operate within the parameters of the offered occasion, but there are individual ways of doing things that can still be accommodated. Specifically, in relation to mealtimes, people may be known to have a small appetite, or to bolt their food, or they may have the flu and not be hungry. Some of these may come to be taken-for-granted behaviors within the family, and only remarked on when guests are present (suggesting the context dependent nature of accounting). Others may be matters for comment on an individual occasion (e.g., having the flu). Here, Mrs. Bruner says in a number of different ways that the meal is too large for her. But her account of herself and her state at this mealtime is not accepted by her husband. Mr. Bruner, on the whole, refuses to validate her claims to this particular type of membership. It seems that Mrs. Bruner is not being treated as an individual person who can judge her own degree of hunger and act in such a way as to be accommodated within the parameters of the meal. Her claims to current identity as a person who is not hungry go unheard. Again, a similar situation can often be seen to obtain with children who (in the case of my own childhood) are obliged to eat the crusts off their bread despite protesting that they do not want them and do not like them. Instead, Mr. Bruner continues with the sort of occasioning statements that might be in order with a difficult child. This suggests that there is a hierarchy of occasioning and face where the full member is prepared to affront the negative face of the less-than-full member in support of the occasion, rather than to promote their positive face. And Mrs. Bruner contests this affront.

So Mr. Bruner uses mainly occasioned talk. The great wash of other talk and noise by Mrs. Bruner is on the whole ignored. Only when she asks him if they are going out today does he respond (Appendix D: Utterances 81–82.). In particular, he ignores a great deal of "mmming", "aaring", and moaning on Mrs. Bruner's part, which I now consider.

Self-Talk Episodes in a Two-Way Conversation

I want to explore two more features of Mrs. Bruner's talk that indicate that there is too much of it. I noted earlier in regard to Tilly that the notion of *talkative* may be related to the density of discourse. I would now also suggest that talking away from turn can contribute to the person being construed as very active in their talk (although not necessarily talkative).

Mrs. Bruner groans and moans a lot in the course of her conversation. Extract 25, contains a further snippet of the lunchtime conversation between Mr. and Mrs. Bruner: The talk takes place about midway through the episode. It will be noted that in Utterances 56 to 58, there is a good deal of talk from Mrs. Bruner that does not seem to be occasioned by the lunch or by the previous utterance.

Extract 25

56. Mr. Bruner:	Come on.
57. Mrs. Bruner:	Oh leave it Dave don't I can't eat it if you keep messing it up ((crossly)) oh no (1.9) mm I don't feel a bit hungry (.) I'd love to go back to bed he he he (.) eeny meeny miny mo oh I'd love to go back to bed (2.3) mm (.) mm (7.3) mm (don't) give me any more Dave it's awful (1.9) no I don't feel a bit hungry (2.6) I'd love to go back to bed he (2.7) I would (2.0) I feel awful (2.6) eeny meeny miny mo (2.2) Oh I do feel bad (8.0) never felt so bad in my life never he er murder(6.7) mmm.(3.1) mmmm (7.2) mmmmmmm (3.3) mmmmmmm (1.7) ar dear (2.5) (Dave) I do feel bad (2.5) oh it's murder mm (2.7) mmmmmmm (3.1.) never felt so bad (2.3) eeny meeny miny mo murder (2.8) mmmmmmm (2.4) mmmmmmmm (1.9) mmmmmmmmm (1.5) What's that Dave? (2.7) What is that supposed to be?
58. Mr. Bruner:	It's a microphone.

Both the beginning of her turn and the end of her turn (and one sentence soon after the beginning) are in the here and now. But much of the middle section of the turn is either moaning, or self-oriented talk, or rhyming talk.

Mrs. Bruner does not really develop or maintain a topic that relates to the other participant, but freely expresses herself without recourse to the other person. Because of their pitch and sequential positioning, we can suggest that the *mms* and *aars* cannot be back channel responses to previous remarks. Her talk appears to be almost self-talk, a mode of talk from which most ordinary members would be likely to desist when they are in company.[12] Most of the talk is quite quiet. The volume only increases at points when when she appears to be specifically addressing Mr. Bruner. We might suggest that if someone is discovered engaging in self-talk, they have to justify what they were doing and have an obligation to reorient to the other. If they do not do, the occasion of a conversation cannot begin. If, however, such talk takes place within what is ostensibly a conversation, then the situation becomes potentially problematic for the other speakers.

Mr. Bruner in no way attempts to influence this episode of talk. During this turn (and indeed a number of other similar turns) he says nothing—no continuers, he makes no contribution whatsoever. The lack of intervention of the normal speaker may well make this stretch of talk seem even odder. By saying nothing, there is no attempt on Mr. Bruner's part to disguise the talk by intervening or to forestall the flow in order to save her face. Having gained a turn, Mrs. Bruner just goes on until something in the room catches her attention. Not only does she disattend to the occasion more than a normal member, but she also presents talk not generally positively sanctioned at such an occasion. Even small children might be sanctioned if they produced such a lengthy string of odd noises. One reason, then, why people may become very active as confused speakers is that the usual restraints on speaking rights are not applied. Conversation might ostensibly be locally managed, but if all the management is dominated by one person, others may tacitly withdraw from participating.

The situation I have described is almost the inverse of those involving minimally active confused speakers, where normal speakers may bid for turn more than they do when participating solely with other normal speakers. In the case of the Bruners, the normal speaker effectively allows the confused speaker to be very active. This may be because for Mr. Bruner to listen in order to figure out what his wife is saying, so as to decide whether to bid for turn himself, is a rather pointless activity—it is not a motivating force in this conversation (Sacks et al., 1978). Indeed, elsewhere in the Bruner recordings, where Mr. Bruner does bid for turn it turns out to be a largely fruitless activity: For example, I noted earlier summoning sequences where Mrs. Bruner summons him from a separate part of the house and ignores several responses to her summons, waiting instead until he is actually copresent. Here, Mr. Bruner's management of his side of the conversation is organized purely in relation to the management of the meal.

In some respects, then, the occasion of lunch is one that Mrs. Bruner fails to do properly. Much of her talk is inappropriate to an ordinary

---

[12] Muttering and self-talk in the presence of others is often used to some purpose, to indicate that the self-talker is absorbed in private activity, and sometimes to convey the *inner person* to others. However, this does not seem to be the case with Mrs. Bruner.

household lunch attended by adults who know each other well. She orients to the occasion as though she is perplexed by it. At the same time there is a dissonance between her claims to full membership and her failure to behave appropriately. The nonoccasioned talk in which she does engage is self-oriented, and would usually be deemed inappropriate at a social occasion. She is not voluble in the same way as Tilly, but if someone talks in such a way as to problematize taken-for-granted understandings, this too is likely to be construed as too much talk.

CONCLUSION

In this chapter I began with an ordinary member's categorization of Tilly and Mrs. Bruner as very active confused speakers. I have tried to explain this supposition by showing that their talk disregards certain constraining influences that limit the talk of normal speakers.

In relation to Tilly, I suggested that very active confused speakers may use dispreferred answers in combination with repetition, thereby producing talk that can be typified as talkative. Tilly's failure to adhere to Grice's maxim of quality generates talk in which the *truth* is contested. With regard to Mrs. Bruner, many of the ordinary occasions of everyday life are mysteries to her. These include management of household routines and even management of her own body in the form of such activities as eating, and getting into bed. The problems generated by this inability to do or understand ordinary activity produce a good deal of talk both in terms of summonses to her husband (to find out what to do) and in often inappropriate occasioned talk when she is copresent with her husband.

In relation to both women I proposed that very active confused speakers frequently have available to them topics for talk that may not generally be available to ordinary members. For such confused speakers, taken-for-granted assumptions, which rarely surface (unless they become marked in some way), *are* treated as available, and thus violate the maxim of quantity (Grice, 1975).

Normal speakers use various strategies for dealing with very active confused speakers. In the face of the type of talkative behavior Tilly produces, Moyra produces more talk too (certainly more than we might expect from an interviewer), and this is talk that in many ways emulates the constructions of confused speakers: It is repetitive, dispreferred and so on. On the other hand, Mr. Bruner at times may refuse to become interactionally available when his wife summons him: and when he is with her, he often seems to restrict himself to occasioned talk. He ignores most of his wife's unoccasioned talk, as it is in no way a motivating factor for him to want to claim a turn. This illustrates another strategy on the part of normal speakers: They may select just one thread of the talk to engage with and ignore the rest.

The lack of rapport that these confused speakers have with normal speakers would seem to relate in some ways to the concept of face. Mrs. Bruner appears to have difficulty in maintaining a line because she has a poor sense of occasion, environment, and even body, despite substantial instruction from her husband. Tilly, on the other hand, maintains a line against all the evidence. Both positions suggest that face-work is likely to be problematic for other speakers interacting with them.

We may therefore suggest that, as with moderately active confused speakers, there are some aspects of normal interactional appearances to be found in the talk of these very active confused speakers. But this structural normality is not enough to make the talk normal.

This chapter has hinged mainly on the question of how some people appear to have more to talk about than others. I hope that I have shown, largely through conversation analysis, some of the machinery of talk that supports very active speakers, and much of what I have said in this respect can be seen to apply to many people who are recognizable as normal but very active speakers. However, the subjects of the chapter were two women who have been identified as being confused, and they are not merely very active speakers, but in both cases speakers who bring to their talk subject matter not generally available to ordinary speakers: Routine occasioned activity is rarely the subject of metatalk, except for the purposes of humor or irony.

As with previous chapters, I would suggest that there are implications for membership when the very active speaker not only utilizes the turn-taking machinery to promote his or her own talk, but reinforces this with an exploitation of the machinery of description that is not bound by context. The extensive use of repetition (which was raised in a rather acute form in the case of Tilly) involves the continuing use of the same topic. As I noted, repetition has a number of legitimate uses, but can also be seen as a way of holding the conversational floor without bringing anything new to bear on the situation. For example, if we suggest that someone is boring, one reason might be that this person has topics for talk that others would either not consider available or desirable or would only consider available for a relatively limited amount of time. I am reminded of a friend of mine who described a party where she had been pinned against a wall by someone for some time—saying to her partner when he arrived to rescue her "John, I'd like to introduce you to Mrs. Smith who was just telling me about her fascinating hobby of mending porcelain plates." I was very struck when I heard this story of how well I identified with it, not being able to get away, not being able to get a word in, not being able to change the subject. Indeed, even the imagery is of being trapped and rescued. If one can take neither equal interactional rights nor equal topical rights then one does, in a sense, become trapped in a conversation that I would suggest is no longer locally managed. Some people battle gamely, putting on an appearance of being an equal (and fascinated) participant, so attempting to maintain face. Others, like Mr. Bruner, effectively withdraw. Yet others perhaps adopt a stance of talking more themselves in order to redress the balance of interactional rights (much as Moyra did with Tilly). Some just walk away.

Perhaps the types of talk used by the two normal speakers in this chapter represent devices that normal speakers bring into play when confronted by a lot of talk. One thing to do is to try to establish one's own credentials and membership as a person who has equal interactional rights here, as Moyra does with her own repetitions and dispreferred answers. But another thing to do is to adopt a policy of minimal responses, working on the basis that nothing you can say will actually make any difference to the management of the talk. These can perhaps be seen as extreme cases, but then the normal speaker response, as I have shown, is based on the options available within an ordinary conversation.

7

Getting Confused?

In this study I examined verbal interaction between confused and normal speakers. In particular, I have been concerned with how talk is recognized as confused and how it is dealt with. The methodic practices that lead to the constitution of confusion have been treated as a topic for investigation and in the course of the book, I have drawn attention both to confused speech as a component of ordinary talk and confused speech that is generated by confused speakers.

Much of the professional and investigative literature in this area sees confusion as pathology. It is concerned with identifying features of confused talk in the abstract, unconnected with any consideration of normal talk. The nature of the latter is simply taken for granted. Yet, a considerable literature is available that shows that normal talk is a complex, context-sensitive, and achieved matter. The work of sociologists such as Goffman and Garfinkel, of conversation analysts, and of philosophers and linguists like Grice, Sperber, and Wilson is of particular significance here. One point that emerges clearly from such work is that the difference between normal and confused talk is defined in the course of social interaction. There can be confusion in normal conversation and intelligible passages in confused conversation: What is crucial is the participants' recognition of confusion and how they deal with it.

Although this study has been about verbal interaction between confused and normal speakers, for the most part, the extracts analyzed do not exemplify the baroque confusion of, for example, Beckett's plays (which, arguably, are not confused anyway because none of the talk appears to be problematic for the participants, only for the audience). In some respects, the talk I have analyzed is only slightly odd. Most of the momentary confusions exemplified are of a kind that can be heard frequently in ordinary conversations representing ordinary troubles; most do not undermine the conversation and bring it to a halt. Normal and confused speakers retrench, regroup and get over the problems somehow. Nevertheless, some participants are routinely to be seen as normal and others as confused. This is a members' accomplishment but it is not one in which there would be much disagreement about who is and is not confused. So how does it come to be that even while relatively normal conversational appearances are being maintained, some people can be categorized as confused and others are seen as normal?

The work of people such as Speier illustrates the interactional consequences of the participation of less-than-full members, many of which are marked and accountable. In some senses, their participation may be seen as a signpost for interactional troubles. I have suggested throughout the study that many of the practices exemplified may have significance for a wide group of speakers who are assigned less-than-full membership. Indeed, it seems to me that membership in talk has been a central feature of the study so that the discussion has implications beyond talk involving confused speakers, and I shall return to this idea shortly. In the case of the confused speakers in this study, with the exception of the Bruner tapes recorded at their home, all the speakers were being interviewed because they were confused. Their less-than-full membership was, in fact, the point of the meetings that constitute these data. Such labeling may suggest to ordinary members, from the outset, that interactional situations of a particular kind may occur. Indeed, they may be ready to attribute any oddities in the conversation to the less-than-full membership of some of the participants.

In the case of the people who feature in this study, regardless of what sort of repair work or rectification the confused speaker undertakes, their efforts may be degraded by the fact that they have already been given the identity of confused person. In a sense, any deviant talk that ensues can be seen to confirm the label they arrived with. Moreover, even though some of the talk produced by confused speakers may have normal features, this may not be given credence. In a sense, this is rather like the situation that criminals can find themselves in: Although they do not spend all their time being criminals their whole identity may come to be determined by that label (Matza, 1969).

The behavior of the confused speakers challenges common understanding of what goes on in talk. In a conversation or interview, ordinary members have a repertoire of strategies on which they can draw, and they also have personal resources that *anyone* has that they can use, such as their own biographies and experience. How they select from this repertoire is determined by their reading of the current situation. People decide what to do by judging what is appropriate at any particular point in time. In an ambiguous situation, especially, they take it step-by-step, attending to contexts and recognizing that they themselves shape those contexts with each utterance they make. Generally speaking, such ongoing local management of the talk is a taken-for-granted activity. Even if many aspects of the talk are preallocated, as, for example, in an interview, participants are still able to choose *how* to respond, although they need to select an appropriate formulation from the many available. When confused speakers participate in situations, however, these ordinary conversational undertakings are called into question. What occurs is analogous to Garfinkel's breaching experiments (1967). Such challenges to the taken-for-granted cause interactional troubles, creating problems for everyone in the form of how to talk and what to say.

When there are interactional problems, in order to save face, participants in any encounter need to rectify how they talk or what they say so as to recover themselves. If they fail to do this, their identity suffers. I would suggest that all the confused speakers discussed in this study have difficulties with this for several reasons. They are frequently unable to bring to an interaction those resources that it is normally assumed everyone has: resources that help people avoid trouble in the first place. Often there are gaps in the biographies they present, or these biographies do not stand up to scrutiny from other participants. In some cases, they appear to be unable to produce a biography at all. If they *can* articulate their biography, they are either unable to present a correct formulation or to choose an appropriate one, so that repair work is called for. All this can be counterpoised to the situation of ordinary members. As a general rule, people's biographies do stand up to scrutiny, are adjusted according to context, do not have gaps and deficiencies (and if they do, identity work is often done to accommodate this).

However, typically, confused speakers do not repair trouble, or their repair work is inadequate. This in itself draws more attention to the original trouble. The markedness of the problem is yet more highlighted. Whereas normal speakers may successfully work to unmark a marked situation, confused speakers do not appear to have the resources to do this. They continue to be *out of face* even when they resort to strategies that ordinary members would use to save face. More than this, though, very often that which they are seeking to repair is of a kind that should not normally cause any trouble. The philosopher Wittgenstein (1969) pointed out that there are certain kinds of information that are givens in our everyday life, indeed, that form the *hinges* on which it works. He used the example of knowing one's own name, but this can be extended to other basic biographical facts, such as how many children one has had, what relation one's daughter's daughter is to oneself, and so on. Such knowledge is constitutive of normal membership. In many ways, getting it wrong is beyond all repair.

A final source of problems is that when ordinary members are talking to someone with an overarching identity of confusion, they can take license to do some unusual things in conversation—engage in test questions, interrupt, present bizarre formulations, and so on. The result of this is that confused speakers may be presented much more frequently than others with conversational situations involving peculiarities that would be difficult for anyone to handle. Indeed, as I noted at the beginning of this book, bizarre nonordinary formulations are often used as a way of rooting out incompetence and otherwise testing people and challenging face. They can be taken as a sign for participants to engage in defensive or evasive talk in order to avoid losing face. And that's all right as long as you are assigned ordinary full membership, because this acts as a sort of guarantee for you. But if you have to deal with a difficult formulation and you have less-than-full membership, whatever you say will be judged from this standpoint. Indeed, as I noted, even when you get *ordinary* things right it becomes a matter for comment: Comment that would be made about no ordinary member.

Confused speakers are faced with a sort of downward spiral. Inadequate resources of personal knowledge tend to cause trouble some of which is difficult if not impossible to rectify. Inadequacy of repair techniques means that they worsen the situation they are trying to deal with. On top of this, a prior degraded identity means that whatever they do is open to interpretation as a reflection of their "confused" identity, and in some cases they are themselves aware of this. All this adds up to chronic interactional trouble for confused speakers. But the problems I have listed confused speakers as having are not merely technical. Each constitutes a threat to face. Through the act of talk, the sense of self as a valued person, and indeed the sense of being a person at all, is constantly precarious. They know, as Mr. Graham puts it, that all the time they are in danger of "blowing the gaffe". On the other hand, normal speakers do not, in general, verbally interact against this background of what we might call triple jeopardy—inadequate resources, inadequate repair, inadequate identity.

At the same time, normal speakers in interaction with confused speakers are themselves confronted with interactional troubles, and these create threats to their face as well. There seem to be several ways in which they handle this. Embedded correction, as depicted by Jefferson (1987), is one strategy, one where the adjustment of incorrect facts does not become the explicit interactional business of the conversation: This promises to maintain face for all concerned. Explicit correction is another option. When correction becomes interactional work, it challenges face but at the same time treats confused speakers in the same way as normal speakers and therefore orients to full membership. (I have a cartoon on the wall in my office of a woman looking down at a tiny child and saying "You're being very childish." That someone orients to you as a full member may not always be a positive experience!) There is also formulation and reformulation of talk to accommodate confused speakers as if they were normal interactants. This too orients to full membership, or perhaps more properly we could say that it mimics orientation to full membership. Finally, there is answering for confused speakers, ignoring them, or challenging their accounts. These strategies seem to orient to the confused speaker as a less-than-full member. As I have suggested there are other groups of people in relation to which these variations in orienting to participants obtain, notably other types of less-than-normal members.

All of the confused talk I have studied *works* in some ways: It has many structurally normal features. The presence of a confused speaker does not mean the absence of a coherent conversation. However, in most of the situations I have discussed, it would appear that no interactional work done by normal speakers (or, indeed, by confused speakers) can result in confused speakers passing as normal members. If a normal speaker has to do all the work to construct full membership for another, then that other cannot be seen as a fully participating normal member, even though the conversation may well appear normal. If a normal speaker has to engage in correction that draws attention to difficulties no normal member would have, then even though this is a normal conversational device, it undermines the membership of the confused speaker. Finally, to ignore deviant talk or otherwise to marginalize it undermines membership of confused speakers, even though it may result in normal interactional appearances for the conversation as a whole.

In these ways, ordinary conversations, interviews, and other forms of interactions can accommodate confused speakers and can often maintain an appearance of normality; but this cannot be done without the use of devices on the part of normal speakers that impair the identity of those they are seeking to assist.

My discussion has largely focused on specific groups of speakers in specific situations. To conclude I would like to draw away to a more general discussion of membership, identity, normality, and confusion.

I want to ask how it is that full members are generally able to remain just that, even if they generate confused talk, whereas less-than-full members are not able to retrieve full membership even when they generate ordinary competent talk? This seems to me an important question for two reasons. First, it is important because it is consequential

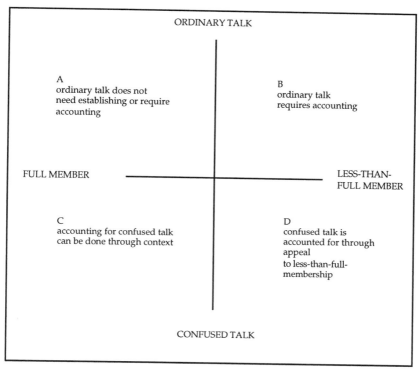

Figure. 7.1. Membership and talk.

for confused speakers themselves; less-than-full membership is a chronic problem for them. Second, it is important because most people have on occasion been treated by others present as less-than-full members and found this situation difficult to overcome, so this can be an acute problem too. My own analysis of the situation focuses on the relation between membership status, confused talk, and requirements for accounting, which I have represented inFigure 7.1.

I think we can use Fig. 7.1. to suggest a number of interesting features about the relation between ordinary talk, confused talk, and membership. When people recognize each other as full, ordinary, competent members ordinary talk is not likely to require accounting (Cell A). When ordinary members generate confused talk, it is likely to be accounted for in terms of the context of the conversation (Cell C) and indeed, I have drawn attention throughout this book to the literature on conversation that emphasizes the importance of context and context sensitivity in the management of talk. I would note too, the many contextual excuses and justifications that exist for ordinary misunderstandings in talk (not being able to hear, being distracted by something else in the environment, and so on). I might also say that even when someone does excuse themself on the grounds of personal deficiency, other participants may well invoke context—"You must think I'm really stupid", "No, most people find this issue very difficult at first." However, when someone is seen as a less-than-full member, then confused talk on their part is more likely to be accounted for in terms of their membership (Cell D). Again, in my examination of confused speakers I have shown that a prior degraded identity may take precedence over the current context of talk, in terms of membership assignment. We can also suggest that even when a less-than-full member produces ordinary talk or an ordinary adequate repair (i.e., an ordinary successful repair whether embedded or as a piece of interactional business), this competence is likely to require accounting in terms of the identity of the person concerned (Cell B). I demonstrated this when I talked about Barry and Edith. Barry made comments about ordinary competence on Edith's part and *marked* it as unusual for her. Of course, extensive use of making ordinary competence a matter for accounting can also be used implicatively to patronize people. Commenting on ordinary competence is category-bound activity usually relating to less-than-full members, and so to do it at all is to imply less-than-full membership.

As will be clear, Fig. 7.1. is designed from the point of view of an ordinary competent member. Using various cells of it, I think it is possible to plot accounting requirements in various kinds of conversations. For example, in a conversation where ordinary membership is assumed, the accounting requirements are likely to be located on the left-hand side of the diagram—either no accounting or contextual accounting. Any other kind of accounting may have pejorative membership implications. In a conversation between a normal member and a confused speaker that is *going well*, we might expect accounting to be located in Cell B, such accounting might be seen in ordinary member terms as positive reinforcement and so on. On the other hand, in a conversation that is *going badly*, we might suggest that accounting options could veer between Cell C (i.e., because in the context of talking to a confused speaker, the normal speaker may also generate confused talk) and Cell D, which locates the degraded identity as the resource for accounting for confused talk.

In an ordinary conversation, or even an ordinary version of specialized talk, participants may, as it were, move between competence and incompetence depending on the mistakes and ambiguities they generate and the extent to which these become interactional business. However, on the whole, ordinary members can invoke and use context as a way of accounting for and retrieving claims to competence.

However, on Fig. 7.1. we can also plot the reassignment of a participant from full member to less-than-full member, that is, in conversational situations where accounting shifts from using contextual resources to identity resources. Also, of course, some participants may assume an identity that they would recognize as implying ordinary full membership, but which is not recognized as such by others (i.e. in some circumstances, women: their talk may discounted or membership reassigned—"Well what do you think girls?"). Here the challenge of accounting is to *regain the left hand cells* that is, to find ordinary competence unremarked, and to account for any confusion locally and contextually within the conversation.

Finally, I would suggest that using such a diagram both integrates confusion within the parameters of ordinary conversation and accommodates for the chronic interactional problems faced by confused speakers as less-than-full members. Everyone generates confused talk: most full members have few problems in overcoming the problems that this brings. They are able to repair confusion, to account for what happened through invoking context, working to side-step threat to face or to save face. And I suppose that this brings me back to the traffic and drivers problem that I discussed at the end of chapter 1. Citing the analogies used by Goffman and Schegloff (1988)—ordinary speakers can blame *the traffic* as the overwhelming problem, but confused speakers appear to have to take total responsibility for their problems as *drivers*. Essentially, the purpose of the book has been to draw out both the traffic and driver problems that are involved when talk is confused.

Appendix A: Research Participants

Names of confused speakers and carers were altered for reasons of confidentiality.

1. Interiews at the psychogeriatric clinic
Mrs. Bowles (client), Mr. Bowles (caregiver/son)

Edith (client), Barry (caregiver/son)

Mrs. Hoy (client), Mr Hoy (caregiver/husband)

Mrs. Inman (client), Mrs. Grace (caregiver/daughter)

Mrs. Pugh (client), Mr. Pugh (caregiver/husband), Mrs. James (caregiver/daughter)

Mr. Toll (client), Mrs. Toll (caregiver/wife).

Mrs. Walker (client), Mrs. Becker (caregiver/daughter)

Pam Shakespeare (interviewer; Open University)

2. Moyra's Interview
Tilly (an older woman, suffering from confusion)

Moyra Sidell (interviewer; Open University)

3. Tom's Interview
Mr. Graham (an older man suffering from confusion).

Mrs. Graham (caregiver/wife)

Tom Heller (interviewer; Open University)

4. Bruner's Household Talk
Mrs. Bruner (an older woman, suffering from confusion)

Mr Bruner (caregiver/husband)

Appendix B: Transcription Conventions

For many of the extracts in this thesis, I used a limited selection of transcription conventions from those developed by Jefferson (outlined in Schenkein 1978), which I have slightly developed in some cases. Additionally, I have used one device suggested by Potter and Wetherell (1987, see point 9 of this Appendix).

1. Simultaneous utterances

Pam:	I used to work there
	[[
Caregiver:	We've always lived there

2. Overlapping utterances

The beginning of an overlap is annotated thusly:

Pam:	I used to work there
	[
Caregiver:	We've always lived there

And where the overlapping stops:

Caregiver:	We've always lived there
	[ ]
Pam:	I see

3. Contiguous utterances

This is when there is no gap between utterances:

Pam:	I used to work there=
Caregiver:	=We've always lived there

4. Contiguous utterances and overlap

Equals signs are used to denote where one speaker's talk continues despite an interruption by someone else:

Pam: I used to work there=
                                [
Caregiver: We've always lived there
Pam: =When I first started teaching

5. Speech characteristics

Here, a colon is used to denote extended sound within words (the greater the number of colons, the longer the extension):

Pam: Can you see the wheel going round?=
Mrs. Hoy: Ye:s.

6. Intervals within and between utterances

1. Intervals within utterances are timed in tenths of seconds and denoted in the following way:

Caregiver: She was oh (0.9) must have been 59 when it first seemed to crop up.

2. Intervals between utterances, also timed in tenths of seconds:

Pam: And what were their names?
                                    (1.3)
Caregiveer: She can't remember.
                                    (0.7)
Pam: Can't remember.

3. Untimed pauses within and between utterances:

Pam: I wonder (.) whether you remember

                                    (.)

Respondent: I'm not sure.

7. Emphasis

Emphasis is denoted by underlining and by capital letters, where something is said much more loudly than the adjacent talk. Where there is noticeably loud talk, for example, where Tilly is really shouting, I have underlined capital letters.

Tilly: It's my own home why shouldn't I be there IT'S NOT RIGHT IT'S MY
                                HOME

8. Brackets

1. Double brackets are used for vocalizations not easy to render in text, or for details of the conversational setting or characterizations of the talk:

Pam:	Do you ((Clears throat)) like it at the day centre?
	((Anteroom door opens))
Mrs Hoy:	((Whispered)) Yes.

2. Single brackets are used where the transcriber is in some doubt as to what was said:

| Edith: | (What do I think?) |

And where no meaning could be imposed:

| Edith: | (   ) |

9. Omission of some aspects of transcript

Potter and Wetherell (1987) suggested using square brackets for omission of aspects of talk and for clarification of aspects of talk:

Pam: And when did you live there?
Carer: [Talks about being a miner in the 1940s]

10. Non-conversation-analysis extracts

Where I have been more interested in what people say than how they say it, I have simplified the transcription in such as way as to leave out many of the conventions relating to turn taking, speech characteristics, and so on, while maintaining the basic column structure used elsewhere:

Pam:	Where did you go in Wales?
Mr. Toll:	Where was it?
Mrs. Toll:	Llandudno.
Mr. Toll:	Llandudno.
Pam:	Had you been there before?
Mrs. Toll:	Years and years ago.

The fuller transcription of the above extract (as outlined in points 1–9 of this Appendix) would be as follows:

1. Pam:	Wh wh er where did you go in Wales?
	(1.8)
2. Mr .Toll:	((Low)) Where was it?=
3. Mrs. Toll:	=Llandudno=
4. Mr. Toll:	=Llandudno=
5. Pam.:	=Ha had you been there before?
6. Mrs Toll:	((Low)) Years and years ago

Appendix C: Tilly's Story

1. Moyra:	[...] How have you been keeping? How are you feeling?
2. Tilly:	Not too good I have rheumatism a lot.
3. Moyra:	Oh.
4. Tilly:	As long as I can keep on that's the chief thing I've got some very good stuff.
5. Moyra:	Have you?
6. Tilly:	Mentholatum Deep Heat I'll show it to you and that's lovely ((Noises)) I've had it her I must get home because my sister's there and I want to know if she's going to be there of what I MUST GET HOME TONIGHT.
7. Moyra:	Alright.
8. Tilly:	And
9. Moyra:	Where's your Deep Heat?
10. Tilly:	Aye?
11. Moyra:	Where is your bottle of Deep Heat you were going to show it to me.
12. Tilly:	You what?
13. Moyra:	Your bottle of Deep Heat.
14. Tilly:	Aye?
15. Moyra:	Your Deep Heat you were going to show it to me.
16. Tilly:	Oh yes.
	((Long silence))
17. Tilly:	This piece of carpet's mine you know.
18. Moyra:	I know oh that's it is it?
19. Tilly:	That's lovely stuff if you've got rheumatism or anything like that
20. Moyra:	Is it?
21. Tilly:	Yes and the heat that it give out and it's clean now I went to the doctor's before I got that.
22. Moyra:	Yes.
23. Tilly:	And he give me some greasy old stuff.
24. Moyra:	Did he?
25. Tilly:	Oooh my dear I messed my vest and my night dress up.
26. Moyra:	Oh dear.
27. Tilly:	And had to soak em oh and I was wild when I had to do that I thought to miself well I don't know.
28. Moyra:	Mmm.
29. Tilly:	But I ne'er went no more after or anything I went and started straightaway to get that stuff.
30. Moyra:	Did you where did you get that from?

224

31.	Tilly:	A chemist.
32.	Moyra:	And what about your headaches?
33.	Tilly:	That's lovely you put that on.
34.	Moyra:	Mmmm.
35.	Tilly:	And the heat it give out and as it cool take all the pain away.
36.	Moyra:	Lovely.
37.	Tilly:	That's the best stuff I've ever had in my life.
38.	Moyra:	Is it?
39.	Tilly:	They give me some stuff at the doctor's er er er a little tin.
40.	Moyra:	Mmm.
41.	Tilly:	Well the rubbish that was absolute rubbish.
42.	Moyra:	Was it?
43.	Tilly:	I you might just as well you know how Vaseline is?
44.	Moyra:	Yes.
45.	Tilly:	That might been just like Vaseline and the tin not not not as big as that round base.
46.	Moyra:	Really.
47.	Tilly:	I'd never see'd a stuff like it.
48.	Moyra:	Goodness.
49.	Tilly:	I thought miself <u>whatever</u> muck have I got here but I soon washed it all off and threw the whole tin in the bin I thought miself let me have some decent stuff and went and got that and
50.	Moyra:	Mmm.
51.	Tilly:	And that put on I was that take all the pain away you know if you got a headache or anything.
52.	Moyra:	Does it?
53.	Tilly:	Just put a little on there that take that away and go to sleep after.
54.	Moyra:	Mmm.
55.	Tilly:	And it sink in.
56.	Moyra:	Well that's good to know.
57.	Tilly:	And there's no no grease nor nothing after just like milk.
58.	Moyra:	Is it?
59.	Tilly:	Mmm clean.
60.	Moyra:	That's lovely.
61.	Tilly:	That' why I like it I shall allus buy that I'll never go to the doctor's no more waste my time and they give you the old stuff all grease oh my word no.
62.	Moyra:	No no.
63.	Tilly:	No mess your clothes up.
64.	Moyra:	Does it well you don't want that do you?
65.	Tilly:	I'll never do that no more.
66.	Moyra:	No no.
67.	Tilly:	I buy that.
68.	Moyra:	You buy that.
69.	Tilly:	You take the top off and smell.
70.	Moyra:	Well oooh it smells nice it smells a bit like Germaline.
71.	Tilly:	<u>Aye</u>?
72.	Moyra:	Germaline I used to have when I was a child.
73.	Tilly:	Oh.
74.	Moyra:	It smells a bit like that do you know Germaline have you.
75.	Tilly:	No I don't know it but that is the best stuff I ever had and you know it take all the pain away and you just go to sleep it's the finest thing out and my limbs are loose and everything and I can move twice now you get I got the stuff from the doctor and that warn't no good at all and that messed up my nightdress and all grease ooh I thought a miself.
76.	Moyra:	Really.
77.	Tilly:	Made me I threw it in the bin and I went and got that.

78. 79. Moyra:	Yes.	
79. Tilly:	I thought to miself I never did see such muck as they tried to slip into me.	
80. Moyra:	Oh dear.	
81. Tilly:	It annoyed me you know.	
82. Moyra:	Did it?	
83. Tilly:	Yes waste of time going there.	
84. Moyra:	Yes.	
85. Tilly:	And then you don't get nothing that do you any good.	
86. Moyra:	Dear.	
87. Tilly:	Oh it ma I so never no more I keep that by me that's lovely you take the top off and smell it.	
88. Moyra:	Mmm.	
89. Tilly:	Would you like a piece of (cake).	
90. Moyra:	Oh I'm droppping it.	
91. Tilly:	Another piece of	
92. Moyra:	No that's lovely a lovely smell.	
93. Tilly:	Get a drop use your finger put it on your hand.	
94. Moyra:	Yes.	
95. Tilly:	On top.	
96. Moyra:	How much does it cost you is it expensive? Oooh it is nice.	
97. Tilly:	It's nice and it get the heat and sink in and that's gone it's clean	
98. Moyra:	Yes.	
99. Tilly:	It's clean no grease or nothing.	
100. Moyra:	No.	
101. Tilly:	No no.	
102. Moyra:	No.	
103. Tilly:	No that's why I don't mind buying stuff like that but when you get that I had some stuff from the doctor oh and that was all grea oh mucky old stuff messed my vest and nightdress I had to soak em afterwards.	
104. Moyra:	Did you?	
105. Tilly:	This is alright this is well I was right disgusted.	
106. Moyra:	Oh dear.	
107. Tilly:	I was really.	
108. Moyra:	Yes.	
109. Tilly:	And that I got there there's no harm in that is there?	
110. Moyra:	No.	
111. Tilly:	And that take all the pain away too.	
112. Moyra:	Well that's what you want.	
113. Tilly:	Yes that's what you want.	
114. Moyra:	How much does it cost?	
115. Tilly:	And I I forget I forgot what it cost me cos I got two or three more things as well.	
116. Moyra:	Other things.	
117. Tilly:	Other things you see.	
118. Moyra:	When did you get that?	
119. Tilly:	I got it at Boots	
120. Moyra:	When did you get it?	
121. Tilly:	Aye?	
122. Moyra:	When?	
123. Tilly:	When oh I've had that for three weeks now.	
124. Moyra:	Have you?	
125. Tilly:	Yes I never put it on unless I have a pain and then I put it on then and go to bed you see.	
126. Moyra:	Yes yes.	

127. Tilly:	But that really take all the pain off and that's the finest stuff I've had that take the pain out soft the pai and you can go to sleep afterwards that's the best stuff I've ever had.
128. Moyra:	Mmm.
129. Tilly:	That beat any of the old doctor's muck old doctor's that they er leave grease on I though a miself I'll allus buy that.
130. Moyra:	You keep that.
131. Tilly:	Mentolatum Deep Heat.
132. Moyra:	Yes very good.
133. Tilly:	You see I forget how much it is but I shall buy some more I shall keep some by me that's the best stuff I've ever had.
134. Moyra:	Mmm well that's good.
135. Tilly:	Well I expect that that save wasting time going to the doctor's when you rub that on.
136. Moyra:	Mmm.
137. Tilly:	Yes.
138. Moyra:	That's right.
139. Tilly:	That's all I want put it on anywhere but that other stuff I got from the doctor's oh I was thoroughly disgusted.
140. Moyra:	Oh dear
141. Tilly:	That was all grease and never warned you or anything else it may have been some old Vaseline stuff you stuck on yourself in fact I believe the Vaseline would have done it just as oh.
142. Moyra:	Who is your doctor Tilly?
143. Tilly:	<u>Aye</u>?
144. Moyra:	Who's your doctor?
145. Tilly:	On ( ) Road that's er one of the doctor's you see.
146. Moyra:	Have you been to see him lately?
147. Tilly:	No I haven't been there I don't often go to the doctor's if I can get the things to put on myself I don't go.
148. Moyra:	You'd rather get your own.
149. Tilly:	I take Aspirins.
150. Moyra:	Do you?
151. Tilly:	I keep them by me and the stuff to rub on Deep Heat that stuff and that take all the pain out of my limbs if they're swollen or that doctor's stuff was full of grease and oh I thought to miself my vest and nightdress was messed up I though this is rubbish stuff I never go I won't go it's a waste of time to go.
152. Moyra:	It is isn't it?
153. Tilly:	Yes.
154. Moyra:	Yes.
155. Tilly:	I won't go and take Aspros you see or Aspr no Aspirin Aspros.
156. Moyra:	Aspros.
157. Tilly:	Yes see and
158. Moyra:	For your headaches do you take those when you get a headache?
159. Tilly:	I know how to doctor miself so it's alright ((Laughs)).
160. Moyra:	You look after yourself don't you?
161. Tilly:	Yes as long as you can keep going.
162. Moyra:	You used to cook didn't you?
163. Tilly:	I used to get it in my head oh and it was terrible.
164. Moyra:	Was it?
165. Tilly:	You couldn't do nothing then I didn't know about that stuff the other stuff I used to rub it on I bought and it but that beat everything you take the top off and smell it.
166. Moyra:	Alright oh.
167. Tilly:	See it's very good.
168. Moyra:	Good isn't it? Very strong.
169. Tilly:	I forget how much I give for it but if you want it you can have it.

170. Moyra:	Oh no love I don't want it.
171. Tilly:	No you don't but if any of your people like tell them about it it is good.
172. Moyra:	Yes I'll tell them.
173. Tilly:	And it's a waste of time to go to the doctor's nowadays.
174. Moyra:	Sometimes.
175. Tilly:	You got (to wait).
176. Moyra:	It depends what you want.
177. Tilly:	I had I did I had I waited I waited oh no end of time in the doctor's I had a tin not as big as that saucer a tin as big as the top of that pot and it warn't a bit of good.
178. Moyra:	Wasn't it?
179. Tilly:	No it didn't give no heat out I might have stuck some Vaseline on miself that's more what it looked like and er I threw it in the bin after I rubbed it on I thought a miself I don't know this isn't much good and in the bin it went I threw it out no heat nor nothing.
180. Moyra:	No.
181. Tilly:	So there you are so I now got I went and bought that in Boots and I said to the man I think I'll have that is that, good? He said well we sell a good bit of it mam.
182. Moyra:	Did he?
183. Tilly:	I say do you? Well that's a good point.
184. Moyra:	Mmm.
185. Tilly:	And that is too you don't want a lot and that take the pain away and you can go to sleep after.
186. Moyra:	Mmm.
187. Tilly:	That's the best stuff I've had just simple to remember Deep Heat.
188. Moyra:	It is isn't it? Yes.
189. Tilly:	And that is deep just get a thumbful and put on your hand and see.
190. Moyra:	Yes I have done love.
191. Tilly:	Did you? Oh there's the heat.
192. Moyra:	Yes it is.
193. Tilly:	That's splendid I can recommend that to anybody in fact my sister Martha what's at home now…

Appendix D: Lunchtime at the Bruner's

1. Mrs. Bruner: It does it looks nice out now (.) What do I do now?
2. Mr. Bruner: Have our dinner.
3. Mrs. Bruner: Ah off you go then mmm(.) ((Sound of a run of notes on the piano and then Mrs Bruner singing)) eeny meeny miny mo (.) What we doing? Aye? Is there only us two?
4. Mr. Bruner: Yes there's only us two today.
5. Mrs. Bruner: Why is that then?
6. Mr. Bruner: Well there always is only us two.
7. Mrs. Bruner: Aye?
8. Mr. Bruner: There's only us two always.
9. Mrs. Bruner: Oh I don't know ma duck what it's all about ah don't know mmm ((Singing)) (what it's all) about ma duck.
10. Mr. Bruner: What it's all about.
11. Mrs. Bruner: Ay don't know he he I'd like to go back to bed I would he eeny meeny miny mo ((Singing)) oh dear I do feel bad I do I'll go back in bed hey ((Singing)) de de dum eeeny meeny miny mo (.) oh it's murder (.) murder mmmmm(.)
12. Mr. Bruner: There you are here's your dinner.
13. Mrs. Bruner: Oh lord Dave Oh you've given me all that.
14. Mr. Bruner: Mmm yes.
15. Mrs. Bruner: Oh Dave I don't know where am going to put it (.) I don't ma duck I don't know mmmmm
16. Mr. Bruner: Now I've put you plenty of gravy on there's some more if you want.
17. Mrs. Bruner: Aye?
18. Mr. Bruner: There's some more if you want.
19. Mrs. Bruner: I don't know what it's all about (.) aye (.) mmm ((Singsong)) (what it's) all about Dave. Have I got to start?
20. Mr. Bruner: Yes you start.
21. Mrs. Bruner: Oh dear don't aye? I don't know where we are ma duck aye? I don't know hey?......I don't know (.) ((Humming)) de da dee de de de dade.
22. Mr. Bruner: Hm hm.
23. Mrs. Bruner: Mmmmmm mmm mmm mmm (   ) you.
24. Mr. Bruner: Do you want a drink?
25. Mrs. Bruner: I'm not going to eat all this lot.
26. Mr. Bruner: Mm mm do you want a drink?
27. Mrs. Bruner: Mm mm.
28. Mr. Bruner: (   ) to.

29. Mrs. Bruner:	Anything I ain't bothered ma duck mmm mmmm (.) don't know ma duck I feel awful.
30. Mr. Bruner:	There you are.
31. Mrs. Bruner:	Mmmm (.) thank you mmm thank you mmmm (.) tmmmmm (.) mmmmmmm (.) mmmmmmmm mmmmmm (.) mmm (.) mmmmmm (.) mmmm.
32. Mr. Bruner:	What's the matter?
33. Mrs. Bruner:	It's boiling.
34. Mr. Bruner:	Boiling.
35. Mrs. Bruner:	Mm.
36. Mr. Bruner:	No I don't think it is.
37. Mrs. Bruner:	Mmmm it is it's all boiling mmmm (.) mmmm (.) mmmmm(.)Dave how the heck I'm going to eat it I don't know mmm ((Sing song)) (.) mmmm (.) mmmmm (.) mmmmmm (.) mmmmm (.) mmm (.) mmmmmm (.) mmmmmmm (.) Have I got to eat all this?
38. Mr. Bruner:	Yes.
39. Mrs. Bruner:	Oh Dave (.) mmmmm I feel about full mi duck
40. Mr. Bruner:	Start a bit there
41. Mrs. Bruner:	Aye?
42. Mr. Bruner:	You've hardly started
43. Mrs. Bruner:	Oh murder mmm
44. Mr. Bruner:	I didn't put you a lot on because I thought you wouldn't eat it.
45. Mrs. Bruner:	Mmmmm (.) mmm (.) mmmm (.) oh I do feel bad he he.(.) mmm (.).mmmmmmm.(.). mmmmmm (.) I can't eat no more Dave he he (.) oh dear not yet he he mm.
46. Mr. Bruner:	Take your time.
47. Mrs. Bruner:	Oh it's murder mm.
48. Mr. Bruner:	Take your time.
49. Mrs. Bruner:	Murder (.) oh I do feel bad he he mmmm he he mmm.
50. Mr. Bruner:	Let me cut it up for you a bit.
51. Mrs. Bruner:	Oh I'm full up ma duck he he.
52. Mr. Bruner:	You haven't eaten much at all come on.
53. Mrs. Bruner:	Oh oh it's murder he he.
54. Mr. Bruner:	Look it's nice look at all that.
55. Mrs. Bruner:	I know but don't leave it hey.
56. Mr. Bruner:	Come on.
57. Mrs. Bruner:	Oh leave it Dave don't I can't eat it if you keep messing it up ((Crossly)) oh no mmm I don't feel a bit hungry. I'd love to go back to bed he he eeny meeny miny mo oh I'd love to go back to bed mmm mmmmmmmm(.) mmmm(.) mmm don't give me any more Dave it's awful no I don't feel a bit hungry (.) I'd love to go back to bed he he (.) I would (.) I feel awful (.) eeny meeny miny (.) Oh I do feel bad (.) never felt so bad in my life never he he he er murder (.) mmmmmm (.) mmmmm (.) mmmmmmm (.) mmmmmm (.) ar dear (.) aye I do feel bad (.) oh it's murder mm (.) mmmmmmm (.) never felt so bad (.) eeny meeny miny mo murder (.) mmmmmmm (.) mmmmmmmm (.) mmmmmmmm (.) What's that Dave what that's supposed to be?
58. Mr. Bruner:	It's a microphone.
59. Mrs. Bruner:	Aye?
60. Mr. Bruner:	It's a microphone.
61. Mrs. Bruner:	Well what's that for?
62. Mr. Bruner:	Well we're taping what we talk about.
63. Mrs. Bruner:	Oh I don't know he he no I can't be bothered he he.
64. Mr. Bruner:	Try and eat a bit more meat.
65. Mrs. Bruner:	Oh I can't he he ( ) on ( ).
66. Mr. Bruner:	Will you have some sweet?
67. Mrs. Bruner:	I don't know he her.
68. Mr. Bruner:	We've got you can have prunes and custard.

69. Mrs. Bruner:	I don't know.
70. Mr. Bruner:	Or apple tart would you like apple tart?
71. Mrs. Bruner:	I don't know ((Indistinctly)).
72. Mr. Bruner:	Come on.
73. Mrs. Bruner:	What's all this about?
74. Mr. Bruner:	What?
75. Mrs. Bruner:	All this I ain't ate any of this.
76. Mr. Bruner:	No you haven't started try and eat a little bit.
77. Mrs. Bruner:	((Crossly)) <u>Well what's the good when I ain't hungry aye</u>?
78. Mr. Bruner:	Well I don't know why you shouldn't be hungry you didn't have much breakfast.
79. Mrs. Bruner:	What's all this lot oh murder mmmmm (.) mmm (.) mmm (.) mmmm (.) mmmm (.) mmmmmm (.) mmmm (.) mmmm (.) mmm (.) mmmm (.) mmmm (.) mmm (.) mmmm (.) mmmmm (.) mmmmm (.) mmmm
80. Mr. Bruner:	(in here).
81. Mrs. Bruner:	Mmmmmm (.) Are we going to go out?
82. Mr. Bruner:	No not today.
83. Mrs. Bruner:	Good job then (.) mmm (.) mmmmm (.) mmm (.) mmmm I'd love to go back to bed he he he (.) mmmmm I would (.) mmmmmm (.) mmmm (.) mmm ((Coughs)) (.) mmmm don't know where we are hm hm or what we're doing mmm (.) mmmm (.) mmmm (.) mmmm (.) ((Coughs)) mmmm. (.) mmmmmmmmmm I'll have lie down I feel awful.
84. Mr. Bruner:	When you've had your dinner.
85. Mrs. Bruner:	Mmm.
86. Mr. Bruner:	You can go and have a lie down.
87. Mrs. Bruner:	Mmmmm I do feel bad he mmm (.) mmm (.) mmmm (.) No (.) I dunno where we are he he mm mmm (.) mmmm (.) mmmmmm Ar don't know ma duck (.) mmmmmmm (.) mm. .mmmmm (.) mmm (.) mmmm (.) mm (.) mmm (.) mmmmmmm (.) mmmmmmmm (.) mmmmmmm (.) mmmmmmm (.) mmmmmmm' (.) mmmmmmmm (.) lie down I don't want to eat any more Dave I've had enough dinner.
88. Mr. Bruner:	No thank you I've nearly finished now I couldn't eat any more.
89. Mrs. Bruner:	Are we going to save this for tomorrow are we?
90. Mr. Bruner:	No we'll throw that away eat a bit more of your meat that will do you good.
91. Mrs. Bruner:	Mmm (.) I can't (.) I can't get at it ma duck (.) no he he he <u>eeny meeny miny m</u>o he he.
92. Mr. Bruner:	Mm.
93. Mrs. Bruner:	Awful oh (look here)?
94. Mr. Bruner:	Yes it's all nice chicken.
95. Mrs. Bruner:	Mm don't know what it's supposed to have been mm (.) mmm (.) mmm ((Coughs very loudly)) Oh I can't get it (.) mmmmm mmmm (.) mmmm (.) mmmmm (.) mmm oh no (.) mmmmm (.).mmmm (.) mmmm (.) mmmmm (.) mmmm (.) mmmm (.) Can't (bury) me away he he mmm dear.
96. Mr. Bruner:	Now then I'll make some custard.
97. Mrs. Bruner:	(.) mmm (.) mmmmmmm (.) mmmm mmmmmmmm (.) mmm (.) mmmmmm (.) mmmmmmm (.).mmmmmmm (.) mi handkerchief he he oh dear isn't it murder mmmmmm (.) I don't think I can eat any more Dave.
98. Mr. Bruner:	OK leave it there or something I'll sort it out in a minute.
99. Mrs. Bruner:	I'm full up ma duck erm ((Both hum).)
100. Mrs. Bruner:	Mmm (.) mmmmmm (.) mmmmmmmm (.) mmmmmm (.) mmmmm he he he he mmmmmmmm What's that? Did you just put it there?
101. Mr. Bruner:	Mm.
102. Mrs. Bruner:	Well I was going to say it ain't mine he he.
103. Mr. Bruner:	Leave it there.

References

Allison, R. S. (1962). *The senile brain.* London: Edward Arnold.

Alzheimer's Disease Society. (1989). *Caring for the person with dementia. A guide for families and other carers.* (2nd ed.). London: Alzheimer's Disease Society.

Alzheimer's Disease Society. (1990). *Questions and answers.* London: Alzheimer's Disease Society.

Anderson, R. J., & Sharrock, W. W. (1984). Analytic work: Aspects of the organisation of conversational data. *Journal for the Theory of Social Behaviour, 14,* 103–124.

Atkinson, J. M., & Drew P. (1979). *Order in court. The organisation of verbal interaction in judicial settings.* London: Macmillan.

Atkinson, M. A. (1973). *Formulating lifetimes: The normatively ordered properties of some life-cycle properties.* Unpublished master's thesis, University of Manchester, England.

Atkinson, M. A., Cuff, E. C., & Lee, J. R. E. (1978). The recommencement of a meeting as a member's accomplishment. In J. Schenkein (Ed.), *Studies in the organization of conversational interaction* (pp. 133–153). New York: Academic Press.

Atkinson, P. (1990). *The ethnographic imagination.* London : Routledge.

Atkinson, P. (1992). *Understanding ethnographic texts.* Newbury Park, CA: Sage.

Bauerle, R. (1979). Questions and answers. In R. Bauerle, U. Egli, & A. Von Stechow (Eds.), *Semantics from different points of view* (pp. 61–74). Berlin, Germany: Springer-Verlag.

Belotti, E. G. (1975). *Little girls: Social conditioning and its effect on the stereotyped roles of women during infancy.* London: Writers and Readers Publishing Cooperative.

Benson, D., & Hughes, J. A. (1983). *The perspective of ethnomethodology.* New York: Longman.

Bilmes, J. (1988). The concept of preference in conversation analysis. *Language in Society, 17,* 161–181.

Blessed, G., Tomlinson, B. E., & Roth, M. (1968). The association between quantitative measures of dementia and of senile change in the cerebral grey matter of elderly subjects. *British Journal of Psychiatry, 114,* 797-811.

Briggs, C. L. (1986). *Learning how to ask. A sociolinguistic appraisal of the role of the interview in social science research.* Cambridge, England: Cambridge University Press.

Brown, P., & Levinson, S. (1978). Universals in language use: Politeness phenomena In E. Goody (Ed.), *Questions and politeness. Strategies in social interaction* (pp. 56–289). Cambridge, England: Cambridge University Press.

Burgess, R. C. (1988). Conversations with a purpose: The ethnographic interview in educational research. *Studies in Qualitative Methodology, 1,* 137–155.

Burns, T. (1992). *Erving Goffman.* London: Routledge.

Chaika, E., & Alexander, P. (1986). The ice cream stories: A study in normal and psychotic narrations. *Discourse Processes*, 9, 305–328.

Cheepen, C. (1988). *The predictability of informal conversation*. London: Pinter.

Cicourel, A. V. (1987). The interpenetration of communicative contexts: Examples from medical encounters. *Social Psychology Quarterly*, 50, 217–226.

Clayman, S. E. (1988). Displaying neutrality in television news. *Social Problems*, 35, 474–492.

Code, C., & Lodge, B. (1987). Language in dementia of recent referral. *Age and Ageing*, 16, 366–372

Coenen, H. (1991). Wandering through the caves: Phenomenonological research in a social world of dementia. In D. R. Maines (Ed.), *Social organization and social process. Essays in honor of Anselm Strauss* (pp. 315–332). New York: Aldine de Gruyter.

Converse, J. M., & Presser, S. (1986). *Survey questions. Handcrafting the standardized questionnare*. Beverly Hills, CA: Sage.

Cook, J. B. (1984). Reminiscing: How it can help confused nursing home residents. *Social Casework: The Journal of Contemporary Social Work*, February, 90–93.

Coulter, J. (1973). *Approaches to insanity. A philosophical and sociological study*. London: Martin Robertson.

Coulter, J. (1975). Perceptual accounts and interpretive asymmetries. *Sociology*, 9, 385–396.

Coupland, N., Giles, H., & Wiemann, J. M. (Eds.). (1991). *Miscommunication and problematic talk*. Newbury Park, CA: Sage.

Dexter, L. (1970). *Elite and specialized interviewing*. Evanston, IL: Northwestern University Press.

Dingwall, R. (1980). Orchestrated encounters: An essay in the comparative analysis of speech-exchange systems. *Sociology of Health and Illness*, 2, 151–173.

Drew, P., & Heritage, J. (Eds). (1992). *Talk at work*. Cambridge, England: Cambridge University Press.

Drew, P., & Wootton, A. (Eds.). (1988). *Erving Goffman. Exploring the interaction order*. Oxford, England: Polity Press.

Earnest, M. P., Heaton, R. K., Wilkinson, W. E. & Manke, W. F. (1979). Cortical atrophy, ventricular enlargement and intellectual impairment in the aged. *Neurology*, 29, 1138–1143.

Edgerton, R. B. (1967). *The cloak of competence. Stigma in the lives of the mentally retarded*. Berkeley: University of California.

Evans, D., *et al.* 1990. Estimated prevalence of Alzheimer's disease in the United States. *The Millbank Quarterly* 68, 267–289.

Feil, N. (1982). *Validation. The Feil method. How to help disoriented old-old*. Cleveland OH: Edward Feil Productions.

Fisher, S., & Groce, S. B. (1990). Accounting practices in medical interviews. *Language in Society*, 19, 225–250.

Garfinkel, H. (1967). *Studies in ethnomethodology*. Englewood Cliffs, NJ: Prentice-Hall.

Giglioli, P. P. (Ed.) (1972). *Language and social context. Selected readings*. Harmondsworth, England: Penguin.

Goffman, E. (1959). *Presentation of self in everyday life*. New York: Doubleday Anchor.

Goffman, E. (1961). *Asylums. Essays on the social situation of mental patients and other inmates*. Harmondsworth, England: Penguin.

Goffman, E. (1963a). *Behavior in public places. Notes on the social organization of gatherings*. New York: Free Press.

Goffman, E. (1963b). *Stigma. Notes on the management of spoiled identity.* Harmondsworth, England: Penguin.

Goffman, E. (1969). On face-work: An analysis of ritual elements in social interaction. In E. Goffman *Where the action is* (pp. 3–36). London: Allen Lane.

Goffman, E. (1971). Remedial interchanges. In E. Goffman *Relations in public. Microstudies of public order* (pp. 95–187). London: Allen Lane.

Goffman, E. (1972) Embarrassment and social organization. In E. Goffman *Interaction ritual. Essays on face-to-face behaviour* (pp. 97–112). Harmondsworth, England: Penguin.

Goffman, E. (1975). *Frame analysis.* Harmondsworth, England: Peregrine/Penguin.

Goffman, E. (1981). *Forms of talk.* Oxford, England: Basil Blackwell.

Goffman, E. (1983a). Felicity's condition. *American Journal of Sociology, 89,* 1–53.

Goffman, E. (1983b). The interaction order. *American Sociological Review, 48,* 1–17.

Goodwin, C. (1987). Forgetfulness as an interactive resource. *Social Psychology Quarterly, 50,* 115–131.

Goody, E. (1978). *Questions and politeness. Strategies in social interaction.* Cambridge, England: Cambridge University Press.

Grice, H. P. (1975). Logic and conversation. In P. Cole & J. L. Morgan (Eds.) *Syntax and semantics. Volume 3. Speech acts* (pp. 41–58). New York: Academic Press.

Gubrium, J. F. (1985). Alzheimer's disease as biographical work. In W. A. Peterson & J. Quadagno (Eds.), *Social bonds in later life* (pp. 349–367). Beverley Hills, CA: Sage.

Gubrium, J. F. (1986). *Oldtimers and Alzheimer's: The descriptive organization of senility.* Greenwich, CT: JAI Press.

Gubrium, J. F. (1987). Structuring and destructuring the course of illness: The Alzheimer's disease experience. *Sociology of Health and Illness, 9,* 1–12.

Gubrium, J. F., & Holstein, J. A. (1994). Analysing talk and interaction. In J. F. Gubrium, & A. Sankar (Eds.), *Qualitative methods in aging research* (pp. 173-188). Thousand Oaks, CA Sage.

Gumperz, J. J., & Hymes, D. (Eds.). (1972). *Directions in sociolinguistics. The ethnography of communication.* New York: Holt, Rinehart & Winston.

Hamilton, H. E. (1994). *Conversations with an Alzheimer's patient.* Cambridge, England: Cambridge University Press.

Hammersley, M. (Ed.). (1986a). *Case studies in classroom research.* Milton Keynes, England: Open University Press.

Hammersley, M. (Ed.). (1986b). *Controversies in classroom research.* Milton Keynes, England: Open University Press.

Hammersley, M., & Atkinson, P. (1983). *Ethnography: Principles in practice.* London: Tavistock .

Hawkins, R. A. & Phelps, M. E. (1986). Position emission tomography for evaluation of cerebral function. *Current Concepts in Diagnostic Nuclear Medicine, 3,* 1–13.

Heath, C. (1988). Embarrassment and interactional organization. In P. Drew & A. Wootton (Eds.), *Erving Goffman. Exploring the interaction order* (pp. 136–160). Oxford, England: Polity Press.

Heritage, J. (1984). *Garfinkel and ethnomethodology.* Cambridge, England: Polity Press.

Holstein, J. A. (1988). Court ordered incompetence: Conversational organization in involuntary commitment proceedings. *Social Problems, 35,* 458–473.

Hughes, D., & May, D. (1986). Order, rules and social control in two training centres for mentally retarded adults. *Sociological Review, 34,* 158–184.

Hughes, E. C. (1977). *The sociological eye.* Chicago: Aldine.

Jefferson, G. (1978). Sequential aspects of story telling in conversation. In J. Schenkein (Ed.), *Studies in the organization of conversational interaction* (pp. 219–248). New York: Academic Press.

Jefferson, G. (1987). On exposed and embedded correction in conversation. In G. Button & J. R. E. Lee (Eds.), *Talk and social organisation* (pp. 86–100). Clevedon, England: Multilingual Matters.

Jefferys, M. (1988). An ageing Britain—What is its future? In B. Gearing, M. Johnson, & T. Heller (Eds.), *Mental health problems in old age* (pp. 1–9). Chichester: Wiley.

Jones, G. (1992). A communication model for dementia. In G. M. Jones, & B. M. L. Mieson (Eds.), *Caregiving in dementia: Research and implications* (pp. 77–99). London: Tavistock.

Kemper, S., Lyons, K., & Anagnopoulos, C. (1995). Joint storytelling by patients with Alzheimer's Disease and their spouses. *Discourse Processes, 20,* 205–217.

Kitwood, T. (1987). Explaining senile dementia. The limits of neuropathological research. *Free Associations, 10,* 117–140.

Kitwood, T. (1988). The technical, the personal, and the framing of dementia. *Social Behaviour, 3,* 161–179.

Kitwood, T. (1993). Towards a theory of dementia care: Personhood and well-being. *Ageing and Society, 12,* 269–287.

Labov, W. (1972). The logic of nonstandard English. In P. P. Giglioli (Ed.), *Language and social context. Selected readings* (pp. 179–215). Harmondsworth, England: Penguin.

Leech, G. N. (1983). *Principles and pragmatics.* London: Longman.

Levinson, S. C. (1983). *Pragmatics.* Cambridge, England: Cambridge University Press.

Livingston, E. (1987). *Making sense of ethnomethodology.* London: Routledge & Kegan Paul.

Lynch, M. (1983) Accommodation practices: Vernacular treatments of madness. *Social Problems, 31,* 153–164.

Lynch, M., & Bogen, D. (1994). Harvey Sacks's primitive natural science. *Theory, Culture and Society, 11,* 65–104.

Mackay, R. W. (1974). Conceptions of children and models of socialization. In R. Turner (Ed.), *Ethnomethodology* (pp. 180–193). Harmondsworth, England: Penguin.

McCracken, G. (1988). *The long interview.* Newbury Park, CA: Sage.

McHoul, A. (1978). The organization of turns at formal talk in the classroom. *Language in Society, 7,* 183–213.

McHoul, A. (1990). The organization of repair in classroom talk. *Language in Society, 19,* 349–377.

Matza, D. (1969). *Becoming deviant.* Englewood Cliffs, NJ: Prentice-Hall.

Meacher, M. (1972). *Taken for a ride. Special residential homes for confused old people: A study of separatism in social policy.* Harlow, England: Longman.

Mead, M. (1943). *Coming of age in Samoa. A study of adolescence and sex in primitive societies.* Harmondsworth, England: Penguin.

Mead, M. (1963). *Growing up in New Guinea. A study of adolescence and sex in primitive societies.* Harmondsworth, England: Penguin.

Mehan, H. (1986). 'What time is it, Denise?': Asking known information questions in classroom discourse. In M. Hammersley (Ed.), *Case studies in classroom research* (pp. 85–103). Milton Keynes, England: Open University Press.

Mishler, E. G. (1984). *The discourse of medicine: Dialectics of medical interviews.* Norwood, NJ: Ablex.

Mishler, E. G. (1986). *Research interviewing. Context and narrative.* Cambridge, MA: Harvard University Press.

Moser, C. A., & Kalton, G. (1971). *Survey methods in social investigation* (2nd ed.). London: Heinemann.

Mura Swan, S. (1983). Licensing violations: Legitimate violations of Grice's conversational principle. In R. T. Craig & K. Tracey (Eds.), *Conversational coherence. Form, structure and strategy* (pp. 101–115). Beverly Hills, CA: Sage.

Nofsinger, R. E. (1991). *Everyday conversation.* Newbury Park, CA: Sage.

O'Keefe, D. (1979). Ethnomethodology. *Journal for the Theory of Social Behaviour, 9,* 187–219.

Ochs, E. (1979). Transcription as theory. In E. Ochs & B. B. Schieffelin (Eds.), *Developmental pragmatics* (pp. 43–72). New York: Academic Press.

Open University (1988). *P577, Mental health problems in old age.* Milton Keynes, England: Open University.

Open University (1990). *P654, Working with older people.* Milton Keynes, England: Open University.

Payne, G. C. F. (1976). Making a lesson happen: An ethnomethodological analysis. In M. Hammersley & P. Woods (Eds.), *The process of schooling* (pp. 33–40). London: Routledge.

Payne, G. C. F., & Cuff, E. C. (Eds.). (1982). *Doing teaching. The practical management of classrooms.* London: Batsford Academic and Educational Ltd.

Pearce, R. D. (1973). *The structure of discourse in broadcast interviews.* Unpublished master's thesis, University of Birmingham, England.

Philips, S. U. (1992). The routinization of repair in courtroom discourse. In A. Duranti & C. Goodwin (Eds.), *Rethinking context. Language as an interactive phenomenon* (pp. 311–322). Cambridge, England: Cambridge University Press.

Pollitt, P. A., O'Connor, D. W., & Anderson, I. (1989). Mild dementia: Perceptions and problems. *Ageing and Society, 9,* 261–275.

Pollner, M. (1975). The very coinage of your brain: The anatomy of reality disjunctures. *Philosophy of Social Science, 5,* 411–430.

Pomerantz, A. (1984). Agreeing and disagreeing with assessments: Some features of preferred/dispreferred turn shapes. In J. M. Atkinson & J. Heritage (Eds.), *Structures of social action. Studies in conversation analysis* (pp. 57–101). Cambridge, England: Cambridge University Press.

Potter, J. & Wetherell, M. (1987). *Discourse and social psychology. Beyond attitudes and behaviour.* London: Sage.

Propp, V. I. (1968). *The morphology of the folktale.* Austin: University of Texas Press.

Psathas, G. (1995). *Conversation analysis. The study of talk-in-interaction.* Thousand Oaks, CA: Sage.

Psathas, G., & Anderson, T. (1990). The 'practices' of transcription in conversation analysis. *Semiotica, 78,* 75–99.

Rawlings, B. (1988). Local knowledge: The analysis of transcribed audio materials for organizational ethnography. *Studies in Qualitative Methodology, 1,* 157–177.

Rayfield, J. R. (1972). What is a story? *American Anthropologist, 74,* 1085–1106.

Richardson, L. (1990). *Writing strategies. Reaching diverse audiences.* Newbury Park, CA: Sage.

Rochester, S., & Martin, J. R. (1979). *Crazy talk. A study of the discourse of schizophrenic talkers.* New York: Plenum.

Ryave, A. L., & Schenkein, J.(1974). Notes on the art of walking. In R. Turner (Ed.), *Ethnomethodology* (pp. 265–274). Harmondsworth, England: Penguin.

Sacks, H. (1963). Sociological description. *Berkeley Journal of Sociology, 8*, 1–16.

Sacks, H. (1972) On the analyzability of stories by children. In J. J. Gumperz & D. Hymes (Eds.), *Directions in sociolinguistics. The ethnography of communication* (pp. 32–345). New York: Holt, Rinehart & Winston.

Sacks, H. (1984) On doing "being ordinary." In J. M. Atkinson & J. Heritage (Eds.), *Structures of social action. Studies in conversation analysis* (pp. 413–429). Cambridge, England: Cambridge University Press.

Sacks, H. (1995a). *Lectures on conversation. Volume 1.* Oxford, England: Basil Blackwell.

Sacks, H. (1995b). *Lectures on conversation. Volume 2.* Oxford, England: Basil Blackwell.

Sacks, H., Schegloff, E. A. & Jefferson, G. (1978). A simplest systematics for the organization of turn taking for conversation. In J. Schenkein (Ed.), *Studies in the organization of conversational interaction* (pp. 7–55). New York: Academic Press.

Schegloff, E. A. (1972a). Notes on conversational practice: Formulating place. In D. Sudnow (Ed.), *Studies in social interaction* (pp. 75–119). New York: The Free Press.

Schegloff, E. A. (1972b). Sequencing in conversational openings. In J. J. Gumperz & D. Hymes (Eds.), *Directions in sociolinguistics. The Ethnography of communication* (pp. 346–380). New York: Holt, Rinehart & Winston.

Schegloff, E. A. (1980). Preliminaries to preliminaries: "Can I ask you a question?" *Sociological Inquiry, 50*, 104–152.

Schegloff, E. A. (1988). Goffman and the analysis of conversation. In P. Drew & A. Wootton (Eds.), *Erving Goffman. Exploring the interaction order* (pp. 89–135). Oxford, England: Polity Press.

Schegloff, E. A. (1989). Harvey Sacks—Lectures 1964–1965. An introduction/Memoir. *Human Studies, 12*, 185–209.

Schegloff, E. A. (1992). On talk and its institutional occasions. In P. Drew, & J. Heritage, (Eds.), *Talk at work* (pp. 101–134). Cambridge, England: Cambridge University Press.

Schegloff, E. A., & Sacks, H. (1974). Opening up closings. In R. Turner (Ed.), *Ethnomethodology* (pp. 233–264). Harmondsworth, England: Penguin.

Schenkein, J. (Ed.), (1978). *Studies in the organization of conversational interaction.* New York: Academic Press.

Sharrock, W. W. (1974). On owning knowledge. In R. Turner (Ed.), *Ethnomethodology* (pp. 45-53). Harmondsworth, England: Penguin.

Sharrock, W. W. (1977). The problem of order. In P. Worsley (Ed.) *Introducing sociology* (2nd ed.), (pp. 477–566). Harmondsworth, England: Penguin.

Sharrock, W., & Anderson, B. (1986). *The ethnomethodologists.* Chichester, England: Ellis Horwood Ltd.

Sharrock, W., & Anderson, B. (1987). Work flow in a paediatric clinic. In G. Button & J. R. E. Lee (Eds.), *Talk and social organisation* (pp. 244–260). Clevedon, England: Multilingual Matters.

Sidell, M. (1986). *Coping with confusion: The experience of sixty elderly people and their carers.* Unpublished doctoral dissertation, University of East Anglia, England.

Silverman, D. (1973). Interview talk: Bringing off a research instrument. *Sociology, 7, (1),* 31-48.

Silverman, D. (1987). *Communication and medical practice*. London: Sage Publications.

Silverman, D. (1993). *Interpreting qualitative data*. London: Sage Publications.

Silverman, D. (1994). Describing sexual activities in HIV counselling: The co-operative management of the moral order. *Text, 14,* 427–453.

Speier, M. (1969). *The organization of talk and socialization practices in family household interaction*. [Authorized facsimile]. Unpublished doctoral dissertation, University of California, Berkeley, CA.

Speier, M. (1972). Some conversational problems for interactional analysis. In D. Sudnow (Ed.), *Studies in social interaction* (pp. 397–427). New York: The Free Press.

Speier, M. (1973). *How to observe face-to-face communication: A sociological introduction*. Pacific Palisades, CA: Goodyear Publishing.

Sperber, D., & Wilson, D. (1986). *Relevance. Communication and cognition*. Oxford, England: Basil Blackwell.

Stimson, G., & Webb, B. (1975). *Going to see the doctor*. London: Routledge & Kegan Paul.

Strong, P. M. (1979). *The ceremonial order of the clinic. Parents, doctors and medical bureacracies*. London: Routledge & Kegan Paul.

Suchman, L., & Jordan, B. (1990). Interactional troubles in face-to-face survey interviews. *Journal of the American Statistical Association, 85,* 232–244.

Tannen, D. (1989). *Talking voices. Repetition, dialogue and imagery in conversational discourse*. Cambridge, England: Cambridge University Press.

Taraborrelli, P. (1994). Innocents, converts and oldhands: The experiences of Alzheimer's disease caregivers. In M. Bloor & P. Taraborrelli (Eds.), *Qualitative studies in health and medicine* (pp. 22–42). Aldershot, England: Avebury.

Taylor, T. J., & Cameron, D. (1987). *Analysing conversation. Rules and units in the structure of talk*. Oxford, England: Pergamon.

Teasdale, K. (1983). Reality orientation. 1. A programme for elderly. *Nursing Times, November, 9,* 49–52.

Tolson, A. (1991). Televised chat and the synthetic personality. In P. Scannell (Ed.), *Broadcast talk* (pp. 178-200). London: Sage.

Turner, R. (1972). Some formal properties of therapy talk. In D. Sudnow (Ed.), *Studies in social interaction* (pp. 367–396). New York: The Free Press.

Watson, D. R. (1992). Ethnomethodology, conversation analysis and education. *The UNESCO International Review of Education, 38,* 257–274.

Webb, L., & Morris, N. (1994). Wilson's model of family care giving. *Nursing Standard, 8,* 27–30.

Williams, R. (1988). Understanding Goffman's methods. In P. Drew & A. Wootton (Eds.), *Erving Goffman. Exploring the interaction order* (pp. 64–88). Oxford, England: Polity Press.

Wittgenstein, L. (1969). *On Certainty*. Oxford, England: Basil Blackwell.

Yearley, S., & Brewer, J. D. (1989). Stigma and conversational competence: A conversation analytic study of the mentally handicapped. *Human Studies, 12,* 97–115.

Zimmerman, D. H. (1988). On conversation: The conversation analytic perspective. In J. A. Anderson (Ed.), *Communication yearbook 11* (pp. 406–432). Newbury Park, CA: Sage.

Zimmerman, D. H., & Pollner, M. (1974) The everyday world as a phenomenon. In J.D. Douglas (Ed.), *Understanding everyday life* (pp. 80–103). London: Routledge & Kegan Paul.

Author Index

Subject Index